*Sir Jason Solway, King's Champion,
has served as Genevieve's bodyguard these five years
since her husband's coronation.
A childhood friend,
he has watched her decline with his own heart breaking,
carrying her fainting form away from the negotiating table
as she lost each much-wanted babe...
each desperately needed potential Heir.
He may be able to solve their troubles...
but doing so may break him,
for all that he loves his monarchs well.*

*

*Sir Adam Loveress, Captain of the Royal Guard,
fiancé to Jason, and closest friend to Damien, has his own
secrets that will bind their bleeding hearts...
or tear them to shreds.*

*

*Time is running out.
Queen Genevieve's declining health may drag her beloved,
soul-bonded husband into death with her.
The nobles are restive.
And there is something deeply suspicious about
Queen Genevieve's attempted negotiations to restore
the Lost Province of Elendria...*

I0779356

THE KING'S CHAMPION

Book Two of the Chronicles of Ilseador

KERRIDWEN MANGALA MCNAMARA

KERRIDWEN MANGALA McNAMARA

This book is a work of fiction. Names, characters, places, and incidents are the product of the author's imagination or are used fictitiously. Any resemblance to actual events, places or people, living or dead, is coincidental.

Also available in eBook and hardcover editions.
McNamara, Kerridwen Mangala
The King's Champion / by Kerridwen Mangala McNamara Indiana: Rising Dragon Books, 2023
384 pages, 2 maps
(McNamara, Kerridwen Mangala. Chronicles of Ilseador; bk. 1)
Summary: Sir Jason Solway, the King's Champion, is the only hope to save the Realm and his king and queen, according to prophecy… but not in any way he ever imagined.
ISBN 978-1-960160-23-2 (pbk)
1. Kings and rulers - Fiction. 2. Rebels and Romance - Fiction
ISBN 978-1-960160-24-9 (hc); ISBN 978-1-960160-22-5 (eBook)

The King's Champion: Book Two of the Chronicles of Ilseador
Copyright © 2023 by Kerridwen Mangala McNamara
Cover art and illustrations by the author
All rights reserved. No part of this book may be reproduced in any format, print or electronic, without permission in writing from the copyright holders.
For further information, email RisingDragonBooks@gmail.com

ISBN: 978-1-960160-23-2
First Print Edition: January 2024
10 9 8 7 6 5 4 3 2 1

For those who have to make their
way through impossible choices

And who still find a way to make it work

A note to sensitive souls:
Ilseador is a land that has been misruled for eighty-three years
by a tyrant who was also an evil sorcerer in every sense of the
word. Up to four generations cannot remember a time before
the old king assumed the throne... and the morals (or lack
thereof) of a country often develop - intentionally or not - from
the example at the top. This is particularly true of the upper
echelons of society, which this story focuses on. The result is
that it's basically an entire nation of traumatized people who
have seen that greed and cruelty and o'erweening ambition are
rewarded. The old king's Apprentice is still around to cause
trouble as well...

Five years into King Damien's more compassionate reign, there
are still far too many scars...

Proceed with caution...

CONTENTS

Chapter ONE

Shocked

THE FIREWORKS HAD ENDED, BUT the drinking would go on all night in some of the city's taverns. Perhaps all over the Realm, for all Jason knew.

Five years – not of peace, for although the Rebels had negotiated an amnesty on the grounds that they hadn't been rebelling against the Realm but against a depraved king, it had taken war to retrieve the Lost Provinces.

Five years – since Damien had been crowned king. A triumph for Jason, Adam and Ciriis... and the people they had recruited to help him reach his throne.

Five years – nearly – since he and Genevieve had retaken the castle, deposed her usurping ex-husband, and defeated Lord Prydeen. All without the help of his Champion or his Royal Guard.

Five years – since the people had begun calling Damien the 'Sorcerer-King'... but with pride and faith in his sorcery.

"They're waiting for us," Adam prodded Jason out of his memories, recalling the tall King's Champion to the present. They were standing on the castle wall where they'd had – not the best possible view of the fireworks, perhaps, but a restful one. Others had had the task of being on guard this evening, allowing Jason and Adam a rare moment of peace and togetherness.

Rosa was home with her husband and her newest babe in Zialest.

Ciriis was in Elaarwen, tending to the ailing Duke Aldred in Genevieve's place, since the Queen's presence was required in the capitol for the festivities and her father hadn't felt up to making the trip.

Damien and Genevieve had invited their Champion and the Captain of their Royal Guard up to the royal suite for a private celebration of how far they had come.

So, it would just be the four of them. His two dearest friends and his beloved Adam. Peaceful.

Jason smiled and followed his love, remembering the day that Ciriis and Adam had told him about the nervous young prince hiding in the Royal Library. The other two had been observing Damien for some time and had come to the conclusion that he was the one they had been looking for: the legitimate Heir that they could *protect* from the depravity of King Reginald and his Court… that they could prepare to be a worthy king.

But Damien had been hiding away in the Library for five years, ever since his parents had been killed. He had come out only when the Royal Librarian – Damien's guardian-by-default – Lady Theresa, forced him to attend 'family dinners' so his grandfather, King Reginald the Ruthless, could observe him.

Lady Theresa. Jason nearly snorted as he followed Adam up the long, spiral stair. There had always been something cold about her, he had felt, even then. But in those days, none of the people assembling to protect the young prince had known that Damien's older sister, Princess Kandra, had planned to marry Lady Theresa's son, Raphael of Cedarwen. Nor had they known that Kandra and her father, Crown Prince Eric, had planned to defect to the Rebellion via Cedarwen following the marriage, taking her mother and Damien along with them. All of which plans had come to naught when the princess was fatally thrown from her horse; her parents had accused the King – Prince Eric's father – of engineering their daughter's death, and had been cut down in the throneroom themselves for their troubles. In front of the entire Court, including a pair of shocked young squires named Jason and Adam… and including their ten-year-old son, Prince Damien. Who had fled into the safest space he knew: the Royal Library.

Baron and Baroness Anvliyar, and young Lord Raphael, had been at Court as well. The Baron was executed forthwith for complicity in Prince Eric's treason. Young Lord Raphael had seemed half out of his mind with grief; his mother, the now-dowager baroness, had literally thrown herself at the King's feet and sworn that neither she nor her son had been made aware of the plan. That it had been hatched solely between her husband and Prince Eric.

Whether that was true, it was impossible to say. Not even King Reginald – feared for his foul sorcery – nor his evil apprentice, Lord Prydeen, had possessed the ability to read in men's minds what was not spoken aloud.

Nor yet in women's, or so it was whispered.

And the King – for reasons that Damien's later partisans learned only too late and to their ultimate sorrow – was inclined to grant clemency. He named young Raphael as Baron of Cedarwen in his father's place, and took his oath as vassal. But King Reginald retained the mother at Court as his Royal Librarian.

There had been no reason to suspect Lady Theresa of being anything other than yet another grieving hostage widow. No reason to suspect she carried an axe to grind against Princess Kandra's long-orphaned younger brother, Damien.

It had been Jason's task to approach the boy. Adam and Ciriis knew quite well that *they* didn't have the patience for it. And it had taken Jason two months of a ubiquitous presence in the Royal Library just to seem innocuous enough that Damien had come out of hiding in his presence. *Another* month before he'd dared speak to the boy, ragged, scrawny princeling that he was. A *full year* before Damien had trusted him enough to leave the Library on occasion at Jason's side.

The lad had taken to riding easily, connecting seemingly instantly with any horse he was introduced to. But it had taken an entire *second* year before Jason had managed to get Damien to so much as take a sword in his hand; the boy had been all too aware that showing any talent or skill that might appear threatening to his grandfather's throne – or his apprentice's place – was a recipe for becoming the victim of a mysterious 'accident'… no matter how carefully he was watched and guarded.

Truth be told, Jason had needed that peaceful, quiet time himself. Luring Damien out of his self-imposed semi-captivity had been healing for him as well, after the years he had spent as Prince Oskar's bodyguard and Champion. The prince had become the younger brother he had never had, trusting Jason as no one – not even Adam – ever had and they had settled into a peaceful pattern.

And that was when Prince Oskar had begun to notice Damien… Jason's thoughts shied automatically away from *that* period as, in the here and now, Adam knocked on the door to the royal suite.

The Royal Guards on duty here were younger men, ones who had been recruited since the coronation year. Jason knew them well, of course – he wouldn't have permitted anyone so close to his king and queen that he did not know well, indeed – but as their captain, Adam knew them better. Genevieve had been pressing to add women to the formally known Guards, and men to the secret cadre; they had been more successful with the latter initiative, as the Royal Guards were one and all belted knights and a woman had yet to meet that standard. Several were close, but the eighty-three years during which King Reginald had refused to award women their shields had taken its toll.

Damien himself let them in, still in his finery from the day's festivities. He clasped Adam on the arm, but shyly accepted a hug from Jason. He'd lost some of the diffidence that had worried them all when he was first crowned; now it showed up mostly when it was just him and his original Inner Circle. The small, neat beard he'd begun to affect a few years ago didn't do a great deal to make him look older to Jason's eye.

Genevieve wasn't in her usual place, and she didn't come forward to greet them besides a brief acknowledging nod.

She was on the far side of the sitting room, leaning pensively against a wall, also still in her flowing, turquoise gown. A particularly extravagant confection of gauzy silk over satin that suited her blue-green eyes and red-gold hair, but that Jason knew she hated from the moment he'd seen her in it. It accentuated her too-slender waist, and his heart tightened, remembering each of the times he'd had to carry her unconscious out of negotiations for the Lost Provinces after yet another miscarriage that followed too soon on the last one.

He knew she was getting desperate to produce Heirs for the Realm and for Elaarwen, but it broke his heart to see her nearly killing herself to try, over and over... and never giving herself time to recover, never pausing in her work on the battlefield or in the negotiating tent.

Not that they had much choice. Damien was best suited to the work of rebuilding the Realm and the nobility from the depravity of his grandfather's reign. Genevieve was the warrior. And... the rulers of the Lost Provinces – and the monarchs of the kingdoms that had all too eagerly accepted them as their own territories – would not negotiate with the 'Sorcerer-King.'

And there was no real Heir to the Realm save Genevieve herself... not that *she* was suited to the position, given that she was soul-bonded to her husband: if Damien should die for any reason, Genevieve would shortly follow. Damien had scoured the Realm, placing the Monarch's Sword into the hands of anyone even suspected of having Alsterling blood – and a great many of his nobles of other Houses as well – in hopes of finding another Heir acceptable to the Sword. But the damned Blade hadn't so much as twinkled, let alone let loose with the coruscating display of lights it gave off when Damien unsheathed it to prove his own worthiness for the throne. Nor the only slightly lesser show it put on for his queen.

Jason looked at her sadly. She was leaning against the cold stone wall, one hand gripping the elbow of her other arm, her eyes turned aside from all of them. Had she been arguing with Damien before he and Adam entered? Surely, she couldn't be *that* angry with her husband about his insistence that she halt negotiations for the reacquisition of Elendria and return for these festivities. If she was, Jason would have to say something to put matters right between the pair of them; he'd been close to insisting on the same thing himself, given how ill and frail she had become.

"I'm glad you could come. We *both* are," Damien said, glancing at Genevieve with an... odd expression. Unhappiness, certainly. Jason resolved to say something as soon as he could work it into the conversation. Let the Queen be angry at *him*.

Adam executed an absurdly florid bow. "What else, when our liege-lord summons us?" He grinned and clapped the young King on the back. "Too bad Rosa and Ciriis aren't here to mark the day with us, but we wouldn't leave the two of you lovebirds *lonely* up here on this tower you refuse to leave..."

The tower suite had been chosen for Damien by Adam himself – and Ciriis, the erstwhile spymistress and Adam's co-conniver in placing Damien on the throne. It was the most securable location in the entirety of Castle Alsterling, having no windows save the skylights that formed part of the cone at the top of the high tower, and with no easy angle to lob arrows or other missiles into the then-prince's living space. A castle improvement project of King Reginald's from the early, still-hopeful, days of his reign had led to even such remote locations having been plumbed for running water – though some of the interior plumbing lower down hadn't been completed until earlier this year – and this suite had originally been designed for Reginald's eldest son, Prince Robert. Supposedly it had also been used to confine Queen Rena – Damien's grandmother – and her son, the young Prince Eric, when King Reginald had managed to have his runaway wife returned to him from her native Dawil.

There were matching suites in several of the other towers – perhaps once intended for other royal offspring – but the others had already been in use when King Reginald had named Damien the Heir and it had finally been feasible for Adam and Ciriis to make sure he ended up in secure rooms.

The reasons for needing that security had changed, five years into Damien's own reign, but not the risk itself.

The prince had immediately discovered a magickal secret passageway leading down from these rooms... though he had taken some five years to share the discovery with anyone else – and then it was only with Genevieve, who had kidnapped him willingly off to a romantic getaway. His reticence had made Jason worry that they had given Damien cause not to trust them, and Ciriis had been beside herself with irritation over the exclusion. But Adam had simply nodded and told the younger man that he'd been clever to have an escape that not even his Inner Circle could betray inadvertently or even under torture.

And, of course, that secret passageway had enabled all of them – and the entire Royal Guard – to escape the castle during the thankfully brief Usurpation by Harold of Siovale.

As well as to allow Damien and Genevieve to sneak *back* into the castle – against all rational advice and without either Champion or Guards. That they'd been successful in overturning the coup, rescuing their remaining people, and defeating King Reginald's apprentice was almost irrelevant to Jason. Both he and Adam had nearly had heart attacks when they realized that the royal pair had snuck off into the night – and *Ciriis* had gone into *hysterics*. They'd all but raised Damien, after all, and Genevieve had been a childhood friend of Jason's.

It had all turned out well in the end...

But keeping the King and Queen's quarters in the tower had seemed only sensible after that. That passage was far too valuable not to keep it accessible to those most likely to need it.

Damien gave his Captain the usual amiable smile. "You know why."

"And it's not like we *need* more space," Genevieve commented without looking at anyone. "Not for just the two of us. Unlike *Rosa* and *Zachary*."

She cut herself off, but Jason exchanged a speaking look with Adam as he silently cursed himself for acceding to her wish to stop for a few nights in Zialest to admire Rosa's newborn second daughter. Even if it *had* been directly on the way back from Elendria. Genevieve had still been sick enough from the latest miscarriage that Jason could have overruled his queen and insisted on not taking the extra time on the return trip; she always recovered better in Damien's presence, likely because of their soul-bond, so there was even a justification besides sparing her the emotional strain.

Damien had gone to the wall and was gently prying her away from it, whispering something in her ear. She shook her head, but came forward without resistance. Almost, Jason thought uneasily, as if she no longer possessed the strength to resist.

The young King guided her to her usual place on the couch, and seated himself as well, waving the other two men to the second couch that had been acquired not long after they had deposed the usurper. It had been added so that Adam and Jason could sit together, once they no longer needed to hide their relationship for fear of King Reginald or Lord Prydeen using it against them... and thereby turning them against Damien. Jason knew that Rosa and Zachary sat here when they visited the capitol, and that Genevieve's father, Duke Aldred, would lie down on it when he was in town. But it had been added for his and Adam's primary benefit; another token of respect and love from their young sovereign.

"A toast?" Adam suggested, pouring out into the crystal goblets already placed on the low table where they had made so many plans. "To old friends."

"To many more joyous gatherings like this one," Damien answered, tapping his glass against Adam's.

"To peace," Genevieve responded in almost a normal tone.

"To ten years since Damien finally learned how to use a sword as more than a bludgeon," Jason added, intending to bring some humor to the moment.

He was completely startled – and baffled – when Genevieve leaped to her feet and fled back to her position on the wall with an anguished cry.

Genevieve, who had never fled from *anything* for as long as Jason could remember.

"Genny, what's wrong?" he asked, but she just shook her head and stared at the floor. Stared blankly, not glared like the Genevieve he was used to.

Damien sighed, and set his wineglass down , then rubbed his fingers through his beard on one cheek in a nervous gesture. "I had hoped to get through this more easily. But... she's... sensitive to references to the passage of time right now."

"What 'this'?" Adam asked warily.

Damien looked back over his shoulder at his wife, and Jason wanted to tell the boy – no, young *man* – to go over there and hold her. But the King turned back to look at them, and as he met those clear, grey eyes, Jason realized that Damien was nearly thirty. Not so *young* after all. An ancient-seeming sorrow was in those eyes for a moment, blinked away by determination and the bone-deep compassion that made it so hard for so many people to meet the King's eyes.

"You know – everyone knows – that we've been trying to have a child. And that we haven't succeeded. You know how vital it is that we produce an Heir to the Realm... and you're aware that the Sword hasn't spoken for anyone."

"You gave Rosa the Heir's Ring," Adam objected.

"We all knew that was temporary," Genevieve replied without moving or looking up. "And with two little girls to take care of... Rosa asked that I take it back." She held up her hand, and Jason saw the dull glitter of the huge grey pearl.

"And we all know why Genevieve wearing the Ring won't work," Damien continued. "Despite how useful it was for her to have it when we faced Lord Prydeen, she won't survive me by long, which does the Realm no good at all. We need someone whom the Sword will speak for, who can take the Throne after me, and who will rule well and wisely."

Jason cocked his head. "You've had everyone of noble birth touch the hilt of that Blade during their public Vassal Oaths, right down to the sons and daughters of families that only rule baronies and likely wouldn't have a clue on how to rule a nation. Even *me*. The whole Realm knows that the Sword hasn't spoken for anyone. Can't you just name another interim Heir?"

And maybe Genny can take a rest and have a better chance at carrying the next child to term, he thought, but did not dare say. He'd suggested as much to her before and gotten a tongue-lashing for it. Nor had she slowed down.

"I can," Damien said quietly. "And I may have to. If the Sword will not speak."

Adam gave him another wary look. "You're not going to make Jason try again, are you?"

Jason gave his love an odd look. Not that he wanted to be Heir to the Throne, but it wouldn't bother him to hold the Monarch's Blade again. He doubted it would prove any more illuminating – literally – than the first time

...though somehow *Adam* had avoided touching the thing, as far as Jason knew. Not that there was much more chance the ancient Sword would Choose a baronetta's son than a countess's. Damien had agreed to stop trying for the families below baronies... in part to spare his Captain, it seemed, and in part because there were simply too *many* to do an exhaustive set of tests. And if Damien couldn't see the thing done *properly*...

The young King shook his head. "We... Genevieve, Aldred, and I... have done some historical research," which meant it was mostly Damien, "and have come to the conclusion that the Blade is highly unlikely to speak for anyone who is not of Alsterling blood."

That wasn't exactly news. It also wasn't exactly *helpful,* given that King Reginald – and his pet sorcerer – had exterminated every last legitimate scion of the royal line. Damien had even tried handing the sword to his bastard relatives to no avail – not that a number of them hadn't tried to parlay that minimal recognition of their parentage into some sort of appointment, or position, or at least wealth. And then, of course, there was Harold the Usurper – who had not been unique in his ambition or attempt, just merely the one with the best backing and most nearly successful.

"Poor planning on the part of the original spell-caster," Genevieve said sourly. "Since its one *useful* function is to identify men and women who will rule *well.*"

"It does more than that," the young King said mildly over his shoulder. She sniffed, and went back to listlessly regarding the flagstones.

"You've met every farthest-flung Alsterling cousin at this point," Adam told him. "Who's left?"

"No one," Damien admitted. "And therein lies our problem. Queen Marian assures me that the Sword *will* speak for one or more of our children. And once it does, I can name a Regent in case of my death."

A strange pass when the word of the ghost of a long-dead Queen was what they had to rely upon.

"But first you need to *have* a child," Adam said dryly. "Or several of them. And Genevieve isn't getting any younger." He folded his arms and leaned back, clearly not-saying 'and what are *we* supposed to do about this mess?'

"No." Damien took a deep breath and stood up. Genevieve made a sort of strangled noise that might have been a sob from another woman and wrapped her gauze-draped arms around herself.

The young King came around the table and sank gracefully to one knee in front of his Champion. He met Jason's eyes with those clear, grey ones, and the knight was thrown back to the memory of himself kneeling in the Royal Library before the nineteen-year-old Damien and pledging himself and his sword to the young prince... Only at that point had they been able to persuade him to move permanently out of the Library at last.

"You've heard the prophecy that Lord Prydeen spoke with his last, dying breath. Genevieve will not conceive my firstborn first. He added a coda to it that only she and I heard: that we had a *Champion* of a problem." He held out his hand to Jason.

"My Champion, my friend, my brother. Will you do this for us? And for the Realm?"

Time seemed to slow, stop.

Jason couldn't even breathe.

His eyes met Genevieve's across the room. His wondering, hers reluctant but drawn.

"Damien, do you *know* what you're *saying?*" Adam said harshly, breaking the spell.

The not-so-young King transferred his gaze to his second oldest friend, and offered his other hand. His voice remained calm, even. "I am asking Jason to father a child with Genevieve. A child to be acknowledged as mine. I am asking you both to make a sacrifice," he cut off Adam's next words, "but in return you will know the child is also yours. And I will name Jason as Regent-Presumptive."

"Damien–" Adam began again, angrily.

"Adam." The King stopped him, but gently. "Do you think I don't know what you've been through? If there were any other way, I would not ask. *We* would not ask. But there is no one else we can trust this much."

"Trust never to reveal the true parentage of the child," Adam said, bitterly.

Damien lowered his eyes. "Yes. You'll watch the child growing up calling me 'father' and you – both of you – 'uncle.' But... the child will exist. And still be yours. And *you* will know." He stood up, and stepped away. "Don't... say anything right now. Talk to each other. Think it over." He turned away, tension radiating from him that said he knew what *Adam's* decision would be. His words were the sort of polite dismissal that Damien often offered as an escape from the royal presence.

"Jase, let's go," Adam prodded, standing up abruptly.

But Jason's eyes were still on Genevieve. His friend, his Queen, who was half-killing herself to fulfill her duty to the Realm... and to her soul-bonded husband whom she loved so well. Her soul-bonded husband... the boy-prince that Jason had half-raised, for all that Damien had legally been an adult when they met.

He also stood, but slowly.

"Jason," Adam said more urgently.

Jason focused on his true love, "Adam. I have to do this."

"Jason, you don't," Adam said, almost pleading. "This is too much for a king to ask."

"Not for my *king*," Jason said softly. "For our *friends*." He put his arms around Adam. "We've... talked about having a child." Well, *Adam* had talked. It seemed... a much more *fraught* issue for Jason than for his love, and he'd kept as silent as Adam let him be on the subject. "For us... there's *this* or adoption."

"Our child, not one who will never even *know..."*

"Adam, beloved," he whispered into his love's ear. "She's growing weaker with each miscarriage. Too much longer and we'll be mourning them both and trying to hold together a country tearing itself apart without an Heir."

"You *want* this," Adam tried to push him away, his eyes filled with hurt and anger and... confusion? "You want *her.*"

He had never lied to Adam... except by omission. "Yes."

Adam froze. Apparently, he had thrown that out there simply to get a rise out of Jason.

"But it's just a *physical* reaction. I don't love her the way I love you. *You* should know *that,*" Jason added slightly reproachfully... and somewhat mendaciously. "I'm yours until the day I die. But... they *need* us. And *I...* need to do this."

Adam sagged, resting his head on his love's shoulder. "I can't like this. But..."

"My heart is yours alone," Jason promised, vaguely thinking that this was too *easy,* then let both Adam and the thought go.

Adam collapsed back onto the couch in a posture of despondence utterly at odds with the alert demeanor he never let slip outside of their bedchamber. Even the Captain's glower at Damien seemed little better than halfhearted... and his eyes seemed... *conflicted,* if Jason was going to try to match a word to the expression.

The King's Champion made his way across the room and stood in front of Genevieve. Lifted her chin. For the first time in five years, he didn't even try to suppress the intense *physical* reaction he had felt every time he touched her, beginning with when he had caught her hand as she climbed onto the royal reviewing stand during Damien's coronation festivities.

His oldest true friend. He trusted her... and he knew how badly Adam wanted a child. That was all this was. All it had ever been. An... anticipation of how he could solve this problem...

Her glorious blue-green eyes met his, filled with mixed emotions. Surprise. Resentment. Relief. Desire... Jason suddenly understood that her harsh denunciation of his attempts to help her after that last miscarriage had been a fear of this moment. She and Damien must have already decided that it was time to ask.

The kiss was as sweet and passionate as five years of waiting could make it.

And she did not touch him with so much as a fingertip, as mindful as he of those who watched them both with aching hearts.

Reluctantly, he stepped away.

"Yes," Jason gave the answer in words. Some things needed to be said aloud to be real. "But not today." He looked at his King. "Genny needs to recover properly from that last miscarriage. She hasn't told you, I'd wager, that I carried her out of the negotiating tent when she collapsed. *Again.*" Damien's stricken look was all the confirmation he needed. "If she really can conceive and carry my child, her body needs to be ready to do it."

Damien nodded.

"Three months," Jason stipulated, looking as sternly as his awakened desire made possible at the truculent Queen. He leveled a finger at her. "Three months of rest. Here. In the castle. Letting others wait on you. Eating properly. No sword-practice. No riding. No sex. No *politics.*"

He folded his arms, and waited while she glowered at him. Then gave one sharp nod.

Jason remembered that glower from the twelve-year-old Genevieve who had wanted to visit the dark underbelly of the city. And the nod, from when she'd agreed to go with him to a secret grotto outside the city and 'learn' swordplay from him instead.

Adam barked a harsh laugh. "Well, I guess I have nothing to worry about. She'll never make three months. Without *politics.*" The sarcastic emphasis implied a world of other meanings.

Jason was across the room in three long strides. "You will never have anything to worry about. Regardless of what Her Majesty does or does not do."

He looked at the King and Queen. Damien's expression was an odd mixture of hope and despair. Genevieve's was... truculent. But Jason knew that the twelve-year-old Genevieve had yielded to his persuasion not to go seeking trouble when he had offered to teach her swordplay. And had not gone back on her word. For three months.

She had already been good, with a natural talent for the blade. And she'd likely been training longer than he had, since they started them young in the mountains of Elaarwen – with swords as well as with much else. And since her father was on the verge of declaring himself in open Rebellion to the Crown, and likely thought his only child would need to know how to protect herself.

Jason had still been better. And, more to the point, there had been no other way for her to practice while at Court, under the misogynistic eye of King Reginald and his sorcerer lackey.

"Thank you," Damien said softly. He had moved to his wife's side, taken her hand. His eyes were on Jason – or was it Adam? – but it wasn't entirely clear to whom he was speaking.

The Champion nodded once, and wrapped his arm about his love. "Let's go."

Adam seared them all with a scathing look and stalked from the room.

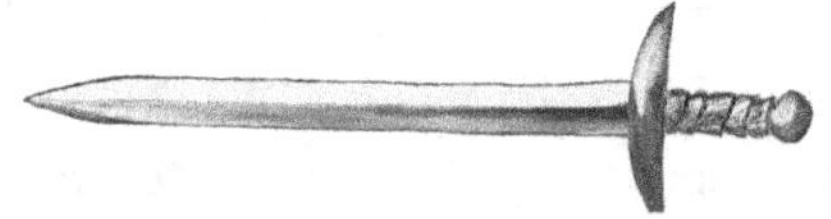

Chapter TWO

Unhappy

Jason caught up with Adam halfway down the stairs, but didn't try to talk. This was far too private – and too secret – for a discussion in a public hallway.

Their own suite of rooms was in a far wing of the castle. They had both wanted a bit more separation from their official roles as King's Champion and Captain of the Royal Guard, knowing how hard it would be to maintain any semblance of a private life in such surroundings.

Adam passed through the nearly deserted corridors and halls like a storm-cloud, and even Jason, who actually topped him by an inch or two, was hard put to keep up with his brisk stride. The Captain's dark humors were well known, however, and neither the occasional servant they surprised in their rapid passage, nor the several tipsy nobles they encountered in the more public corridors, interrupted their progress. Jason just hoped the physical movement would wear off some of his love's fury.

Once they were securely in their own rooms, the heavy, oaken door closed and latched, their swords racked properly and automatically, and the wards set against prying eyes and ears – Damien's gift from the early days of his reign – Adam whirled on him.

"*Why,* Jason?" His face, his voice, were angry, but Jason knew him well enough after fifteen years as a pair, and five before that as close friends, to see the hurt and bewilderment.

Hurt and bewilderment... and something else that Jason couldn't lay a name to.

The Champion tried to take his love into his arms, to soothe, but Adam was having none of it and brushed him off. Walked to the far side of the sitting room and poured himself a drink from the sideboard. And Adam never drank when not in company.

Jason sighed, and sat down on the overstuffed sofa.

"I should have waited and discussed it with you."

"Damn straight, you should!" Adam threw back the drink and poured another.

"Love, Genny is wearing herself out trying to bear an Heir." Jason stared down at his hands. "She's fainting all the time. The army Healer added a midwife specialist to her staff just to keep an eye on her. I had to carry her out of the negotiating tent last month because she'd collapsed. It wasn't the first time. You know that. I've told you."

Something besides hurt and anger found space in Adam's eyes. "Is that why the negotiations for Elendria were put on hold? It wasn't just for the anniversary celebrations as was proclaimed, was it?"

There hadn't been time to discuss this before – Jason and Genevieve and their troops had arrived late the previous evening. Time... or willingness. After so many months apart from his love, political concerns had been at the bottom of the Champion's thoughts. And then Adam had needed to rise so early to see to the final preparations for the anniversary celebrations...

Jason shook his head. "She couldn't get out of bed for *three days* this time, Adam. She tried... and fainted again. *Twice*. I've never seen anyone be so pale and still be alive." The memory still terrified him. The only bits of color in Genevieve's face had been her freckles, and they had stood out like tattoos against her deathly pallor. "I had to bring the Countess of Elendria and the Ambassador from Deltheran in to see her lying there unconscious before I could get them to put off the negotiations and bring her back here. I don't know whom they might accept in her place... but at least they won't be surprised when *she* doesn't come back." He frowned deeply. "I didn't notice Rosa give her back the Ring when we stopped in Zialest. I don't know how she could do that to Genny, after seeing..."

"Perhaps," Adam said bitterly, "Rosa hoped to *precipitate* this."

Not that it sounded like Damien and Genevieve had shared their dangerous solution even with Rosa...

"Seeing her babies was enough for that. Genny knows how to cry very quietly, but – I know, too. She cried herself to sleep every night after our stop in Zialest."

"Jason..."

"I slept on the floor next to her bed after she fainted in the camp trying to get up. I'd *still* be doing it if I didn't trust Damien to *feel* something going wrong with her, their marriage-bed or not." The Champion looked the Captain in the eye. "I *failed* my King when Harald usurped the throne, Adam. I *failed* him again by not being at his side when he took it back. And so did *you*. We've spent the last five years trying to make up for that. You, by keeping Damien safe, and I, by looking after Genny. But... *anyone* could do what we're doing. This... he's right. Prophecy or not, we're the only ones they can trust with this. This... *this* will make up for our failures."

Adam looked away first. "It won't work anyways. Any child you have with her isn't going to look a whit like Damien. Blue eyed and blonde and *tall*..."

"Who else?" Jason persisted. "Zachary of Dalizell? Tim Ancellius?" He paused thoughtfully. "Damien takes after his mother. The rest of the Alsterling line has always been blondes. There's no reason a child of his wouldn't look more like Prince Eric."

He and Adam had been on guard duty as squires the day that Crown Prince Eric and Lady Miria had confronted the old King about their daughter's death. Jason had gently probed his younger friend's memories and knew that Damien didn't remember any details of the day besides the horror of losing his parents – that he didn't remember *Jason* and *Adam* standing there, too shocked to move... to react... to try to help the orphaned boy.

But the tall Champion remembered a handsome, golden prince and his tiny, lovely, fierce-eyed lady. Prince Eric had worn the Heir's Ring at the time, which was perhaps why he had dared to face down his father. He must have known that he – *and* his Lady *and* his young son, so long as he touched them – had protection from magickal attacks because of the Ring. He must not have believed that his father would have the *Heir* summarily executed by a regular knight in the *throneroom* during full Court.

Prince Eric hadn't been a child, but a man of over forty years. How had he so misjudged?

A man of over forty years... and a father desperately grieving the death of his treasured daughter...

Jason still remembered the look of fear in Lady Miria's eyes when she realized what was about to happen.

How she had thrust her young son away from them and said *"Hide."* And so, he had...

Jason remembered that look dying in her eyes as her head lay on the floor, separated from her body, and somehow ending up near his own feet where he'd stood frozen on one side of the royal dais, with Adam opposite him on the other. They'd often been assigned the decorative duty, both being tall and blonde, practically a matched set. The only small mercy had been that the King had called upon one of his full knights to accomplish the task, and not on his horrified young squires.

The King's Champion at the time, likely, though Jason's own memory of the day was uncertain. It hardly mattered. There had been any number of men – and women – who would do whatever King Reginald asked. Or implied. But not *hinted* – *that* sort of personal initiative had caused the perpetrators' heads to roll when it turned out their interpretation was wrong. King Reginald's Court had been a place of fearfully fine distinctions.

Adam and Ciriis had winnowed through the ranks of knights and nobles alike to find men – and, for the Secret Cadre, women – who could be trusted with Damien's safety and honor. It hadn't been an easy task. Damien himself had taken up the winnowing on a grander scale after his coronation; the oath of vassalage as taken from his hands was a *spell,* binding his nobles to the good of the Realm and their people *(though he refused to bind them to himself, out of his own sense of honor and obligation).* It simply wouldn't take on people who attempted to swear dishonestly. In some cases – such as the duchy of Reyensweir – Damien had ended up unable to confirm both the former ruler and her favored Heir, finally administering the oath to someone farther down the local line-of-succession who could bear it in good faith.

But... it had taken four *years* for Adam and Ciriis to remember Damien's existence after that dreadful day when he lost his parents. And a *further* year for them to bring him to Jason's own attention. Another failure on their part. And on *Jason's.*

Adam flung himself down on the opposite end of the sofa. Not a chair, that would completely prevent Jason from sitting beside him, but not coming close either. Yet. Hopefully that was only a *yet.* "If it were anyone but *her,"* he said softly, bitterly.

Jason gave him an ironic tilt of the head. "Anyone other than our *soul-bonded Queen* would feel less threatening to you?" He paused. "A *woman* bothers you at *all?"*

Adam glowered, but some of his heart wasn't in it. "You know what I mean. It's *Genevieve.* Your *Genny."* No, he hadn't been happy that the obvious division of their duties had put Jason and Genevieve together so much of the time. Adam was all too aware of their history, their friendship, platonic though it had always been. And what he wasn't aware of...

Jason gave him a crooked smile. "This won't help, but did I ever tell you that there was talk of betrothing us that Summer she was at Court? Our families have been close friends for generations. If Mother hadn't been such a staunch supporter of King Reginald..."

To his surprise, Adam looked torn. "You'd have gone back with them to Elaarwen instead of earning your shield. I'd never have met you. But... you might have been spared... Oskar."

Jason couldn't suppress a shudder. Though not all of that shudder was for the things Adam would think it was. "And he might have turned his attentions to *you* instead. Not a good trade, Adam." He paused. "But Genny wouldn't have married Harald."

Adam grunted. He loved their queen dearly as well, but Harald of Siovale was water under the bridge to him.

Jason shook his head, his eyes shadowed by memories he was refusing to allow himself to consider. Ones that even Adam – *especially* Adam – would never understand. "Oskar damaged my body, Adam, but I always knew you were still waiting for me." Even when he hadn't wanted Adam to... "And it was for a mercifully short time, all told. Do you not wonder why Genny is so desperate to conceive that she won't even let her body heal before trying again? Do you not wonder why Damien hasn't insisted she do so before? Harald damaged her *soul*, my love, and he did it by hammering on the idea that she was worthless, useless, because she could not conceive. And he had *eight years* to do it in. And *she* had no one waiting for her. That she knew of."

Damien had been, of course, but she hadn't known.

Adam looked stricken.

"Oskar may have been more... inventive," Jason went on, "but Harald was a master of his own arts of hurt. Not that he skimped on the physical pain either."

"She... told you?" Adam was startled.

Jason shook his head. "Rosa did. She didn't want to, but after spending so much time with Genny, there were things I could see... things I could recognize, having been through something similar myself. Rosa gave me enough details that I could do a better job taking care of her, know what might trigger her fears and compulsions. Rosa... knew that I would understand. Damien confirmed other things," he admitted, "in a roundabout way, though I'm sure he knew what I was asking about."

Adam stared at his hands.

"I don't want to lose you, Jase."

That was so raw, so honest, so... vulnerable. The powerful, sardonic Captain had laid himself bare for once, letting go of the hurt and anger and resentment and guilt... and whatever all the other things were that had been a part of his reaction tonight. Rarely did he let himself relax this much, even with Jason.

He'd once been more open and easygoing, Jason recalled sadly. Even after watching what had happened with Prince Oskar, Adam had been... determined. Resolute. But not... so deeply hurt that he hid layers of his heart even from Jason.

No, *that* had taken the break with his family. With his much-adored *parents,* who couldn't accept who their eldest son had fallen in love with. Or rather... couldn't accept that Jason was a *man.*

Not that the Champion didn't have a similar problem with his own mother and older sister... but Countess Solway would gnaw off her own arm before she gave up control over her son. Jason could only *wish* she would refuse to speak to him as the Baronetta and Lord George had done with Adam.

"You won't," Jason said softly. "One night with Genevieve isn't going to break what we have between us."

The other man whuffed a laugh. "I may not know much about women, but I know they don't always 'catch' on the first try."

Jason's heart twinged. He still wasn't being completely honest. But he knew no way to explain the strange passion that he felt for Genny without utterly terrifying Adam. "A couple of nights, then. I'm still yours. And always, *always,* will be." He paused. "Don't you think Damien is fighting down the same fear?"

"Damien," Adam said dryly, "is a pragmatist at heart. Besides, he knows he can set a soul-bond against a night – or a month of nights – and have nothing to fear."

"*I* would have said he's an idealist," Jason retorted. "And do you truly think a night – or a month of nights, as you put it – can stand against how much I love you? Against nearly twenty *years* together?"

"No..." Adam wavered, then looked up, his eyes shadowed. "You said you *wanted* her, Jase. Not just wanted to *help* her. *Wanted* her. In your *bed.*"

He *would* remember that. "It's a physical reaction. Not an emotional one. Use it up and it'll be gone."

Lies… but Jason had gotten good at telling himself those lies. Surely, he could fool Adam if he could practically fool himself.

"Will it? Or will you suddenly discover that what *we* have, what we *do*, isn't as satisfying?" The stern, sarcastic Captain of the Royal Guards gulped like an anxious adolescent. Like he had been, the first time he'd told Jason how he felt, when they were seventeen and eighteen. "You've never lain with a woman before. What if… you find out you *prefer* it? Her?" Adam had never shown any sense of insecurity at this level. Never.

"Adam," Jason said gently, "if Prince Oskar couldn't convince me to swear off making love with you, Genevieve is not going to." More prevarications… but Adam didn't want to know, he'd made it clear in the past… The Champion made a wry face. "And actually, I *have* lain with a woman before. Prince Oskar… required it."

Adam looked at him askance. "You never said."

"I've told you as little as possible about those days, love." Because Adam had never really wanted to know.

Adam came into his arms at last. "I'm sorry I reminded you."

Jason shrugged, setting aside again the things Adam wouldn't, couldn't, ever understand. Not telling him was easier than trying to explain those things, as he knew from experience. "It's long ago. You've healed most of the holes in my soul."

The other man sighed, and laid his head on Jason's shoulder. "And now you're going to tell me that you *need* to do this," no question what 'this' was, still, "to heal the hole in *Genevieve's* soul that Damien can't help her with."

Jason wisely stayed silent.

"I still can't *like* it…" Adam said after a long moment.

"I don't think any of the four of us 'like' it," Jason said dryly.

"And… the child? She won't be 'ours,'" Adam said with sadness.

"'She'?" Jason was amused.

"I don't like saying 'it.' Even odds I'm right, anyways." Though he sounded… evasive. And more quickly resigned to this odd request than Jason's stubborn, determined love ever was. Adam had obstinately clung to positions for *years* that he'd have done better to set aside. This… swift readjustment was almost unbelievable.

On the other hand, they'd spent so little time together these last few years and Adam had been more deeply involved in the political realities of helping Damien run the country; perhaps he'd grown a bit when Jason wasn't looking. After all, it was only in affairs of his *own* heart that Adam had ever dug in his heels. In any and every *other* sense, his sharp intellect was almost gymnastically flexible, with protecting Damien, Jason, Genevieve, and the Realm set higher than any other goal or moral... not necessarily in that order. Adam loved fiercely and completely...

"She *will* be ours," Jason told him, yielding to his choice of pronoun. *"I'll* be the one who teaches her to use a sword, and *you'll* protect her night and day. We'll be with her day in and day out. She might call us her 'uncles,' but what more could a *parent* do?" He sighed and pulled Adam a little closer. "Given our duties and responsibilities, could we even find the time to care for a child all on our own? Given how much *Damien* and *Genny* do, could *they*? Maybe this is all for the best." He paused again as Adam... didn't object the way Jason had anticipated. "If this goes according to the sorcerer's prophecy, there will be other children. Other princes and *princesses*. We'll have to show them all the same level of care and affection."

A whole family's worth of children, and the pair of them inextricably embedded into it. Adam had been campaigning for them to adopt for... years. Surely this should sate his love's child-hungry soul.

"Will *Damien?*" Adam began, then shook his head, snuggling closer. He answered his own question "Of course he will. Damien loves everyone." He sighed. "I can't believe we're basing all of this on the dying words of an evil sorcerer who nearly destroyed our Realm. *Twice.*"

Jason stroked his lover's hair. "That *is* the weakness in the whole scheme. But at least it's a hope. The alternative being civil war when something inevitably happens to Damien."

"He's expressing a great deal of faith in *you,* you know," Adam said quietly. "Naming you as Regent-Presumptive. It... sounded like he meant for *whichever* child the Sword speaks for, not just *ours.*"

Jason felt a cold shiver. "Gods forfend. I don't know anything about ruling."

He felt Adam smile into his chest. "You've only been at the side of one or the other of them night and day for five years – and will be for years more. You see everything, you know which pots are boiling and whose fingers are in each one. And you have that ability to make everyone *like* you, much like Damien."

"I think you're biased, my love."

"Jason Solway, is there any person in this Realm who counts you as an enemy?"

Jason snorted. "I don't think your mother or mine are particularly happy with me for denying them grandchildren..."

"Not what I meant..." Adam sighed. "They'll have their wish and never know." That awful, aching wistfulness that he usually hid so well when speaking of his parents was... out there in the open.

Jason hesitated. "We could find someone else... Have a child we could claim..."

"Absolutely not! Giving you up to Genevieve is bad enough."

"Temporarily."

"Temporarily," Adam conceded... but again, there was something Jason couldn't interpret in his voice.

"We *could* adopt," Jason said somewhat reluctantly. He barely wanted to admit to himself, let alone Adam, his reasons for not wanting to have primary responsibility for a child. And if this was something his love *needed* in order to make the rest of this work out... "There are all those thousands of orphans from when we were fighting the Rebellion... and from the old King's cruelty." And Oskar's...

Adam tilted his head up to give Jason a sardonic look, that almost terrifying *vulnerability* starting to disappear back into its usual place. "*Your* mother would never accept an adoptee as her grandchild. And mine *couldn't* if that child would be my Heir." Because Adam was still Heir to Lynncrag and nevermind that he hadn't spoken to anyone from his family in over ten years. "Besides, weren't you just trying to convince me that we don't have the ability to raise a child on our own?"

Jason conceded the point. "Not now, maybe. But in a few years... we could retire. I'm sure Damien would grant us a cottage somewhere. We could adopt *older* children..."

Yes, and that sounded even more terrifying, given his own reasons for avoiding parenthood... though again, if this was what Adam *needed* to have *his* heart be whole...

Adam chuckled. "I'm not sure I can see *us* keeping house and domesticating a pack of half-feral orphans."

Jason shrugged. He rather liked the idea, now that he'd thought of it. He had too good an idea of what fate orphaned children faced on the streets, or unwanted in the homes of relatives. While they didn't have quite the same fears as Damien had lived with, their day-to-day existence was much less predictable. Helping Damien had filled a deep need in his soul, but the boy was grown now, and there were others...

Still, he could suggest they revisit the thought in a few years.

"Oh?" he said teasingly. "I rather like the idea of coming home to find you in an apron, with an apple pie cooling on the windowsill and supper on the table."

Adam's head came up off his shoulder, his eyes blazing with yet another intense emotion. "I'd have to learn to cook." He paused. "I could do that. *Just* an apron?"

Jason blushed fiercely, and Adam laughed. "I suppose not if there are children about. Mmmmn. Maybe I should talk to Damien about a little place for us to... hmmm... learn to *cook?*" Adam paused as Jason searched for a suitable way to extend the metaphor while very – *very* – distracted by the picture he was imagining.

"I love you, Jase," Adam said softly.

Jason responded wordlessly – but entirely unambiguously.

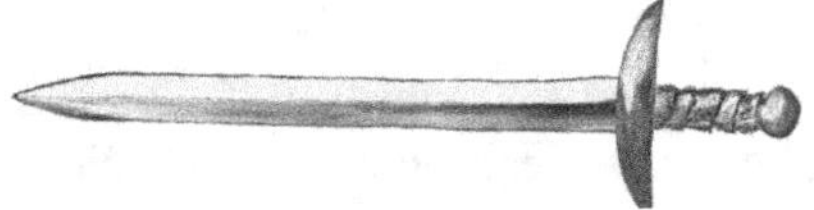

Chapter THREE

Restless

FOR THE FIRST WEEK, GENEVIEVE seemed to enjoy her enforced rest. She really *was* exhausted, both physically and emotionally, and had little strength to object. Damien doted on her, passing off his responsibilities to his Royal Council in order to spend more time with her. She spent most of her time in bed, and he brought her books and flowers and sat reading his favorite tales to her for hours on end. They took breaks to feast on small, rich foods designed to help her regain her weight.

By the end of the second week, he had resorted to hiding her leathers and her weapons. She had strength enough to wander around the castle for short periods. Damien had to return to some of his duties as king, and Jason was returned to his Genevieve-watching responsibilities. The Champion was stricter than his King about what she was allowed to do, and admitted to Damien that he found a certain relief in being able to give her a certain *look* when she tried to pull rank on him; for this little while he held the upper hand over his headstrong Queen.

By the end of the *third* week, Duke Aldred and Ciriis had been sent for, because it was obvious that keeping Genevieve from exerting herself was going to be a fulltime effort for Damien as well as Jason. The King had had to set up a separate office, where reports could be delivered to him without her getting hold of them, instead of simply using the desk in their sitting room as he had done until now. He had occasionally brought some reports with him to read while she slept the first couple of weeks, but by this point she wasn't drifting off at random intervals, and she was far too inclined to try to sneak the reports away from him to read herself. Damien was sympathetic to her boredom and need to feel useful, but it was easy to see how the emotional effort of reading and responding to the information exhausted her – even if Jason hadn't forbidden politics in return for his aid.

It was especially important to keep word away from her about the negotiations with Elendria and Deltheran. She had been making some headway with people known to be notoriously hardheaded, and now they simply refused to reopen the discussions. The army camped on their border didn't seem to overly worry them – they knew that Damien didn't want Elendria destroyed in the process of restoring it to his Realm. The King was fighting with his Royal Council to appoint a new negotiator; *he* wanted Tomas Elsevier, Duke of Siovale, but some of the Councilors still could not wrap their heads around the fact that Tomas had been enspelled to assist his younger half-brother, Harald, to usurp the throne, nor did they believe in Duke Tomas's utter loyalty to Crown and Realm.

It wasn't because of Duke Tomas's former Rebellion against King Reginald – it was hard to even imply that, after all, given that Queen Genevieve had been the leader of that Rebellion. And besides, the Councilors' choice of replacement negotiator plenipotentiary was Duchess Rosa Miramar of Dalziallest, another former Rebel. But Damien refused to draw his friend away from her newborn child… or suggest she take the babe into a potentially dangerous situation.

There were times when Damien truly regretted vesting so much power in the hands of the Council.

When he left the Council chamber after more hours of haggling that had gone nowhere, and headed straight for a drink in his new office for the third day in a row, Adam put a hand over the cork. The Captain had been faithfully dogging his heels, standing at his side during the meetings at which he was now – despite his own protests – a voting member.

"Damien, this has to stop. Just appoint Tomas and be done with it."

The King looked wearily at his friend. "You don't want him there either. You voted against the notion I-don't-know-how-many times. Move your hand, Adam. I need a drink. If Genevieve gets a sense through the bond of how this is going, I won't be able to keep her out of the Council chamber."

"Maybe you need her in there," Adam told him, not moving his hand. "With the voting structure you set up, the two of you together can overrule the rest of the Council. This country needs a king who can get things done, not government by a committee that can't agree on what color the sky is."

Reluctantly, Adam yielded to the King's tug at his hand. Damien picked up the entire bottle and took a swig, shuddering slightly at the taste. He'd never liked the bitter flavor of alcohol. But lately that bitterness had been easier to deal with than Genevieve's questions on top of the Council's bickering. So long as he could put aside the stresses before he returned to her – and keep her from telling how the stresses stuck with him after the Council meetings – he could put her off, persistent though she was.

"I put the power in the Council for a reason, Adam," he reminded the Captain. "No one man should be able to do what my grandfather did."

He wandered away from the sideboard where the wine was kept towards his desk, taking another swig and shuddering again. He knew from too much recent previous experience that it would be a while longer before the slight numbness set in that dulled his emotions and made it possible to hide things from his soul-bonded Queen.

Adam followed him, frowning with worry. "So you've said, many times. But it wouldn't do any good. A sorcerer could take power with or without the legal means to do it. And in the matter of Duke Tomas, I'm biased. *I* know that. *You* know that. The whole damned *Council* is biased against him after Harald's usurpation. Except, for some reason, you and the Queen. You have some way of knowing that the rest of us don't. You should make the decision and let us all move on."

He stopped in the middle of the room, arms folded, in an exaggerated parade-rest posture while Damien wandered aimlessly, too tired to focus on anything, but all too aware of the growing backlog of other work. Some of it was what was being put off while they sorted out a negotiator for Elendria, and some was work Genevieve would otherwise be taking care of, even if the reports had to be sent to her in some remote part of the Realm. He hadn't realized how much she did... until she didn't.

"I think Tomas will do a superb job as a negotiator," Adam threw in candidly. "I just don't trust him."

"If you *don't,* and the Council *won't,*" Damien mumbled, setting the half-empty bottle down and slumping into the chair at his desk. "Why would Countess Miraly? Or Queen Estelle?" He sighed, leaning forward and resting his forehead on his folded hands. "I *have* to trust in the process, Adam. If I just step around it every time it doesn't work out the way I like, we're right back to where we started."

"That's the other thing," Adam complained. *"First,* you give over all this power to the Council, *then* you add in Councilors to represent the Guilds and Trades. *Now,* you're planning elections for the Council members who represent the various provinces instead of just letting you or even their liege-lords appoint them. It's almost as if you're trying to give over *all* the monarch's power."

"Got it in one, Adam," Damien mumbled.

The Captain's jaw actually dropped in shock for a moment.

The King raised his head and gazed at him sleepily. Adam read practically everything Damien did, and had for at least the last three years, had proofread all the edicts Damien made out, had been a voting member of the Royal Council. If he hadn't been so tired, the younger man would have been surprised that his sharp-minded friend hadn't seen the pattern for himself. Unless Adam had been intentionally avoiding drawing the obvious conclusion.

"Just think, Adam. A powerless monarch wouldn't need to go to ridiculous and unfair lengths to have an Heir. The children and grandchildren of a powerless monarch would be free to live whatever life is best for them. No more fear. No more political games around bloodlines."

Adam came around the table and pulled Damien to his feet. "You're out of your head with exhaustion," he muttered, conveniently ignoring the long-laid nature of his King's plan. "And wine on an empty stomach. Genevieve will have my ears."

Damien laughed tiredly. "Give her something to do..."

The Captain looked around for a place to lay his King down, and finally settled on a thick rug on the floor. It was better than leaving Damien to slide off the table and hit his head... but not by much.

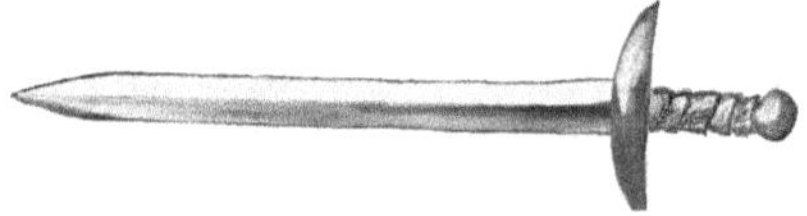

By the end of the fourth week, the Champion and the Captain were almost done in themselves.

Jason was discovering that keeping Genevieve safe on a battlefield was actually less strenuous than trying to keep her quietly occupied in a castle with nothing to do. He tried engaging her in chess, but only Damien or Ciriis could keep her challenged enough not to be bored; Damien didn't have time, and they were still at least a week away from hearing back from

Ciriis in Elaarwen. She hated embroidery with a passion, although she was skilled at it to his untutored eye; he kept her entertained for a full two days by asking her to teach *him* how to do it, but then her restlessness was back.

She wanted *physical* activity as much as *mental* activity.

Tired of fighting her, Jason relented a bit and suggested they go for walks to rebuild her stamina. To his lack of surprise, and Genevieve's utter disgust, she couldn't make it around the castle's curtain-wall without a good long rest... twice. But *on* the curtain-wall he had to fend off well-meaning questions from the castle guards and anything that might tell the Queen how the situation was deteriorating in Elendria.

Adam was in little better shape. Damien was working himself to the bone trying to keep up with his work as well as Genevieve's. No matter how much he delegated, things seemed to keep coming back to him for final approvals. A country trained to defer to the whims of a tyrant moved but slowly to believing that their 'new' king was a reasonable man.

A couch long enough for Damien to sleep on had been installed in his new office, but he was collapsing there at least daily. Adam had quietly had the wine replaced with fruit juices and herbal teas, which had helped some... but not enough.

And to complicate it all, due to the soul-bond both King and Queen were completely aware of the other's condition, adding the stress of worrying about each other to the whole mix.

And there was something else...

"It's doing this every time we're near each other," Damien sighed, as the four of them met one evening in the royal suite. Little sparks of white fire fizzed and popped around him and Genevieve.

"All night long?" Jason asked with some alarm. It seemed like a fire hazard to him.

Genevieve nodded. "Damien is hardly getting any sleep."

"Neither are you," the young King retorted with amiable exhaustion. "And here I always thought that keeping my wife awake all night would be a good thing. Or at least *fun.*"

She rolled her eyes.

"It's the soul-bond," Genevieve explained to the others. "We've tried this, this *abstaining* before. We're not *complete* fools, you know," she added with a sharp look at Jason. "We knew I needed more recovery time before trying again. But the magick of the soul-bond doesn't care."

Damien sighed again. "Based on past experience, we have maybe another day or so before we won't have a choice. And Genevieve conceives immediately every time."

"What do you mean you 'won't have a choice'?" Jason asked at the same moment as Adam asked sardonically if they'd never heard of contraceptives.

Damien blushed as bright as his wife's hair. "The bond... does to us approximately what it did in the very beginning," he mumbled.

Adam snickered. "Meaning you can't keep your hands off each other."

"*Hands* wouldn't be a problem," Damien told him dryly, his face still scarlet. "We've tried everything – yes, including contraceptives – to avoid another pregnancy."

"*Everything?*" Adam asked archly.

"The Royal Library is quite... extensive," Genevieve replied with a hint of a smirk. "And Damien is *very* well-read." Even Adam had to choke a bit on that one, which left Genevieve the only person *not* blushing furiously.

"So, what can *we* do?" Jason asked. "You're nowhere near ready for another pregnancy," he told Genevieve bluntly. "The midwives have told me more than once over the last several years that you should have at *least* three months to recuperate, and longer would be better."

She didn't disagree, which told him more than words about how she was actually feeling. That... and that she was more or less lying down on the couch, with her legs stretched out and her feet resting in Damien's lap.

The young King looked uncomfortable. "I don't know. I'm so tired... It's hard to think. To *remember* what I've read." That was quite an admission for a man who seemed to have inhaled the entire Royal Library and have the cross-references ready to hand at any instant.

Genevieve sighed and reached out to caress her husband's head to a disconcerting crackle and hiss as sparks of white fire went flying – landing alarmingly close to Jason, though neither King nor Queen seemed to notice. "He remembers what he's found. He just doesn't want to tell you. Neither do I. We're already asking too much."

Adam gave them both a wary look.

Jason just sighed.

"Tell me." He glanced at his love. "*Us,*" he amended.

Adam rolled his eyes, but gave Jason a small, tight nod of appreciation for the inclusion.

"As near as we can tell," Genevieve said reluctantly, "this correlates with the two to three days when I'm most able to conceive. There doesn't seem to be any power in the world able to prevent a soul-bonded couple from conceiving during that time."

"Or from *trying* to," Damien looked at the floor between his feet. His elbows were on his knees, and he looked... heavy... somewhere between despair and despondency. It was a sharp contrast to how he usually had to contain his excess energy by pacing or bouncing on his toes.

"Will power – just simply doesn't exist. I can't not touch her."

As he continued on, the King's hands balled into fists. It was the greatest display of frustration Jason had ever seen from the younger man... who had, after all, learned to hide unhelpful expressions of his emotions in the cruelest lesson possible.

"I've tried. *We've* tried. Locking the doors, staying in separate parts of the castle... it's like there's a... a *blankness,* and then when we're aware again, we're together." Damien winced, looking as if there was more he *could* add but *wouldn't.*

Jason supposed the royal pair were both aware enough of their surroundings during these periods of 'blankness' that they could countermand any orders they might have earlier given their Guards to keep them apart. On the other hand, even if they weren't, would any of the Royal Guards – Secret or otherwise – be willing to bar either monarch from doing *anything,* even if they'd been told to do so?

Surely with Damien's penchant for nighttime wanderings, the Guards were alert to the idea that they needed to protect him from his own potential muzzy-mindedness.

Though likely neither of the pair had wanted to admit to such a weakness...

"What happens if you're in different parts of the Realm?" Adam demanded. "That's been the case rather a lot these last few years." There was a note of resentment in his tone, since Damien and Genevieve's separations involved himself and Jason also being kept apart.

The young King spread his hands. "I'm sorry it's been this way, my friend. There's been so much to *do...* being able to have one of us in each place and still communicate through the bond... it's made sorting things out so much easier..."

"Easier, hah!" Genevieve interrupted. "Say *'possible.'* Our negotiations with Alpinsward and Minglemere went so smoothly because, even though they wouldn't talk directly to Damien, I could get enough from him through the bond to be able to answer the legal and economic questions right away. If not for that, we'd still be drawing up a framework with Alpinsward *today.''*

Damien gave her a grateful smile. "As she says. I've hated keeping you two apart almost as much as I've missed Genevieve myself... but haven't you noticed that somehow, within a month of her last miscarriage, she would always wind up back here with me? For some perfectly acceptable reason?"

"We didn't *plan* it," Genevieve answered the looks in the Captain's and Champion's eyes. "In fact, these last two times we planned for me *not* to come back. For a good long while."

Jason looked away, remembering how he had used the excuse of the five-year celebration to get her back here where he thought she could rest and recuperate. She'd been too dizzy from blood loss to read Damien's letter saying how much he would miss her during the festivities, so the Champion had been more deceitful than he could remember ever having been in his life and read it to her selectively to make it sound like a summons to return. And then he'd used that 'summons' mercilessly to force Genevieve to eat and rest enough that she could ride out from the Elendrian border, rather than in a carriage... or on a stretcher.

Once they were well past the border and most of the likely spies, he'd told her that her options were the carriage, the stretcher, or the front of his saddle. She'd chosen the carriage, of course, though she'd insisted on riding into Emeralsee so that 'the people wouldn't worry.'

"It doesn't matter," Genevieve said, reaching as if to touch his hand reassuringly, then pulling back quickly before she did so, her gaze flickering to Damien and Adam. "If not for you, there would have been something else."

"Three years ago, during the Alpinsward negotiations, it was the attempted coup at Cedarwen – that took both of us to resolve," Damien said.

"Two years ago, during the negotiations with Minglemere," Genevieve went on, "the Baron took sick and then we had that scare over Papa... then later the Minglemere lakes flooded and we had to wait until that abated." She bowed her head. "Minglemere hasn't had flooding that bad since before Queen Marian's time. Last year it was the hurricane that flattened half the coast, and Damien needed me here to help coordinate the aid we were sending." She looked like she felt guilty over the natural events.

"You're conflating things," Adam scolded, though his tone was gentle if exasperated. "You both know better than to assume you're responsible for things like Duke Aldred's heart attack and natural disasters. The Gods maybe, but you two aren't *Gods*."

"Queen *Marian* says we aren't imagining the connection, Adam," Genevieve flared at him.

Adam's mouth twisted dryly at the reminder of the ghost of the former queen that supposedly haunted the castle and advised her descendants.

"Maybe *you're* imagining Queen *Marian*," he suggested.

Damien winced, glancing at a particular bit of air over the chair to Adam's left. "Please, Adam, apologize. She has a very piercing voice for those of us who can hear her."

"Which includes *Papa*," Genevieve reminded the Captain. "And it's not like *he's* as flighty and imaginative as you seem willing to accuse *us* of being. Nevermind, Grandmother," she sighed. "*I* probably wouldn't believe in you either, if I couldn't hear or see you." She gave the same spot of air that Damien had been looking at an ironic expression, then shook her head and focused on Adam again. "*Rosa* says the correlations are too frequent not to be linked. We've sent the dates to Ciriis to look over... she hasn't gotten back to us yet."

"You're serious..." Jason raised his eyebrows and shook his head in wonder. "You really think the flooding in Minglemere – and the hurricane – happened just to force Genevieve to come home."

"Come home and *conceive*," the Queen corrected him somewhat bitterly.

Adam leaned back and crossed his arms. "I still don't see anything we can do about this. Anyone can look at Genevieve and see that she's not healthy enough to carry a child yet. If you were trying to adjust the timing we all agreed on."

"We're not," Damien said quickly. "Jason's points were all spot on. She's stronger now than she's been–" Genevieve nodded, "–but we all know how far she has to go."

"Then what?" Jason asked.

Damien put his face in his hands.

"Sweet love," he said to Genevieve. "I can't *do* this. It's hard enough to *think* of..."

"Shhh..." she soothed, drawing a line of white fireworks down his back. "I'll do it." She looked grimly at Adam. "We think – we *hope* – that the magick can be fooled. It should be only the pair of *us* that are so infernally fertile together. Jason could use some form of contraceptive and it should work."

Damien's faint skeptical expression suggested that he didn't agree. Or agree entirely. But with which part?

"But we can't do this alone," Genevieve went on. "And even if *Jason* agrees... it's not enough. Damien... isn't going to be himself. We're *supposed* to be together. We..." she faltered. "Have you never wondered why we host all those dances and don't dance at them? Jason, you *know* how much I love to dance."

He gave her a halfhearted smile as he absorbed what she was, what *they were,* asking him to do. This time. A month of nights indeed. "It's both of our jobs to know where the two of you are at all times and make sure you're safe. We're well aware that you sneak off to dance privately in the nearby hallways."

She nodded. "Where somehow the music can always be heard. Did you notice that first year, that we had all the musicians' stands repositioned, so it would be?"

Jason hadn't. Though Adam didn't look surprised – he was more musically inclined.

"Even during normal times, when we aren't... sparking," Damien said to the floor, "I can't bear to see another man touch her. Even so little as in a dance."

"And I'm just as bad," Genevieve hastened to add.

"Oh, hardly," the young King laughed self-deprecatingly, but his voice was colored with shame. "You didn't abuse *your* power and assign knights to far reaches of the Realm just because they *looked* like they wanted to kiss your hand." His eyes flickered to Adam. "Too much power for one man..." he murmured, and the Captain twitched slightly.

She snorted. "Need I mention pretty little Maree?"

Damien winced, and Jason lifted an eyebrow curiously.

"The knife-sharpener from the kitchen," Genevieve explained. "She helped us re-take the castle, took out one of Prydeen's bullyboys with a frying pan as he battled Damien, making herself a Hero who had Saved the King's Life, so far as *she* was concerned anyways. So, *then* she decided that *Damien* should be her reward." She gave her husband an ironic look. "Not that he had any particular reputation for chastity at that point."

"Oh, *I* remember," Adam had a look of enlightenment. "The little tart who kept trying to sneak past my men."

"She succeeded," Genevieve's tone was very dry. "And more than once."

"Genevieve... was not particularly gracious," Damien said euphemistically.

"Elista made sure she found other gainful employment," Genevieve commented with prim distaste. The woman's promotion from senior maid to castle Chatelaine had been well-deserved. "Down in the City. At least *men* don't throw themselves like that at Damien," she sighed. "Or at least the magick doesn't care. It doesn't make me wild to see *men* around him."

Jason noticed to his private amusement that his young king gave her a sideways look and breathed very slowly when she said that. Adam caught his love's eye, and the amusement was shared. Damien was a very handsome young man, after all, as well as the center of power and prestige and privilege. And while he had only ever taken female lovers to Jason's knowledge, Damien was openly accepting and encouraging of himself and Adam, and notoriously open-minded about everything.

It would be... *surprising*... if he hadn't been propositioned by some of his knights or young lords.

Something else clicked. "But you have *me* following Genny around all the time," he noted. "For Gods' sake, Damien, you watched me *kiss* her a month ago."

The young King looked very... tight-strung.

"Yes," he said, and left it at that. A hint of the internal struggle that presumably went on every day.

Genevieve gave the Champion a poignant smile. "But that *was* a month ago, before *this* came back..." She ran a finger over Damien's shoulder to harvest another curl of white sparks, and as he leaned into her touch, Jason realized that the fire didn't bother *them* at all. In fact... they seemed to be *enjoying* it. "And, under normal circumstances *you* don't touch me, Jason. Not unless it's a matter of saving my life."

Of course, he didn't. Avoiding physical contact between the two of them was all that had made the last five years bearable. Adam gave him a speculative look, but Jason suspected that whatever conclusions he was coming to about the reasons for that omission were going to be rather different than the truth. At least, he hoped so.

"It... helps..." Damien admitted. His eyes told a different story.

Jason realized that the young King knew *precisely* why his Champion avoided even casual contact with his queen, and felt a surge of guilt that he hadn't found some way to explain things to Adam.

Please, he prayed to whatever Gods might be listening, *please take this 'reaction' away once it's sated. Let us be friends again, the way we were as children.*

"So, you want... what?" Adam asked. "*I'm* supposed to restrain Damien from doing damage while Jason and Genevieve try to 'trick' the magick?"

The Captain didn't look *happy,* of course.

But he almost looked... resigned.

And... surprisingly unsurprised. Though Adam *did* spend the better part of every day at Damien's side – playing confidante and adjutant and secretary, as much as Captain and bodyguard, to listen to his nightly complaints. Adam had been passing off a larger portion of his own work to his Second, he'd told Jason, to keep the Royal Guard from falling apart while he supported their increasingly exhausted young king.

Damien went bright red again, and buried his face in his hands. Abruptly he stood up from the couch and went to their bedroom, closing the door firmly behind him.

Adam raised an eyebrow, but Jason was all too afraid he understood his young king's reaction.

Genevieve sighed.

Jason decided to try to change the subject slightly. "Genny, why haven't you been staying quiet and still here in the castle once you knew you'd conceived? I can understand that first time – there really wasn't much choice about re-taking the castle," he suffered her triumphant smirk graciously, since he and Adam had both argued vehemently against it, "but since then? Women who *don't* have trouble carrying babies to term are more likely to lose them when riding and fighting."

She leaned back into the leather couch and brought her knees up to her chest, wrapped her arms around them. Dressed as she was, in a gown, it was a profoundly vulnerable position. He began to understand her preference for her hunting leathers – gowns provoked a protective reaction in the men around her, one that she didn't usually appreciate.

Right now... their perception of her was clearly the last thing on her mind.

"Because it didn't *matter,* Jason. Queen Marian could see that there's been something wrong with the child every time. She showed Damien how to tell also – for him, it's connected to his Healing abilities, and believe me, he's tried to fix every last one." Genevieve looked... too worn for tears. "Our best hope has been to keep us far apart from each other after the inevitable miscarriage. And you see how well that's done."

The Queen took a long, slow breath. "Sometimes I feel like it's been so long since we've been together that it would be easier to just stop *breathing* than to keep this up. A soul-bond isn't meant to be stretched this much."

She tried a laugh that didn't have any humor in it as Jason fought down a surge of panic at that desperate, desolate description.

"When the bond first... happened... I resented it, did you know that? I didn't want something tying me to a man I'd seen *once* when we were both children. Even if the reason that I'd *come* here to find out if he was the kind of king we were hoping for – the reason I believed he *might be* – was the memory of his eyes that had haunted me in all the years between..." She shook her head, swallowed, turned her head away and rested it on her knees. To hide – what? A resurgence of that resentment would surely be understandable since the soul-bond was possibly dragging them to their deaths.

Or if not resentment... resignation? Because she'd given up hope, even with this mad scheme?

Jason had known that Damien had been infatuated with the idea of Genevieve since he was a child. It had been impossible to miss, even if he hadn't confided in Jason in a way that he never had to Ciriis or Adam. He hadn't known that *Genevieve* had also remembered that brief encounter...

Adam cleared his throat. "What does all this have to do with him storming out of here?"

"Love," Jason said softly. "That wasn't *storming*. That was *fleeing*."

"'Fleeing'? Fleeing what?"

"You, I think," Jason told him.

"*Me?* Why?" Adam was baffled and more than slightly irritated. Even offended. "I've already signed off on this insanity, haven't I?"

Genevieve looked back at him and shook her head. "Not *this* insanity."

She put her feet back on the floor and stood up to glare down at them, seated on the other couch. The advantage of height wasn't usually something that could be used against him, tall as he was, and Jason found himself distinctly uneasy to have to look up at her. His mother usually insisted that he sit when she scolded him for just this reason.

"Blast it all, *Captain*. Do you think this is something we invented to *inconvenience* you? Don't you think I'd rather have a child – or two, like Rosa, or even one a *year* and be nothing but a womb on legs – than go through this over and over and *over*? Than to have to come and *beg* for your help? And then, this... we'd *hoped*... we'd *planned*..." She threw her hands up and spun away, walking to the desk on the other side of the room and half-sitting on it, tense and frustrated... and clearly unable to stand unsupported for any longer than it took to walk that little distance.

"Genny..." Jason tried, after a moment of silence so thick he could have cut it with his boot-knife. "Damien said the grotto was special. Sacred. Shielded, even. Have you ever tried to have one of you go *there* to avoid this..."

He wasn't sure what to call it. Mating frenzy seemed correct... but massively inappropriate when referring to his sovereigns.

She eyed him darkly, but he saw the shift when her gaze turned thoughtful. "No. I don't know. From what he and Queen Marian have explained to me, though, magick should work better to *amplify* what is natural, rather than hold it back." She blushed, unaccountably, at some memory of her own.

"We could ride out there and see if... it makes any difference," he offered.

Genevieve gave him a sad smile. "Dear Jason. And if it doesn't? You and I there, alone – or so I presume. And Adam here with Damien?" She closed her eyes. "I'm sorry. I'm *so* sorry to have put you both through this. He's right. We can't... we..."

She shook her head, squeezing her eyes tightly closed and tilting her head back. Keeping back tears, it was all too obvious. The tall Champion hadn't seen her shed a tear in years, even through all those increasingly horrible miscarriages. Not since... not since he'd arrived too late to save the day and she was brushing away tears at having thought her father slain before her eyes by Lord Prydeen's bullyboys until Damien's Healing powers proved equal to the task of saving the old duke.

"I think I'm missing something here," Adam said bemusedly. He frowned at Genevieve, then looked at Jason with a raised brow. "But I seem to be the only one."

Jason looked back at his love and sighed. "Adam, my love, Damien isn't going to be *raging* because Genevieve is with me... at least where he can't see us. He's going to be reacting to what he feels from her, through their bond, and be overcome with *desire.*" He paused to let that sink in. "And since the hope is to fool the soul-bonding magick, the hope is that his *desire* can be sated without Genevieve."

Adam gave them both a horrified look. "You're joking." He looked at them again. "You're not... this is insane. Damien is... is like a little brother to me!"

There was something... just slightly off with Adam's dismay, even though he'd said all the right things, had the right expression... Almost as if he'd *expected* this? No, that was impossible. Jason was just trying to find ways to justify the whole bizarre situation and tell himself Adam wasn't as disturbed by it all as he was. As he himself was also. Really.

Genevieve waved a hand to dismiss the thought without opening her eyes. "We'll find another solution. Somehow. We've had word out to other kingdoms. Eventually we'll get word about how to cope with this. Or we'll find some sorcerer willing to help – one strong enough to block the bond for long enough..."

That... seemed like an extraordinarily bad idea. Adam dropped his furious glare at the door to the royal bedchamber to purse his lips at the floor, and Jason knew exactly why. The Captain had decided that, in order to keep his king and queen safe, it was critical for him to understand more about magick. He hadn't shared everything he'd learned with Jason, but one fact had stood out as crystal clear: Damien's link to the Realm made him one of the most powerful sorcerers in the *world*. They were all blessed that, unlike his grandfather, he had no interest in using that power for his own gain or amusement – or to build an empire. But to find another sorcerer, even more powerful than he, in hopes that said sorcerer would *also* have the Realm's best interests at heart... they didn't need another Lord Prydeen any more than they needed another King Reginald.

The lamplight flickered as Damien came back into the room, and took his wife in his arms. She seemed limp, and the flickering shadows cast her face in deeper relief. He bent to scoop her up and carry her back to the couch, completely ignoring the renewed sparks and trails of magickal white fire. Genevieve didn't object.

The young King was strong – Jason had seen to that himself when Damien was little more than a boy; he continued to make sure the younger man kept up with his sword practice when he could, and assumed that Adam did the same when he was gone – but Genevieve was nearly as tall as her husband, and all muscle. Damien should never have been able to pick her up that easily.

The Champion thought about how much effort it had been to carry her out of the negotiating tent in Elendria... and how much *less* effort it had taken for him to move her more recently when she abruptly ran out of energy on one of their walks.

She wasn't *regaining* the *weight* she'd lost. She was *losing* the *muscle*.

When was the last time he had seen Genevieve sit up straight – or stand without leaning on something for more than a moment, Jason suddenly wondered. Ten miscarriages in five years... he knew she was worn out, but for the first time he wondered if she was damaged inside. She couldn't be, he argued with himself. Damien would have Healed anything that happened to her.

And yet... Damien wasn't all powerful. He couldn't fix whatever was wrong with the children they conceived, for example.

"She's not stronger, is she." He heard himself saying, not asking. "She's worse off than when I brought her home. You should have come to us sooner. Before she was so ill."

Damien looked over his shoulder from settling her on the couch, tucking pillows around her – those silly little throw pillows that had appeared all over this room shortly after their marriage. Genevieve's eyes were shut, and her breathing was even... but shallow.

"She wouldn't let me. Not that *either* of us *wanted* to." The young King sat down cross-legged on the floor at her side, and leaned back against the base of the couch to face his oldest friends, looking nearly as weary as his wife. Nearly as *worn out*. His face was full of the knowledge that they didn't have another chance after this one.

"Jason..." Damien hesitated, then gave up and extended his hand. The grey pearl of the Heir's Ring gleamed in his palm. "Take it," he added when his Champion made no move.

The tall knight looked at the Ring. "Damien, I can't." He reached blindly to his side, and felt Adam take his hand. "I'm just a knight."

Damien shook his head. "You've been at my side or Genevieve's for the last five years. You know as much as I did, then. And you have a gift for getting people to trust you," he smiled in memory, "as I have reason to know."

It was all the arguments Adam had given him after the last strange conversation in this room. Jason wanted to shake his own head, but couldn't even bring himself to move that much as he stared at his king. Adam's fingers squeezed in counter-pressure – was Jason shaking or tensing too tightly? He couldn't tell.

"Dammit, Jason," the King flared, that flash of temper so rare that his Champion could honestly not recall the last time he'd seen it. "There's no one else I can trust this to. There's not anyone of Alsterling blood – however distant – to whom I'd trust the Realm, and the Sword agrees with me. Rosa gave it *back*. My next choice would be Tomas, but I can't even get the Council to approve him as a negotiator – what chance would he have as king?"

Adam sucked in a breath. And looked harder at the sleeping – no, *unconscious*, Jason realized – Queen. And at the shadows beneath Damien's eyes that weren't all from the extra work he'd been doing.

"Heal her," the Captain said harshly.

Damien laughed without humor, much as Genevieve had done. "Don't you think I've *tried?*"

His eyes were too bright, silver more than grey, as he looked over his shoulder at the woman he'd loved since he was eight. "This happens all the time now. At least... I don't think I could bear what Duke Aldred has lived."

Genevieve's mother had died when she was eight, twenty-five years earlier. The soul-bond would ensure that Damien didn't face such a lonely fate because *he* would die soon after his wife.

"Put the damned Ring on, Jason. If I'm willing to name you Regent – and you're willing to accept *that* – then it shouldn't come as a surprise that I name you Heir on your own recognizance." He gestured to the desk. "I wrote up a proclamation and we both signed it earlier. She agrees." He looked at his wife again, briefly. "I'll have it copied and distributed tomorrow, so you'll have less trouble when the time comes." He gave Adam a wry look. "It may be that you'll have to divest the Council of its powers. I'd follow Adam's advice on that if I were you."

"Not that *you* do..." Adam muttered, trying to cover up his stunned tone with disgruntlement.

Damien flashed him a smile that was almost as charming as the one they were used to. "Ah, but *I'm* not *Jason*. I'm the 'Sorcerer-King' – Chosen by the Sword and Bound to the Realm... What I can get away with won't work for *him*. And vice-versa."

Jason looked at his love. "Adam..."

Adam swallowed. "Take the Ring, Jase. Someone has to wear it until our daughter's old enough." He slid off the couch to half-kneel across the low table from his king. "I'll do whatever you need me to, Damien. Whatever you *both* need."

Which wasn't anything more than he'd pledged – than they'd *both* pledged – to the younger man when he was nineteen. But there was something different about this repetition. Adam's voice and posture somehow suggested a surrendering of... *something*... that had been held back? *Something*... that he'd *known* he would be called on to give?

Jason couldn't begin to guess how he was getting all of that from watching his love kneel to the young man they'd worked to set on the throne. Adam had knelt to Damien a thousand times in the last ten years, surely... this was no different in any measurable way...

The young King's smile grew a bit strained. "I honestly think it's too late, Adam. Jason is right. We waited too long."

Jason took the Ring out of his friend's hand and slid it onto his own finger. "Where there's life, there's hope, Damien."

Genevieve stirred. "Jason suggested that the grotto might shield us from each other, love," she murmured. "I could ride out tomorrow to see..."

"No!" All three men said it at once, then exchanged a bemused look.

"No," Jason said again, more gently. "You're not going anywhere for a long while, Genny."

"*Jason* will take *Damien* there tomorrow," Adam told her decisively. "*I'll* stay here with *you*." He paused. "So long as my King approves?"

Because they didn't dare chance those white fires engulfing Jason and forcing Genevieve to conceive too early. That *should* only be possible with her soul-bonded... Jason decided not to think about that point too hard.

Damien carefully kept his eyes on his wife. "Jason?"

Jason gave his love a long look. Adam didn't bother to try to feign innocence. Or ignorance. "It's just a scouting run. To see if you can feel the bond while you're in the grotto."

The young King nodded heavily. "Very well. We'll leave after breakfast."

Chapter FOUR

Surpises

JASON HATED TO ADMIT TO physical failings, but he was hard put to keep from yawning as his huge warhorse cantered alongside Damien's dressage-trained steed.

The young King's palfrey was as tall in the shoulder as Jason's warhorse, but much less massive, and seemed positively dainty in comparison: she was a beautiful, elegant bay mare by the name of Sunset, with a fiery spirit, but gentler than a lamb with Damien. The horse had been a gift from Duke Aldred when he and Genevieve had wed; Siovale was more famous for its horses, but Elaarwen's breeding was clearly not to be scoffed at. Jason had taken to riding his own huge chestnut on the campaigns with Genevieve, the gelding's bulk and muscle being up to the task of hauling him around in full plate armor to overawe the enemy. The giant drafthorse he had ridden back to the castle during Harald of Siovale's usurpation had sold him on the value of heavier steeds than the average knight would ride; Jason's current mount was a warhorse-drafthorse crossbreed.

It had been late when he and Adam had returned to their own rooms, and they had stayed up later still, having a discussion that wandered closer to the edges of an argument than he wanted to admit. Not that they hadn't had their share of disagreements over the years... usually, he realized, with a feeling that bordered both dismay and amusement but wasn't quite either, in the context of Damien.

The first child they had tried to raise together, for all that he'd been fifteen and nearly a man by the time they found him.

Hopefully *only* the first.

Though it had usually been *Jason* who was feeling exasperated and worn out from dealing with the frightened boy-prince and his interminable fears and fear-born stubbornness. Not that he'd ever let Damien – or, indeed, anyone other than Adam – see how tempted he was to give up. Despite the hot temper and sharp tongue that had made Adam cede the project of taming the half-feral prince to Jason, it was Adam who had never flagged in his faith and his compassion for Damien. All that experience with his younger brothers and sisters, no doubt.

As usual, Damien slowed down once they were outside the confines of the city, although he'd been the perfectly kind and generous young king as they had traversed the crowded streets and marketplaces. He was known to stop and answer questions and his people had no qualms about doing just that, from the least little urchin in the street to the most pompous merchant. The exact opposite of his grandfather – precisely and intentionally so.

He greeted every citizen with a smile and sincere interest, but sped up just enough between times that it was obvious he had somewhere else to be.

Outside the city, though, and beyond the press of people and the urban sprawl that extended a few miles past the city-wall... the young King's demeanor changed.

The countryside was beginning to show the first touches of Autumn – color-washed leaves in every shade but green, a few bare branches, fields shorn of their crops, and cattle grazing on the crop-stubble. A faint haze of dust rose beneath their horses' hooves, smelling of chaff and dry leaves, to be caught up by the light, cool breeze.

It was peaceful enough, Jason supposed, but Damien seemed to see an entirely different place. His expression grew relaxed, losing lines of tension around his eyes that had become so constant that Jason hadn't even noticed them until they eased. He looked years younger.

"I've missed this," the young King admitted. "Even after all this time, I forget that I'm allowed to leave the Castle."

"We should have gotten you out more when you were a boy," Jason sighed.

To his surprise, the young King shook his head. "You did exactly right. The last thing I – any of us – needed was for my grandfather to realize there was anything worthwhile about me." He shuddered slightly, then opened his eyes wide to the open fields as if he could absorb them a bit more that way. A deeper breath almost suggested he was trying to inhale them as well. "Lord Prydeen suggested once that King Reginald would have taken me as his apprentice if he'd realized what I might become. And then where would we all be?"

"Still in the middle of a civil war," the Champion answered. "With Genny on the other side."

"Or... worse," Damien said soberly, and as Jason wondered if he should ask what 'worse' might have been, went on. "I... suspect that I'd have been drawn to the Sword eventually. It was right there in plain sight in the City, after all. Or Genevieve would have been. It would have spoken for her if I hadn't been there, or if I were... no longer worthy. And she and I would have been drawn together once we were in such close proximity. And then the soul-bond would have kicked in."

Jason's eyes widened. "And King Reginald would have had Heir, Sword, and Rebel Duchess all in one hand."

Damien nodded. "Genevieve would like to believe that she came to look into my eyes because somehow that would tell her whether I was the king she hoped I was. *I* don't think that was it at all. *I* think she was drawn here by the soul-bond and the Sword. And... I don't believe she could tell anything about me by *looking into* my eyes." He smiled wryly. "Except, maybe, how much I love her."

Jason wasn't so sure. Damien's eyes had a quality to them that seemed to shine from the depths of his soul. "She told us that she remembered your eyes from when you met as children."

The young King snorted. "We never *met*. At least not so that we were introduced. I was the youngest of a herd of my cousins, all lined up to do honor to the Duke of Elaarwen and his daughter, come to Court at last. Our gaze met, once, though *I* saw *her* any number of times that Summer. I'm more surprised that she had a clue who *I* was enough to connect that one glance with my name when I was crowned. Even if she remembered my *eyes.*" His tone was very dry and he gave his Champion an odd, sideways look before returning those *eyes* to the road ahead of his horse. "*You* spent much more time with her that Summer."

Jason took the hint as it was intended. "My family and hers have been friends for generations. Our residences in the City are next door to each other. I saw Genny climbing out of the Stellarine townhouse the first night they arrived and followed her, thinking to keep her out of trouble. We'd been introduced earlier that day, though I'd seen her across a room a number of times when we visited back and forth."

Jason hadn't been important enough for Countess Solway to give his name to the duke and his daughter, but she'd never been willing to leave him home in Brindlewell. At least until she sent him to be a page... and then when she realized he might be *useful*...

"My mother was talking about seeing if Duke Aldred would be interested in betrothing us." The tall knight smiled faintly. "We were caught, and I was put on bread and water rations. And read the riot act about my behavior and how I had likely ended any chance of a betrothal. Not that any of that meant a thing to me at thirteen – *I* just wanted to earn my shield."

And be away from his mother, terrifying woman that she was.

That, at least, hadn't changed.

Five years ago, Damien would have had suppressed panic in his eyes at the thought of having lost Genevieve before he'd ever really met her. Today, he just seemed interested in hearing the story from Jason's perspective.

"The next night Genny snuck *into* my room," he went on. "She'd gotten much the same treatment, except the part about being confined to her room. Since they were on an official trip to Court, Duke Aldred couldn't really do that and present a proper face. So, she'd used her freedom to raid their kitchen of sweets and brought me a knapsack-ful to apologize for getting me in trouble."

Damien laughed aloud. "It didn't occur to her that this might make it *worse?*"

"Apparently not," Jason admitted. "It did to *me*, though." He chuckled with the ease of having many years between the incident and the present. He could *remember* his adolescent fearfulness now, but it wasn't the visceral terror he'd felt at the time. It *wasn't*. "I really can't imagine just how badly my mother would have taken it to find Genny there. In the end, the only way I could get her to *leave* was to promise to go with her somewhere the next day when we were both free."

"She's... persistent," Damien said, feelingly.

Jason nodded. "It turned out she wanted to go down to the docks."

Damien paled. "You didn't."

Cleaning up the underworld of crime that seemed to have made the docks its own was always near the top of the King's to-do list, but it had thusfar been eclipsed by other, more urgent, priorities. Still, his connection to the Realm meant Damien was all too aware of what went on there.

Jason shook his head. "I knew better than to do that. I offered to teach her to use a sword instead."

Damien frowned. "I thought she'd been learning swordplay since she was seven or eight. Four or five years *before* she met you."

The blonde knight sighed. "How was *I* supposed to know that? None of the girls *I* had grown up around knew – or *cared* – about learning to fight. I'm not even sure why I suggested it to her, except... Genny wasn't *like* any other girl I'd ever met."

"No..." The King chuckled. "So that's why you told me never to play cards with her."

"What – when did I say that?"

A wry smile. "When you found us in the grotto. Five years ago. You both told me some of the story then, too. But I was wondering... what?"

Jason was staring at him. "Damien, do you ever forget *anything?*"

The dark-haired man shrugged self-consciously. "Sure, I do."

"It doesn't seem like it."

Damien shrugged again. "Does it matter?"

Jason just shook his head in wonder. He had helped raise this man; how had he never understood just how remarkable he was? Genevieve had tried to tell him, and more than once, but he'd blown off her opinions as those of a woman in love. Jason had watched his boy-prince be crowned, become a sorcerer, and finally mature into a wise ruler. He was constantly startled by just how *much* Damien knew.

Why was it only *now* that it all came together, and he could see this larger picture of the king and man that his protégé had become?

Now, when it was such a risk that he might lose him?

It was abruptly obvious that a big part of how the naïve young prince had so quickly been able to grow into his role was due in no small part to that prodigious memory. Jason recalled Genevieve's comment last night about Damien being *very well-read...* presumably from all that time he'd spent hiding in the Royal Library. They'd all seen his ability to recall and correlate random-seeming facts in Royal Councils and private strategy sessions, but it hadn't seemed remarkable... perhaps because Damien himself was so diffident about it all, apparently believing that book-learning was somehow inferior to 'wisdom' attained in field-practice. And this, despite the fact that he proved that idea wrong, day in and day out.

The idea of trying to fill Damien's shoes was suddenly even *more* intimidating.

The Champion shook his head again in dismay.

"You were wondering something?" Jason asked, feeling almost as if he was trying to prove that he, too, could keep track of things.

Damien looked at him sideways again. "Why? Why spend all that time with a girl you'd just met? Why offer to teach her swordplay? And why keep going back when she knocked you on your ass?" Which *Jason* hadn't mentioned, so clearly *Genevieve* had at some point.

Something compelled a truth from Jason that he had barely acknowledged to himself. "If you're asking if I was in love with Genny... I don't know. I was only thirteen. And she was twelve. She was... *interesting*. It's the age when most boys and girls are beginning to be... *interested*. But there was never any other girl, or woman, who..."

"Yes..." Damien said quietly. Understandingly.

Too understandingly. "I never wanted more than friendship from her, Damien."

"Until five years ago."

"Even then." Jason paused. "She told you." It wasn't a question. He hadn't known until the night before, but the look in his friend's eyes then had made it obvious to him.

"There's no place for secrets like that in a marriage, Jason." The young King was looking down, his eyes glued to the road, and didn't see his Champion wince. "It nearly destroyed us at the beginning when she *didn't* tell me. Though since we'd known each other for all of two days, I can see why it wasn't... easy to bring up. But I saw the way you looked at each other that first day after the soul-bonding bubble released us, and... I couldn't bear it. I nearly killed us both out of stubbornness, trying to deny the soul-bond."

Jason shuddered. His memory of the pair of weeks he had spent watching his two friends fall apart... *knowing* he could only make things worse... *trying* to cope with this strange new desire... without letting *Adam* see how he was reacting...

And as they – and Ciriis – tried to hold together Damien's fragile new regime in the face of Lord Prydeen's grab for power... despite how uncharacteristically distracted their young King had suddenly become...

"Have you ever talked to Adam about this?" Damien asked, and Jason almost fell out of his saddle. Could the young King read *minds* now, *too*? Was he *more* powerful than his grandfather or Lord Prydeen had ever been?

"Here's the trail." Jason guided his horse onto it. A good distraction.

It was more of a game-track than a trail, but somehow it never overgrew to block the passage. Jason hadn't been here since early Summer, when he had been home for a few weeks at Genevieve's side and had managed one very special night out here with Adam. It wasn't really a convenient place to talk, there being just enough space to ride single-file on the narrow, twisting path through the trees. The ground was relatively flat, the bushes to the sides were neither prickly nor particularly grasping, but the track nearly doubled back on itself more than once, and there were a couple of spots where it almost seemed to diverge into a second trail if one wasn't watching.

Unfortunately, Jason was all too familiar with the trail, and so was his horse. Following it wasn't *enough* of a distraction to put the conversation out of his mind.

They reached the usual small meadow that was a perfect place to leave horses, just before the game-track curved steeply around a rock-outcropping, and then even more steeply down into the grotto itself. A tiny stream, that probably fed into the larger one in the grotto, provided water. The grass was thick and lush, even this late in the season; clearly mowed regularly by deer or other forest creatures, it was, as always, at the perfect height for the level of tenderness that horses preferred. The trees and scrub around the small area were too dense for contented horses to want to push through, and the trail that continued on, too steep. A fallen branch pulled across the game-track they had come in on served to close the meadow off as if it were a pen, and the horses could then roam freely therein.

The two men removed the gear they had brought – some food, blankets, a tinderbox with flint and steel – and unsaddled the horses. Jason didn't plan to spend the night, but it was wise to pack as if one did at this season, and they weren't sure how long it would take to test their hopes. If Damien attempted some magick... he was usually tired and hungry after.

Jason made as if to start down the trail first, and Damien let him, though there was a sense of gentle tolerance in his deference to his Champion's effort. As if he knew, on some level deeper than Jason could understand, that there was no cause for concern in this place.

Come to think of it, there had been no surprising the young King *anywhere* since the usurpation. Jason knew that something had happened to Damien and Genevieve the night they had returned to the castle; whatever it was had attuned the young King to his Realm and his surroundings most finely. On more than one occasion, he had seen Damien staring impatiently at a door, as if waiting, until a messenger burst in with unexpected news... unexpected to everyone but their young King, clearly.

Genevieve, too, seemed to have some sixth sense about Elaarwen, and, to a somewhat lesser extent than Damien, about the Realm at large.

"Since you didn't answer my question," the young King said, as he followed his Champion around the rock, "I think I can assume the answer is that you *haven't* spoken to Adam."

Jason wondered if he could get away with pretending to focus on negotiating the slippery path. Probably not. It wasn't *that* slippery, and if *he* could read Damien and Genevieve as well as he thought, *they* could probably read him, too. The problem with knowing people so long and so well.

"No."

Damien didn't ask him why not. Instead, "You're going to have to at some point."

"Do I? Is that an *order,* Your Majesty?" Sarcasm never seemed to roll off his tongue.

Damien didn't reply.

After a moment, Jason felt his shoulders sag from tense resentment into shame. "I'm sorry. That was unworthy of me."

"Hmmmn. Perhaps. But also, understandable."

They had reached the bottom of the trail and the grotto spread out before them.

To Jason, it was as it always was: the special place he had discovered and shared with a few special friends. Genevieve. Adam. Damien had been brought here by Genevieve. Rosa, Ciriis, and the knights who had served as Damien's initial Royal Guardsmen when they were all escaping the usurpation.

He suspected that some of those others had brought someone special here as well, but he had never run into anyone else here, or even evidence someone else had been here recently.

He had never shared, even with Adam, just why he had been ranging so far outside the city at the tender age of thirteen. Why he had *needed* a special place that no one else knew about. Though he suspected that Adam might have guessed.

"Does anything feel different yet?" Jason asked.

Damien shook his head, but didn't speak. He wandered around, looking into distances that didn't make sense to Jason.

"I've never come here without her," the King said at last.

"Can you feel her?"

"Hmmn? Oh, yes, of course. I can *feel* her at the farthest reaches of the Realm. And probably well beyond. *That's* not the question."

Well, that was what *Jason* had thought the question was...

Damien continued to wander around, seemingly absently. He wandered a few dozen yards down the stream to check on the beaver pond, spent some time smiling enigmatically and reminiscently at a small clearing along the way, then wandered back to the central area.

Bemusedly, Jason followed him. He had his own special memories of this place, after all. Many, many hours spent playing with Genevieve the Summer that they were children here. Fewer, but more intense, hours – though perhaps more, all told, over the course of nearly twenty years – with Adam.

"Shall we go back to the city, then?" Jason asked at last, when Damien seemed to have come to a stop and was smiling thoughtfully at a bit of rock wall, still with that enigmatic expression.

"What? Oh. No. Not yet. Are you hungry yet? I'm famished."

They dug out the food. Jason found a boulder to sit on, but Damien just dropped gracefully to the dry ground – a thin layer of dry soil and almost-scratchy moss over the rock shelf that was the floor of this part of the grotto. The amount of food that the young King put away made Jason wonder if he'd been doing some kind of magick while they wandered around. He was used to seeing Damien eat a lot when he had to use those powers, though he hadn't done anything that Jason could perceive since they arrived.

"So, you 'taught' her swordplay all Summer long?" Damien asked after he'd slowed down a bit.

Jason nodded. "She surprised me the first time – and yes, she knocked me on my ass." He grinned wryly. "But I was better than her," he added without false modesty.

"You still are," Damien commented. Then, dryly, "Of course you're better than *everybody*."

The Champion shrugged. "That's why you gave me the title, isn't it?"

"Not really," Damien surprised him by replying. "But it helped in explaining it to other people."

His young King noted the surprise. "You've been my Champion since you first showed up in the Library, Jason. No one else cared about what happened to me. No one else has sacrificed so much for my sake."

The tall knight surmised that no one had ever told the young King the truth about what happened in Zialest the year he was chosen as Heir... and why. Not that Jason wanted to do so himself...

"Until Genevieve."

"Until Genevieve," Damien confirmed. "But that's different." He shook away some tension and smiled again. "You could have been the worst swordsman in the Realm instead of the best, and I would still have named you my Champion."

Jason digested that. For so long he'd measured his worth by his skill with the sword. It was... disconcerting... to find that that wasn't what Damien valued him for at all.

"So… when did you know Adam was 'the one'?" Damien asked after a moment.

The blonde knight blinked at the change of topic. "Why?" he asked quizzically.

The younger man shrugged. "You've never talked about it. It seems the sort of thing friends know about each other. *I* told *you* about Genevieve when I was fifteen."

"Sixteen," Jason corrected. "You didn't say a word to me for the first year."

Unaccountably, Damien blushed.

"I hadn't spoken to *anyone* in years, Jason, not beyond a 'yessir, nosir' to my grandfather when I was summoned. I didn't know *how* to talk to anyone. And you were… you are…" He stopped and shook his head, still blushing.

Jason's eyebrows went up. He'd never guessed that Damien had had a crush on him at the time, but it all made sense, he supposed. Damien had been the right age, and Jason the first person who paid attention to him – well, better on him than a crush on the traitorous Lady Theresa, though cold as she was, that would have seemed unlikely. There had been other boys – and girls – with a similar reaction, after all, inevitably ones whom he had paid attention to for some reason or other. It was just the nature of many children of that age to fixate on someone.

As always, the knight discounted his own good looks, charisma, and inherent compassion as any part of the explanation.

"At that point, Genevieve was more of an abstract concept for me," Damien went on hesitantly. "I knew her name, and what she looked like… I listened enough and read the updates in the Royal Archives to know that her father was leading Elaarwen in Rebellion against the Crown." His eyes fell. "I knew she'd been married a year or so before you showed up."

Jason cleared his throat uncomfortably. It could have been *him* Genny was wedded to instead of Harald of Siovale, if his mother had had her way. If she had followed Duke Aldred into Rebellion. Alexa Solway and Aldred Stellarine had been friends since childhood; Jason still wasn't sure why she hadn't followed her old friend's lead. He couldn't regret that it had brought him and Adam together… but it would have spared Genevieve those years of abuse from Harald. Not to mention the rape when Harald 'reclaimed' her during his brief coup.

Damien was well aware of that back-story. Likely he was as torn over the alternate possibility that hadn't happened as Jason was.

Genevieve had apparently never looked back. She was stronger than either of the men.

"About my third year in the castle – I was a squire by then, and so was he – they started pairing me with Adam for things like honor guard duties. Things where you just want everything to look nice. We matched well, of course – both tall and blonde. And nearly the same height at the beginning, though I outpaced him a bit before long, of course, since he's a year younger. At first, I was slightly annoyed by it all. We all wanted the attention of the *older* squires and knights, not the younger ones. But he tended to scare off, well, *girls...*"

It was Damien's turn to raise his eyebrows. *"Girls?"*

The Champion shrugged. "Girls, women. I don't know why, but they would always try to flirt with me when I was standing duty. And other times. They didn't seem to believe I couldn't be interested in them. But when I realized that if Adam was with me, they veered off... well, it made me interested in spending more time with *him.*"

Damien snorted. "Adam's followed *me* around for years and it doesn't seem to help."

Jason gave him a wry look. "They probably imagine there will be some sort of advantages to being the one who ends up in your bed. *I* was just a poor squire."

"Not that poor. The Solway family is one of the most prosperous noble houses."

Jason's turn to look down. "I'm the younger son, not the Heir."

Damien, who had been born nearly as much junior to his older sister as Jason was to Megan, waved him to go on.

"Anyway, we'd gotten to the point where we spent a lot of time together. He didn't seem to mind me using him as girl-repellent." Damien snickered, and Jason ignored it. "I started to realize I enjoyed his company. I wasn't thinking about him romantically. He waited until shortly before I was knighted before he told me how *he* felt." Jason closed his eyes with a smile. That was one awkward conversation that had turned out very, *very* well. "It just seemed right after that."

He firmly decided that, if Damien pressed for more details, he would skip over the suffering of the next few years when he had been assigned to the unlamented Prince Oskar. Watching Adam watching him had been worse in some ways than living through it himself – and more terrifying, since he knew Adam's temper. Discouraging – or ignoring – the younger knight hadn't worked at *all...* for which he was now profoundly grateful, of course. But it hadn't been until Oskar was demoted from being Heir and Jason was free that they had truly found each other.

"He said you looked like someone had poleaxed you and he was terrified you were going to either laugh at him or avoid him thereafter." Damien informed him.

"Wait, you talked to *Adam* about this?" The tall knight wasn't sure how he felt about that.

"We've spent a lot of time together over the last several years," Damien said dryly. "About as much as you and Genevieve. Though I don't think he's ever felt it necessary to sleep on the floor beside my bed." He paused. "Not that I'm criticizing that decision. I've considered tying her up on any number of occasions."

Jason's eyebrows flew up and Damien blushed.

"To make her lie down and rest," he elucidated.

"Was I supposed to be imagining some other reason?" Jason asked archly, and Damien blushed harder until his friend laughed.

"What did it feel like to have the soul-bond happen?" the tall knight asked, once they'd settled again.

Damien smiled slowly. "Like everything I'd ever dreamed of and yearned for finally fit into place. Like there was hope and glory in the world."

Then he sighed. "If you asked *her*, she'd have a different answer. Genevieve had... a whole different set of dreams. None of which," he added ironically, "prominently featured a pair of grey eyes, regardless of what she tells you. As far as I can tell, she'd completely forgotten me until the announcement of my grandfather's death and my upcoming coronation. She claims she started having recurring dreams about me then. At least she calls them *dreams* instead of *nightmares*. Though I believe she's used the term 'haunted' several times."

"So cynical," Jason chided with amusement.

"Practical," Damien countered. "Somewhere in this fairytale there needs to be some practicality."

"Speaking of which..." Jason looked around them pointedly. "What *are* we doing here, Damien?"

"Testing," Damien replied.

"Testing *what* for the Gods' sake?"

"Several things," Damien stretched out his legs and leaned back on his elbows in the soft, damp moss, scratchy or not. "Firstly, whether Genevieve is injured further by my absence. As fragile as she is, *that's* my prime concern."

Jason nodded soberly. He couldn't disagree with that at all.

"Secondly, whether being in the grotto without her makes the soul-bond's demands easier or harder to bear. Third, whether the Council can manage without me for a day or two, because if we're right it's going to take at least a few days before I'm able to be useful again... and we all know how well things *didn't* go the last time I left Emeralsee for awhile and the Council was in charge." The pair of them exchanged winces in memory of that debacle.

"And lastly..." Damien shook his head. "Nevermind."

Jason looked at him curiously. "That... always makes me want to get the answer out of you."

Damien gave him a crooked smile. "I know."

Jason waited, but nothing seemed to be forthcoming. "All right then, what about the other issues? Or at least the first couple. I don't imagine you can tell how the Council is doing until we get back."

Damien snorted with amusement. "Oh, I'd know if there were any *major* disasters, but you're right, and I fully expect to need two days of catching up just to make up for being gone today."

Jason tilted his head. "Is it really worth it, working with them like this instead of just making decrees and issuing edicts?"

The King chuckled. "Like my grandfather, you mean? Adam's always onto me about not giving away all my power. But the Council actually had *more* power under Grandfather's rule than now, because he didn't care or pay attention. They had more *fear*, too, of course, because if he didn't like their work, he was liable to just have them killed." He chuckled again. "Adam disagrees, but I think that's mostly because he hates that I made him a voting member."

"That... might be half of it," Jason admitted. He'd listened to enough complaints from his lover that he knew the Council's work actually fascinated Adam. "Why did you anyways? Make him a voting member of your Council?"

"Training," Damien said softly, "So he'll be ready to support *you*."

Jason frowned at him. "I thought the whole point of *this* exercise," the tall knight waved around the grotto, his distraction and anxiety over the conversation making it a bigger gesture than he was usually prone to using, "was to eliminate that possibility. Besides which, you're just handing the problem of an Heir off onto *me*. And it's not like *I* can produce one more easily than you can."

He didn't want to think how long Damien had been considering the possibility of Naming him as Heir. Adam had been added to the Council three or four *years* ago.

"I surely hope you *can*. Or this 'exercise,' as you call it, is pointless," Damien retorted.

Jason could feel his own face warming at that reminder, but that was not, apparently, the King's point.

"*You* could appoint anyone you want as Heir, Jason," Damien told him, "assuming the Sword doesn't make some sort of preference extremely clear. Though I think it's unlikely to. The Alsterling dynasty will come to an end, and good riddance. Have the Council elect one of their number, but only for a set period of time – a year, two years, it doesn't matter. By the point they need to do it, they'll be used to making decisions for the Realm."

"Adam said you were talking about handing over all power to the Council, but I hadn't believed it," Jason breathed. The audacity of the idea blew him away. Half the Council was not noble-born, and he could just imagine his mother's reaction to the idea – or that of his sister, the Solway Heir.

"It probably *wouldn't* work as long as there's an Alsterling on the throne," Damien admitted. "At least one that the Sword has chosen and who has been properly Bound to the Realm. And there *are* benefits to a ruler with those attributes. But even the monarchs that have been so Bound haven't all had the same depth of connection that I do – Queen Marian certainly didn't, and we can see where that got us all. My grandfather *could* have, since he had more of a gift to work magick, but the Sword rejected him." He shook his head. "It's better to disperse the power so no one man or woman can harm so many people. Never again." His eyes glowed silver with determination.

"It makes sense when you put it that way," Jason admitted.

Though he could see why Adam hated this plan. All that effort to get Damien on the throne…

"But to answer the first question," the King went on after an acknowledging nod, "Genevieve has been resting soundly under Adam's supervision." He grinned. "I gave him a stack of my most boring reports and told him to read them aloud to her until she fell asleep. In the most droning voice he could manage. I think it worked."

Jason had to chuckle at that, and he wondered if Adam had put himself to sleep as well.

"As for the other... Whether it's harder or easier to bear, here in the grotto..." Damien sighed. "Yes and no. Lord Prydeen told me that the Realm had eaten my grandfather up, which is why he couldn't keep himself young and strong the way most of the Powerful evil wizards do. That no matter how they raised Power to feed to him, the Realm just *took* it. I could see the damage that tainted Power did to the fabric of the Realm when I... completed my Binding to It the night we re-took the Castle. I've spent much of the last five years trying to fix that underlying structure.

"The *problem* is that the Realm was never supposed to receive Power like that. It's like feeding someone a diet of dried bread and stale beer. It leaves them hungry all the time, even when they're full... but they develop a craving for the beer."

Jason tried to wrap his mind around the idea of the Realm being like a living creature. "So... how do you change the diet to something more nutritious?"

Damien gave him a wry look. "My first thought was to feed it *me... All* of me. Genevieve... objected, and I've come to realize she was right. I could have worked on the problem from the inside, but I could never have finished the job. There simply isn't enough of *me*. Of course, now I may not have enough *time...*"

He shook himself, and Jason belatedly realized that Damien was speaking literally, though how he could have gone *inside* the web of living magick that he claimed underlay the entire Realm, Jason could not imagine.

"Anyways," Damien went on after a moment, "what the Realm *really* wants is Power that's been raised in a healthier manner than the way my grandfather and Lord Prydeen did it. Ultimately all the Power becomes the same – 'flavorless' you might say – but there are different amounts of 'nutrition' initially."

The King looked upwards, his eyes focusing at distances where Jason could see nothing at all.

He seemed ageless in that moment... Ageless, and yet old and weary as the mountains. Not the young man that Jason knew so well.

"The Realm seems to feed and sustain itself on Power raised from... I'll call it 'happiness' for lack of a better word. Rightness. Plants and animals – even rocks and soil – generate that just by their very existence. They don't plan ahead, so they are never *unhappy,* even when they're *physically* miserable. The Realm uses that Power to keep Itself healthy – clean the waters, rejuvenate the fields, heal, prevent disease, that sort of thing.

"We humans, though... we create *voids* in the fabric of the Realm with our unhappiness. Our unmet expectations, our cruelties to each other, large and small both. That lack is usually made up – rewoven, if you will – by the Power we raise through our more intense 'happiness.'" He smiled. "Every love-marriage celebrated, every child born to eager parents... every night lovers spend together. It all feeds the Realm."

This seemed rather far off the topic of the soul-bond that was driving the King and Queen to their deaths. "Damien, what does this have to do with–"

"I'm *getting* there, Jason." He flickered a reproving glance at his Champion, who settled down with an odd sense of having the tables flipped on him by his *former* protégé. "It's not a simple answer. I've spent the last five years reading, learning from Queen Marian, and testing my theories to figure all of this out."

Jason subsided uneasily. He'd already learned more about magick in the last few minutes than in the rest of his life – he didn't really want to know *more*. This felt a bit too much like Damien trying to explain things to him in the event that he had to take the King's place.

Not that there seemed any polite way to stop him.

"Those of us who are Bound to the land in one way or another," Damien was going on, "rulers, priests, a few others – are given an ability to use Its Power in return for the responsibility to replenish it more than others. Some lands can be made fertile and prosperous with enough attention that would be dry and dead otherwise. And then there are lands like ours, which have been damaged *by* the ruler. *We're* just incredibly lucky that my grandfather wasn't fully Bound or the plains of Siovale and Reyensweir would be dust-bowls and the mountains of Elaarwen and Alpinsward would be barren, jagged peaks."

He paused. "I know I seem distracted a lot of the time, Jason. It puts a heavier burden on the rest of you, and I'm sorry for that. But with the Realm as damaged as It has been, I have to feed It Power directly and channel that Power to the right places... things a healthy Realm would usually be able to handle without direction."

"I understand that, Damien, and none of us mind–"

"*Do* you understand?"

The King focused his full attention on his Champion, and Jason shifted uncomfortably. Damien so rarely gave anyone his *full* attention, that he'd forgotten how intimidating it could be.

"Do you *really*? I'm sure everyone would be thrilled to know I stopped a potential plague arriving on the docks, and made sure the crops in Siovale were thriving. But how would *everyone* feel about the effort I spent stopping an outbreak of mange among the squirrels in Cedarwen, or the leaf-smut on a tiny forest plant that no one has ever bothered to name in Elendria?

"*Those* are my responsibility also – and it's part of why we need the Lost Provinces back. When I was Bound to the Realm, they were *still included.*" Damien paused, then sighed a little. "And it's why you need never worry about me trying to build an empire – even if it weren't too much work, the Realm Itself has decided its boundaries." His eyes glittered, the grey gone silver with sparkles in the waning afternoon light – *white* sparks? But Genevieve was far away...

"Oh." Jason didn't know what else to say. Squirrels and unnamed plants?

Damien looked upwards again, taking some of the pressure away. "This grotto – it's a concentrator of sorts. What Power is raised here echoes around and stays, except for what eventually drains away into the Realm." He frowned. "There's some sort of amplifying effect I don't understand also. It's as if each pulse of Power is reflected from the walls bigger and stronger than it was to begin with. Which makes no sense... the Power has to come from *somewhere*..." He shook his head. "It's not important now.

"What *you* wanted to know is if the grotto makes the soul-bond's requirements on me and Genevieve easier or harder to bear."

Jason nodded, wondering if his king would actually *answer* the question this time. He hadn't heard Damien speak this much at once... ever. Even the speeches he gave were shorter. As if all those years alone in the Library had taught him a value in staying silent.

The younger man stood up and unsheathed his sword.

The Sword.

The Monarch's Blade.

Jason had felt a certain consternation, several years back, when he'd realized that Damien wore the precious thing all the time, as if it was some ordinary blade. At least he also *practiced* with it – which he had to, for prudence's sake, if that was going to be the sword he had with him. And at least it didn't light up like a bloody prism with the sun shining full on it when he drew it for ordinary purposes.

Damien held the Sword balanced on his palms, looking at the shining steel. "I think... that, yes. It's easier here. You have to understand, Jason, it's the Realm, not the soul-bond, that's demanding this of us. Of *me,* though she is also Bound. The soul-bond alone... could be denied or delayed, but the Realm needs to be fed Power. By the Bound monarch. Power raised *joyously*." He snorted. "Did you never wonder why my grandfather wedded seven times and fathered all those bastards on top of it? If he had actually *loved* any of his queens, he'd only have needed one. Instead, the Realm fed on *him*."

Jason eyed his friend, holding that Sword, with some concern, and tried to sort through all of that verbiage for an actual answer. "So... 'yes' means that you're *not* feeling as pulled upon here?"

Damien looked up at him in surprise. "Oh, no, I'm still being 'pulled on' as you put it. But *Genevieve* isn't."

"Well, that's something, I guess," Jason muttered, trying to make sense of all the pieces. He frowned. "Are you telling me that because... because you and Genevieve haven't been making love, the Realm has been feeding... on *you?*"

The King looked somewhat relieved that his Champion had figured that much out. "Before, when she'd come back, when you'd *both* come back, we'd wait as long as possible. All of that 'everything' she mentioned last night," he said, flushing. "And *that* fed the Realm as well. But she's been so *fragile* this time, I haven't dared do more than hold her. There's been more fear and worry than... 'happiness' to feed the Realm. So... it takes what it needs. And because she's also Bound as Queen, it's taking from her also."

He sheathed the Sword, and Jason took a deeper breath. He hadn't *really* thought Damien would do something... drastic. But the King was acting so very fey, he wasn't sure *what* he thought.

"The Sword is a focus," Damien explained. "The Castle is a concentrator, like this grotto. It focuses the Power of the Realm into the Throne, which then focuses it into *me*, or into the Sword, as the situation demands. I don't dare sit on the Throne without Genevieve touching me," he said dryly, but without further explanation. "But between the Sword and this grotto, I should be able to feed the Realm without affecting Genevieve. She's Bound to Elaarwen directly, but to the Realm only through me. I should be able to keep it from trying to feed off of *her*..." He looked away from Jason again. "But not alone."

Jason gave his king a long look as the meaning of that sank in. His usual reaction to unexpected news was to freeze, internally, until he could determine how he was supposed to feel or what he was supposed to do. But apparently Damien knew *him* as well as he knew the younger man. All this talking in circles, touching on the topic by little bits and pieces...

"*This* is why you told me about how you felt about me in the beginning. Clever to work it into the conversation."

Damien sighed. "I could ask you instead to fetch one of those girls who drive Genevieve wild with their attentions to me. I swore to her I'd never have another woman in my bed, but to save her *life...*"

Jason raised his chin. "It wouldn't be as effective, though, would it? Just as it wasn't effective for King Reginald? Even if I were willing to play the part of the king's pimp." Damien winced, but didn't disagree. "But you'd be feeling guilty the whole time. And then your firstborn would be a bastard on top of it all."

"And that's what Harald did to her," the King said quietly. "I think it would be *better* to die than put her through that again. From *me.*" He looked away. "But it would also fulfill the letter of the prophecy, though I suspect the Gods don't accept legal arguments." He looked up at his Champion again. "*You* were meant to father her firstborn child. If I hadn't been on the lower level of the reviewing stand – where you and Adam *had* told me not to go – she'd have touched *your* hand first. And she'd be *yours.*"

Jason looked at him, stunned. And Adam...? Ten years by then of love and promises... plans and trust...?

Damien gave him a wry look. Apparently the Champion's thoughts were visible on his face. "*Genevieve* was in love with Rosa when the bond happened to *us.* Two years they'd been together. Two very *intense* years, I've gathered..." He closed his eyes for a moment, then gave Jason another of those disconcerting, direct looks. "What you have with Genevieve isn't likely to *fade away,* Jason. Or *get used up,* or... whatever you've been hoping."

The tall knight looked at his king and tucked these uncomfortable thoughts away for later as he rose to his own feet, restoring the usual difference in height between them. "That's neither here nor there right now. You know perfectly well I'll do whatever is necessary to save her life. Or yours."

He surveyed Damien from top to toe, vaguely amused by how the younger man twitched under his gaze. He'd usually reserved that look for use as the king's swordmaster, and followed it with critiques of the younger man.

Young*er,* but... as he'd realized not so long ago, no longer *young.*

Jason put aside his internal images of his friend as a half-grown boy, ragged and unkempt and unsure of anything to do with people. This was a wise ruler, a powerful sorcerer, a skilled swordsman... a clever politician. Mature, confident, capable, and... a very handsome man.

He'd never been attracted to anyone besides Adam.

...And Genevieve.

And... one *other*... Though *that* hadn't exactly been *attraction*...

Gods, what a mess.

Damien sighed at whatever he saw in his friend's face, and began to turn away.

One kiss. Jason decided he could manage that much. He'd kissed Genevieve after all.

He closed the gap between them before he could think about it too hard. Took his king – no, *Damien* – by the shoulders, and kissed him.

Barely a touch of the lips. It was almost chaste. Or... it would have been if Damien's arms hadn't encircled him. If he'd thought five years of yearning for *Genevieve* had made that kiss sizzle a few weeks ago, this was nearly *fifteen* years from the younger man's perspective. Somehow, he put a more complete surrender into the kiss than Jason had imagined possible.

"Well, *that* woke her up," Damien said mildly when they moved apart.

He didn't try to hold on to Jason. Didn't try to confine or constrain the tall knight in any way.

Only... only Adam had ever understood how important that was... And in Damien's eyes there was none of the bitterness that still tinged his love's gaze when Adam was reminded of *why*...

"*Most* people *outgrow* their childhood infatuations," the blonde knight muttered, trying to ignore away the increase in his own breath and heartbeat.

Damien gave him a shy smile that the taller man hadn't seen in years. "I had no one else to think about. Or fantasize about. For *years*. You... made a strong impression." He hesitated, then reached out. "Jason... was that too much? I... held back as much as I could."

"You... oh, Gods..." If *that* was holding himself back...

"Jason...?"

The next kiss was not the slightest bit chaste.

Chapter FIVE

Fantasies

DAMIEN CAME BACK TO HIMSELF to hear Jason asking if he was okay and waving a hand in front of his eyes. He jerked back, and would have tripped if not for those strong arms that caught him.

"I'm fine," he managed. "I told you about the blackouts, I know I did."

Actually, no, he hadn't, there having been plenty of other things to worry and dismay Jason with… though he and Genevieve had alluded to periods of 'blankness.' But Damien had learned that his nearly-perfect memory didn't distress people as badly if they suspected he had slips. Nor would *they* admit that they couldn't recall any such conversation if he phrased it just right…

"This happens *every time?*" Jason said with dismay.

Damien blushed furiously. "Only when it's been a… long time. And when it's… very good."

He hadn't dared kiss Genevieve when Jason had brought her home. Had barely dared *hold* her for fear of letting loneliness combine with the demands of the soul-bond and the Realm… It had been three months since she and Jason had left for Elendria and close to another since they'd been home; Damien was nearly as starved for simple *touch* as for… anything else. Sex was more about love and tenderness than a mere physical release that he could readily secure for himself, after all.

His Champion stood back and ran a hand through hair that had escaped its usual confinement as a tail – from having had that done too many times while Damien was unaware?

"Well. That it was." Jason's smile was equal parts worry and... attraction? Maybe? Damien's emotions were too involved here to be able to tell. "Perhaps you should sit down." The tall knight gestured. "Since you seemed practically rooted to the ground, I set up a bit of a camp while you were... out."

The sky was still bright autumn blue, but the shadows were long indeed. Evening came early deep in the grotto. And it was darker for him than it probably was for Jason...

Usually his 'blackouts' didn't last nearly so long... but then neither had the Realm been denied even the merest 'taste' of a proper 'meal' in quite so long either. At least the sudden, eager draining of magick from him always froze his muscles so he didn't collapse... and thank the Gods that Genevieve was nearly as strong as Jason, given that he hadn't been in as well-balanced a position as was wise the *first* time they'd discovered this problem.

Damien looked around at the fire, a small pot bubbling on a metal tripod over it, and... *one* set of blankets. He looked at Jason questioningly and received a self-conscious one-shouldered shrug in answer.

"The walls of the grotto glowed for awhile," the knight said conversationally as Damien sat down on the blankets. He dished up a bowl of soup and a piece of the bread they had brought with them and handed both to his king. "A minute or two, perhaps."

Damien nodded as briskly as he could manage, given that he was feeling more than a little lightheaded. "Good. It might be working then."

He began to eat, rapidly and neatly, aware that the magick had again left him drained. The Realm was still taking more from him than he had to give, though the fact that enough of it had stayed to light up the grotto suggested there was hope. The fact that the glow hadn't lasted very *long* made it clear that mere kisses, however delightful, would *not* be enough. He regarded his oldest friend from under his lashes, trying to look as if his focus was entirely on the food.

"Only 'might be'?" Jason frowned. "Can't you tell?"

"You'd better eat some of that before I finish it all," Damien warned him. "I'll check as soon as I can, Jason. We... opened a door. Normally I have some control over how fast the Realm can feed off of me. But when I make It an offering of more... 'happiness...' It can reach past that. I'm too famished to even see magick right now." After a few more bites he added, "Which is saying something, because normally I can't *not* see the magick around us." He held out his bowl with a pleading look.

"Hunh." Jason refilled it and put together food for himself. After taking a bite, he asked tentatively. "What does it look like?"

"Magick? Sparkles of light. It's really beautiful." Damien smiled. "Genevieve can see it, too. And some of my vassals, once they've been Bound to the land. I suspect they have some latent ability to use magick themselves." He looked at Jason. "You do, too, I think, though since you haven't land to be Bound to, I can't check that way."

"Me?" The knight was clearly startled. Did he really think Damien had asked him to be his Heir without believing he had any abilities of his own? He'd looked uncomfortable earlier when Damien had been describing the Binding of the Realm... the King had thought it was because Jason was imagining that happening to *him*... But perhaps not. Was he merely uncomfortable with *magick* at all?

Gods, but that might make things even *messier*...

Damien nodded, finished another bite. "Thank you for this, by the way. Rich broths are about the fastest way for me to absorb nutrients and rebuild strength. Yes, you. Magick is everywhere, but the ability to use it seems to be a combination of intelligence, imagination, and some third quality I'm still trying to understand. Imagination seems to be the most important part, though."

"I don't think I'm particularly imaginative," Jason said dryly.

Damien hid a smile. "You're throwing me straight lines now. Adam would never let that one go."

"Adam..." Jason looked pensive. "He's not going to like... this."

The King gave him a gentle smile, hoping to hide his own awkwardness. Just because he'd played with the idea since he was fifteen didn't mean this was what he really *wanted*. Damien's life had seemed fairytale perfect when Genevieve agreed to marry him...

"No. But he was expecting it." At Jason's frown, he went on, "I saw the look he gave you yesterday. I'd lay even odds you argued about it half the night, too. *He* wasn't willing to come here with me. He knew what would happen."

Jason was silent, looking at his food, but barely eating.

Damien tried a shy look instead. He was more than a bit shy about this, after all, no matter what they all seemed to think about him. "It wouldn't have been the same. It wasn't *Adam* I was dreaming about for all those years." Not strictly true, but Adam had *terrified* him.

Jason kept eating, slowly.

"Actually, he kind of terrified me," Damien went on, beginning to feel like he was trying to fill up all the silence on his own, which was something else he wasn't used to doing. "Sometimes he–"

"Damien," Jason said quietly. "You're babbling."

He kept his eyes on his food, and the younger man shut up, feeling like he'd made everything worse.

They ate in silence for a few minutes. Damien didn't bother refilling his bowl a third time; he just finished off the stew in the pot directly.

Jason had finished eating, but appeared to be deep in thought. Damien quietly collected the dirty items and rinsed them clean in the stream, then sat on the bank for a little while, watching the sparkles of magick that were once again visible to him. Night had fallen while they ate, and he always loved most to watch the magick at night in the grotto – his own private fireworks show, he considered it. Genevieve called them fireflies, and after seeing those almost-magickal insects during a Summer visit to Elaarwen, he had agreed there were similarities.

It *had* been too much to ask after all. The young King bent his head in resignation. Break his vow to Genevieve and break her heart? Or let her *die?* She hadn't had an answer for him the last time they had discussed it, and he feared to bring it up again now that she was so weak.

And Jason had been right in his guesses – it would be hard for him to raise enough Power with another woman. The ones who were willing weren't really in love with him, they were in love with the idea of being the king's mistress. The ones who had actually loved him were all married now, and it would not be fair to their families to lay a cuckoo's egg. And the ones who were really young enough to still be infatuated – were far too young for him to seriously consider.

There was still Lena... he felt shamed even for thinking it. She had never completely recovered from the blow to the head that she had taken during Harald's Usurpation: her sense of humor, her cleverness, her maturity had come back when Damien Healed her, but she would believe anything anyone told her. *Do* anything anyone told her. Her memory was fine, and she looked back with dismay on what had happened each time... He and Genevieve had spent the last five years trying to find a job that suited her unquestionable talents – and where she could do no harm accidentally or as the victim of callous humor. Currently she served as Assistant Royal Librarian, and that had seemed a stable position for nearly a year.

She might make a wonderful mother, and was perhaps the one woman whom Genevieve would be unlikely to resent. But Damien couldn't ask her – because Lena had no ability to say 'no.'

Was he stuck with making a series of women happy, then, and breaking his true love's heart over and over and over? Was this a piece of the path his grandfather had tread? Damien had never been able to find out much about how King Reginald had become entangled with the abuses of power and Power, and with Prydeen... but Reginald Alsterling had been a man of thirty when he was crowned: married and a father. There had been some hints in the chronicles that it was the death of his first wife, Princess Lindrea, that had hardened his heart. Or perhaps it was merely wishful thinking on the part of the chronicler.

King Reginald had raised Power through bedding more women than Damien had ever been able to determine. And through torture. And possibly by the raising of demons, though the notes that the old king and Lord Prydeen had left had been written in a code that Damien had yet to fully break. What the young man had seen in the dungeons, and in their private quarters, had been enough to convince him that whatever those efforts had accomplished, it wasn't worth it. The few poor souls he had been able to Heal enough to release had never been able to re-enter society.

He had... known that this was too much to ask of Adam and Jason. But... they cared about him, and about Genevieve. And *he'd* harbored these adolescent fantasies long enough, though he'd tucked them away long, long ago out of respect and love for the two of them as his friends and colleagues. He hadn't wanted to take them out and air them where he would have to face ridicule or rejection...

But he also didn't want to lose the wife he loved so deeply. Nor to abandon the work for the Realm that he knew he would never finish, not really... though he had tried to keep faith that there would be someone able to carry it on after him.

Damien had hoped that some of those things combined – or at least the magick generated from his own emotions – might be enough to create sufficient Power to feed the Realm that Genevieve would have time to recover enough...

To recover enough to bear a child to *Jason*. And – according to the prophecy Lord Prydeen had given them – at least one other, because the Sword would not speak for that first. At least *two,* preferably, because Prydeen had claimed Damien and Genevieve's youngest would be his own 'true Heir,' suggesting that child would follow in his great-grandfather's footsteps and use magick for evil purposes.

But if there were only *two* children, it would be the younger one who would also be acceptable to the Sword. Damien's plan to hand over his secular power to the Council to prevent another tyrant wizard-king wasn't at all for idealistic and hypothetical reasons.

Even if Damien also couldn't imagine a child he raised and loved becoming a monster... he had to plan for the worst.

He had long ago ceased wishing that he didn't have to be king.

Or so he had thought.

"Damien." Jason's voice. He sounded... strained, but decisive. "Aren't you coming to bed?"

Sighing, Damien picked up the metal camping bowls and spoons and pot. Surely Jason must have separated the blankets into two spaces. And the young man could not blame his old friend. If their positions were reversed, he wasn't sure if he could ignore Genevieve's preferences.

He snorted slightly. That was *exactly* what he was trying to do. So apparently, he could.

But his Champion was a man of sterling principles and not the pragmatist Damien had been forced to become...

Jason had not separated the blankets.

He was in them. And judging by the neat pile to one side, his clothes were not.

The cookware fell from the King's suddenly nerveless hands. The noise startled him, and he scrambled in the dark, just past the ring of firelight, to pick up the scattered items.

Jason gave him a wry smile as Damien set his burden down more carefully and in a more findable location. "I don't know that I can live up to several years of fantasizing, but... we can see."

Damien felt himself blushing. Knew Jason *probably* couldn't tell in the firelight that turned his blue eyes violet.

"Are you *sure?*" the younger man asked quietly, coming over to kneel at the edge of the blankets.

Jason sat up, and no, he wasn't wearing anything. Damien had seen *most* of that well-muscled frame before during arms-practice. His heart beat a little faster. A *lot* faster.

The blonde man put an arm around Damien and pulled him in for another kiss. "I'm sure."

The grotto began to glow.

"Damien, are you always this... *diffident*... when you're with Genevieve?"

A silence. "That's... that's different."

"Is it?"

Another silence.

A delighted laugh. "Now *that's* more like it."

"Damien, are you always this... *diffident*... when you're with Genevieve?"

A silence. "That's... that's different."

"Is it?"

Another silence.

Chapter SIX

Misunderstandings

J ASON WOKE AS ALWAYS WITH the first light of dawn – though it was still pitch-dark at the bottom of the grotto, only the dim glow of the banked fire providing any light though the sky directly above had brightened.

His friend – his *lover,* Jason now supposed he could call him – was shivering, despite being on the side of the fire and having Jason wrapped around him. Somehow all of the blankets had ended up on top of the tall Champion.

He frowned, never having been a blanket-hog in all the years he had slept beside Adam. Had Damien somehow, in his sleep, *given* over all the blankets to keep Jason warm? A sweet thought, and it fit his king's compassionate personality.

Compassionate and... *passionate,* Jason thought with a small smile as he tucked the blankets back around Damien's chilled form, being careful not to snag strands of the fabric in the King's short, stiff beard. It was time for Jason to get up anyways... though now Damien was snuggling in tightly to him. For warmth, surely, but with happy little sleeping noises. He'd done that when he was a boy and prone to nightmares, huddling for comfort between Jason and Adam... Better to put *that* memory well out of the way; this was awkward enough.

Not that it was a *bad* memory.

Nor was last night.

He waited until Damien's shivers had stilled and the young King was sleeping more deeply again, then rose and dressed. His morning calisthenics were next – one did not retain one's flexibility and strength enough to retain the title of best swordsman in the Realm by skimping on one's morning exercises. Certainly not after the age of thirty. Or perhaps twenty-five. Or ever, if he was honest with himself about it.

Next, Jason surveyed the campsite and inventoried the food they had brought. Not enough for breakfast. Not *near* enough at the rate his king was scarfing it down. He'd have to ride to town for more.

But he wouldn't leave while Damien was sleeping.

Even if this was as safe a place as his king always claimed, he didn't want Damien to think he'd been abandoned. He knew that was the worst possible thing he could do to the younger man, and not merely because they had slept together. Abandonment lay at the depths of Damien's fears, enough so that he'd talked about preferring to die than live without Genevieve – it was a thing lovers sometimes said, but there had been something in his voice that suggested he truly meant it literally.

"Damien." Jason squatted down and shook the other man's shoulder. "Damien. Wake up."

The dark-haired man made some more rather adorable whuffling noises and buried back into the blankets.

Champion, knight, lover... and swordmaster. He could put the last hat on and be a little cruel to be kind. Jason seized the blankets he had so lately tucked around his friend and jerked them off.

Damien yelped as cold air inundated him, and sat up straight, blinking.

"Oh, Jason," he said with relief, and grabbed for the blankets dangling from Jason's hands. Successfully, too, since the goal had been to wake him, not torture him. He was shivering again, Jason noted somewhat guiltily.

"Damien. I'm going to ride to town to get us some breakfast." He kept his tone firm.

"You half-froze me, Jason." The dark-haired man grinned up sleepily. "Don't you think you should warm me up?" The look in his eyes was unmistakable.

The tall knight sighed. "Are you insatiable? I'm not sure I have anything left. Besides, you'll be insatiable in another way shortly. We're almost out of food, and with the way you eat..."

His voice trailed off as Damien made a casual gesture and several trays of steaming food appeared on the far side of the fire. "Enjoy," he muttered, kicking at the blankets to spread them out properly and curling back up.

"Did you... just... *create* all that?" Jason asked, awed.

"What?" The King half-sat up and looked at the spread of pastries, porridge, fruit, sausage, tea. "No, of course not. That's from the royal kitchens. And I left a note so they'd know it wasn't stolen. *I* barely know how to make porridge." He snuggled back into his nest, looking appealingly at Jason. "I've made sure it'll stay hot. Are you *sure* you don't want to come back to bed?"

Jason stared at him. The man was *half-asleep* and he'd done this. And not forgotten to leave a note. He had seen Damien Bind his vassals over and over again; had only missed seeing Damien take the Sword from the carved stone statue of Queen Marian because he'd been facing the wrong way; had seen Damien engulfed in the white fire of the soul-bond; had seen him Heal people; and had been told how the King had glowed after defeating Lord Prydeen. For that matter, Jason realized that Damien was glowing slightly *now*, and *had been* since he'd woken up, though the increasing light from the sky was making it harder to tell.

But somehow this casual, even offhanded, use of magick impressed Jason more than all the rest. It suggested that *King* Damien could afford to spend magick on such trivial things and that to do so was nearly as easy as breathing.

"I've never seen you do anything like this in the castle," Jason said quietly.

"Hmmmn?" The King was already half asleep again.

"I said, I've never seen you do anything like this in the castle."

"What? Fetch breakfast?" Damien sighed and sat up with the look of a man who knows he isn't getting to go back to sleep. "It seems to bother people. Even Genevieve. So, I try to remember not to when other people are around. Which *is* pretty much all the time."

He folded his legs into tailor position and ran both hands through his hair in an attempt to tame it that only made it stand up in more odd directions than it had been. Damien kept his hair shorter than most any other man at Court.

Jason sat down beside him a bit more heavily than he'd intended. "You don't have any idea how amazing you are, do you, my – Damien."

Raised eyebrows under that wild thatch of hair was rather amusing to see. Kissable even. "That's... a little more than I was expecting."

Jason flushed. "I was going to say 'my prince' but that's a little out of date. It just slipped out."

"Ah." Damien looked up at the sky. It was bright enough up there, but still fairly dim in the grotto. He blinked quickly a few times as he looked up into the brighter light.

"So... how are you feeling?" the knight asked cautiously.

Damien grinned and stretched luxuriously, that glow around him brightening. *"Glorious."*

He saw Jason's expression and the glow dimmed a bit. "Better. And not half so hungry. The Realm fed on the Power we raised, not on *me*. And not on Genevieve," he added before Jason could ask. It might be just the slow brightening of the grotto, but his glow seemed to dim yet another notch.

"I'm going for a swim," the King said abruptly, rising, and snatching at the pile of his clothes that Jason had automatically folded this morning.

"Damien, that water is freezing...!"

He was gone.

The grotto seemed much emptier and colder.

"We can go back when you're ready," Damien told his Champion as he ate. He needed more food than he'd expected. Knowing that Jason was tracking how much he ate, he reluctantly passed on a third bowl of porridge and eyed the last two sausages with disguised longing. The pastries didn't tempt him at all – he needed the heavier foods. "I think we should have tamed those sparks for a while."

That wasn't exactly true, and Genevieve's fertile period was likely to start today or tomorrow... but one did what one had to do. The... Power raised the night before *should* help.

Jason eyed him sideways. "How long is 'a while'? And is the Realm likely to be 'feeding' on you again if we do? I counted your ribs last night, Damien. You haven't anything to spare, and Genny is worse." He sighed as he noted the younger man's attention to the nearly denuded platters. "Don't stop eating on my account. You still look hungry."

With a little sigh of relief, Damien picked up another sausage.

"I told you: *this*... isn't really about Genevieve getting pregnant. It's about what the *Realm* needs. It's the soul-bond that will ensure she conceives." He took a bite while Jason nodded. "You were both home in early Summer before leaving for Elendria. It's now mid-Fall. We should have three or four months before it's critical again."

Before exactly *what* would be critical in three or four months, he left deliberately vague. Throw enough semi-relevant information at people and you could usually bury what they were really asking about and still make them think you'd answered. Yet another skill of 'politics' that made Damien's teeth ache to practice, but it had saved him a number of useless arguments. Genevieve had told Jason and Adam both that it was her fertile period upcoming that was increasing the risk, but Damien could switch the emphasis to spare them all...

Jason gave him a dry look that said *he* hadn't so easily been thrown off the track. "But it's also been taking from you directly that whole time. And... can you compare how much Power you raise with her compared to... um, what we did?"

He paused, looking uncomfortable. "Does it even store the stuff up to use later, or is it like trying to eat too much food at once?" Jason actually laughed as Damien's hand froze on the way to pick up the last sausage.

"Don't stop on my account, Your Majesty," he said again, but he was smiling this time.

Jason's laughter eased a bit of the tension in Damien's shoulders. Clearly his plan was working. They'd switched focus to the abstract and away from the all-too-personal.

"It's a big Realm; It can take a lot of Power before It runs out of 'space.' I suspect It does do better when It's fed regularly instead of at these long intervals, but..." He shrugged. "As to the other... no, I can't compare directly. I feel less drained than I did when we came here, and I know that Genevieve has been sleeping properly for the first time since she came home."

And *that* was a deep satisfaction in and of itself. No matter what else, no matter what awkwardness resulted... it would all be worth it for Genevieve to have even this much of a real rest.

"But it could start drawing on you both again as early as tomorrow."

"Or tonight," Damien shrugged again. "It is what it is."

Sometimes one had to let these things play out a bit or the other person realized you were building a façade of words. And then they pushed harder to see what was hidden behind...

Jason refilled his king's bowl with porridge and piled it high with nuts and honey and finely chopped fruit, handing it to Damien just as he finished the sausage. The younger man was three spoonfuls in before he realized how quickly he was still eating. He looked up at Jason with trepidation.

"We *can't* go back," the tall knight said softly. "Not yet."

Damien lowered his eyes to his food.

"We need to build up enough of a stockpile of this Power you talk about," Jason went on. "Enough to protect you both. To let Genny recover. Three months' worth."

"Hmmn." Damien kept eating. At least he'd managed to distract Jason from the real risk. So, his subterfuge was *half*-working.

"I don't want to try to fill your shoes, Damien. I'll do what's necessary. Including stay here with you as long as we need to."

Damien sighed and stirred all those good things into his porridge. This... wouldn't work. No matter how wonderful and possible everything had seemed when he'd woken up. He needed to give Jason more explicit reasons for why it made sense for them to go home.

"I *really* need to be getting back, Jason. We still have to appoint a negotiator for Elendria, not to mention all the other work that they probably piled on my desk yesterday. And already this *morning*." He looked up as if the idea were just occurring to him, though he'd been toying with it since he knew his wife and Jason were coming back early from the negotiations. "You were at Genevieve's side the whole time. It should be you."

"Me!" Jason's eyes went wide. "I've never negotiated anything more than the price of a tunic!"

"But you've watched and advised her for four years while she brought two provinces back into the fold." Damien decided to add the real carrot. "You could take Adam with you. He's skeptical enough to make you look through everything twice before agreeing to anything. Adam and... hmmm... Master Fenric. He knows the Realm's legal precedents and treaties backwards and forwards. As a team, you should be able to handle almost anything."

Jason frowned. "But Adam is Captain of your Guard."

"He has a Second, doesn't he? Sir Marcus can use a little more practice at leadership. What's the point of having a Second if he doesn't have the experience to be able to lead in case of an emergency?" Damien had heard Adam and Jason both use that argument themselves several times over the years.

The knight seemed rather taken – or at least taken aback – by the novel idea for a moment, but then he narrowed his eyes at his king. He was a far from stupid man, after all, though he tended to leave critical work to Adam outside of the practice-ring.

And he was thoughtful, careful, and compassionate... which was why he would make an excellent king in a few months.

"And what will happen to you and Genny then?"

Damien shrugged with careful casualness. "You'll need to come back before Winter hits. Elendria is no place to face Winter storms in mere tents."

Likely they'd be back sooner than that. For Jason's coronation.

"Two or three months before Winter." Jason said. "Two weeks travel each way. It took *Genevieve* a month just to get them to agree as to where the negotiating tent would be set up. And with the cold weather coming on, that will be to do all over again."

The King tipped his head. "You never call her 'Genevieve' in private. Or in public, for that matter."

"In public she is my Queen," the knight reminded him. "And I don't do anything that could undermine her authority. Nor yours. In private... it is my duty and my privilege to call you both out on foolish and wrongheaded ideas. Like sending Adam and me away for a negotiation we all know isn't going anywhere while the Realm devours you both or you decide to sleep with half the starry-eyed daughters of your vassals."

Damien flushed.

"Jason..."

"Or having us head back before you've solved the problem enough to not send us back out here in a couple of weeks." He paused. "Actually, a couple of weeks would be preferable to a couple of *months*. It'll be *damned* cold out here by then."

Damien waved his hand and the chilly grotto was comfortably warm. "*That's* not the problem."

Jason blinked. Apparently, he hadn't correlated the unusual arrival of breakfast with other possibilities.

"Then what *is?*" Jason demanded in frustrated bafflement. "Last night – even this morning – you seemed to want nothing more than to get me in bed. And now you're pleading work and suggesting I leave town for three months. What changed, Damien?" And now his tone held a hint of... hurt? offense?

"Nothing but my perception, Jason," Damien kept his voice even, calm, pleasant, his shoulders relaxed, easy. He had a lifetime of practice in concealing his emotions. No reason it shouldn't work now. "Thank you for your help, my head is clearer now."

Jason's eyebrows flew up. "I thought I knew you better than this, Damien," he said in a disappointed tone.

A lifetime's practice hiding emotions warred with over a decade of this man training him to ride and fight... and longer than that of wanting to impress and please him. Damien felt his shoulders hunch, and stared at the remnants of porridge in his bowl. The porridge Jason had prepared just the way he liked it without even being asked. Just like a thousand other things Jason did for him – and for Genevieve. Most especially... last night...

He owed Jason an honest answer, not a pleasant screen of excuses. No matter if it would be easier if his Champion would simply accept those excuses.

"You... don't want *me*," he said at last, still staring into the bowl. "Not... like this. I knew that. But... this does no good if there isn't joy. And there's no joy in being... a chore." Damien's mouth twisted in a wry smile. "It was a bad idea to begin with. We're both naturally monogamous–"

Jason snorted. "*You?* Damien, you bedded every woman in your Royal Guard."

The King looked up sharply. "Serially monogamous, then. That wasn't *my* idea, and you know that." He caught the skeptical expression. "Wait, you didn't? But Ciriis said..." He thought back carefully. "No, I guess she didn't say *you* had agreed with her. She said *Adam* had."

"Agreed about what?" the tall knight asked almost irritably. Damien knew his habit of sorting memories out verbally drove Genevieve and Adam slightly crazy, but he hadn't realized it also bothered Jason.

He switched the topic slightly. "You know that Ciriis was... my first?" Jason nodded. "But do you know why?"

An amused look. "I assume for all the same reasons as every other young man has gotten a beautiful woman into his bed."

Damien gave him a withering look. "Jason, I was still half-terrified of people at the time. And more than half in love with *you*, for all that I knew that wasn't going anywhere. And Ciriis is... fairly intimidating at the best of times." He took a deep breath. "It was when Adam and Ciriis took me to visit his parents at Lynncrag. I... didn't know why at the time..." his eyes apologized to Jason, "I was just so happy to be going *somewhere*. I hadn't left the City – hell, I hadn't left the *Castle* – since I was ten. I'd almost forgotten what forests and fields looked like. What places without stone walls and *brick* looked like.

"And then Adam's family was so friendly and warm–"

Jason snorted again. Though there was a certain wistful sadness in it.

"Well, they were to *me*," Damien told him. "Ciriis and Adam had me use another name, and I look like Mother, not any of the Alsterlings. I don't think his parents knew they had a prince under their roof until the last day."

A day he would *not* talk to Jason about, since it involved Adam having a huge fight with his parents over the lover he was going back for, instead of staying for the girl they wanted him to marry... and Adam telling them Damien's real name.

"I... didn't want to come home. So, I wrote to my grandparents – my *mother's* parents." He met Jason's eyes again. "You've been to Lynncrag. You know how... relaxed everything is. I was able to post the letter without Ciriis or Adam knowing. And I waited... hoping. And then I got the word from my grandmother..."

Damien had to stop and close his eyes. The lump in his throat had to be swallowed several times. It still hurt. It still hurt *very much*.

He went on without opening his eyes.

"We'd lived with them until I was eight or nine. Kandy had grown up there. I thought, surely they would let me come back. Let me come *home*. I understand *now...*" he added, trying to find a steady voice again. "Genevieve and I visited them years ago."

Jason... had probably been with them on that visit. For some reason... Damien couldn't quite remember...

"My grandfather was the youngest son of the Baron of Elderwyld and a failed knight: he never made it past being a squire. And my grandmother was a blacksmith's daughter, a prosperous family, but not wealthy. They'd lived on his father's estate when they married, and by the time my parents met, Mother had half a dozen younger siblings. Grandfather – King Reginald – granted them a small town on royal lands, mostly farms. It was technically for my parents, but they brought her whole family there and willed it to them.

"By the time I wrote to them, my aunts and uncles had married local farmers, and my grandparents were old... they were afraid my grandfather – the king – would evict them if they helped me. Or worse."

Damien opened eyes full of tears. "But all I knew – at seventeen – was that my last hope in the world had written back to tell me never to contact them again. I thought about trying to run away to the Rebellion, but I didn't have any money, or... or *anything* that didn't belong to Adam and Ciriis, or his parents." He attempted a wry smile. "Though, I suppose the horse I'd ridden there was my grandfather's.

"Ciriis found me crying in my room. I couldn't tell her why. After all the kindnesses all of you had done for me – that I knew about *then*," his eyes apologized again, "I couldn't tell her that I was trying to run away from the plans she was making for my future. But she let me cry myself out on her shoulder... and then gave me something else to think about." He smiled slightly. "I would have done anything she wanted of me *then*, which I suppose is the normal response."

"Damien..." Jason's eyes were troubled.

The King bent his head again to avoid that gaze. "And then we came back and you... Adam was so bitter, and Ciriis was angry, and they... they wouldn't tell me what had happened to *you*. I had to sneak into your room to find you."

"I remember," Jason murmured, and his eyes were far away for a moment.

"I thought you were going to *die*, Jason," Damien went on at last. "Even after you said you weren't. You looked..." He shuddered. "And then Ciriis and Adam found me there and she took me out... and told me exactly what had happened to you. And why."

Jason's lips were tight. "She shouldn't have done that. You didn't need to know. That was half the point. You weren't *supposed* to know." He shifted closer to the younger man and put an arm around him. "It wasn't your fault, Damien. I made my own choices, and I knew what I was getting into. What Oskar did... is on him." He kissed the mop of dark-hair. "Protecting you was worth it. Having you grow up into the kind of king – the kind of *man* – that you are, was worth it. *Is* worth it."

Damien couldn't help trembling in the reassuring circle of Jason's arm. "So you've said before. I... couldn't bear to have anyone touch me after that. All I could think about was what had happened to you. At that point I was convinced I was in love with you, and I felt guilty about Ciriis anyways, and terrified of Adam."

He tried for a chuckle. It didn't come out well. It had all been *his fault* after all. Adam and Ciriis had taken Damien away. Jason had stayed behind to be a screen of protection for their departure... for *Damien's* departure.

"I knew that you and Adam were supposed to be together, but... well... I was seventeen. And an absurdly shy and sheltered seventeen. I didn't know how to sort it out in my head." He heaved a sigh. "I just knew I didn't want Ciriis to touch me anymore. It... seemed to irritate her."

"I'll bet," Jason muttered. There was a grim note to his voice, and Damien wondered why.

"She kept... trying to interest me. And eventually I gave in. But it was never as magickal as it had been at first. And we just sort of... stopped after a while." Damien remembered that Ciriis had seemed disgruntled about that, too. He'd gone back to hiding in the Royal Library again, which had

had the side-benefit of making it more awkward for Ciriis to badger him about sleeping with her.

"I tried to stop thinking about you... that way. *This* way. I went back to dreaming about Genevieve... And then I was named Heir, and you all started assembling my Guards. I suppose you must have known it was coming and were prepared. You've *always* been prepared, somehow." Damien smiled, but felt Jason's arm around him twitch slightly. "I came back to my rooms after the official coronation as Heir and... Lena was in my bed. I didn't know what to do. I hadn't asked, didn't want... But *she* did."

Damien felt himself relax. It was one of the things he had done that he knew had gone right in his life, with no ambiguity. "Ciriis explained, later, what Lena had been through. She'd been one of my grandfather's and Lord Prydeen's... victims. Ciriis said I could help Lena figure out how to be okay with touching again. That... I would understand because I knew what *you'd* been through."

He closed his eyes again and leaned into Jason's shoulder. "I don't know if Ciriis knew what she was really asking. Lena needed to re-learn that *love* was real, not just the... touching. But it's easy to love Lena." He smiled sadly. "I... told her about Genevieve. Only Lena. And *you*, of course. She told me if I ever gave up on the dream-girl, she *might* be willing to marry me. We laughed about it, of course. We both knew that if I survived so long as to be married, it would have to be for the good of the Realm... not to a squire's daughter like my mother was, or like Lena is."

Jason twitched in that odd way again.

Damien twisted to look up at him. "They were all like that, Jason. Lena, Aryllis, Felena, Terellie, Sasha, Elsa, Emerie, Thielda, Nalda, Kamauri, Licia, Mirabelle. Ciriis sent them to me and I did my best to love them enough to let them begin to heal. To give them a piece of *me*, so that they *could* love again." He paused. "I couldn't help *you*... that was Adam's place. But I could try to help *them*. And... it turned out to be good practice for understanding Genevieve, after what Harald had done to her." He paused again. "But I haven't so much as noticed what another woman is *wearing* since I laid eyes on Genevieve." A chuckle. "That's caused a few problems, like when I was supposed to compliment the Ambassador from Vindalia on her dress..."

Jason looked torn. "Damien..." Abruptly he pulled away, and rose up to kneel humbly, head bent as if in shame. "My king, I *did* know what Ciriis was doing, but it *wasn't* as innocent as you describe it."

Damien put a hand on his Champion's shoulder. "You mean that she was trying to control me through sex?" He laughed at Jason's shocked look. "I *did* grow up in my grandfather's Court, Jason, even if I spent most of those years in the Library. I was never as innocent as all that. And I was at an age where I was probably going to fall for *some*one. Better her than one of the other courtiers."

The knight controlled his expression, then went back to looking grim. "There's more to it than that. Ciriis... and Adam... knew you were writing to your grandparents. They... told them what to reply." His eyes were pleading. "*I didn't know until later.*"

Damien went very still inside.

"Damien?"

He'd let all these things out to tell Jason... putting them back in their cubbyholes in his memories was hard... and now he needed *new* cubbyholes...

"Damien – my king?"

"It was the right thing to do," Damien said very quietly. "My grandparents' fears weren't baseless. And... *I* needed to be at Court. Needed the three of *you* teaching me how to survive."

Not how to be a king, though they'd tried. That had happened by a combination of his voracious reading in the Royal Library – despite his friends' claims, he hadn't read quite *everything* it contained – and the wisdom of Genevieve and her father. Though Genevieve still insisted it was a natural gift of Damien's own.

Jason didn't move. "You could have learned what you needed in Elaarwen. Probably better than anything we could do. We should have taken you there."

Damien just looked at him, trying not to think too hard about that. It still felt dangerous even to imagine, for all that he was king himself now and there was no 'higher authority' to threaten his safety or those he loved. A plan to run away to Elaarwen was what had gotten his parents and sister *killed*. Didn't Jason understand that *that* was what had truly held him off from making his own attempt during that visit to Lynncrag, as much as a lack of resources and an awareness that a lone, naïve traveler on the road was a target? Simply taking the trip to Elaarwen – *after* they were married and he was duke of the province as Genevieve's husband, as well as her being queen as his wife – had given Damien anxiety attacks. Genevieve had apparently managed to keep even Adam and Jason from knowing about those, just as she'd promised...

"When? That was the only time I left the Castle, and I'm well aware that Adam was chastised by my grandfather for having removed me even briefly without his approval. If you hadn't been the chain to bring them – *us* – back, I don't doubt Grandfather would have had more severe consequences for him than a tongue-lashing. But he knew that Adam would never abandon you."

Jason's eyes were wide with shock again. They'd gone to such extents to hide how they felt in public... "How did he – surely he didn't *know...?*"

Damien gave the tall knight a grim smile. "Grandfather gave *me* a tongue-lashing after as well, and *told* me that was why he hadn't bothered. He knew *I* didn't have the ability to run away on my own, and since *Adam* would have to come back... I don't think it even occurred to him that Ciriis might have helped me. We all know how little he regarded women in general." The King looked down. "I wasn't such a fool as to let him see how *I* felt about you. That would have been more dangerous than him simply being pleased to be able to lever the two of you against each other, should he decide to do it."

Jason sat back down heavily. "He *knew...*"

Damien nodded. "He knew. If there was a piece of information anyone could be blackmailed with or tortured with, he collected it. Most were never used.... but his files were extensive. For some reason he felt the need to write everything down," he added bemusedly.

"Most of us can't remember everything like you, Damien," Jason told him, looking like he was still feeling rather dazed.

The dark-haired man shrugged. "In any case. I'm having just as much trouble with *this* as you are." He waved a hand around the grotto, then smiled wryly, "Except I suppose, that *I* spent all those years dreaming about you. But there's no joy if it's a chore – for either of us. And without the joy, it means less – *much* less – Power is raised. And then there's no point."

"No joy..." Jason looked confused. "What are you talking about?"

Damien gave him an almost pitying look. "I know you were probably imagining Adam in your arms last night, and I–"

"If you say you were imagining Genevieve, I shall be very... *confused...*" Jason said dryly.

Damien blushed, "No, of course not. But you clearly didn't want to have anything more to do with me this morning..."

To his surprise, Jason began to chuckle. "Is *that* what this all comes back to? Damien, sometimes you still seem very young indeed."

That... was almost offensive.

He frowned. "Why?"

"Or perhaps that soul-bond of yours changes things," Jason mused, unilluminatingly.

"Jason, *what* are you talking about?"

"I'm older than you, Damien," the knight explained patiently. "I told you that first thing. I don't have your... I suppose stamina *is* exactly the right word here."

"Oh." Damien's voice was very small.

"I wasn't putting you off or ignoring you," Jason went on. "I'm just used to getting up and moving first thing in the morning. Adam is used to that. He usually has to get to things right away also. It didn't occur to me that you might not understand."

Damien had never been able to completely train his body to follow other people's rhythms. Adam claimed it was all those years in the Library without any responsibilities that had apparently permanently set him onto an erratic schedule. He knew it drove the servants – and Genevieve – crazy when he wandered through the Castle at odd hours, but he was careful not to interfere with the late-night work of the staff and his wife was gone so much... he assumed Adam was informed as to his night-time wanderings, since at least one of his Guards trailed him everywhere, but they had never discussed it. Mornings were not always Damien's friend.

Hope sparked. "Then... you *did* enjoy yourself last night?"

Jason's eyebrows flew up again. "As if you couldn't tell!" He pulled Damien close and murmured, "And it *wasn't* Adam I was thinking about, either..."

A great deal later, Damien stirred and murmured "I love you, Jason," before falling back to sleep.

The tall Champion carefully freed one hand to run through the blonde hair that had gotten loose again from the tail in which he usually wore it. No real surprise, that. Neither the hair, nor the sentiment.

It was impossible not to notice that his young king – his *beloved friend* – was falling asleep almost as easily, now that he was out from under the weight of his royal responsibilities, as Genny. Adam had mentioned that Damien's stamina was shot; that he was taking more naps throughout the day, but didn't seem to be wandering as much at night either.

But Adam *hadn't* mentioned that those naps segued from healthy sleep into brief periods of unconsciousness... also just like Genny. Perhaps the sharp-eyed Captain hadn't noticed. Or perhaps this was new.

Either way, it was troubling.

When he'd agreed to come out here, Jason had assumed it would be a day-trip. Or maybe an overnight exploratory mission. No matter what Damien claimed Adam had understood, the Champion doubted that his love had realized how close their young King was coming to breaking.

The strain of the office alone was a nearly incomprehensible weight. But add in these *magickal demands* of the embodied Realm itself on Its Bound King...

Jason brought his free hand to where he could soberly regard that huge grey pearl sitting innocently in its band of pale gold. The Heir's Ring, marking him, Jason Solway, Countess Solway's unwanted son, as the Heir to the throne of Ilseador.

Insanity.

And a burden he had neither the desire nor the skill to bear. *Adam* would do a better job at it than he would, and the Champion had no idea why Damien hadn't Named his love instead.

An incentive for Jason not to abandon this mad plan that walked the line of threatening both Damien's marriage and his own long-term relationship? That was hardly necessary. Even if the knight wouldn't do just about anything to protect and care for his king and queen, even if Adam didn't so desperately want to be a father... there was still Jason's unwanted, and thusfar unrequited, passion for Genny.

If he could somehow give *that* up, perhaps... though there would still be the other things.

But... this was really more than a king should ask of a simple knight like himself. Jason wasn't fit to be a king.

And... he really *had* counted Damien's ribs last night. To the tune of happy, mostly-asleep mumblings, he recalled with a wry smile. If Genny's loss of weight – and muscle – had shocked him day before yesterday, Jason was now even more shocked that Damien had managed to lift and carry her even that short distance in his own state.

Any last thought had fled now of using this interlude – and it *was* going to be more than a day or two, it was clear to Jason – to begin working on the young King's strength and *physical* stamina *(ahem!)* or testing how much skill he had lost at swordplay. Damien needed *rest* as much as his wife did, and the best thing his Champion could do would be to see that the young King exerted himself as little as possible.

Jason eyed the shining, silver-plated trays and teapots and tureens that had held their breakfast. Surely doing things like *that* couldn't be wise, though he had little idea of how else to provision the pair of them otherwise. He couldn't possibly leave Damien alone here – no matter how safe the grotto seemed – to ride to town for more food. That would be an entire dereliction of his duty to guard his king.

And… he had to admit that it hadn't seemed to steal anything from Damien to bring the food.

The younger man had used an analogy of the Realm having previously been fed on dry bread and stale beer – but now that It was getting what It 'wanted,' was it more like a torrent of rain falling on parched land? Brindlewell was just far enough back from the confluence of the Emerald and Sapphire rivers that they didn't usually suffer from the backflow flooding during the Spring melts, but their soil was thin and didn't absorb water terribly well in the late Summer after a dry spell. Jason hadn't been home much since he was eleven, but he remembered the dry washes becoming deadly with flashfloods after a heavy rain and the water pooling up everywhere, even in the castle courtyard.

Damien had said something about it probably being better to feed the Realm more regularly… was that because too much of the magick just ran off uselessly if it was only provided at rare intervals? That might explain why the young King had so much to spare – he was clearing away the flooding before it did damage by using it up in trivialities.

Something about that idea *felt* right to Jason.

And, more, that this grotto might serve as a reservoir, filling up with magick, and then allowing it to drain into the rest of the Realm at a rate that was more beneficially absorbed. Was it possible that the glow that had followed that first kiss – or when they'd made love – had measured how 'full' that reservoir was? Was it the length of the glow or its intensity?

Jason resolved to pay attention to both and monitor them for progress in his young king's recovery.

Because there was no way he was taking Damien back to Court until the younger man's own reservoirs were replenished and the leaks that were draining him so badly were staunched.

To do anything else was clearly to risk Damien – and Genny – dying. And himself being stuck with the whole mess himself.

This solution might make Adam – and himself – unhappy, but there was simply no other option that Jason could see. At least... it had been long enough that Jason had forgotten the – ah – *side-benefits* of sleeping with a Healer; this might be *possible*.

He snuggled in around the sleeping – and thankfully not *unconscious* – form of the handsome younger man and Damien smiled in his sleep, relaxing as if a part of him had been expecting Jason to leave him alone. It occurred to the tall knight that perhaps a part of the young King's nighttime wanderings that so distressed his Guards were simply that he couldn't bear to be *alone* at night. Certainly, there were fewer complaints from his detail when Genny was home and in bed with him...

Which argued that all Jason might need to do to keep Damien resting was stay in bed with him, even while the younger man seemed otherwise deeply asleep. That... didn't really seem like anything to complain about, the tall man mused, his lips curving into a slight, pleased smile.

Though keeping up his own sword-practice might be more of a challenge than Jason had anticipated...

Chapter SEVEN

Secrets

D AMIEN FELT LIKE BOUNDING UP the spiral staircase to his apartment, but restrained himself to a sensible pace. While he *felt* more energetic than he had in months, he knew his physical reserves were still tissue thin.

He knocked politely before entering, which amused his Guards standing to the sides of the door. Their expressions grew serious again as Jason appeared around the curve of the stair behind him. The King might not mind their amusement, but the Champion and the Captain took a much more dim view of levity at His Majesty's expense.

Adam was already halfway across the sitting room when Damien came in. They nodded at each other distractedly, their attention each on the unseen person beyond. The King paused on the threshold of his bedchamber to enjoy the sight of Adam flinging himself into Jason's arms before heading for a less exuberant, but no less heartfelt reunion with Genevieve.

She looked better. Not *all the way* better, but some color had come back into her cheeks, and the shadows were gone from under her eyes. She'd sensibly stayed in bed, and he paused just to drink her in with his eyes.

"I missed you," he said quietly.

Genevieve's lips quirked into a wry smile. "Really? That's not what it felt like." Damien blushed, and she laughed, apparently more at ease with the situation than he was himself. "Come here. Adam has threatened to hide all my clothes if I stir from this bed for more than a trip to the washroom."

Damien shucked off his boots, and climbed up on their bed beside her. No visible sparks, just the usual little fizz they had each felt every time they'd ever touched. Desire, yes, but not the overwhelming, will-destroying thing that they had been fighting before.

She snuggled into his shoulder, and all was right with his world again.

He'd left the door open intentionally, so after several long moments Jason and Adam drifted in, as Damien had expected.

"We're heading out," Jason informed them. "I need a bath in water that isn't icy cold. And clothes that have been sitting in a clothespress or a closet instead of dangling from bushes to dry."

Genevieve gave Damien a look, and he shrugged. His own clothing was in much better shape since he had made use of his magick to fetch fresh items from his own closets and drawers. "I offered, but he said he didn't want me to get him fresh clothes while we were... gone. He said the food was enough. And we both agreed that heating the pond would be cruel to the beavers."

Adam was giving him a very strange look, and the King found himself ducking his head as if he were young again.

"I *did* heat the air in the grotto," he said diffidently. "It got pretty cold at night, and I didn't think it was worth freezing to make a point."

"What are you talking about?" Adam demanded.

"I'll explain later, love," Jason promised, gently pushing the other man's shoulder to turn him back towards the door. He'd grown used to Damien's casual use of magick, but wasn't wholly comfortable with it.

"Adam?" Damien called out softly, and his friend and Captain looked back over his shoulder questioningly. "Thank you." There was a world of meaning in his words.

Adam nodded brusquely, then said. "You look better. Less like something we dragged out of the dungeons." He stepped out of the room, Jason following, since their fingers were still tightly laced. The Champion took the time to give Damien one last, sweet smile.

They closed the door behind them.

"Was Adam... all right?" Damien asked his wife.

Genevieve waggled her head, neither nodding nor shaking. "Anxious. Not particularly happy when you were gone overnight. Not happy that you were gone a full week. But... not as bad as I feared."

Damien nodded. "And you?" he asked, holding his breath.

"*I* knew you were okay." She smirked, though he could *feel* that that it was somewhat forced. "Rather *better* than okay."

"That's not what I meant," he said, but she'd made him blush again.

"I missed you every minute and hated that *Jason* got to touch you and *I* didn't." Genevieve sighed. "And... I hated that *you* got to touch *Jason* and *I* didn't," she added apologetically, which explained some of why she was taking things so 'well.' "If I hadn't had to keep Adam occupied with taking care of me, I'd have been a real mess. But it was pretty much a fulltime job keeping him busy."

Damien's sneaky, cleaver queen grinned. "Those reports of yours were pure genius, by the way. Both of us are now absolute experts on potato production in eastern Siovale and historic weather conditions in Cedarwen. The hardest part was staying awake until I knew *he* was about to fall asleep... and setting that spell you taught me so I would wake when he did."

A spell he'd come up with that first time she'd conceived, and they were still hoping that Lord Prydeen and Queen Marian were both wrong... the idea being to wake when their baby did. Genevieve's talent for magick was greater than her desire to learn how to use it, but she was very creative in applying the small things Damien had shown her.

"We'll use it for its intended purpose eventually," she said softly, feeling how still he'd gone. "That's what this is all about, right?"

"Almost two more months..." Damien sighed. "And then..."

She snuggled closer. "Yes. But after that it's us. *Just* us."

He shook his head, but didn't elaborate. He'd tried explaining his theory that she and Jason would have developed a soul-bond if he hadn't encountered her first, and it had upset her. She, like Jason, seemed to have based a necessary personal mythology around the idea that they simply needed to meet the demands of desire and it would go away. Time would tell.

"So..." Genevieve said after a few minutes. "Awkward topic to get over with. I could feel that you were enjoying yourself. Was he... good?"

Damien wriggled uncomfortably. "It's Jason. Have you ever known him to be *bad* at anything?"

"Embroidery," she said promptly, startling him into a laugh. "He made me give him lessons for two days a few weeks ago. I'd show you what he created, but it was so laughable that he burned it before anyone else could see."

Damien squeezed her gently. "Well... let's just say this wasn't embroidery."

"Hmmn," she said thoughtfully. "And... was there enough Power? Will it last?"

"I hope so," Damien said soberly. "The Realm is going to sleep right now, as it always does in the Autumn, but it uses Power more erratically in the cold season. There're more diseases among humans in Winter, more fights and cruelties, big and small, when people are trapped indoors together. The plants and animals don't usually need much extra care, but the humans... I never know." He raked the hand that wasn't holding Genevieve through his hair. "This isn't fair to Adam. To either of them, but particularly Adam."

"Yes and no," she said, surprising him. "Adam and I talked a lot. He wants a child desperately. He's been pushing Jason for them to adopt, but they've been so busy and had so little time together..."

Damien winced, but she shook her head. "He doesn't blame us. Or not much, anyways. We live the example, after all..."

"This child... can't know Jason is its father." Damien said slowly. Toddlers... were not known for their powers of discretion.

"Her," Genevieve corrected wryly.

"What?"

"Her. Adam is convinced it's going to be a girl. It's easier to just go with it than disagree with him, and he's got even odds of being right. We spent *hours* going over names," she added with some bemusement.

Damien blinked. "That sounds much more bought-in to the plan than I had guessed."

She waved dismissively. "It's Adam. He always sounds cynical and irritated."

"Except around Jason."

"Well, of course."

After a few minutes, Damien asked, "So... did you come to any conclusions?"

"Me? About what?"

"You and Adam. About names for... our daughter." He felt warm all over thinking about it.

She laughed. "The two of you are going to fight over her, I can just see it. It will be up to Jason and I to make sure she's not spoiled rotten."

Damien thought of his grandfather and his uncle, Prince Oskar, and shuddered. "No chance of that." He cuddled his wife closer. "So. Names?"

"My mother's name was Giendra. He likes that. And his grandmother was Marguerite. I like that, but we agreed we should be careful about choosing names from his family or Jason's."

"Hmmmn." Damien ran through the relevant family trees in his head. *"My* mother's mother was named Alexa in honor of your great-grandmother... and that's Jason's mother's name as well. The name fell out of favor for some reason."

They exchanged a wry glance. No, it hadn't been common to name children after Genevieve's great-grandmother, King Reginald's most likely rival for the throne. Countess Solway was just old enough that her parents might not have realized the potential problem with that name... either that or they'd been making a political statement that their daughter later disagreed with.

"There's a variation of Marguerite somewhere..." Damien mused. "Ah! My other grandmother, Queen Rena, was a princess from Dawil. *Her* mother was named Marlerite. With an L."

Genevieve smiled. "That sounds lovely." She was used to his prodigious memory by now, though she occasionally asked him why he'd bothered to read, let alone remember and be able to compare, certain obscure facts. At this point, every genealogical tree in the Realm apparently didn't faze her. Let alone the more distant details of his own.

"Did you think of names for boys at all?"

"Eric, for your father," Genevieve said firmly. "Grandmother Marian and Adam both agree on that." She hesitated. "And Miria for a second daughter, if we have one. Miria *Kandra.*"

Damien felt tears prick his eyes, and he squeezed her gently again. "We're not going to keep having children just to honor our dead, love. Your health is more important than that."

"Heir and a Spare," Genevieve reminded him. "If my parents had managed that, Elaarwen would be getting the attention it deserves. And since the Sword has to speak for one to be your Heir, and we've been assured that it won't be our first, that sort of asks for a minimum of three."

"And Harald made *such* a valuable contribution to Siovale as the second child," Damien rolled his eyes and resolutely put aside the other part of Prydeen's prophecy about his youngest child's future. *"One* child that the Sword will speak for. And our eldest gets Elaarwen. If she wants it. Do you think the Sword will speak for them as babies?"

"Queen Marian says they need to at least be toddlers. But since it didn't speak for any of hers, I'm not sure how certain she is."

Damien thought about that. "I'm surprised she didn't insist *her* name be on your short-list for girls." He nestled into her hair. "For *daughters.*" He liked that word better, he decided.

Genevieve sighed. "Since Adam was insisting on me staying in bed and milady has sworn to stay out of our bedchamber, she was sort of limited to weighing in when he remembered to leave the door to the sitting room open. I... decided I was too ill to remind him." Damien snickered, and she grinned ruefully. "I'm sure I'll get to hear all about it when she decides I'm strong enough. I know she was fairly put out that Adam got to come in here."

"Poor ancient spirit," Damien said without sympathy. "Where did Adam put himself to sleep reading reports, by the way? Not in *that* chair?"

The one chair in the room was fairly low-backed; it was matched to Genevieve's dressing table and was there so her maid could do mysterious and exquisite things to her hair. Several of the newest of their Secret Royal Guards absolutely *loved* playing with the queen's hair. Last he knew, she hadn't yet bothered to set them straight on her lack of enthusiasm for being subjected to such things; it hadn't seemed worth it, given how little time she'd been spending at home, and this last month she hadn't been well enough to sit for long periods of time, nor had there been any formal events that she had needed to attend.

"He tried," Genevieve said with a grin. "But after he woke up with a terrible neck cramp... a couple of times... he yielded to logic and sat beside me. It may have helped that I insisted he keep getting up to come show me the charts and numbers." It was her turn to snicker. "He seemed *very concerned* that I would 'make an attempt' on his virtue."

"I suppose that's fair, considering," Damien said, and then "Ow!" because she had punched him in the abdomen. It hadn't hurt, because she hadn't put any real force behind it – he wasn't sure if she had any force to *put* behind it just yet – but it was a game they had developed over the years.

"Oh, Damien," Genevieve sighed, leaning deeply into his shoulder. "Tell me that it's all going to work out..."

It wasn't like his practical Rebel Duchess – his warrior-Queen – to ask for this kind of reassurance. For pretty lies and hopes wrapped up together in promises.

"It will, my love," he whispered. "Somehow, I'll *make* it work out."

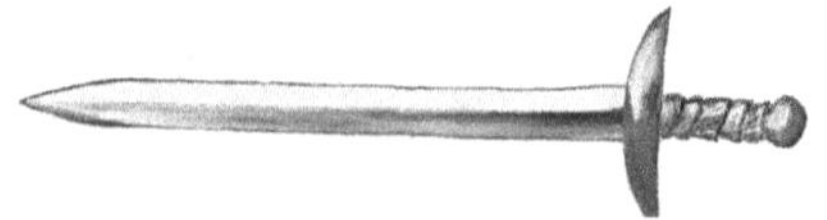

Duke Aldred and Ciriis arrived, to everyone's relief, a few days later.

Genevieve was always happier when her father was close by, and the old dowager duke could spend his days at her side without shirking any other responsibilities. While he and Ciriis managed Elaarwen for Genevieve, she had a very capable cousin from her mother's side of the family who was their chatelaine, with the understanding that Lord Adsel also served as Regent during Genevieve and Duke Aldred's frequent absences.

Ciriis had gone over the dates Damien and Genevieve had sent her and confirmed their and Rosa's analysis. The correlation between Genevieve's miscarriages and natural disasters and health crises with other people was too strong to ignore. It might be irrelevant now that she was staying in the capitol and strictly resting, but it served to convince Adam in particular.

Their presence introduced new problems, however. Both were sharp-eyed and intelligent, and there was no plan to enlighten them about Jason's intended contribution to the Alsterling-and-Stellarine family tree. Jason had been Genevieve's assigned protector for the last several years as she conducted negotiations, so it was just barely plausible that he would hover over her while she was so ill, even back at home.

However, *Adam* had developed a much closer relationship with Genevieve over the week when Jason and Damien had been gone... and a vested interest in her future as the mother of his daughter. He had developed a habit of checking on her several times a day and bringing her treats from the kitchen or scraps of gossip he thought would make her laugh. Even after they were back, and he was not on fulltime Genevieve-watching duty, he continued doing so... and *that* was a great deal harder to explain, especially to Ciriis, who knew him so well.

Despite years of working closely together, Adam had never been this easy around Genevieve. To be perfectly honest, he wasn't this comfortable around *anyone* other than Jason or Damien, and it was an obvious and marked difference. But none of the other three wanted to suggest he stop.

Even Jason found Adam's transformation somewhat bemusing, and it seemed more than likely to arouse the newcomers' suspicions. Especially when they heard about Damien and Jason's mysterious missing week, and there was no way to prevent them from hearing about *that*. Ciriis tended to suspiciousness as a general character trait, though she had handed off her official responsibilities as Spymistress to Lady Aryllis Ancellius some years back in order to serve as Duke Aldred's assistant, and Duke Aldred was always aware of anything surrounding his daughter.

It was only a matter of time before the awkward questions would start.

For the first couple of weeks, Duke Aldred was so shocked by his daughter's appearance that he focused on little else than keeping her restful and feeding her constantly. He also noted how Damien had lost weight, but seemed to assume it was largely out of worry for Genevieve, or perhaps some tangle from the soul-bond. Both of them were looking better at last, but to the duke, who had not seen them since the Spring Festival, the changes were both dramatic and traumatic.

It was in the third week after their arrival that Ciriis finally heard about Damien and Jason's disappearance and confronted *Adam* about letting them leave without proper escort. That went spectacularly poorly when he told her that if she wanted to have any say in such things, she shouldn't have left her position at Court. The shouting match that ensued had everyone creeping around the castle to avoid both of them for the next few days, but Genevieve, Damien, and Jason had a good laugh about it privately. The tall, blonde Adam and the short, dark-haired Ciriis were well-matched in ferocity.

Jason was much *less* amused when she tried to face *him* down about it. But instead of fighting with her, he merely listened while she said her piece, then turned and walked away. It was a technique guaranteed to make Ciriis grind her teeth in frustration, but it gave her no hooks to hang any theories from.

Damien began to hide out in his apartments, hoping that Ciriis wouldn't dare to beard him there, with the risk of upsetting Genevieve. Unfortunately for him, that just meant he ended up facing both Ciriis and the duke simultaneously.

"What were you *thinking*, Damien?" Ciriis exclaimed quietly. The door to the bedchamber, where Genevieve was resting, was barely open – just enough so that they could hear if she needed anything – so they kept their voices down. "We taught you better than that. Just because you haven't faced any serious attempts on your life since the usurpation doesn't mean you're *safe*. Jason is a brilliant warrior, but any one man can be overwhelmed, and even *he* has to sleep *sometimes*."

Duke Aldred sat beside her on the second couch, listening but not yet commenting.

"It wasn't that big a deal, Ciriis," the King attempted to say, though her point that *'even Jason had to sleep sometimes'* had him fighting down a blush.

"You were gone a week! A *week*, Damien! And no one knew where you were. *Anything* could have happened!"

"Genevieve and Adam knew," he said defensively.

He didn't need to explain himself to her, he told himself, nor even to Genevieve's father. He was the king, and he was not responsible to either of them.

It didn't help very much. He had spent too many years obeying the tiny, elegant woman, and had completely relied on Duke Aldred's wisdom for the first two years of his reign.

He evaded the old man's eyes.

Ciriis drew breath for another expostulation, but Duke Aldred unexpectedly put an arm around her shoulders. "Now, Cirii, the King must have had his reasons. I'm sure he'll share them with us when he's ready." One of those iron-grey eyebrows lifted in a gentle invitation for Damien to do so. "Yelling at him isn't likely to advance that moment."

And, surprisingly, Ciriis settled. Not happily, and her glower would have fried rats, but... she settled. Damien eyed the old duke with renewed respect... and some consternation.

"*Well?*" Ciriis demanded after they had sat in silence for several minutes.

Damien sighed, stood up and walked around the couch to his desk. "No. This had nothing to do with you, Ciriis. And I don't need to explain myself to you anymore."

"*Aryllis* couldn't find out where you were! Are you going to tell me it's none of *her* business?"

"If Lady Ancellius has concerns, she can bring them to me directly."

"She says she tried. And that you shut her down."

Damien hid his frustration. Ciriis' persistence had been a big part of what had put him on the Throne. "Then that is between me and my Spymistress. The which you are no longer, Lady Celavell."

"*Damien–*"

"Papa?" Genevieve had opened the bedchamber door all the way, and Damien was at her side in a flash. He could *feel* across the soul-bond that she was 'rescuing' him by providing a distraction none of them could ignore, and he felt more than slightly guilty that she needed to do so.

Well, guilty and grateful.

"Love, you're not supposed to be up. What's wrong?"

She shook her head, her long red-gold braid twisting enticingly over her shoulder and down her breast. "Papa," she said again, "When were you and Ciriis going to tell us?"

And for the first time in *Damien's* memory, Ciriis Celavell blushed. Her dark-complected skin didn't show it as well as Genevieve's pale, freckle-dusted face, but it was distinctly a blush.

His own eyebrows rising with his suspicions, Damien *looked* at her in the special way Queen Marian had taught him... The way that had confirmed the inviability of each of his and Genevieve's conceived children... The way that also allowed him to tell who needed Healing and how and whether it was beyond his abilities.

This time, however, what he saw was much more optimistic.

"You're pregnant!" Damien smiled at his old friend, sliding an arm around Genevieve's too-slender waist to provide extra support should she need it. And, invisibly, he sent her a tendril of love and support down the bond. He looked at Duke Aldred, whom he now realized had been *hovering* slightly whenever Ciriis was nearby. "Yours, I assume?"

The apparently-not-so-old-as-he'd-thought man nodded serenely enough at the King, but looked at his grown daughter with slight anxiety in his eyes. "Genevieve?"

"I'm so happy for you both," Genevieve smiled. "You've been alone since Mama died. I'm glad you're not anymore."

Her smile was open and honest, and Duke Aldred smiled with relief. But then Genevieve's eyes went suddenly wide.

"Damien?" she said, her voice startled and slightly alarmed, and he had just enough time to scoop her up as her knees buckled.

"Back to bed with you, my love," he said. He nodded at the other pair, "Duke Aldred, Ciriis. Congratulations." Then he stepped back through the doorway carrying Genevieve and kicked the door shut between the rooms as soon as they were through.

"You sneaky creature," he said admiringly as he deposited her on the bed. "Thank you."

"What, *me?*" his beautiful wife laughed, holding her arms out for him to join her. "I could feel you starting to panic, and why. It seemed a good time for a diversion."

Damien shook his head. "Not *panicking,* so much as walking the line between exerting my authority as king and being rude to two people we care for very much. How did you know Ciriis was pregnant?"

He sat down on the mattress and lay back to put his head in Genevieve's lap. He flicked the tail of her braid and gave an admiring look at her through the thin fabric of her sleeping gown.

"You're very fetching in this, you know... though you might consider putting on a robe before appearing in public. Not that *I* mind," he added.

"There didn't seem to be time to look for one." She combed the vagrant lock of hair out of his face with gentle fingers. "I don't think I'd figured it out until just now. A lot of little clues, I suppose." She sighed. "I *am* happy for them, but this will pose us some problems."

Damien laughed. "Let's hope that's not an understatement. Your father isn't Duke of Elaarwen except by courtesy, since it was you I Bound and confirmed... but he's there more than you are and he's still doing much of the work. He *and* Ciriis. There is bound to be a movement to name their child as Heir to the province."

Genevieve sighed again. "Perhaps this *solves* our problems, rather than making them worse, love. Their child will be as much a descendant of Queen Marian as either of us," she added wistfully.

Damien's eyes widened. "I hadn't made it that far. Another claimant to the throne."

"Potential only. The Sword still has its say."

He gave an ironic laugh. "I've put so much effort into making the Realm less dependent on a monarch... but the idea that someone other than *our* child could rule after me is putting my hackles up." Damien sighed. "I'm not as far along in my perspective as I had thought."

He looked up into her beautiful blue-green eyes. "If I thought this could save you any pain, I would jump on it. But we'll still have the same problem we've been having. I still need to feed Power to the Realm, and the soul-bond won't be satisfied until we've produced a child. Jason... is a temporary solution for both of us."

She ran her fingertips down his chest, and he shivered. "Just under a month left of this *waiting...*"

Damien caught her fingers and kissed them. "I want it over, too, love. But I'm still not eager for the day I have to put you into Jason's arms and close the door."

"Once I *am* pregnant, though, there's no reason *we* can't make love." Genevieve's eyes sparkled, and Damien caught his breath.

And kissed her fingertips again, because he didn't dare kiss any other part of her.

"Is the Power holding?" she asked, taking a calming breath herself.

"So far." The King sighed. "I shudder to think of trying to get past your father and Ciriis for another little trip."

She chuckled. "Oh, I suspect we've spiked her attempts to 'solve' your disappearance for a while. But Papa... may not be so easily put off." She seemed to hesitate.

"Do you think we should tell him?" Damien asked her seriously. "Tell them both?"

Before Genevieve could answer, there was a knock on the bedchamber door.

Damien gave her a wry look, and got up to answer that knock. It could only be one of a handful of people who could come so close without triggering the web of awareness that he had developed – an intellectual offspring of the way the Realm communicated with him about its own needs. Damien had needed to have a less alarming manner to explain how he knew things... and annoying as it was to wait for a messenger to come in with news that he had known for days or weeks, it made dealing with his Royal Council and other subordinates easier.

He wasn't omniscient, after all, and he wanted neither their fear that he was nor their reliance upon him to be so.

As he had suspected, it was Jason at the door, looking slightly breathless, as though he had run up all the stairs. His eyes were a tad wild. "Is she alright?"

"As you see," Damien opened the door wider to admit his Champion.

Only Genevieve saw him roll his eyes as Jason stepped into the room. She muffled a smile as the knight came and sat down beside her, quietly asking what had happened, how she had come to collapse.

Damien had begun counting in his head when Jason knocked and hadn't reached a full one hundred when Adam burst into the room. He was also slightly breathless, but his expression settled on sardonic as he saw Damien leaning casually against the doorframe, clearly waiting for him.

"I've been had, haven't I?" the Captain asked, crossing the sitting room to join the others.

Damien looked at his wife. "I think we'd *better* tell them before Ciriis cooks up something that makes it even more obvious to everyone. This won't be much of a secret if you two dash up here like this," he chided his Captain and Champion mildly.

"The Queen's health should always be our first concern," Jason asserted. "That's just our job descriptions. And you're both our dear friends as well. It's perfectly natural for both of us to want to check on Genny when we hear something has gone wrong."

Damien rolled his eyes again, this time not bothering to hide it. "Did Ciriis at least tell you in private that Genevieve collapsed?" he asked. "Or was it out in the middle of the Great Hall where anyone and everyone could hear why you turned and dashed up here?"

"It's Ciriis," Adam's voice was very dry. "She's always careful. At least when she and Duke Aldred told *me,* it was privately in my office."

"They just sauntered in, casually dropped the news, and you were out of there like they shot you from a bow?" Damien sighed. "I thought *you* were more skeptical, my friend."

And more careful, he didn't need to say. Clearly the entire castle would have seen the two of them galloping up to the tower, two steps at a time.

"Two steps at a time, Jason?" Genevieve grinned.

He flushed. "Three, actually." He had long legs. They both did.

"I suspect they're on their way back up here already," Damien folded his arms and looked at the two knights. "Do you want to be here for this conversation?" He flickered a glance at his lovely wife. "So much for spiking Ciriis' curiosity by outing her for carrying your father's child."

Jason and Adam both looked utterly stunned.

"Ciriis... is... *what?*" Adam managed after a moment.

Damien just shook his head, counting again.

One hundred fifty. He went to the outer door and opened it just before Ciriis knocked. He took one look at his father-in-law and looped the man's arm over his shoulders to help him into the room. The knights on Guard duty outside the royal apartment looked incredibly curious, and Damien sighed internally.

"Papa, you shouldn't be going up and down so many stairs so quickly," he chided. "It may have been two years, and I've Healed what I could, but your heart still shouldn't take such strain."

"Much less of a strain here in the lowlands than in Elaarwen," the old man wheezed, not objecting as Damien settled him on the couch. Damien gave Ciriis a reproachful look as she brought the duke a glass of water.

"What was I supposed to do?" she asked, defensively. "I asked you straight up."

"Did it never occur to you that this *really* might not be any of your business, Ciriis?" Damien said in exasperation. He knelt by the couch as he kept a hand on Duke Aldred's, checking the health of his heart and the general 'rightness' of the rest of his body. The old man was healthier than he had a right to be, at his age and after his long incarceration in Siovale, not least because Damien checked on him as often as he could.

"Don't blame her alone, son," the duke said, having caught his breath at last. "We both want to know what's going on with you and Genevieve. Secrets," he added with a sterner note, "are rarely good for the Realm."

Damien sighed, raking his hair out of his face. "And sometimes they are absolutely critical for the good of the Realm. Jason," he called out to the bedchamber. "Bring Genevieve out here if you please."

There was a moment of small, bustling noises – Damien restrained a grin as he guessed that Jason and Adam were hunting for a robe to cover that *very* thin sleeping gown – and then Jason carried the Queen out of the room. Without looking at anyone, he carefully deposited Genevieve in her usual space on the couch. Damien crossed over and sat down next to her, pulling her legs up across his lap so that she could lie down a bit more. Jason busied himself with tucking pillows and a warm throw in around the Queen.

"Adam," Damien called while this went on.

No, his Captain wasn't going to get to hide in the bedchamber while the rest of them had to explain things. The other tall, blonde man came to the door and looked out with a more trepiditious expression than the King had ever seen on him.

Damien snorted. "You've faced battle and death, Adam, these are just friends... and family."

The King waved both knights to sit down as he took his wife's hand. Jason sat nervously in what had once been Damien's favorite chair. Adam seemed inclined to try to hold the wall up, but came forward reluctantly to sit in the chair opposite Jason when Damien gestured more pointedly.

The King fixed the erstwhile duke and his lover with his complete attention. "You have questions, Your Grace. I'm not sure I can give you all the answers you want."

Duke Aldred bore up under Damien's gaze, but Ciriis wilted a bit. "All the answers I *deserve,* then? As a *Peer* of the *Realm?* Or as Genevieve's *father?*"

The Queen spoke before her husband. "You're no longer a Peer of the Realm, Papa. Not that we'd be sharing any of this with Tomas Elsevier, or even Rosa Miramar. If you receive answers, it will be because you are my father, and only that."

She'd said it gently, but it seemed like the old man took it as a blow anyways. Ciriis took his hand, petting it soothingly, and gave Genevieve a scathing look. The Queen ignored her. She and Genevieve had been *allies* during the overlap of their tenures in Emeralsee, but hardly comfortable ones... although they worked well together, putting the well-being of the Realm – and of Damien – above their personal feelings.

"What *will* you tell me then?" Duke Aldred demanded. "Has a man not a *right* to know about the health of his only child?"

There was a slight quaver in his voice for the first time that Damien had ever noticed. Even after Lord Prydeen had all but killed him, the old man's voice had been steady, if weak. Damien had checked him for the obvious results of his rapid climb of the tower stairs, but was there something more subtle to be concerned over?

... and then the old man transferred his gaze back to Damien, a challenging look in his eye as he added in that same, slightly quavery voice, "About how her *husband* is *treating* her?"

Damien would have cared more about Duke Aldred's condition, if the old man's second statement had not nudged his temper to an immediate boil. He didn't dare move, certainly not jump to his feet to pace as he dearly wanted to. Not with Genevieve's legs stretched across his lap.

He felt her alarm, saw both Adam and Jason shift from nervous despondency to almost battle-readiness. Ciriis shrank against Duke Aldred's side, though *she* looked more confused than the men or his wife. Apparently all three of them could read his reaction from body language or expression nearly as well as Genevieve could across the soul-bond.

They – and Duke Aldred – were also looking over Damien's shoulder with expressions of shock and fear.

"Damien, my love," Genevieve gripped Damien's nearer arm with both hands... a reminder that she really wasn't strong enough to handle a great deal of emotional stress.

He swallowed his wrath, tamped it down. Was startled to hear a tinkling as if of a dozen wineglasses being set down with some care.

"I am taking care of Genevieve." Damien stated it carefully and slowly in as even a tone as he could manage. "I am taking care of my responsibilities to the Realm. I am grateful for all you taught me about how to rule, Aldred, and for giving me the care that my own father no longer could. *But you may not question my motives and actions until you can answer how you could let Harald of Siovale torture Genevieve for* **eight long years** *and* **under your own roof.**"

Things they had never spoken of...

Duke Aldred's expression was a curious mixture of guilt and truculence as he clearly tried to come up with a reply. Damien didn't bother to look at anyone else... but he could *feel* Genevieve's calm demeanor cracking... She was always most open and vulnerable when her father was here anyways...

Abruptly – or so it seemed – the soul-bond shut-down. Or at least Damien could no longer *feel* his wife's reactions.

The King took another slow, careful breath, then looked again at the man he had called 'Papa' for five years, and the woman who had been his first lover... in some ways – though not all – his first love. "Lord Aldred. Madame Celavell. You are dismissed from Our Presence. We shall see that you are summoned when your attendance upon Us is desired."

There was stark and utter silence for a long moment as the former duke stared almost uncomprehendingly at his son-in-law and king. Ciriis was pale with shock.

At last, Adam stood up, asking Damien's permission with a glance. He received it with a brief, sharp nod.

"Let me help you to your quarters, my lord," he said, taking Aldred's elbow and urging the old man to rise.

"Genevieve...?" her father asked, hesitantly, that quaver in his voice an entirely different timbre than the earlier one that now sounded so contrived to Damien's memory... but he didn't seem to be trying to explain... *or* to ask forgiveness.

The Queen's expression was carefully neutral, and she did not speak, though she met his eyes.

Adam silently escorted the pair out of the room.

There was another long moment of tense silence.

Damien didn't know how to break it. Didn't dare look his wife in the face to see how angry she would be for how he had treated her father. Didn't want to know that she had only backed him up because it was her duty as queen. Didn't want to look at his oldest friend and see how much his loss of control had disappointed the older man.

"Thank you," Genevieve said at long last, surprising him into raising his eyes to look at her. "I... I've wanted to ask him that for a long, long time. I just... couldn't."

Tears began to trail down her face, as silent in their escape as the ones she had shed during her long, abusive first marriage, and she hugged one of the throw pillows to her chest. "I knew why *I* didn't do anything about Harald. But..."

"But he's your father," Jason agreed, slipping off his chair, and coming to kneel on the floor beside her. "He should have protected you."

"He *did* tell me the marriage was a bad idea," she temporized. "He told me I could change my mind, even the night before..."

Damien wanted to take her in his arms... and didn't dare.

He was still trembling with the effort of controlling a temper that had rarely ever seen the light of day... Normally he nipped these reactions before they even really budded. It had always been too dangerous to show his own hurt or anger or frustration; a lifetime in his grandfather's Court had taught him that. And Adam... Adam had taught him how to cope better when Damien's inevitable failures at learning the sword or dealing with *people* had overwhelmed him as a nascent adult. Though Adam's solution had been a bit... dramatic. And it wasn't an option right now.

"He left you to your own devices after that?" Jason asked, and shook his head. "A man – or woman – is responsible for what goes on under his roof."

Damien thought about the hundreds of people who lived and worked in the Castle. About the hundreds of *thousands* of people who lived in Emeralsee's city and province. The *millions* who lived in his Realm. Without the web of magick that he was Bound to, it seemed like being responsible even for the former would be well beyond him. Duke Aldred – *Lord* Aldred, who had violated his oaths to his former king when he formed the Rebellion – had not been so Bound. But it wasn't the doings of the scullerymaids and potboys that was in question here, it was the safety and well-being of his own daughter, his Heir and only child.

Jason had risen up to hold Genevieve as she cried.

Damien didn't dare touch her. With both of their emotions loosed like this, what chance that he – *or she* – would be able to maintain the willpower not to yield to what both Realm and soul-bond had never ceased demanding?

His beautiful, hurting, soul-bonded warrior-Queen – who never, *ever* cried...

He needed her.

And *she* needed *him*.

And he *didn't dare touch her...* but *Jason* could.

Abruptly it was all too much, and with a gesture – a thought, really – he was alone on top of the tower. He sensed Genevieve's brief dismay, then a wash of understanding. She was still crying, but somehow, she still had the capacity for compassion for *him*, worthless husband though he was proving in her hour of need.

She was still crying, and Jason was holding her.

She was still *crying*...

Damien rested a hand on one of the crenelations around the top of the tower and stared out over his Castle. His City. His Realm.

The lights from a hundred thousand homes made the faint mist that always rose up from the ocean at night glow. He couldn't see as many stars from here as from other parts of his Realm, but each star that he missed was replaced by one of those lights below. Each one representing the prosperity of his capitol, and of the Realm beyond it, for the City of Emeralsee was a concentrator of wealth, just as the Castle and Throne concentrated magick.

A prosperity that was his to guide and to guard.

Though at what cost...

He felt the other's approaching presence through the web of the Realm, and his own now-hyperalert web of awareness, even more than he heard the footsteps.

"I won't let that happen to my children, Jason," he said without turning. There were only two whose feet would be able to find the invisible, intangible staircase that led up here, and Genevieve wasn't in any shape to make that climb. "They will not wed for anything less than love, and if that love goes sour, I'll be there to help them get free. I swear it as king."

"A heavy oath," the other man said, stopping close behind. "And if they don't want your help? Or won't listen when you offer your wisdom? Will you intervene between husband and wife without being asked?"

Damien's head dropped. He put a hand up on the other crenelation, holding himself suspended in the embrasure between. "You found the passage up here, I see."

"She told me." His Champion's tone was bemused. "Adam came back and she practically flung herself into *his* arms, then told me how to come up here. I'm not sure which of us was more startled."

"She doesn't dare touch you for long any more than I dare touch *her*. Especially when there are strong emotions involved."

Damien dug his fingers into the unyielding rock. He couldn't even comfort his *wife*.

His eyes were dry, though they burned in the crisp, cold air. His stomach and chest felt constricted, knotted... almost too tight to swallow – or breathe – let alone seek the release of tears that he surely didn't deserve...

He nearly jumped when he felt Jason's hands on his shoulders, his neck. Thank the Gods the walls of this Castle were so thick – thick enough to walk through without being seen from either side, as Damien well knew. Surprise didn't risk a deadly fall, even from the top of this highest tower.

"Jason... stop."

"Damien, your shoulders are tight as bowstrings. Let me help."

The dark-haired man shook his head. "Not right now... I can't... this will only end one way right now."

"I know." Jason's fingers continued to work magick on his shoulders through tunic and shirt. His breath on Damien's neck... dear Gods. More than breath...

"Jason... no..." His fingertips were going to be *bloody* if he squeezed the rock any harder...

"You scared us all, earlier, Damien," Jason said quietly. "Did you realize you lifted every piece of glassware? Just a few inches... and you set it all down safely, but... *all of it.*"

Those tinkling noises he had heard when he tamped down his fury.

He tried to huff a laugh. "I suppose that was why Ciriis and Du– *Lord* Aldred looked so shocked. A bit much, but it seems to have made my point."

Actually, they had looked half terrified.

Jason and Adam had looked *shocked* as well.

The King didn't want to believe he'd seen *fear* in the faces of his oldest friends as well. Or on Genevieve.

"Damien..." Jason's fingers paused briefly in their massage. "It wasn't just in that room. Adam says it was everything in the *castle*. And they'd just started getting reports of the same thing from the city."

In horror, Damien sent his awareness out into the Realm to look for echoes, ripples... dear Gods, he had affected *the entire Realm*. What might have happened if he hadn't controlled his temper? If... be real... if *Genevieve* hadn't recalled him to his duty?

Damien sank down into a squat, resting his elbows on his knees, his face in his hands. Away from the embrasure and its tempting height... no more need to worry...

Except that wasn't fair to *Genevieve*...

Or to the Realm, which was depending on him to Heal it and find himself an Heir to carry on that work...

Or to these beloved friends who had worked so hard for the benefit of both himself and the Realm they also loved, if in a more abstract sense...

Jason knelt down behind him. "My sweet prince. You need to release some of this tension... before anything else happens. And *that* I *can* help with."

He wrapped his long arms around Damien, careful not to overbalance him. His arms were as secure a place as Emeralsee Harbor was for all those trade ships out there – as safe a place as they'd been fourteen years ago for the terrified boy who'd finally dared to speak to this tall, gentle man who had so patiently outwaited him.

The King set one knee down on the deck of the tower to stabilize himself; physically if not emotionally. Jason was absolutely right. He had to get control of himself. The business with the glass made that... hunh. *Perfectly clear.*

"I can't even hold her to comfort her, Jason," Damien said sadly. "I don't dare. *She* doesn't dare."

"I know," his Champion soothed, kissing his hair.

"Adam..."

"Doesn't want to see the castle fall down around *his* ears either," Jason said dryly. "He told me to come up here and do 'whatever' I needed to do to 'put you back together' was his wording. He knew what he was saying."

"I can't keep *doing* this to you... *Both* of you..."

"My sweet prince," Jason murmured into his neck. "Trust me, you won't be the only one *doing...*"

Damien shuddered as those words and that touch built images in his head, and made himself relax into the other man's embrace. It wasn't entirely sexual tension, but that was a part of it. And perhaps the only part he could do something *about.*

"One of these days we'll find a place with a proper bed," Jason chuckled. "Unless..." He looked down through the clerestory windows that formed the glittering, pointed top of this tower at Damien and Genevieve's bedchamber. "No, Adam's settling her in there."

"Oh, if that's what you want..." Damien waved a hand, and a mattress, complete with blankets and pillows, nestled in the bare stride's length between the base of the windows and the crenelations.

He didn't dare look down through those windows himself. The soul-bond had cracked open enough to let him *feel* Genevieve a little again... she was still *crying.* He didn't want to think about that.

He *couldn't* think about that right now or the Glassmaker's Guild would have a great deal more to do than merely replace every piece of stemware in the country...

Jason laughed. "Much better. Now if you'd like to do something about this cold air...?"

Chapter EIGHT

Confidences

LATER... MUCH LATER... JASON WAS drawing lazy designs on Damien's abdomen, his arm reaching around while his breath was warm on the younger man's neck.

"I do love you, too, you know," the knight said at last. "It's not the way I feel about Adam, but..." The smile was in his tone. He said it again, warm and generous and without any more implied caveats. "I love you, my lovely liege-lord."

Damien sighed. "I still feel like I've done something terribly wrong. You've only ever been with Adam... and now I'm–"

"And Oskar," Jason interrupted.

Damien waved that off. "Prince Oskar doesn't count, he–"

"He most certainly *does* count," Jason corrected gently. "He taught me how to be a lover, after all."

Damien twisted to look up into the other man's face in consternation. "But..."

"Hush." Jason kissed him gently again, then tucked Damien back into his chest. "I hadn't done much more than exchange kisses with Adam before I was assigned as Prince Oskar's bodyguard. Oskar... had a long view of what he wanted from me, so he took the time to make sure I was happy. Enjoying it. Except for not having a choice, of course."

He sighed. "Which didn't matter as much to me then as you might think. He was nearly as handsome as you, though more in that classical Alsterling way. Quite nearly as charismatic as you as well. And just enough older than me that he had some of that older-and-worldly-wise feel to him to make him very... alluring. I'd heard all the stories, of course, but he was... kind. And tender. And gentle. And like you said about Ciriis... you get all starry-eyed after your first time."

"You... fell in love with him." Damien couldn't even make it a question, though he desperately wanted to. Or rather, he desperately wanted to deny that any such thing was even possible. He didn't want to know about a kinder, gentler side of his uncle. Not after hearing about the horrors the man had visited on Rosa and her family. Not after helping so many of his Secret Cadre of Royal Guardswomen recover from Prince Oskar's 'attentions.' Not after seeing what Jason had looked like when Prince Oskar was done with him the *second* time.

"He planned it so," Jason agreed, and his tone... was more regretful than bitter to Damien's dismay. "Before long, I would have done anything he asked. I *did* do anything he asked. And what he asked started to become... more exotic. When he wouldn't let me fight at the battle of Siovale – *me*, the best swordsman in the Realm! – I convinced myself it was because he loved me too much to risk me. And after all, there's a difference between sparring in the ring and fighting a war. I'd never killed anyone. I wasn't particularly eager to do so, though I didn't like to be sidelined. But when I objected, he took a couple of camp-followers into his bed and shut me out as punishment."

Jason snorted softly. "It probably seems odd to you that it was *my* punishment that they took my place. But at the time it was... very effective. I begged him to forgive me and take me back." He paused and kissed Damien's shoulder. "I don't know if you can understand this..."

Damien realized he'd gone tense, and relaxed back into the loving warmth of Jason's body curving around his. No matter how *he* felt about his unlamented uncle, there was something here that Jason wanted to tell him... Or maybe... *needed* to tell him.

And... Prince Oskar clearly wasn't *unlamented*. Not if Jason's tone meant anything...

"Genevieve..." Damien said softly. He'd learned enough of her first marriage to understand how this sort of manipulation could work... and to sympathize, rather than blame or be horrified. "You've... never told Adam this, have you."

Open, honest Jason... who hadn't told the love of his life about his unacknowledged passion for the wonderful woman he'd nearly been betrothed to as a child. Of course, he hadn't shared his unresolved attachment to the prince who had nearly destroyed him.

Nearly destroyed them *both*. Damien could remember all too well... watching Adam fall apart when he was out of Jason's sight, after the second time, but only when Adam thought he was entirely alone. At only seventeen, Damien – with his own neglected, confused, pubescent heart – had still been struggling to trust them all, to understand his physical reactions to Ciriis and his emotional reactions to Jason... and not *just* to Jason...

The young prince hadn't known how to help either of the men he loved and depended on. It had also been utterly terrifying to see them as so much more vulnerable. So much *not* the perfect protectors he needed them to be.

So much more... human.

That might have been when he began to think of Jason and Adam – and Ciriis – as guides and friends. When he began to see himself as an actor in the drama of his own life, rather than merely a bit character. When he began to realize that someday – if all went according to his *mentors'* plans – he, Damien, would be King of Ilseador, and they would only be his advisors. When he began to think of himself as a prince.

Both Adam and Jason seemed to find some comfort in his presence; so he'd tried that for awhile, snuggling close and reading to Jason or letting Adam wear him – and Adam himself – out in the practice court... But then Ciriis had tried to re-kindle the romance she'd begun with him in Lynncrag – and when she hadn't taken his timid refusals as the final word, Damien had retreated to the Royal Library so that she couldn't pressure him.

And the familiarity and comfort of that space had been too hard to leave again after such a traumatic reintroduction to the world of his grandfather's Court. It had felt safer, too, than staying out and about where his uncle or Oskar's mother, Queen Eliza, who was just as bad, could notice him. If Prince Oskar do such terrible things to the tall, strong, knighted *Jason,* what hope had Damien who was small for his age and barely knew which end of a sword to hold? His hopes of a reprieve from the Court had been dashed at Lynncrag... he had to *survive* to become the King that Adam and Jason and Ciriis had told him he might.

It had taken Jason healing enough to come to the Library to lure him back out again with patience and kindness...

Jason... and two more *years*. Damien had come out for Court functions during that time, taking care to seem ineffectual and shy. He'd acted reluctant to learn more swordwork from Adam and Jason, to their continual frustration, but nudging them to fence each other as much as possible where he could watch – and then trying what he saw them practice at night in the Library when he was alone. And Damien had also spent the intervening time reading through sections of the Library that he'd never covered in as much detail; most particularly certain ancient treatises on political philosophy that had turned out to be incredibly useful in keeping himself from drowning in the eddies and whirlpools of the Court... and the very occasional missteps by his three mentors.

When he'd finally emerged from the Library – at nineteen – for good, he'd been far better prepared.

But he'd never forgotten what Prince Oskar had done to Jason – nor why.

These... revelations... fit into the mosaic, but they were changing the overall picture. How drastically, the King wasn't yet sure.

He felt Jason nod in answer to his not-question about whether Adam knew. "No. I've told no one else, ever. Who would understand?"

Another soft snort tickled Damien's neck, but the topic muffled the reaction the younger man might otherwise have had. "When I heard Oskar was dead, I cried. I went to the grotto and cried, all by myself, because I couldn't do that in front of anyone. I didn't love him anymore... but... I'm not built to hate. Not even after all he did. To others. To... to *me*."

The King wasn't so sure that his Champion was being honest, even with himself, about what feelings he might still harbor for the dead prince.

But now, tonight... it didn't matter in any way that would change anything.

Tonight... what mattered was what Jason needed *now*.

Which was the assurance that *he* wouldn't be derided for *not* hating Prince Oskar.

"Jason..." Damien reached a hand up to touch the other man's rough cheek. "Genevieve cried every night until we buried Harald's remains. She waited until she thought I was fast asleep." He intercepted a warm droplet, brought it to his lips. Salt. "*I* cried when my grandfather died," he added quietly. "I couldn't have explained why."

And Damien felt a certain relief for being able to say that aloud for himself.

Jason's arm tightened around him in gratitude for the acceptance. "When we came back after Siovale, things were... different. Oskar was made Heir, and he was sure of his power over me, I suppose. Both temporal and emotional. He started... leaving me chained up."

Damien wanted to tell him to stop. He didn't want to hear this. Didn't want to *know*...

But Jason had carried this burden in his heart for over fifteen years.

Alone.

The King stayed silent.

"Spreadeagled. Naked. On his bed. Sometimes for days." Jason shuddered... but there was a weird sense that it wasn't all out of remembered horror. The feel of his body against Damien's suggested... that he found even that horrible a memory... *arousing?* On some level anyways...

Damien tried to keep himself open and non-judgmental... and suppress his own sickened reaction.

Instead, he focused on the technical aspect.

"But that would surely get... messy... If he didn't let you up to... um..."

"He didn't care. He laughed at me. The servants would come in to clean and carefully not look. Except when he ordered them to. He had his own cadre of 'special' servants, of course. No one dared disobey. And eventually he would unlock me, and let me clean myself up. I'd be lightheaded with thirst – he'd feed me by hand, like a pet, but I couldn't drink in that position without choking.

"And he'd stand there drinking water and waiting for me to beg..." Jason's face buried into Damien's shoulders. "And I would. But I wouldn't be begging for water. I'd begging for... *him.*"

He took a deep breath. "And then... then he started requiring me to lie with others for his entertainment. Women, men. And I did it, hoping he'd decide to pay attention to *me* again. When he discarded me and chose Sir Edmund his bodyguard and Champion... I wanted to die. If it hadn't been for Adam... and Ciriis... I don't know what I would have done."

Jason paused. "And you, my sweet prince. Adam was going out of his head trying to show me how much he loved me, but you... you *needed* me. You didn't spend all your time swearing about Oskar and threatening vengeance... *you* just needed time and gentleness."

Because Jason hadn't just been dealing with the aftermath of physical and emotional abuse. He'd been dealing with a broken heart.

The timing struck Damien. Prince Oskar had shown his true colors after the battle of Siovale, as had Harald. But Prince Oskar had had no reason not to discard the lover he no longer wanted, whereas Harald's entire fortune had rested upon controlling Genevieve, heart and soul.

"You gave me all the gentleness and time I needed," Damien said, and smiled so that Jason would hear the change in his voice. The love and... *gentleness* that he had given so unstintingly to the terrified boy-prince in the Royal Library. After five years of attention from only a woman who hated him, how could Damien *not* have fallen in love with him in return? "I never understood how you couldn't see how I felt about you... but I guess I understand now."

Jason kissed his neck, and Damien shivered. "Can you also understand why I went back to him when he started showing an interest in *you?* I talked Adam into taking you to Lynncrag..."

"Yes..." It had clearly been as much about jealousy as about protecting the naïve young prince. No wonder Jason had never talked to Adam about this. "But it wasn't the same, was it." Damien paused. "*He* wasn't the same."

Jason shuddered again, and this time it was more of a normal shudder. "No. This time he had no need to be kind. *Or* gentle. And... his tastes had grown even more... exotic. I wasn't his bodyguard or his Champion – he was wearing the Heir's Ring again, but he didn't even offer me the title, though I could have defeated his so-called 'Champion' of the time blindfolded. I had offered myself to him without asking anything in return, and he took everything he cared to without giving anything back. And tossed me out again."

"Oh, Jason..." Damien ached for the re-breaking of his friend's heart.

"It... *wasn't* as hard as the first time. No matter what it looked like. No matter what Adam and Ciriis think. Oskar was much, much harder on me physically the second time – he had me addicted to half a dozen different aphrodisiacs in those few weeks you were gone, among other things." Jason snorted. "Not that he'd needed to use them on me since I was half dying to please him, but he found it amusing. He didn't bother trying to feed my emotions either, so I could more clearly see what... he was."

He was still nestled close in to Damien's shoulders, and the younger man could feel his back growing very damp.

"I hadn't wanted to the first time. To see the *real* Oskar. I had kept trying to believe it was something *I* did. No matter what Adam and Ciriis said. It... hadn't helped that my mother berated me for losing such a prime position as Champion to the Heir. She would rather, apparently, have my expenses covered by the Crown than support a knight for whom she had no use."

Damien swallowed. He knew Countess Solway wasn't very warm with her son, but Duk– *Lord* Aldred had only the best things to say about the woman who had been his childhood friend... and perhaps his first love. The King couldn't quite understand how a parent could treat their own child so cruelly. He loved his own children fiercely and *they* weren't even born yet.

And it wasn't as if Jason were unlovable in any way...

"I could finally see just how awful Oskar was. And how very *good* Adam is." Damien could hear the wry smile in his friend's voice. "He tries so hard to hide it behind that prickly, cynical exterior..."

"I know..." Damien was smiling as well. "Did he tell you that he and Genevieve spent the week we were gone picking out names?"

Jason laughed. "No. But it doesn't surprise me."

Damien wriggled around to face his friend.

"Better?" he said, with all the compassion he could muster.

Jason blinked as if he'd been dazzled by Damien. "Tone that down a bit please, dearheart."

Oh. Apparently he had.

Damien lowered his eyes, but Jason had fingers tilting his chin up for a kiss.

"*Much* better. Thank you for listening."

Damien gave him a wry grin. "What else could I possibly do for the unacknowledged Hero of the Realm?"

"Hero...?" Jason raised an eyebrow.

"Well, you probably stopped me from causing some sort of disaster. Or at least breaking all the glassware in the Realm," Damien said dryly. "Though the Glassworkers' Guild might not agree that that's a good thing."

"Are you planning on telling them?"

Thank the Gods it was too dark to see him blush. "No."

"Ah. Then they'll never know how close they came to riches," Jason said wisely. "Not that glassworkers are anything less than prosperous anyways..."

"They earn it, every bit," Damien said earnestly. "Have you ever been to a glassworks? Hot, hard work and incredibly dangerous... what?" Jason was giving him a fondly annoyed look.

"I'm surprised you and Genevieve managed to conceive once, let alone ten times, if this is what you talk about in bed."

"She does it, too," Damien muttered, flushing again, but for a different reason.

Jason rolled his eyes. "Oh, what I have to look forwards to."

Damien closed his eyes, trying to shut that image away. Not that she was ever far from his thoughts... but...

And he was reminded that he was still coming between Adam and Jason. Though perhaps he had done *some* good for them by letting Jason unburden himself to a sympathetic and non-judgmental ear.

"You're still worrying," Jason said with amusement. "I told you... what I did... not only because it helped me to be able to talk about it at last, but also so you could see that what Adam and I have *isn't* fragile. It stood up to Oskar. It stood up to me not really believing in how important he was to me. We'll weather this as well."

"Lovely company," Damien muttered.

"What you and Genny have isn't fragile either," Jason added.

"Hmmn."

"But my *other* reason for telling you is so that you'd know that not everything I took from my time with Oskar was terrible." There was a mischievous glow in Jason's eyes that Damien had rarely seen in his quiet, often too-serious friend. "He could be quite... inventive. And... delightful. And Adam... much as I adore him... is entirely too conventional to try certain things. But I think maybe you would appreciate some... creativity?"

Damien eyed him dubiously. On the one hand, everything *else* he'd ever heard about Prince Oskar... on the other hand... *Jason*. He trusted Jason. With his life, his honor, his Realm... his *wife*.

Slowly, he nodded... and felt his pulse and breathing speed up in anticipation of... whatever Jason planned. A part of Damien's mind protested that they should agree on how and when to *stop* before Jason proceeded with this; but the rest of him was well aware that although the knight could easily *physically* overpower him, Damien's magick meant he was at no particular risk. Likely it was a conversation they *should* have... but was it really worth disturbing this rather delicate moment when there was no real danger? It would only be this one time, after all...

Jason's smile became positively wicked.

"Oh, my lovely liege-lord," he breathed. "I was hoping you'd say that."

His fingers slid across Damien's chest, circled his nipple a couple of times, then *pinched*. It should have hurt – and it did, some – but it was so incredibly *arousing* that he barely noticed the pain. He cried out, but it was a cry of pleasure.

Dazedly, Damien snapped a sound-shield around the bubble of warm air he had trapped around them. This... he didn't want anyone to hear them. And he didn't want to *share*.

Jason's smile was knowing. "Nothing that will leave a mark," he promised. "Nothing that will leave you hurting tomorrow."

Damien nodded again, not daring to speak as his breath and his pulse sped up, and Jason's fingers began to travel again. He held his breath, then whispered, "And for *you?*"

Jason's wicked smile softened. "Tonight is for you, dear one. *Next* time I'll show you how to do things for *me.*"

And Damien nearly lost his *entire* ability to breathe because it was *Jason's* plan that there should be a 'next time.'

Chapter NINE

A Tangled Web

DAMIEN AND JASON CAME DOWN the magickal stairwell in the light of pre-dawn to find Genevieve asleep in Adam's arms in the center of the bed. With one look of perfect understanding exchanged, they each climbed in and snuggled up to their own true love.

For once, Damien had no fear of losing control. He was so tired and... *sated*... that there was nothing at all for the magick of the soul-bond to work on. And the Realm... was likewise *sated* and undemanding. It wouldn't last long, but for now he could enjoy the smell of Genevieve's hair without worrying that she would have to face another unintended and debilitating miscarriage.

She curled towards him and into his arms automatically, without waking up. He noticed Adam doing the same with Jason, and was glad as never before that he had such a *large* bed. The King smiled and settled into a light doze, happy and with everything right in his world for the moment.

It wasn't long before Adam was stirring, of course. The Captain was used to being up at first light, and simply sleeping in the wrong bed – and one he had grown used to in the week he had been on solo Genevieve-watch – would not disrupt his internal clock.

To Damien's surprise, his Captain wasn't the sort to wake up easily, but seemed to climb up out of sleep as if he were fighting it. His own light doze didn't last, and he felt Genevieve stirring against his chest.

"Jason?" Adam muttered. He seemed bleary-eyed and somewhat confused. "Jase?"

"I'm here, love." Jason *was* the sort to be disgustingly wide-awake as soon as his eyes opened. Or perhaps he'd just been in as light a doze as Damien. The King couldn't say, despite their weeklong 'camping' trip, since Jason had always been up and moving long before he pried his own eyes open. And often deep in dreams long before Damien could fall asleep... though he'd always managed to fall asleep wrapped *around* Damien, so discreetly rising to pace or even just twitching to use up some of his restless energy hadn't been an option for the younger man.

"Where are we – oh." Adam had sat up and looked around to orient himself. He groaned and fell back onto the pillows. "Damn. I was hoping yesterday was nothing but a bad dream."

Jason had propped his head up on his elbow. He smiled at Damien, seeing the King was awake, and shook his head with a smile. *He* didn't feel the same way.

Damien gave his friend... his *lover*... a shy smile back.

Genevieve was also the kind to come all the way awake at once. Damien knew, more because of the bond than because of any physical change that he could consciously detect. He had long ago guessed that this absolutely perfect emulation of sleep was something she had trained herself to do while she was married to Harald. Self-defense of another sort.

He remembered Jason's words of the night before, but his lips still tightened thinking about it.

"The Guards at the door are going to be wondering what happened," Adam was complaining at the ceiling. "And the word is probably all over the castle that there's been a falling out between Their Majesties and Du–Lord Aldred and Ciriis. We'll need to get on top of this before the rumor mill gets completely out of control."

Managing the rabid hotbed of rumor in Castle and City – and Country – was technically Aryllis' job. Adam had begun to work closely with her on it a few years ago, their talents and official capacities dovetailing neatly. And in this case... they couldn't ask the Spymistress' aid without revealing *why*...

Genevieve relaxed slightly, and rolled to be able to see Adam, shifting to stay close in Damien's arms to his infinite, if silent, approval.

"And here I was thinking *I* was your nightmare from yesterday."

She said it with a smirk.

Adam looked at her, threw his arm over his eyes and moaned softly.

Jason raised an eyebrow. "Something you want to tell me about, love?"

Adam lifted his arm enough to glare one-eyed at Jason. "Seems that could go two ways."

Jason's smile took on that smug, wicked look Damien had never guessed his friend had in him until last night. "Fine by me. Shall I go first?"

Adam's arm went back over his eyes as he went very red.

"I... couldn't stop crying last night," Genevieve offered after an awkward moment. "Finally, Adam kissed me to shock me out of it." Her expression was wry. "It was a shock all right. For both of us." She focused on the miserable man. "Thank you ever so much for not going with the usual glass of cold water in the face."

Damien stifled a laugh, and Jason snorted.

Adam glared at his love. "I didn't know what else to do. She wouldn't let me go so I could *get* a glass of water... and I was afraid that might make her catch a cold on top of everything else. I've never kissed a *woman* before," he moaned.

"Then that makes you the only person in the room who hadn't," Geneveive said a little tartly. "Stop thinking of me as a 'woman' and think of me as a 'friend.'" Her tone softened. "You were there when I badly needed someone who would hold me. Thank you."

Damien felt his insides go cold again. *He* hadn't been there when she needed him...

"Was it a *good* kiss?" Jason purred to Adam suggestively, leaning on his chest and pinning him down.

"Jason... not in front of..." Adam flickered an embarrassed glance to Damien and Genevieve, who both quickly looked away.

"As good as *this* one?" Jason proceeded to provide a sample for comparison.

Damien felt a spiral of curiosity and amazement from his wife through their bond. She met his eyes and for once he could hear the actual words that she was thinking as well: *Whatever did you do with the quiet, serious Jason we've always known before?*

The King blushed and shrugged. *Listened to him, mostly. I think this has always been there. And Adam got to see him like this. He's just comfortable letting **us** see it now.*

Genevieve glanced back over her shoulder, and Damien followed her gaze. They were murmuring softly into each other's ears now, but Adam was still bright red. *He might be, but I don't think **Adam** is...*

I have absolutely no sympathy, Damien told her, kissing the tip of her nose mischievously. *Do you remember how Adam walked in on us the day after we bonded?*

Her eyes crinkled at the memory. *You have a point.*

Aloud, she sighed. "But Adam does have a point, love. If we don't do something about the rumor-mill, it'll eat us alive."

How angry are you still at your father, love? Damien asked silently. *He and Ciriis have given us most of the excuse we need... if we should choose to use it.*

She gave him a look of consternation. "Not *that* upset... but *you* still are, aren't you?"

"These half-silent conversations of yours are extremely difficult to follow," Jason commented dryly, "but in this case, I think I can surmise that you're discussing whether to toss Lord Aldred and Ciriis to the hounds of gossip."

"Starving *wolves,* more like," Adam noted. "Jason, let me *up.*"

He was still pinned, and while he doubtless *could* get free, it would involve more athleticism than any of them cared to subject Genevieve to right now.

"Later..." Jason told him, and it wasn't so much a *hint* as an entire *promise* in his words.

Adam nodded very quickly, and Jason let them both sit up, though he kept an arm around his love's abdomen. Damien saw the muscles contract beneath Adam's shirt, and smiled to himself at his Captain's extremely distracted expression. For all that he needed all of their full attention just now.

The King also pulled himself into a seated position and stacked pillows around his wife to help her sit as well. She sighed somewhat bitterly, but suffered him to provide the care.

"I am so *sick* of this... nothing..." she said.

"When boredom is *all* that's afflicting you, love, we'll all be relieved." Damien kissed her forehead. "You're looking better, but you've a ways to go yet."

"That's a different problem," Adam put in, "but I want it clear that you're not galloping around the Realm once you're carrying *our* child. Those stupid Elendrians can damn well start dealing with Damien, if they're willing to accept him as their king."

"I agree entirely," Damien said instantly.

Genevieve looked deeply aggrieved. "They just want to be sure that they're not being unduly influenced in the first place."

The King smiled at her. "I know. And I've yielded to that logic. But we have the examples of Alpinsward and Minglemere, and we've made those treaties public. Countess Miraly should be aware that we deal in good faith. And... I think I can show them a thing or two that might change their minds."

Jason had a peculiar look on his face. "They might not have noticed if their squirrels have mange, Damien." Adam gave his love an odder look still.

Damien waved that off. "*Other* things, Jason." He paused. "Though that one... mange is contagious across species, and even to humans. Not that I'd let things get that far."

"Fine. You can do *my* job," Genevieve groused. "And I'll do *yours* and run the Council while you're gone – so long as the three of you deem it not too *strenuous* for me."

The Queen rolled her eyes. "We've at least a month yet before *any* of this is a problem. Can we please look at the *current* problem? Papa and Ciriis having a child is an issue for the inheritance of Elaarwen, but I don't want blame for my current weakness to fall on them. That wasn't a *real* collapse, remember, I faked it to keep Damien from having to explain everything *else* to them."

"Well, your *first* one may not have been real, but your *second* one definitely *was*," Adam retorted. "And it would explain about *half* the goings-on yesterday to connect those dots for Lord Aldred and Ciriis as well as the rumor-mongers... though both of *them* seemed to know you were faking the first one. They both were too calm when they talked to *me* anyways."

His face showed his chagrin for having been so easily taken in by a pair he knew to be wily.

Wily – but always before entirely trustworthy.

Jason nodded. "That should have tipped me off as well," he admitted with some embarrassment. "If you'd *really* collapsed, your father wouldn't have been walking serenely through the Great Hall."

Damien rubbed his hand over his face. "So, Adam, *you* didn't light out of the Great Hall like all the armies of the Sea-Goddess were after you, but Jason, *you* did?"

The Champion gave him a slightly offended look. "I *walked,* thank you very much. Quickly, but I walked. Well, until I got to the stairs," he admitted. And there shouldn't have been anyone else on the stairs up to the royal apartments... except for their own closemouthed Royal Guards.

"All right," the King said, accepting it for what it was. "So, we have Lord Aldred and Ciriis calmly leaving our apartments, talking to Jason, who comes up here quickly. Then going to find Adam, who comes up here even *more* quickly – I know exactly how long it takes to get from the Great Hall to your office and from your office up here, Adam," he added as his Captain tried to say something. "A hundred heartbeats is cutting it close, and that's not even counting time for them to actually give you the news."

Adam subsided, looking somehow both disgruntled and embarrassed.

"Then Lord Aldred and Ciriis come *back* up here, also quickly. I help them in, and then they leave again shortly, in great distress, with Adam. Who returns. And then none of the rest of us leave all night long." Damien looked around at the grim expressions. "Is that about it?"

"As usual, your memory leaves nothing to chance, Damien," Jason sighed. "It looks... messy, doesn't it?"

"You *are* forgetting one thing," Genevieve said quietly. "You've all been referring to my father as 'Lord' Aldred, when you've only ever called him 'Duke' before, certainly in public. No one else may have heard... yet. But someone is bound to notice almost immediately any of us go out."

Kindly, she didn't mention that Damien had also referred to him as 'Papa' in private the last several years.

"We could go back..." Jason suggested uncertainly, watching his king's face.

Damien shook his head adamantly, but it was Adam who answered. "Not a good idea, Jase. We've a potential alternate heir to both Elaarwen and the Crown to worry about here. We aren't trying this hard to prevent a civil war for *lack* of an Heir," he flicked the Heir's Ring on Jason's hand, which was the one around his waist, "just to end up with one for having *too many* Heirs."

Jason looked at the Ring. "I'd... forgotten that any child of... Lord Aldred's could be a contender for the Throne."

Genevieve gave him a wan smile. "It's why the Rebellion was so dangerous. My claim, and Papa's, was as good as any of King Reginald's line, and without the taint of being descended of him. Though we'd have welcomed Prince Eric and his family," she added, reaching for Damien's hand and squeezing it reassuringly. Not that she'd ever held his lineage against Damien, not after the soul-bonding.

"Especially if he brought the Heir's Ring with him," Adam said dryly.

The former Rebel Duchess inclined her head. "Of course. Political realities."

"Which is what we have to face now," Damien said with a sigh. He looked at his wife. "I'm sorry, beloved. I don't see a way out of this without either exposing *our* plans or placing the blame on your father."

Genevieve looked down. "If... anyone else knows... we'll have no end of trouble getting anyone to accept *any* of our children as Heir."

Not to mention that *Lord* Aldred might not take well this very non-traditional arrangement the four of them were developing. If he decided that his daughter's honor was at stake... or that this compromised the integrity of the Alsterling line... he might very well reveal their secret himself.

Damien opted not to mention any of that. His wife was the strategist of the family. If she hadn't seen all of that for herself, it was because she couldn't bear to think about it.

"Or Genevieve as Queen..." Adam added grimly. "And Damien won't be taken seriously as King."

Damien looked wry. *"That* won't last." He lifted a hand and fire blossomed in his palm and then danced in multiple colors around his fingers.

Adam glared at him. "Seriously as a *sorcerer* is different from seriously as *king.* You'd be relying on their *fear* to gain compliance."

"It's not a road we want to go down, either way," Jason said in a mollifying tone. He took on a slightly disapproving look. "Besides, they've brought this on themselves."

Genevieve looked wistful. The part of Damien that had slowly begun to thaw froze up again. It wasn't fair that it was this hard... not that any of *them* had reason to believe that life was fair.

"So, the story *could* be that they told Genevieve about their baby and she collapsed," Adam suggested, looking at Genevieve with less of his usual sharp cynicism and more of the gentleness he'd once shown a certain skittish boy-prince. "I doubt there's anyone who doesn't know how much these miscarriages have grieved you both. And *you* told them to go get *us,* being more concerned about her than about *why–*"

"I suppose I could have been in the other room and not known why she collapsed," Damien said dubiously. "But they went down far too calmly the first time, if Aldred was really worried about Genevieve. And – no offense – but why would I send for *you?* Everyone knows that I can Heal, and it can't have been too bad if her own father wasn't concerned."

Jason stretched his legs out on the mattress, leaned back and put his arms behind his head, looking up at the canopy thoughtfully. "Everyone also knows that we've both spent a lot of time looking out for Genny. Is it really that surprising that we'd hurry up here to make sure she was okay? We can remind everyone that she's been like a little sister to me since we were children."

The Queen winced slightly at that description. "That might – *barely* – fly as far as you're concerned, but what about Adam?"

Adam rubbed his face. "I need food before I can think."

"Damien, no!" Jason exclaimed, sitting up quickly, but the mattress was already covered with trays and steaming dishes.

Genevieve just sighed. Adam raised an eyebrow curiously.

"Breakfast, I assume?" the Captain asked.

"From the kitchens," Damien answered, "with a note to explain. It's how I kept us fed while we were... gone."

He didn't look at Jason, reaching carefully for a cup and the pot to pour out some tea. He'd thought his Champion had gotten used to this... to his casual use of magick, but apparently not. Genevieve didn't appreciate it either, but didn't complain. Much.

"Very convenient," Adam said, seemingly without a hint of a qualm. He picked up a plate and began to load it. "Are you planning to return the empties the same way, or will you have the maids come retrieve it all?"

The King gave him a sharp look, but Adam was entirely engaged in filling his plate and didn't even notice.

"Does it matter?"

"It depends on what we decide," Adam told him. "But having the maids come up and see that we all had breakfast together – openly – would make the point that we aren't hiding anything. I wish I'd known you could do this before," he added thoughtfully. "I can see other ways to use this sort of ability." He looked up to see his king giving him a look so overwhelmed with gratitude that it was almost embarrassing. "What? I should have asked, I suppose, about what all you can do. Jason said you vanished *yourself* to the top of the tower last night."

The Captain's eyes were filled with an understanding of why he must have done that – and Damien felt grateful all over again.

It was Adam who had taught him to absent himself from a situation when it became too overwhelming; the young prince had known better than to breakdown where anyone might see, though he'd become less careful with his two male mentors. His initial lessons with the sword – before the

Lynncrag trip – had been so *frustrating,* given that Damien was starting some six or seven years later than any of the boys training to be knights ever had… and he'd begun to emulate Jason's habit of pretending to be a blank wall when things overwhelmed him.

Adam had taken him aside and explained why he didn't dare do that if he was to be king someday: it might just be a façade, but to a Court trained to fear a king who ruled with seeming dispassion, it would be a terrifying signal. When that hadn't been quite enough, Adam had finally told him how Jason's pretense of not reacting to anything had made it so much harder for him to *actually* react in any positive way… and that it was a defense he'd developed for dealing with the eternally unsatisfied Countess Solway.

'I know you think he's close to perfect, Damien,' Adam had said quietly. 'So do I. But Jason is still letting his mother control him. Do you want your grandfather to control you – even when he's long in the grave and you're a man grown and a king?'

Genevieve flicked Damien's arm. "Are you going to hand me that tea before it's cold, or am I allowed to move around and feed myself?" Wordlessly, he handed it to her, and she took a sip, settling the cup back in its saucer before adding, "Adam, I don't understand why you don't play better chess. You have a knack for seeing the realities of a situation."

The Captain half-shrugged, balancing his food. "Too boring. I'd rather do something with real consequences or real products."

Jason started getting his own food, and Genevieve nudged Damien with her foot and a raised eyebrow until he began doing the same for her. He knew Jason was trying to catch his eye, but kept his eyes on the serving dishes. It wasn't Jason's – or Genevieve's – fault that they felt uncomfortable with magick. But he could wish that they could accept him as he was.

Genevieve had tried to suggest that it was like using Jason's massive broadsword to chop onions. But for Damien *not* using magick was more like trying to chop those onions with his off-hand. With a blunt knife.

Genevieve also worried that these 'frivolous' uses wasted Power that they needed to keep the Realm fed. That was true when he was so low that it was stealing energy directly from him – and her. But the rest of the time the King had realized that *he* was as much of a concentrator as the Castle or the grotto; the Power was just there, whether he used it or not, and he couldn't store it up against droughts. He'd heard there were magickal objects that could store undifferentiated Power, but Damien had no idea how to make such a thing – his few experiments had been unsuccessful in the extreme, though he had picked up the trick of storing a single spell in an object, such as the wards he had set in a few places around the Castle.

Adam's casual acceptance of his use of magick was... a gift.

"*Now* I believe you're doing better," Jason commented, and Damien looked at him in surprise and forced himself to suppress the desire to shrink away from the disapproval he expected to see.

But Jason had moved on to other thoughts, and was nodding at the fact that Damien wasn't stuffing himself. Had, in fact, been lost in thought and ignoring the food entirely, after giving Genevieve hers.

"I haven't been eating so much for *weeks* now," the King said, starting to fill his own plate.

"You aren't quite so starvingly thin either," Jason agreed. "I couldn't count your ribs quite so easily last night."

He said it in a straightforward way, as if it was perfectly natural for him to have been doing that.

Jason, apparently, had decided it was time to just accept the situation as it was. Damien kept his eyes on his food to avoid looking at Adam's reaction. Jason might be the only one of them who had come to that level of ease.

"I think it's time for you to get back to sword-practice," Jason added.

Damien hadn't been working out, let alone sparring, since shortly after they had left for Elendria in early Summer. He simply hadn't had the energy to spare.

"Good idea," Genevieve put in. "At least *one* of us should be able to get some exercise."

Surprisingly, it was Adam who objected.

"Not in the open," the Captain said firmly. "You need to rebuild some strength and stamina before we let anyone see how much you've lost," he told his king. "I'll clear some time to work with you... no. We don't want anyone to notice." Adam rolled his eyes. "Those night-time wanderings of yours can finally come in handy. Mik and Rodney are nightowls like you, which is why they're on night-duty so often. They can work with you." He gave an evil grin. "And Marcus. He can see what this side of the job is about."

Genevieve laughed and lifted her tea-cup. "To training our Seconds to put us out of a job."

"Hear, hear." Adam paused. "Wait, who have you been training to take *your* place at the negotiating table, Genevieve?" He followed her amused look to his love, and found Jason studiously digging into his fried potatoes.

"Ah. I see." The Captain fell silent, clearly working through how this changed things.

"Damien mentioned it when we were... gone." Jason admitted.

"More months..." Adam sighed. "I suppose it was inevitable. One or the other of us would have to go along to guard Damien if he's doing the negotiating anyways."

"Actually," the King smiled. He was going to enjoy this. "I'd proposed that *you* go along with him. And Master Fenric to review the legal aspects." His smile turned into a grin. "After all, the Heir will need protection as much as Genevieve and I."

Adam's eyebrows flew upwards, and a slow smile grew.

"Marcus *could* use more experience," he agreed. "And the Elendrians will be happier to talk to Damien *after* the treaty is signed. Say, when he comes out for the Binding and Confirmation of Miraly as Countess of Elendria."

"Maybe a little earlier," Damien suggested. "For a visit anyways. The Realm still thinks it includes Elendria. I don't know if Queen Estelle is Bound to Deltheran the way I'm Bound, but if she is, it should be easy to convince her to return the county."

Jason was still pushing his food around. *"I* still think I have no idea how to do this."

Adam gave him another one of his evil grins. "You'll figure it out. And I'll be there to make sure you don't fall on your face. Or somehow give *our* Realm to Queen Estelle."

Damien choked on a laugh.

"Everyone has to start somewhere," Genevieve said with rather more sympathy. "I'd send Papa with you if he were in better health..."

There was an awkward silence.

"And... we're back to where we started," Damien sighed.

"We have to sell this to Aryllis also," Jason added.

Because keeping one's allies in the dark was unwise, especially one's Spymistress. Though they surely couldn't tell her about just why Jason and Adam were so involved in Genevieve's health any more than they could anyone else. Aryllis – and her husband, Sir Timothy Ancellius – were utterly trustworthy, but the fewer who knew a secret the fewer who could loose it accidentally.

"Or give her a story she'll believe." Damien closed his eyes at this additional complication.

If only they had left the old man and Ciriis in Elaarwen. Not that it would have dealt with the issue of a competing Heir... though other women than Genevieve also miscarried and the problem might have resolved itself. Not that Damien would wish such heartbreak on anyone else, let alone his father-in-law and his first love, no matter how much trouble this was going to cause him personally.

The King could feel his beautiful soul-bonded steeling herself to make the decision no one else wanted to... He could feel her heavy sadness... There was only one way to protect her from having to do that, though she would have the excuse to hate him if she didn't speak the words herself...

The King stood up and faced away from the bed.

"Here's what we're going to say happened. We'll start with what Adam outlined: That Duke Aldred and Lady Ciriis came in to tell the Queen about their unborn child. She collapsed in shock – no one will be surprised that that was shocking to hear. I had been giving them some privacy, so I didn't know what had passed between them and sent them to fetch the Heir – Jason – in case she'd had a relapse and I'd need him to run the Council for a time."

He turned back to look at them, to see Jason's face go pale at that thought. Apparently, it hadn't occurred to the tall knight that being the Heir meant that might be one of his responsibilities. At another time, Damien might have smiled at his expression.

"And I also had them fetch Adam, because it was clearly time for him to rearrange Guard details to cover Jason. Duke Aldred thought I was overreacting, but when he and Ciriis came back up to check on Genevieve, I had found out what they had told her. And... I threw a magickal tantrum and moved all the glassware. In the whole Realm." Damien carefully didn't meet anyone's eyes. None of the others had yet known just how far-reaching his reaction had been and he wasn't quite ready to see their shock. Or their disappointment at his lack of self-control.... Or, worse, their *fear.* "But the reason we'll give out for my... tantrum will be that it was because they are setting up to contend with us.... with *me*... for the Throne.

"Not that I quite believe that," he assured Genevieve. "But it's plausible."

Damien looked away again before she could respond. "We'll put it about that I made it clear to them that Duke Aldred had kept his title only by courtesy. That it was Genevieve who was confirmed and Bound as my first vassal, and that Aldred is an oathbreaker since he had sworn to my grandfather before he founded the Rebellion. That he and his," and at this the King had to take a deep breath, "his *doxy* are stripped of their titles and no longer welcome in my Court. At that point, Genevieve pleaded for mercy, and I relented – some – and said that they may return for the naming of my natural-born Heir.

"And then Adam escorted them away, and he and Jason stayed up here all night because I was still raging around and they were keeping me from doing anything more extreme... and took turns keeping watch, because I'm known," he favored Adam with a dry look, "for wandering around at night as it is.

"Did I miss anything we need to explain?" He fixed each of them in turn with his gaze until they looked away.

"And by morning, you were feeling badly about making us spend a night on those lumpy, leather couches, so you fetched breakfast up here?" Adam looked thoughtful. "It might work."

"Will Aryllis buy it?" Genevieve asked. "She's seen you stay awfully cool in extreme circumstances, love." Such as when Damien had burst in to save Aryllis herself from Harald and re-take his throne. "And she *has* been trying to discover where the two of you went – and why."

Jason snorted. "Not something she'll be able to discover."

"Except by elimination," Genevieve pointed out. "You didn't disguise which direction you took when you left, or which direction you returned from, I'll bet. She knows where the grotto is."

"Hmmn," the tall Champion looked much less sanguine all of a sudden.

"Then I'll keep her too busy to bother about resolving such a minor mystery," Damien said firmly. "She and Tim may also have to make a trip to Elendria. *Her* Second doesn't know about the grotto, and the longer it takes before Aryllis works herself around to checking the memories of the people who happened to be out and about those days, all of them should be foggy."

"We could go for a few more rides," Jason offered. "Different directions, different days. Make it harder for people to remember which trip was which."

"Don't go overboard with the idea," Adam said to him dryly, his glance flickering momentarily to the King. "Damien's never gone for countryside rides regularly before, so *that's* going to stand out, even if it makes the first trip blend in." He looked at Genevieve. "You... probably don't get to say goodbye to your father. We haven't been letting you leave these rooms, and it... would fit the story for Damien to refuse to allow him to come back up."

She nodded, looking unhappy. At Duke Aldred's age, *any* goodbye might well be a permanent one.

"And *you...*" he turned to Damien, "are going to have to come down and stalk around looking furious." He raised an eyebrow. "Do you even know how to *do* that?"

Damien blinked in surprise. "I'm... not sure."

Anger... had always been an emotion he couldn't afford. Not since his father had moved them to the Castle, anyways. Not as a forgotten young prince, hiding away in the Royal Library. Not as a less-forgotten prince trying to build a façade of a reputation as a moderately dissolute dandy. Not as the Heir to the Throne, subject to the whims of the king who had slain Damien's parents when his own father was Heir. Not as the young King precariously trying to rebuild a nation and survive the machinations of his nobles in order to do so. And not as the Sorcerer-King.

Definitely not as the Sorcerer-King.

Last night had proved that. Had there been any doubt.

Self-control had been Damien's path to survival.

No, he hadn't dared anger. Nor hatred... Not that the latter had ever seemed that useful to him, though he acknowledged now that he came close to hatred when remembering Harald and what the bastard had done to Genevieve. And apparently Duke – *Lord* Aldred – for what he *hadn't* done to protect her... though that was complicated with the honest love and respect he felt for the old man.

Damien had *thought* he hated his uncle, Prince Oskar, but Jason's tangled story had unwound some of his perceptions of the man and he hadn't rewound them into a new shape yet.

Lord Prydeen... he had feared and felt deeply determined to defeat, but the man had given him and Genevieve a gift in the end, the key to solving her string of miscarriages. Genevieve seemed to blame Prydeen for casting a 'curse' upon them, but Damien suspected that telling them his prophecy, even with that malicious glee, had been the one good deed the man had ever done in his life. The 'apprentice' sorcerer had had no other even mildly redeeming trait... but Damien couldn't quite find it in him to 'hate' Prydeen when his cruel words might keep Genevieve from dying.

And his grandfather... it had taken him years to emerge from the fear and realize that his grandfather had actually given him the time and space to grow up. That he had known where Damien was and left him there in relative safety... and in isolation from the intrigues of the Court. Had known who his friends were later and allowed them to teach him... and not interfered as they schemed to put him on the Throne. Had given him the

Heir's Ring... and had not involved him in any of his temporal or magickal abuses of Power.

Lord Prydeen had made it clear that *he* had known nothing of Damien's potential as a magick-wielder... but Damien had found hints that King Reginald had at least suspected; indeed, that he had suspected Damien's father Prince Eric to carry the same potential. That, perhaps, he had hoped that one of them might be able to fix the broken Realm.

Either that or that on one of them would bring him the Monarch's Blade and give him greater access to the Realm's Powers, allowing him to break it further.

There were hints in those partially decoded journals that King Reginald had even *loved* Queen Rena – Damien's grandmother – in some sense. That he had loved their son and thus regarded his grandchildren – Kandra and Damien – more fondly than the rest of his horde of scions. Only the old king's rare mentions of his first wife – Princess Lindrea – and the children from his first marriage, including his eldest, Damien's Uncle Robert, had more such hints.

King Reginald's entry for the day he'd had his son and daughter-in-law slain – and which Damien had decoded and read out of a morbid curiosity – had been... regretful. And more than moderately ambiguous, since he referred to having had the deed done *'to spare the boy, as he is all I have left of Rena. She fainted on hearing and regained her sense, but not her sensibilities thusfar. I had no choice, with what Eric planned. I dare not look weak, but I have spared whom I could. The boy must remain heart-whole or it is all for naught. All this I did to spare the boy.'*

Small doubt he had meant Damien – Reginald seemed from other writings to have despised Oskar and his youngest queen, Oskar's mother Eliza, nearly as much as did everyone else. After much internal wrangling, Damien had been forced to conclude that his father's confrontation of King Reginald before open Court had made his own treasonous intentions to defect to the Rebellion too obvious to ignore. In the end, the old king had spared Kandra's intended, Raphael of Cedarwen, even elevating the man to his father's seat and accepting Lady Theresa's contention that neither she nor Raphael had known of the plan.

And he had spared Damien.

And neither the corpses of the baron nor of Damien's parents had been nailed up on Traitor's Wall – with their remaining sons required to set the first nail as proof of their innocence and refutation of the traitors... nor, worse yet, had they been kept alive and Damien and Raphael required to do that to their *still-living* parents.

No, in a *'fit of bad-temper'* that had clearly – according to Reginald's journal – been wholly manufactured, the old king had ordered all three slain and the remains cremated before even Lord Prydeen had dared to suggest the more usual route.

There were more than hints that Reginald's relationship with his 'apprentice' had deteriorated into a subtle and deadly rivalry by then. Certainly, there was no one else who might have dared rebut the Sorcerer-King in such a mood, but Reginald's journal suggested that he had felt haste was of the essence before his efforts might be wasted.

Damien's opinions of his grandfather had become at least as tangled as his impressions of Prince Oskar.

In the here and now, Adam was rolling his eyes. "Really, Damien, you take 'mild-mannered' to an extreme that–"

"Leave him be," Genevieve almost snarled. "He's perfect just as he is."

Perfect? Surely an exaggeration, but he had to work with who he was. And what.

"Will *'icily furious'* do, Adam?" Damien asked. "I think I can manage that. As if I'm overcontrolling? And... as the reports start filtering in from other provinces, it ought to be obvious why."

Jason's eyes widened. "You... weren't joking when you said you affected the whole Realm. Were you."

Damien shook his head, hardly daring to look his Champion in the eye.

Genevieve, surprisingly since magick made her just as uncomfortable as it seemed to do Jason, gave him a sardonic smile before turning to the tall knight. *"I* could have told you that. He's had to work hard to be able to isolate one part of the Realm from another in his perceptions. If he's not paying attention, it's going to be the whole thing." She lifted her chin slightly. "I haven't put much effort into it, but I can usually get a sense of direction if something is wrong somewhere. It's sort of like one of those itches that you can't quite locate and you end up scratching your whole leg to soothe and it still doesn't go away. Damien can locate the original bug bite, but only when he's trying."

Damien gave her a bemused look, but didn't disagree. The Realm did feel like an extension of himself, and it *did* take effort to identify the geographical or topographical features that matched with the way he perceived the underlying magick. Not that he'd realized he could affect the whole Realm the way he had last night, though *It* invariably affected *him.*

"If he's *not* paying attention..." Jason muttered, looking disconcerted.

Adam was looking at the King speculatively, however, and seemed entirely unfazed. "Icily furious seems more in keeping with your style anyways. Good call."

There was a moment of silence as they all considered the various parts of the plan.

"Can... can we somehow let Papa know that this is temporary?" Genevieve asked at last. "That – we're not *really* angry at them?"

Damien looked away from her. He could feel Jason's and Adam's eyes on him. "We do have to let them know that their exile is over when *our* baby is born."

He could *feel* his wife tasting the word 'exile' and finding it bitter indeed. But it was what it was. And they had brought it upon themselves, as Jason had said – had neither of them considered using a contraceptive? "There's something to be said for making that declaration in public. Perhaps in the courtyard, as they're leaving."

A pause. "And...?" she said softly.

The King met his wife's eyes reluctantly. "I *am* really angry with them, Genevieve. I was prepared to overlook the fact that they were nosing into things that were none of their affair, on the grounds that he is your father and concerned about you. I was even prepared to try to explain... *something*... of what we are doing, though in retrospect I'm glad I didn't have a chance. And for five *years* I have tried to overlook the fact that he put the success of the Rebellion above the health and sanity of his only Heir, which is not the act of a man who should be king – and I know quite well that is where the Rebellion was planning to take things.

"It was the thought of *that* which pushed me over the edge of control last night." Damien nodded sharply. His instincts and reasoning had gelled on this issue while they discussed it.

"But what I *cannot* overlook is that he is walking perilously close to treason – and taking one of my closest friends with him – in setting up an alternate claimant to my throne."

And Damien would do everything in his power to prevent *Lord* Aldred from irrevocably crossing that line – a second time. Not only because of his own complicated feelings for the man and for Ciriis, but to spare his beloved wife the necessity of proving her own innocence.

After all, Damien could hardly be less merciful and compassionate than his grandfather – the Evil Wizard they were now starting to call 'Reginald the Ruthless.'

"He's not a stupid man, Genevieve. The more I've thought about it, the more I'm convinced Aldred knows *exactly* what he's doing. He thinks *we* can't provide the Realm with an Heir, so he's determined to provide one himself."

Genevieve looked... appalled. "He wouldn't..."

The King shrugged. "It's probably for what he considers to be the best of reasons. We told him about my research that suggests the Sword won't speak for someone not of Alsterling blood. So, he assumes that if there's another Heir of the right lineage, then *you* don't have to keep going through these miscarriages. He doesn't know that would doom us both to death. We didn't explain all that. And he probably assumes – correctly – that one or both of us would be 'unreasonable' about his 'solution,' so they came to us with a *fait accompli.*

"But he's put me in an impossible position. And he's done the same to you, as Duchess of Elaarwen. Are you ready to fight an insurgency in your mountains – but from the other side? Or will you cede your rule to your half-sibling, instead of this first child of ours for whom the Sword will not speak?"

"No..." Genevieve agreed. "Not if we have a child to inherit each seat. Elaarwen is mine now, not his. But to *exile* him, Damien...?"

"I will not turn him out of *his* home," Damien told her, "though there would be few who would disagree I've the right to do so after this. But I will ban him from *mine* for now, and good riddance."

She looked stricken... but spoke no other word of protest. And... shed no tear. She... had that look of introspection that she took on when feeling out her province.

Jason and Adam both shifted uncomfortably in Damien's peripheral vision, but the King kept his eyes on his wife until she came back to herself and gave him a sharp nod. He relaxed. He had felt her probing and knew she had been testing for Elaarwen's connection to her father. In the early morning hours, when he *still* had not been able to sleep, Damien had done the same. Genevieve had found that connection wanting, as had he.

The province wanted Genevieve, wanted her offspring, and would accept no substitute without some significant magickal intervention. Why, he had no idea.

He looked at his Captain. "Adam. Go ahead and let Lord Aldred and Madame Ciriis know that they are to leave within the hour, and make whatever arrangements are necessary."

Adam started slightly at his decisive tone, but rose immediately, snatched up his boots, and headed into the sitting room.

"Have the Guards send word to Madame Elista to have someone clean our breakfast up as well," Damien added.

"As Your Majesty commands," Adam's voice drifted back from the sitting room and for once had not the slightest hint of irony in it.

The King turned to Jason. "I want you behind me when I bid our erring kinsman farewell. Go put on some fresh clothes."

Jason stood up, also snagging his boots and heading for the door, but paused on the threshold, his head cocked slightly to one side. "Will I be there as Champion or as Heir?"

Damien smiled slightly. "We need to resolve this and properly crown you as Heir."

He saw the faint panic in Jason's eyes, as much, he guessed, for the thought of losing the chain of the Champion for which he had worked so hard as for the thought of gaining the coronet of the Crown Prince. The latter was still largely abstract, after all.

"Another day for that. Dress as befits my Heir... but be sure you still wear your sword." As if Jason would ever, ever go anywhere without it anyways.

The tall man nodded. "As Your Majesty commands," he repeated Adam's words, and vanished into the next room himself.

Chapter TEN

Bound

THE KING TURNED TO HIS wife. "Can I trust you to stay here, and stay in bed?"

Genevieve gave him an amused look. "What, *I* don't get orders?"

Damien's return gaze was reproachful. "As my Queen you are above such things." But he gave her the gentle smile he could feel she wanted to see and added, "But as Duchess of Elaarwen and my vassal... I'd rather just trust you, love."

Genevieve grinned. "It's not often you actually issue orders. Especially not to Jason and Adam. Did you see how quickly they jumped?"

She reached out to him and he came to sit on the side of the bed at her side. At that point she faltered, dropping her arms and her eyes, and his heart ached to see it. "Is it safe, yet?"

In answer Damien took her in his arms. And, greatly daring, he kissed her.

It almost undid them both.

"Are we at four weeks left?" Genevieve asked breathlessly. "Five?"

"Four and a half, I think," he answered, but... "Love, you still seem very, very weak."

"If you'd let me get up and move around..."

"We tried that."

"Now that the Realm isn't feeding off of us both..."

"Beloved," he said, back to holding just her fingertips and daring nothing more, "It's out of your control *and* mine. I'll do nothing to make Jason change his mind about the timing. And that means I am *not* bringing you downstairs to go through what is going to be a horribly emotional and draining scene with your father in front of half the Castle's staff and every noble who hasn't a pressing engagement elsewhere."

She sighed. "I had to try."

He kissed her fingertips. "I know."

A few minutes later, Damien sat back down to let her fuss unnecessarily with the collar of his tunic, and the set of the small coronet he wore for semi-formal occasions that didn't require the heavier Crown of the Realm. It was a sufficient reminder for most situations, and more than he wore on a daily basis.

He dared another kiss as he stood up, but Genevieve caught at his hands as he stood to leave. "Damien... *look* at Papa before he gets in that carriage. This... it may be his fault, but it's still an awful shock. Don't let him leave if he's ailing." The words didn't leave room for disagreement, but her tone and the look in her eyes was pleading.

Damien smiled at her. "I'd planned to. I may be angry with him, Genevieve, but I still love him."

She relaxed. "Tha–"

He touched her lips. "Don't say it." He didn't want to be thanked for a Healing he might not perform, for a heart attack he might have precipitated in the old man.

"And... I'll be doing one more thing..." he added, as he carefully removed from his wardrobe the scarlet and miniver cloak that only the Crowned and Anointed king – or queen – might wear.

Genevieve gave him a very dry look. "In *that* outfit? I should never have guessed." She sighed briefly. "I suppose I should have taken care of it myself, years ago. It would have averted, well, *some* of this mess."

"But you didn't, for all the same reasons *I* didn't. No regrets, my heart. It will be done with." They exchanged a somewhat rueful glance and he headed out.

Lady Alanna, a new member of the Secret Cadre of Royal Guards, was just escorting the maids in to retrieve the breakfast dishes as Damien strode out. He nodded to her, remembering just in time that he was supposed to be icily furious.

He wasn't as close to the women and men who had slowly replaced his original twelve ladies. Impossible, since they didn't share the same history...

and they had never and *would* never share his bed. But he made sure to know them all – and his more obvious Royal Guards as well – and he trusted Adam and Jason... and now Aryllis... to choose them, train them, and place his and Genevieve's lives in their hands.

"Lady Alanna," he said over his shoulder as he stepped out the door. "Do you stay with Her Majesty until I or the Captain or the Crown Prince returns. Don't let her exert herself."

She bobbed a curtsy, acting the part of the slightly ditzy lady-in-waiting that he knew she wasn't. Intelligence and cleverness were the second and third traits after loyalty that Adam looked for, after all.

"Of course, Your Majesty." But her eyes widened as she realized he meant Jason. The word had filtered out only slightly more quickly than people had noticed the Heir's Ring on Jason's finger... but this was the first time he had publicly given his friend the proper title.

Damien realized he hadn't done that in front of *Jason,* even when they were discussing it a few minutes earlier.

The door shut behind him, the two Guards – Sir Everett Ladler and Sir Drake Milbourne – were clearly torn. Usually, their king was quiet and congenial, and today he was anything but. Usually, their Captain or the Champion... the Crown Prince?... came to escort him, and they knew one of them was supposed to tail him anywhere he went, but the Queen was still inside the apartments...

Damien solved their conundrum for them. "Sir Drake, with me. Sir Everett, Lady Alanna is on duty with the Queen, and We have utmost confidence in her abilities. But We shall send you a replacement for the door in order to maintain the proprieties."

There had been some complaints, Aryllis had said, that the members of the Secret Cadre were not being treated with full respect by the newer members of the official Royal Guards. Adam and Aryllis had been planning to have the young ladies and gentlemen do some arms-practice with the knights – figuring that having them dump the knights on their asses a few times would resolve the situation. It had worked for his previous sets of Guards.

But all those plans had been put on hold when Genevieve had come home and Damien had needed Adam's attention elsewhere. Perhaps expressing his confidence in Lady Alanna would go some distance.

He swept down the stairs without waiting for a response.

Damien had timed his departure from the royal apartments finely; his goal was to stalk through the Castle at a good pace but clearly without haste.

He wanted the word spread that the King was on the move and possibly intending to confront the mysteriously disgraced Duke Aldred as the latter was being hurried off. Damien wanted an audience in the courtyard by the time he got there, and he wanted everyone else to be there first. *They* should be awaiting *him,* not the other way around.

The King fine-tuned his progress through the Castle by pausing occasionally to have a word with various courtiers, who shrank from his path or confronted him as was their wont, tearing down the latter and giving a word of reassurance to the former as often as not. Damien had an advantage in determining his exact pace and timing – his sense of the Realm had grown so strong within the Castle that he could now, when he chose to, pinpoint individuals by location and mood. He would arrive in the courtyard after Adam had hurried a half-packed and complaining Ciriis out the door in order to meet Damien's deadline, but before either she or Lord Aldred had actually entered the carriage. He could tell that Jason was already standing at the top of the stairs to the entry hall, looking out over the gathering chaos with a certain grim amusement.

And a crowd *was* starting to gather.

Good. Set some of the rumors to rest and let new ones start, all at once.

Damien strode out of the main doors, the doorkeepers pulling them open hastily as it became obvious he would not break his stride to give them time. Poor Sir Drake was flapping in his wake, trying to keep up.

The King looked forward to being able to laugh over that with Genevieve later; his latest crop of Royal Guards underestimated *him,* in addition to doing so with the Secret Cadre. They had all heard how he and the Queen had re-taken the Castle in one night on their own, freeing allies as they went and defeating Lord Prydeen at the end... but they were young enough, some of them, that they had not even been at Court at that time and the rest had been newly made squires. They had never themselves seen their King as anything but a mild-mannered administrator.

And since he never sparred with anyone other than Adam or Jason – or Genevieve, until this last year as she had grown weaker – they had no idea how well he could hold his own in a fight. *Those* three knocked him on his ass regularly, and these more callow youths, who had not had to fight a secret internal rebellion to protect their prince, had not yet noted how *long* their quiet king lasted against the best swordsmen in the Realm.

The King paused at the tableau presented before him.

A well-appointed carriage awaited Lord Aldred and Madame Ciriis, and Adam held the door for them, looking relieved when he saw Damien arrive. Aldred was actually beginning to help Ciriis into the carriage, but turned when he noted Adam somewhat overdramatically freeze and stare towards the Castle's main entrance. All around them, servants and men-at-arms in the Elaarwen colors scurried about in the frigid late morning air of Autumn, loading horses and carts.

A small and swelling crowd of onlookers gathered at the margins and peered from windows.

Jason, dressed in his finest – but it was definitely time for a proper Heir's coronation to get him the proper accoutrements for a moment such as this – stood as he had been, at the top of the wide low stairs that descended from the formal entrance to the level of the courtyard. His arms were folded, and he might have been a disapproving statue save for the acknowledging nod he gave his king when Damien arrived beside him. And the step he gave way for the King's precedence.

Damien descended the steps slowly, stopping before stepping all the way down onto the cobbles of the courtyard. His eyes remained fixed on Aldred; Jason was one step behind him the entire way. Ciriis had stepped down from the carriage, and the old man had his arm around her as if to protect her.

"Lord Aldred." Damien said clearly and coldly.

A ripple of shock went through the crowd, and the old man raised his greybearded chin in slight defiance. The Rebel Duke indeed. A grim humor gripped Damien within – his father-in-law was going to play his part very nicely.

"As was made clear to you last night, We have banned you from this Court. Your title of Duke – retained only by courtesy as the father of the Queen, who is the sworn and Bound Duchess of Elaarwen – is rescinded, as it was by Our grandfather, King Reginald, when you did break your sworn oaths to the Crown and the Realm by rising in Rebellion. Your current perilous flirtation with treason and your incitement of the Queen into relapsing into the illness that has plagued her are sufficient and more than sufficient cause." Damien could hear the murmur of speculation running through the crowd. Well, he'd satisfy their curiosity soon enough.

"We have, again for the sake of courtesy and kinship, declined to request and require your Vassal's Oath as has been required of every other man and woman of noble birth in this Realm. That privilege is also hereby rescinded.

"Kneel, Lord Aldred of Cloudcroft, and proffer to Us your hands that you may be sworn and Bound."

He waited, maintaining his perfect, icy demeanor as the meaning sunk in, and the old man stumbled forwards to kneel on the cobbles at Damien's feet. It would have been a kindness to have had a small rug placed to protect his knees from the cold, rounded stones with their sunken mortar. The King was not inclined to be kind. Like his grandfather before him, Damien could not afford to look weak before his nobles.

He sensed, more than saw, Adam preventing Ciriis from rushing to her lover's side.

The hands Duke Aldred offered up were shaking, but not palsied. It was shock that caused the trembling, and Damien could see it in the blue-green eyes that matched the ones that the King loved so well.

Shock for having precipitated Genevieve's collapse.

Shock at being accused of near-treason by the son-in-law he loved.

And *shock* at being publicly stripped of his title and granted the least of his former holdings – though Damien had chosen to leave him Cloudcroft because of the family history.

That was the cottage where Grand Duchess Alicia had held the ducal-Heir, Lord Siegfrid, hostage throughout a cold, deep winter. And where the pair of them had conceived Aldred before the snows melted and made it possible for their irate parents – Duke Emmeren and Princess Alexandria, a.k.a. 'Erawan the Kind Robber' – to retrieve their erring offspring. The cottage had been renovated several years ago and was far warmer, more secure, and better stocked than when Aldred's parents had nearly starved while snowed in there for half the winter.

It was also, not coincidentally, remote from the rest of Elaarwen and an unlikely place to begin building *another* rebel movement.

"Aldred Stellarine, wilt thou guide and guard my fair property of Cloudcroft as its lord, placing the needs of thy people before thy own and caring always for their prosperity and well-being?"

"I so swear."

"And wilt thou take me as thy liege-lord, accepting the rule of my fair property of Cloudcroft in my name? Wilt thou further swear to be a loyal and faithful subject of this Realm and to raise arms only in the defense of thy people of Cloudcroft or of this Realm?"

"I so swear."

"Then accept my fair property from my hands unto thine and rise. From the Power granted me by the Gods as King of this fair Realm, I create thee Aldred Stellarine, Lord of Cloudcroft."

Damien felt the Binding spell flow from his hands into Aldred's, saw the old man's face transform as he was Bound to the Realm. Because Aldred had himself been a potential Heir to the Throne, even to the Sword having once spoken for him as a toddler, the Binding was deeper than his link to the small property of Cloudcroft would suggest. And that Genevieve's talent for magick came through him was unquestionable, since his eyes now went unfocused and then refocused on the sparkles of it that were everywhere in this courtyard. The old man squinted as if nearly blinded… which he likely was.

Lord Aldred's face took on an almost anguished expression as he struggled to his feet. Damien kept his hands to discreetly help him up, knowing that the Realm was giving him its own version of a tongue-lashing for his various sins. Knowing also that his father-in-law had not entirely believed them when he and Genevieve – and others – had explained that the Vassal's Oath from Damien's hands was entirely different from what King Reginald had done. Had Damien's grandfather been able to use the magickal version of the Oath, with the wording then in use, then-Duke Aldred would not have been *able* to Rebel. Under Damien's wording, it was entirely possible – and without breaking the Oath at all – but only if Damien became a tyrant. There would be no further incursions that walked the line of treason from this man.

The moment of assisting Lord Aldred to stand also gave the King his opportunity to fulfill his promise to Genevieve and ensure that her father was as healthy as was possible. His promise to his wife – and to himself, since he loved the old man dearly, no matter how angry he was for Aldred and Ciriis' presumption.

"Our Queen has appealed for mercy upon your behalf, Lord Aldred." Damien continued. "Your exile will be ended when the Queen has given birth to Our natural-born Heir. We will not deny Our child the pleasure of knowing their grandfather.

"In the meantime, however, you will hie yourself and your *doxy*," he had to fight himself not to look at Ciriis, nor wince at the word, "to Cloudcroft, there to remain until We require and request your presence.

"We are not without mercy," he added. "And We are aware that Cloudcroft is but minimally attended. You therefore have Our leave to make a *brief* stop in Elaarwen, there to collect a midwife and whatever other servants and supplies you may require."

And there was the rest of what the scavengers around the courtyard were waiting for. Ciriis' demotion from Lady of the Court to the mistress of an unimportant lordling, and her pregnancy. Just what Ciriis had been to *him* was hardly a secret, after all.

"You are dismissed, my lord." He beckoned Adam to assist Lord Aldred back to the carriage and then ignored Captain, Lord, and Ciriis all together.

Carefully, Damien removed his royal cloak, handing it to Jason, who draped it carefully and respectfully over one arm. Underneath, the King wore the colors of Elaarwen: silver-trimmed violet. The coronet he wore was similar to the ducal coronet of Elaarwen – the same shape, but gold instead of silver – and it was clear he was now standing in proxy to Genevieve as Duchess.

It wasn't a role Damien often had cause to assume, but one of his titles *was* Duke-Consort of Elaarwen, and as such it was he, not Aldred, who was liege-lord to the men-at-arms who wore the purple-and-black of Elaarwen. They had come down from the duchy with the old man and Ciriis, and were going back with him. They were good men, and he knew most of them from the frequent visits he and Genevieve had made to the duchy. More to the point, *they* knew *him,* and knew he would not request anything of them without Genevieve's explicit consent.

This time, Damien stepped down from the stair and went to the cluster of men-at-arms.

"Is the Duchess well, Your Grace?" their captain asked as soon as he had come within range. "We had hoped to see her while we were in residence..."

Damien clasped the man's arm. "She is *getting* better. She wanted to come down here, but agreed it wasn't a risk she should take as yet."

Another of the men – a childhood friend of Genevieve's – nodded. "We've all been worried for her, milord. My own wife had a string of miscarriages. We decided to adopt instead... but I suppose that's not a choice you can make."

Damien shook his head ruefully. "You have it to rights, Istvan. Would that we could, and not have the Realm fall to wrack and ruin over it. I'd do it in a heartbeat to spare her further pain."

"We know you would, milord," Istvan nodded. There was a twinkle in his eye. "Not that it does Elaarwen any good, but are you officially adopting that great galumphing fellow over there, now he's your Heir?"

"Jason?" Damien laughed, then paused. "I hadn't thought of it. His appointment is temporary, of course, but officially adopting him might solve a few other problems." He gave Istvan a nod. "I'll think on it. Thank you for the idea." He looked at them all. "For now, though, you can spread the word at home," he saw their smiles that he would call Elaarwen 'home,' though he hadn't specified his or theirs, "that Genevieve is resting. We had to hide all her leathers to make her do it, but we're insisting she recover before she tries again for a babe. I've tried before..." He added, a sliver of his frustration forcing itself through his measured, planned words.

"We know Her Grace is a stubborn lass," one of the others chuckled. "Guessing milady had to be nigh half-dead before she'd admit to any weakness."

Damien nodded. "You know her, Raymond. In some ways you *all* still know her better than I do," he acknowledged. "And..." he brought the point back around, "we all know her father would never do anything to hurt her. But I don't think he realized what having another child will do to Elaarwen, if not the entire Realm. He knows *now*, but..."

"We've been in Rebellion, Your Grace," the captain said. "We've no desire to go back for anything less than a tyrant on the Throne. And we trust you and her Grace not to let that happen." There was a murmur of agreement. Damien firmly put aside thoughts of the prophecy that his youngest child would be Lord Prydeen's 'true Heir.'

"Did milord Aldred really make Genevieve relapse?" Istvan asked.

Damien looked sober. "Not too badly, but yes. She collapsed, and I put her to bed. But then we had to talk to him again, and she ended up crying half the night." They all looked perturbed – their Duchess wasn't a woman to cry over much.

The captain straightened. "Orders, Your Grace?"

Damien smiled. "Easy ones, Captain. Escort Lord Aldred and... his woman... back to Elaarwen,. Give them three days to get their affairs in order. Make sure they acquire a midwife to see to the child. A *good* one, with references and experience with births in the highest altitudes. I would not have it said that Genevieve's half-sibling received anything but the best of care.

"Then escort them up to Cloudcroft. Maintain a force of at least six up there. You may exchange men with Elaarwen as need be, and the servants are welcome to come and go. Lord Aldred and his woman must remain. And at least one midwife must be in residence until a month after the child is born." He gave them an apologetic smile. "I know it will be a bit crowded. Genevieve had the 'cottage' renovated a few years ago, but it will still be tight. Rely on the mountain-folk for what you feel you can. I would trust them with my life or hers – or theirs."

Several of the men-at-arms stood up a little straighter at that. Men of mountain-blood or -breeding.

"As you say, Your Grace," the captain said formally... then dropped his formal manner for a moment. "Tell Genevieve we miss her, milord, and bring her back to us as soon as she is able."

"Our dearest wish, both of us," Damien hesitated. "Well, after her healthy recovery and a safe and successful pregnancy." Nods all around. They couldn't fault his priorities. "If she isn't able to travel in the Spring, I'll come by myself."

"Thank you, Your Grace," the captain said. "We've no complaint with Lord Adsel, but Elaarwen needs its Bound and sworn leaders."

"Good man." Damien clapped him on the shoulder. "Elaarwen is always first when I look through the Realm." The reminder of his Power caused an uneasy stirring, but also some appreciative murmurs. "I have to go put back on my other hat now. And the *King* is far more upset with Lord Aldred than is the *Duke*. And not at *all* with Elaarwen. I'll send a fast rider ahead to let Lord Adsel know the lay of things. Go with the Gods, all of you."

They bowed, and Damien turned back to his Castle, striding away without a backward glance. Putting the icy expression back on his face was harder than he would have expected. The pure absurdity of the situation was beginning to tell on him.

Jason had clearly had to hold back Sir Drake from following Damien down to speak to the Elaarwen men-at-arms. He was explaining quietly to the young knight as the King swept past.

"—as the King, but as Duke of Elaarwen. And dukes have neither Champions nor Royal Guards. And they trust their sworn men-at-arms, just as the King trusts us." They fell into step behind Damien. "It would be a grave insult to Elaarwen for you to follow him in among his own people as if you don't trust them."

"How am *I* supposed to know when he's being which?" Sir Drake complained.

"Today, it should have been easy. He took off the royal robes and was wearing Elaarwen's colors." Jason paused. "You *have* memorized all the colors and devices of the noble houses by now, of course. I believe you were tested on that before you were accepted as a Royal Guard."

Sir Drake mumbled something to the effect that he hadn't known he was *still* supposed to be able to recall that information. Damien had been on the receiving end of one of Jason's disapproving silences often enough to sympathize with the effect it was surely having on the younger man, though not on its cause.

He stopped in the entry hall as he spotted Aryllis.

148

"Lady Ancellius," the King summoned her. "Lady Alanna is currently attending upon the Queen. Kindly arrange a roster of Her Majesty's ladies-in-waiting to ensure that the Queen is not left alone when the Heir and I are otherwise occupied."

Aryllis curtsied perfectly – as one would expect of the Mistress of Protocol. She had a steely look in her eye however, and Damien knew the slender, platinum-haired beauty was not happy about her friend and predecessor's summary dismissal and humiliation. He wasn't too happy about it himself for that matter, but Ciriis had brought it on herself.

"As Your Majesty commands," she said, and drew breath to say something else.

But the King wasn't done. "It is time and past time that we arrange a proper coronation for the Heir. Set a date some three weeks hence and send out the word for the noble families to assemble – those that are available to do so. We shall entrust the details to you and to Madame Elista."

This would likely be even more effective at distracting his clever Spymistress than a trip to Elendria – and arguably this was even more urgent and necessary. After all, Elendria had been a Lost Province for nearly three decades; a few more months, or even a year, would not make much of a difference. Not that the *Realm* agreed with that assessment...

A look of suppressed panic appeared in the back of the willowy woman's usually serene eyes as she curtsied again. Less than a month was not much time to plan such an event, especially when it required her to wear her Spymistress hat as well as fulfill her duties as Mistress of Protocol. It was *barely* enough time to send word to the more remote nobility in time for them to arrive at all speed. But Damien's tone did not invite suggesting that the celebration be postponed even slightly.

In fact, he had already turned away as Adam came up beside him. "Captain. Sir Everett has been standing duty alone for the last hour. See to it that you find him a replacement for my tail here." Damien didn't even bother to glance at the hapless Sir Drake. "And it appears the Royal Guards need a refresher course on regalia of the noble houses and the relevant appropriate etiquette."

He didn't envy Sir Drake as Adam looked past the King with narrowed eyes.

"I'll take care of it, Your Majesty." Adam said a bit grimly.

"And it's time to start expanding the Royal Guard," Damien added. "We've been relying too heavily on Our Champion's skills alone to protect the Queen, and the men-at-arms of Dalzialest to protect Duchess Rosa when she wore the Heir's Ring. As I've been reminded–" by Aldred and Ciriis "– even Our Champion must sleep betimes, and now that he wears the Ring he should have his own protectors. The Heir to the Throne – of whatever age and skills – should be fully under Our protection. Plan on doubling the Guard by Midsummer and trebling it within two years."

Adam looked stunned, even falling back a pace, but his eyes registered what *else* the King was telling him: they needed a larger force prepared before the child they all hoped for was born. Adam's daughter, if he had the right of it.

And by giving him the command in the middle of the Great Hall – just as Damien's command to Aryllis regarding Jason's Coronation – the word would be spread quickly amongst the Court's gossip-mongers. In this case, that might have the extra benefit of making it clear that there would be a great many openings available in the Royal Guard – Adam might not even have to officially solicit applications.

It was also more evidence, for the gossipy types, of Damien's temper: that he should treat with both his *Captain* and his Mistress of Protocol – and former lover – in such manner and in *public*. Likely his high-handedness would result in some brief surge of jostling amongst the lesser nobles in case Aryllis or Adam should prove to have lost the King's favor... and keep them all too busy considering their own possible advancement to bother with paying attention to what Damien and his Inner Circle were up to. Keeping the lesser nobles off-balance was an unpleasant but necessary part of ruling...

Damien was making these adjustments to the plan he had roughed out over breakfast on the fly – though Genevieve was enough in touch with his thoughts that he could sense her approval in the back of his mind. It wasn't so much *instinct* – no matter what Genevieve thought – but rather a number of subconscious clues and some background reasoning coming together. These were both things that needed to be done – that he'd been putting off dealing with out of exhaustion. The fact that it would throw Aryllis off of following directions he didn't want her to, and that Adam had reacted with genuine surprise and thereby enhanced the effect of the whole passion play, were merely side-benefits.

"As Your Majesty commands," the Captain bowed correctly, speedily recovering his usual *savoir faire*... though a *look* in Adam's eye suggested there would be some... *discussion* later. "And where may I send a second Guard to keep duty on your royal person, if I may ask?"

"We'll be in my office. Come along, Jason," the King said, heading now for the secondary office he had begun to find convenient even when not hiding reports from Genevieve.

The taller man caught up with him within two strides, his long legs making up the difference without looking like he was hurrying overmuch. The royal cloak still draped over his arm neatly, and he kept his demeanor serene.

The King paused only once more, this time to sow more confusion by catching one of his Councilors who had the misfortune to be in his path and instructing the man to inform the rest of the Royal Council that they were to convene over lunch. Oh, and to send word to the Castle's Chatelaine, Madame Elista, that lunch was to be served in the Council chamber.

They made it to Damien's office, shutting the thoroughly befuddled Sir Drake into the hallway as Jason remanded him back to door-duty.

The tall, blonde knight sealed the heavy door and triggered the wards that Damien had installed here as well, to prevent eavesdropping and spying. Then he turned to face his King with an amused smile.

"You certainly created an effective set of distractions, Damien," he said with a chuckle. "Including for Adam."

Damien had already seated himself at his desk and he didn't give in to the temptation to burst into relieved laughter. "Sit down, Jason, we're not done here by a long ways."

His oldest friend and mentor – and now his Champion and Heir – carefully hung the royal cloak from a hook on the wall, then took a seat without arguing, raising only a single eyebrow in eloquent interrogation.

The King relaxed enough to smile. "You have no idea how much I appreciate that. Unlike certain *other* people – you just *do* what I ask and ask questions *later.* Even in private."

"Not always," the Champion demurred, a slight smile on his face.

"No, and sometimes you *do* need to call me out," Damien agreed, and refusing to let himself blush as that look recalled their week in the grotto. "But not *every* time, and not simply for the purpose of arguing. Which is what it starts to feel like."

He leaned back in his chair and brushed his hair out of his face. "Now. We've been letting the business with Genevieve subsume everything else. You should have been introduced to the Council as a voting member immediately. With full proxy rights to act as my surrogate when both Genevieve and I are unavailable."

"Wait, what?" Jason sat up straight with a look of consternation. "I thought this was more in the nature of a legal fiction." A look of dawning horror crossed his face and Damien winced, internally. "You're *serious* about a coronation ceremony and assigning me Guards. And... Damien, Heirs *have* Champions. They don't serve *as* Champions."

"I know," Damien said sympathetically. He let Jason take his time, knowing the other man had more to say. If it had been him, he'd have been out of his seat and moving, but Jason wasn't a pacer.

It also wasn't as bad a surprise as Jason wanted it to be. Just as with that first awkward conversation in the grotto, Damien had been nudging him into a slow realization of his new role. Not that there was any way to make these last steps anything less than stunning, not given who Jason was and what his self-image was composed of.

On the other hand, it had been a careful enough introduction that Jason wasn't *frozen* as he tried to sort the newness out in his mind. He could at least give voice to his consternation.

"Damien... all I wanted... all I've *ever* wanted was to serve as your Champion. I'm *happy* this way." The tall knight looked down at his fingers, his capable, skillful hands that were born to wield a sword. He caught up the chain that marked his title as King's Champion and stared at the links, at his hands holding them.

The King waited.

Jason looked up, almost in tears. "*Why?*" he asked.

"For all the reasons we talked about before, Jason," Damien said quietly. "There is no one else I can ask who could do the job of Heir. And no one else I *would* ask to be Regent for my child. For *our* child – our *daughter,* if Adam is right. But for you to be able to do *that* job, you need to give up *this* one," he indicated the chain that Jason now clutched as tightly as if it were his hope of life and love. "Accept what comes with being the Heir, and learn to rule."

"*You* didn't do any of this. Except the coronation ceremony."

"No, and we all saw what came of that. I lost my throne within a month of being crowned and had to re-take it by force." The King leaned forward on his elbows. "Will you wish that on our daughter because you will not learn – now?"

"Of course not." The words were almost ripped out of him, but Damien knew Jason meant them, no matter how much he feared and resented this imposition. Had he waited too *long* after Jason accepted the Ring? It had been nearly two months. Was that long enough for his friend to have come to the conclusion that he need do nothing else than wear it? Apparently, it was *not* long enough for him to get used to the idea of being Heir.

"Jason." Damien tried again. "You have been my Champion since the day you walked into the Library and let me know I wasn't alone anymore. You will always *be* my Champion, regardless of what title you bear, or what piece of jewelry goes with it. But now I need your fine intelligence rather than merely your brilliant swordsmanship."

The knight looked at him dubiously. A sense of self-worth built from personal, physical skill was not easily set aside. No one else had ever particularly lauded his intelligence; his mother and older sister had been especially cutting about his lack of it when he was a child, Damien knew. The King could see Jason's struggle to master his emotions, knowing that eventually his friend would come back to his sense of duty. Duty had carried Jason through every hill and valley so far...

"What do you need me to do?" he said at last, and Damien sighed. The war was far from won, but the battle was over for now. And at least Jason hadn't shut down and presented a blank wall of expressionlessness – so he wasn't quite as overwhelmed as all that. Yet, anyways.

"For now – we'll just introduce you properly to the Council over lunch. For the *rest,*" Damien favored him with an evil grin. "You read reports. You can start with these. I've finished this set."

He nudged a stack across the desk that was several inches high. Jason blanched, then visibly braced himself and reached out to take the first one.

Damien picked up another from the stack that he had yet to peruse, watching Jason through his lashes until he was certain that the other man was actually reading. After a few more minutes, he pushed a pen and ink-pot and an empty, bound notebook towards the other man.

"The pages are already numbered. Use the back page to list which page has notes on which report." A trick he had seen Genevieve using, though he rarely needed to use it himself.

Jason nodded absently, adjusting the ink and pen to where they were more convenient to reach.

Damien went back to his own reading.

But he was distracted with another thought: the Elaarwen man-at-arms – Istvan – had suggested an idea that the King wanted to consider. But he needed to research it a bit first and talk to Genevieve. He noted a list of tomes he would need to have brought from the Royal Library on the legal precedent of adopting an Heir. The principles were clear in the King's mind, but he wanted to be sure he hadn't missed anything in his original reading

– at fourteen, his interest had been in being adopted *away* from the King's house, not *into* it. That goal had turned out to be impossible, and he might not have paid sufficient attention to the passages relevant to his current question.

He took the note to the door and told Sir Drake to have a page take it to Lena in the Royal Library. The *kindest,* most *responsible* page he could find.

Damien read again for a few moments, then remembered he needed to send the note to Elaarwen, and took pen to parchment to quickly write it up. He reviewed it for errors and possible misinterpretations, signed, sealed, and took it to the door to have Sir Drake – or his new companion, Sir Angelos Eldridge – send it by fast courier to Lord Adsel in Elaarwen.

He wandered back to his desk, picking up the abandoned report yet again. He felt eyes on him and looked up to see Jason watching him bemusedly.

"How do you get anything *finished* like this, Damien?" he asked.

The King frowned. He'd just dealt with two other tasks; he was getting plenty done! But he knew what Jason was talking about.

"I'm just restless," he admitted.

Jason nodded. "It is definitely time to get you back into sword-training. Use up some of that frenetic energy."

"Hmmn." Damien didn't disagree aloud, but decided he would give Jason no more reasons to think he had to run him ragged on a practice-court. Despite what the older man thought he was seeing, Damien's reserves of physical energy were still paper-thin. Adam's plan to have him practice with a couple of the Royal Guards in the middle of the night would be better for him right now than trying to fence with Jason. Until he rebuilt some stamina, anyways.

He settled down to his reading for a full ten minutes before there was a knock on his door.

Damien bounded up to answer it.

Lena herself, bearing the requested books of legal precedent. She smiled at them both, handing Damien the heavy volumes. "I've noted a few others you might want to look over when you're done with these, Damien," she said cheerfully, handing him a note.

"Thank you, Lena," he said, giving her the most relaxed and heartfelt smile he'd worn since he left Genevieve's side.

"Anytime, dear," she showed herself out, with a last smile for Jason.

Damien started to read again.

This time perhaps fifteen minutes had passed when Sir Drake knocked to announce that the Council was met and Madame Elista was serving lunch.

"Time to go," Damien was out of his chair in an eyeblink, a wicked grin on his face before he tamed his expression back to something slightly milder than the icy fury of the morning.

Jason just heaved a sigh and followed.

Chapter ELEVEN

Solutions

"You want to adopt Jason."

Genevieve's tone was probably as disbelieving as she knew her expression was, though Damien couldn't see her face. She was snuggled up against his chest, her head tucked under his chin and the short, stiff hairs of his beard tangling in her hair as the two of them enjoyed the chance to be close while the opportunity lasted... before the magick of the Power-hungry Realm or the child-hungry soul-bond rose up to try to drown them once again.

She remembered that she had once hated the soul-bond for stealing her choices from her. That she had read the stories of soul-bonded pairs as a young girl and felt resentful on behalf of the young couples who were so bound. And in those stories, everything always worked out so beautifully...

Whomever had composed those tales had *no idea*.

If only she and Damien could have met and fallen in love in a more normal way. There was no doubt in her mind that it would have happened. If it could have.

But there would have been no 'normal way' for the two of them to meet once Prince Eric's plan to defect with his family to the Rebellion had come to such a disastrous end.

If she hadn't come to look into the young King's eyes to test her private hypothesis that it was *his* eyes that haunted her dreams – an effect of the soul-bond, she surmised – they would have met over the negotiating table as King and Rebel Duchess. They might even have ended the Rebellion through an arranged marriage of state.

But without the soul-bond... she wouldn't have dreamed of those clear, grey eyes until she was half-mad to know who they belonged to... and *he* wouldn't have spent sixteen years dreaming of *her*.

Without the soul-bond... and her foolish, dramatic decision to sneak into his coronation festivities... perhaps Damien wouldn't have *survived* his first month as King, and *she* would now be leading the Rebellion against whatever puppet-king Lord Prydeen installed. Probably Harald. Who would have her father to use as leverage against her *and* the Rebellion.

Without the soul-bond... they would never have met as just two people, with open hearts and opportunities.

"It's not *necessary*," Damien was saying into her hair, his arms clasped contentedly around her. "I named Rosa as Heir, and no one complained. But Rosa is a Duchess, trained to rule, and a former leader of the Rebellion. No one doubts her ability to lead if she needed to take the throne. Jason... isn't well-known. And what he *is* known for is his sword-skills, not his leadership abilities. He's a younger son of a prosperous, but fairly minor, noblewoman, whose political star has been in eclipse since I took the throne... by the by, do you have any idea *why* Alexa Solway supported my grandfather so staunchly? I thought she and your father were the best of friends."

It was getting off topic and Genevieve was aware that one of Damien's usual techniques was to introduce a bold idea then back away from it, talking around it until it had had time to settle in the minds of his listeners and they accepted it as less than startling. Since she *was* still wrapping her own mind around the idea – and since she'd long ago realized that, when her husband did this, it *did* give her time to think through things properly – she again let him get away with the tactic.

"I ended up going through some of Papa's personal papers when we all thought he was dead. I found love-letters from Countess Alexa. Mostly from when they were little more than children, but she'd started up again after Mama died. She'd divorced her own husband by then – Jason's father, whomever he was. Megan's father died of what were apparently natural causes, though I've heard speculation that he was desperate to get away from Alexa."

Genevieve snorted. *That* was an arranged marriage that hadn't gone so well. Not that Countess Solway's second marriage had gone any better. Jason never spoke of his father, even to name him.

"What I found in Papa's papers… It was *more* than love-letters. She offered to betroth Jason to me, and said it'd give her the excuse to move in with us, since Jason was still a minor. She said Megan was old enough to serve their county – she's even older than him than Kandy was older than you, you know." The Queen sighed. "That Alexa *meant* she could move in and serve as my father's mistress, was *all* too clear. I don't doubt that she's going to be *far* angrier with Ciriis – and Papa – than we are."

Damien sighed. *"That's* a mess. Do you…" He hesitated, and she could *feel* him trying to decide if he should ask his question. That he was wondering if it was any of his business. "Do you know why she's been so cold to Jason all these years?"

"Not… really." Genevieve pondered. "Though I know that Megan is just as cold to him… except when she's fussing at him the way you might expect Alexa to do as his mother. There's that huge gap between their ages, so maybe she had the care of him when he was small, and it's a habit that she resents? A number of women seem to resent a child who spoiled their health – or their mother's health – by being born, but I've never heard that Alexa had any miscarriages, or even a particularly difficult birth. And I think I've heard the story of just about *every* woman in the Realm who's had that sort of troubles at this point."

She rolled her eyes. Understanding of the difficulties she was having was nice. Gruesome details… not so much. "She divorced Jason's father not long after he was born, I think."

Damien frowned. It amused Genevieve that she could tell what his face must look like through some combination of body tension, voice, and the bond, though cuddled up against him like this she couldn't actually see him. "He's not listed in the Solway genealogical records. I double-checked this afternoon. It takes a particularly awful crime to be wiped out of family records like that. Especially when there are children… and presumably another entire set of grandparents, cousins, connections." He paused. "Could… they be punishing *Jason* because of something his *father* did?"

That didn't make sense, but the Queen knew that emotions clouded judgment and Damien often now had an almost uncanny sense about these things. Her own feelings about Harald and anything relating to her time with him were still not… entirely rational. And Countess Alexa's relentless, and, for such a dignified woman, entirely shameless pursuit of Duke Aldred suggested that there might be some serious clouding going on.

Perhaps Jason's birth and this mysteriously vanished husband had had something to do with Genevieve's father? They had both been grown by then, the rulers rather than the Heirs to their respective lands… and it would have been about the same time that Duke Aldred was falling head over heels in love with a certain Lady Giendra Topasirre.

Had Countess Alexa married Jason's father out of spite – or to make Duke Aldred jealous? And then… discovered too late that she was unsuccessful, pregnant, and disliked the man she'd taken on for her ploy? A man who also made her daughter miserable? Or…

There was nothing but rampant speculation here. Certainly nothing that could help Jason.

"Does it matter?" Genevieve asked, at last.

"It might," Damien answered. "Alexa Solway – and Megan Solway – will be very uncomfortable relations for the Heir to the Throne… or the King. And with this mysterious father and whatever family *he* came from… Jason could have people coming out of the woodwork to place claims on him."

"They could do that even if his last name is Alsterling," she pointed out. "The ties of blood will still be there. And we'll be making an enemy of Alexa and Megan Solway."

He shrugged. "She accepted the Vassal's Oath. She can't work against the best interests of her land and people."

"I think you put too much trust in that Oath and Binding," Genevieve said with some asperity. And not for the first time. "Especially since you don't use the part that binds them to you and *your* best interests."

"I decided not to before I knew it would be a spell-Binding, Genevieve. Your father shouldn't have had to be an oathbreaker to protect Elaarwen from my grandfather."

"I know." She caressed his hands as they lay on her – still flat and empty – abdomen. "And I respect you for it. But it does leave room for interpretation, and we don't know how the spell will react if the Oath is twisted, let alone broken."

"I don't think it *can* be–"

"Any lock, any binding, can be broken with enough effort," she overruled him verbally. "Or enough sacrifice. And it's Alexa you've Bound. Megan placed her hands between yours and swore the Vassal's Oath, but since she was only the Heir, she wasn't actually Bound, or so you've told me." She twisted to give him a wry grin. "That *is* the loophole that kept me – and Rosa, and a number of others – from being oathbreakers, if you recall. We hadn't sworn to King Reginald at all, our parents having made those choices before we were old enough to do so."

"Hmmmn. There are other reasons to adopt Jason, though. And to make sure he isn't potentially jumping into having to sit the Throne with no real preparation."

"*You've* managed to be a successful king without any real training beforehand," Genevieve reminded him. "All the people who supported you will support him."

"My dear love," Damien said very dryly, "That was very much in doubt for the first several months, you may recall. Even you and Rosa weren't completely sure that the rest of the Rebellion would come around to following an unproven princeling. Even with a soul-bond to you to prove my good intentions."

"And you think the Alsterling name made the difference?" she said skeptically.

He shook his head. "No. If anything, it made it harder. But it suppressed other serious claims to the Throne long enough to consolidate my power." He paused. "And to find the Monarch's Blade."

Genevieve drew in a sharp breath. "Love... you don't think you can fool the Sword into accepting Jason if he bears the Alsterling name?"

"Not... exactly..." His voice became very earnest. "I think I can do the adoption such that the Realm would accept him as my Heir. As if he was *born* of Alsterling blood."

"Damien..." She didn't doubt he had a very good idea of what to do. But there was no guaranteeing the result. And... it sounded like whatever he planned would have to change something about Jason. Something fundamental. Who knew where such changes might lead? "You said his introduction to the Council went well. And you chose him in part because he's been at your side or mine while we've been working for the last five years."

"Sweetheart, he could end up as *King* in less than a year."

She went very still. "You don't believe that any of what we're doing will actually work."

The *current* King's arms tightened around her. "As has been pointed out on numerous occasions, we're basing an entire strategy on the dying words of an evil sorcerer who had no reason to help us and every reason to try to destroy us." He paused, and she felt a different sort of fear chasing him in mental circles. "And... women don't always survive childbirth, my Genevieve. And you're... not so young for a first child."

She hadn't thought that far ahead. Or rather, she'd been determinedly *not* thinking that far ahead. Enough to simply not lose the child before the third month. But her husband, the Healer... and the *King*... had to look ahead.

"Why not just acknowledge my father's child with Ciriis as Heir then, and my father as Regent?" she said softly. "He ruled Elaarwen for twenty years. He'd make a good regent. Or even king."

"Because I don't trust his judgment," Damien said, more bluntly than she had expected. "Even if the Sword would still speak for him – and I don't intend to put that to the test – he will make the same mistake as King that he did as Duke."

"And that was...?" Once, she would have said it defensively. She had to admit that her father's judgment had been questionable of late, but she had thought he'd done a fine job as Duke of Elaarwen.

Damien laid his head against hers and sighed. "He – and Ciriis also – will put the Realm above your half-sibling. Just as he put Elaarwen and the Rebellion above you."

"Damien, that's not fair–"

"It's entirely fair. He should have simply forbidden you to marry Harald once he saw what kind of a man Harald was. Later on, he should have had him marched on foot to your borders rather than see Harald destroy you, piece by piece. Hush."

Her husband laid gentle fingers over her lips as she tried to protest – again – that it had been her choice.

"I'm not saying this because I love you and it drives me wild to know that all this happened to you – well, not entirely because of that," he admitted. "I'm saying it because his first duty *as Duke* was to ensure that his Heir was healthy – physically, emotionally, and morally – *as well as* well-trained.

"By failing you, he failed Elaarwen. And had the Rebellion succeeded in setting him upon the Throne, he would have failed the Realm. I know he loves you and made sure you had all the preparation you needed to administer and lead Elaarwen. I've benefitted from his caring and tutelage as well – he filled the place my own father should have done. But Lord Aldred has repeatedly chosen his ambitions and duty to the duchy before his duty and care for you.

"I have to assume that the wonderful person you grew into owes more to your mother than to him, and that *she* always put you before Elaarwen. But your half-sib will be reared by Ciriis Celavell, not the Duchess Giendra, and I know for myself about the lengths *Ciriis* will go to for what she believes is what is needed... and how she will put that above the needs of the *real people* around her.

"But the Realm is made of real people, Genevieve, and I have to look beyond who will rule after me, to who will rule after *them.*"

She was silent for a moment, digesting this. "And who will rule after Jason? It's not exactly easy for him to produce his *own* Heir."

Damien was silent in turn. "I told him that, if he couldn't find anyone he trusted, to gradually hand over power to the Council. He's far younger than your father. He should have decades to make it work." That *Damien* had wanted to be the one doing it... over decades... went unsaid.

Genevieve let out a slow breath. "Just as we discussed, back in the beginning."

It was a conversation they'd had while they were still feeling out the soul-bond. At the time she had felt it was a mad scheme, but had been enchanted by the breathtaking scope of his vision. Not that there had been much about him she hadn't found enchanting then... *or now...*

Though Damien's grand idea had come to him when he understood how the Rebellion was organized... The way *Genevieve* had setup a governing council and run things by a messy sort of consensus after her father had vanished with Harald. Every smallest constituency that had come to her banner had had a voice. Though she'd done it that way simply as a means of keeping her chary and awkward coalition together; in most cases all that had bound them into a single Rebellion was fear of King Reginald a trust in her father's leadership... and once Duke Aldred had disappeared...

Giving every smallest holder and merchant a voice on the Rebel Council had been a necessity and had drastically reduced their effectiveness. War by committee wasn't easy, and even determining whether to send help to flooded Cedarwen – at the edges of the Rebel territory, but still pledged to the Crown because of Duke Raphael's hostage mother – had become impossible.

Raphael might have been swayed – for the good of his people, as had other lords and ladies before him – but the Crown had sent aid first, in a remarkable break from previous policy that she had later learned had been the only real contribution Damien had been allowed to make as Crown Prince. Because King Reginald had ceded no power to anyone who might see their way to unseating him... and given away nothing more than he'd ever had to. Why he'd yielded to Damien's plea for Cedarwen in this case... Genevieve still wasn't sure.

Her husband and King nodded. "No one man – or woman – with more power than their morals can cope with."

They sat in silence together. Genevieve wanted to tell him it would never work, that people wanted a King or a Queen... but she knew his plan was to do it so incrementally that it felt like things had always been this way. It *could* work, though it might well take *generations* instead of the mere decades her pragmatic, yet still idealistic, love envisioned.

"There's a plethora of reasons *not* to adopt Jason," she said at last, deciding to make a stand around this topic instead of one of the more ephemeral – if also more essential – side-issues. "Beyond making an enemy of Countess Alexa and Lady Megan. And of my father, for that matter. The first one being that I don't think he'll agree. He's older than either of us, and – for God's sake, Damien! He's sleeping with *you* and he's supposed to father a child with *me*. As if this situation isn't awkward *enough*..."

"Erm, yes..." Damien sounded abashed and she felt him bury his face in her hair. It appeared that her husband wasn't as sanguine about all of what they had realized they had to do to survive as he tried to pretend.

"Jason will already have Adam's support, and that of the Army and the Guards, both Royal and Castle," she went on. "He's befriended the men-at-arms of most of the provinces – which may not sway their liege-lord, but it might slow them down and give him time to consolidate his power. He'll have the support of Tomas in Siovale and Rosa and Zachary in Dalzialest." Genevieve hesitated, and she knew that her omission of Elaarwen in that list was glaring.

"As your adoptee, you could name him Heir to Elaarwen also," Damien suggested.

"It wouldn't be a good idea," she disagreed. "He has no interest in the mountains. So there's nothing to bind him there. Adsel should be Heir to Elaarwen until we have at least two children."

Damine nodded. "That makes sense. You should write to him and see if he'll take it for now. I... actually was thinking of naming Jason Duke of Emeralsee... it's traditionally the duty of the Heir to the Throne, but I've held the title since I had no one to pass it on to." Emeralsee was the province that included the capitol, the personal territory of the Alsterling family. "It would also give me the excuse to Bind him to the land during his Heir's Oath."

Genevieve nodded. "I like *that* idea much better. Then – *if* the Throne does come to him – the shock of being Bound to the whole Realm should be less. It was for me."

"But can I really do that if he's not an Alsterling?"

164

She twisted around again, and reached a hand around his neck. "Damien, my love," she said with a smile. "I think you've proven that you can get away with nearly *any* crazy idea you want these last five years. The people love you, and the nobles are chary of upsetting their Sorcerer-King."

He winced at the epithet, but smiled at her. "So long as it's not the other way around, I suppose I can live with it. But if you think so, then I have a *different* 'crazy' idea for you to consider..."

Chapter TWELVE

Proposal

"**M**ARRIED?"

Jason felt stunned, but Adam's eyes were shining.

"They've been doing these sorts of weddings in Dawil since my grandmother was a girl," Damien said with a shrug. "No reason for us to continue on with our own barbaric exclusionary approach. Genevieve agrees." He sounded as if he was trying not to make it seem that using her opinion was his trump card.

The three of them were in the solarium where Genevieve trained with the Secret Cadre when she was home and not ill. Adam was still trying to arrange with Sir Marcus and Aryllis to plan secret nighttime re-training sessions for the King, but their plans were coming together only slowly in the wake of Damien's demands for the Heir's coronation and a doubling of the Royal Guard. Not to mention the need to determine *where* to train... without waking up half the Castle or letting too many people notice unusual goings-on.

In the meantime, Adam and Jason had decided not to let more time slip past; they were planning to claim two hours of the King's time each day, together or singly, working it around his other commitments. Though they all knew that the solarium was not impervious to prying eyes – having spent two weeks at the young King's side as he tried to watch his soul-bonded without her knowing it early on – it was more private than most of their other options. Though Damien's first act in the solarium had been to install wards that fogged peeping eyes and listening ears, which suggested they might use it at night as well. He'd looked mildly amused that they hadn't thought to ask him to do so in the first place.

"I thought the priestesses have said it goes against the Will of the Gods?" Jason asked. He tried to keep his thoughts from making themselves clear on his face. Whatever they were. He had, quite literally, never spent more than a passing moment considering the possibility.

His young king shrugged again. "It's not against the Will of the Gods in *Dawil*. And we worship the same Gods, if some by different names and aspects. I found a very senior priestess who is willing to do the ceremony. If you want her to." He paused, his expression much less certain as he looked back and forth between the two of them. "I... had hoped to include it as part of the coronation ceremony. It's... rather dry by itself, as you know. You'd be setting an example for the rest of the Realm." Damien paused again. "And since your families will both be here..."

Adam sheathed his sword and sat down, hard, on a wicker chair that was never meant to take such punishment from a man of his size. He didn't seem to notice the creaking and groaning of the woven reeds, though at least they held and he wasn't dumped on his rear for his carelessness. "I don't know if they even got an invitation. This... might make them prefer to stay home."

Blame his own mother's conservatism, Jason thought, that was safe. Everyone knew about Countess Alexa. And then he could avoid saying anything *himself*...

"My mother – and my sister – won't approve either." The Champion reached a hand towards Adam, though he was too far away to reach him... an acceptable distance, since he carried his unsheathed blade in his other. "Neither family has ever... approved of us choosing each other."

Adam barked a bitter laugh. "I haven't seen *mine* since we visited when you were seventeen, Damien."

Over twelve years... and before that he'd written them nearly every day and visited Lynncrag several times a year.

"I wish we didn't see *my* mother so often," Jason muttered, hoping it would serve as a distraction from... all the rest.

The King sighed. "I can send them both a 'request and require your presence' letter." He eyed Jason. "Or just the Loveress family. I suppose Alexa and Megan Solway will be here regardless." His tone echoed Jason's own 'whether we like it or not' feelings.

"With David and my nieces and nephew," Jason agreed, feeling guiltily relieved that his distraction seemed to have worked. "I've received word that my mother expects me to have the townhouse opened up and ready for her arrival."

"Personally," Adam added with a sardonic grin.

Damien frowned. "Have Madame Elista make the arrangements, Jason. I need you here, not skittering around town looking for... what's involved in opening up a house anyways?"

"Hiring temporary staff, making sure the pantries are stocked, the linens aired and everything cleaned," Jason ran down the list. He had done the task nearly every year for the last twenty or so, before his mother arrived – with or without Megan – for the Summer social season. Part of him relished the idea of passing what was essentially scutwork off to someone else. The other part winced, knowing that Countess Alexa would Not Approve. "It's not a big deal, Damien. Elista's busy with preparing the Castle. I can handle Solway House."

"You misunderstood me, Jason," the young King returned, one eyebrow raised. "That wasn't a *suggestion.* You're the Heir to the Throne, and you have more important things to do. And I hardly expect Madame Elista to handle it herself; give her your family's accounts and she'll hire someone trustworthy to see to it. If the Countess wants a *personal* touch," Damien added dryly, "She can send Lady Megan or Lord David on ahead. Or even Lady Elaina. Send her a letter to tell her what's going to happen."

Jason dropped his eyes.

"She may direct her complaints or appeals to *me,"* Damien added.

That wouldn't stop her from giving Jason a tongue-lashing as soon as she could get him alone. Probably followed by one from Megan, though he might be able to avoid *her.* Adam's expression was a curious mixture of sympathy and unholy glee; he'd been telling Jason to quit bowing to their every demand for years.

"Your oldest niece must be over twenty by now, am I right?" Damien went on. "And the others – there was a bit of gap, wasn't there – fifteen and twelve?"

"Elaina is twenty-two. Roger is thirteen. Esmerelda is eleven," Jason recited dutifully. "Rudolph would have been nineteen if he were still alive." They were too much like their mother for him to really appreciate them, though David – their father – had always been kind to Jason.

The King looked speculative. "Roger isn't too old to become a squire. And Esmerelda is exactly the right age to join the pages." Jason gave him an incredulous look.

"Good luck with *that*," Adam laughed. "Megan's precious babies doing something *useful?*"

Damien turned that silver-grey gaze on his Captain. "We're doubling the Secret Cadre also. What about Elaina? Serving as the Queen's lady-in-waiting has been helpful for other unmarried young ladies."

Jason restrained a snicker as Adam looked like he was choking. It was officially someone else's job to handle the pages and squires, but Adam personally worked with Aryllis to train the Secret Cadre. "Please tell me that *this* time you're only *suggesting*, Damien. Or joking. Joking would be better."

"What would be more natural than to invite Our Champion and Heir's kin to serve in the Castle?" Damien dropped the innocent look and laughed. "Oh, I know they'd be an utter disaster. Or a set of disasters. But I'm still tempted. Elaina might be a lost cause, but the younger two..."

"Megan's held them close since Rudolph died," Jason answered. "And even if she agreed somehow, my mother would veto any such plan." He winced. "She still complains how much it cost her to put *me* through the training." And it still hurt that although he had risen to the highest position a knight could aspire to – and now *beyond* – that the money was all she cared about.

Damien's expression grew positively wicked. "I believe I shall offer them a *scholarship.*"

Jason covered his eyes with his free hand. His mother would be furious. But... she'd be forced to send Roger and Esme. Maybe it *wasn't* too late for them to learn some useful skills. Of course, then he'd have to see them regularly... Perhaps they'd learn not to shrink away from his approach.

"So long as you don't make *me* work with Elaina," Adam shuddered. "She wouldn't even do as a *regular* lady-in-waiting with that chip on her shoulder. Much less *our* kind."

Jason waved his sword at the other two. "Enough rest. Back to work."

If Damien was bent on these mad plans, it would all fall out that way. But if these were just spur-of-the-moment ideas, perhaps they could be ignored out of existence.

No such luck.

Also, Damien hadn't yet enough stamina to last more than a few more passes. But his mouth and brain were under no such constraints of energy.

"I'm not such a fool as to believe that you're lucky to have family available to attend," the young King panted. "But sometimes people *do* change." At least, Jason thought guiltily, he was focusing on Adam. On the other hand, Damien knew Jason's own family rather too well to try this line of reasoning. "Sometimes they feel *badly* and want to make *amends* to their children."

"Your Majesty," the Captain said irritably, "would you kindly *stuff it?*"

Damien shrugged. "As you say." He looked at Jason. "I'm heading up for a quick wash and a change of clothes. I'll meet you in the office after. We need to go over the agenda for the next Council meeting, and I want a draft of the letter to Countess Solway on my desk before I get back."

Jason reflected that Damien had become much less... *diffident* lately. Less distracted or abstracted or... something. More *present*. It had these unfortunate side-effects of him trying to reorganize everyone around him, but was probably a good thing for the administration of the Realm overall. *Probably.*

"Yes, Your Majesty." A draft... that meant Damien was going to insist on a firmness of wording in the final version that would leave no ambiguities. His mother was going to be furious. Absolutely furious.

"Remember when he followed *our* lead?" Adam sighed ruefully after the door had closed behind the King.

"It's to our credit he doesn't any longer," Jason replied quietly, trying to convince himself. It was easier to believe when Damien wasn't ordering him to do impossible things. Like face down his mother. Or...

"True..." Adam stared at the door a moment longer. "But he seems to have changed in the past few days. He's shaking everything up, almost as if..."

The Captain shook his head, and focused on his love. He crossed the floor in a few quick strides and slid his sword-free arm up under Jason's to pull him close for a kiss. He'd re-engaged the wards after the King had left the room, so their privacy was assured.

Jason's free hand wrapped automatically around Adam as well. The other man had been tall as a boy, which was part of why they had been matched as sentries and 'ornamental' guards so often despite the difference in their ages. But they had evened out as adults and had a scant two-inch difference in heights despite the fact that Jason was taller than any other man at Court. It made certain things very... convenient.

"Jase," Adam said after a moment. "You didn't answer Damien about including our wedding in your coronation. You didn't say *anything*, actually."

Of course, he would have noticed.

But perhaps this didn't have to be about *Jason*...

"Your parents and siblings have written you scores of letters in the last twelve years," Jason replied softly. "You haven't read any of them."

Adam stepped abruptly away. "I read the first few. I don't need to see that sort of thing over and over."

He turned his back on Jason, his fists clenched, his head bowed. Adam had been the cherished eldest of a tight-knit clan. Losing his family had been incredibly difficult for him, but not once had he given Jason reason to believe he had regretted choosing him over them.

He had taken Jason home – once – a year before they had sent Damien there for safety. The beginning of the visit had been wonderful; Jason had known that other families were warmer than his, but he had never been made to feel a part of one of those families before. Adam had introduced him only as a 'friend' initially. A few days before they were to leave, Adam had taken his parents aside and explained how much more than 'friends' they were, and it had all fallen apart. His mother had cried for the rest of the visit, refusing to leave her room, while Adam spent countless hours sitting at her bedside, begging her to understand. His father had refused to speak to him at all. His younger brothers and sisters, none of them full adults yet themselves, had hovered, unsure of what they were supposed to do.

When he had come back a year later with Damien and Ciriis, but no Jason, his parents had assumed he had 'come to his senses.' Jason knew from Ciriis that Adam had been overjoyed to be able to just be part of the family again, despite his worry for what Jason was undergoing back in the capitol at Prince Oskar's tender mercies.

It wasn't until the last day that his parents had actually confronted him – that since he clearly wasn't interested in Ciriis, who now had Damien following her around like a lovesick puppydog, why wouldn't he stay and marry the girl they'd picked out for him? Or another girl. *Any* girl.

But *stay*. And *marry*. And give them *grandchildren*. And take his place as his mother's Heir. Finding out that he was still just as attached to Jason as ever... had resulted in a shouting match that ended with Adam swearing never to set foot under their roof again.

And some just plain swearing, Ciriis had reported sadly.

Jason sighed. "They write to *me* occasionally now, too."

Adam's head popped up.

"Did you know that your sister, Desirée, is married and has two little boys? They both want to be knights like their uncles." Jason paused. "She's been sending me their drawings. Mostly pictures of you fighting dragons.

With me standing with them on the side-lines." The King's Champion smiled wryly, then added very quietly, "They write the names of everyone in the picture down, so it's clear that Uncle Adam is Fighting the Dragon. And *Uncle* Jason is the knight standing with them."

Adam had turned back, and his eyes were full of tears. "Why didn't you tell me?"

"I tried, Adam. You shut me down every time." Jason looked at him with compassion.

Adam had burned those first few letters, likely as much so that Jason wouldn't see them as much as to let go of what they had said. But the Champion had probably heard most of the same comments from his own family over the years, since they *wouldn't* stop talking to him.

There was more, though, if Adam was finally ready to hear it. Twelve years of family news – or at least eight, since Desirée had begun writing to Jason. "Charley left home to become a forest ranger, but he's come back recently, and he's courting some girl from the local village that Desirée says he's always been sweet on. Lorry married, divorced, married again, divorced again. Fontaine nearly pledged to the priestesshood, but changed her mind before her final vows."

"And the babies?" Adam breathed, his beautiful golden-hazel eyes hungry with longing.

Jason almost hated to tell him. They'd been six and eight when he'd seen them last – the youngest hadn't even been born when he'd left to become a knight, but Jason had seen how much Adam adored her. "Martin has a gift for Healing, it turns out, and Marianna... has asked me to submit her application to be one of the Queen's ladies-in-waiting."

Adam's face was shocked. "When were you going to tell me that? Does she know what they really *do*?" Although they reported to Aryllis on a daily basis, Adam was Captain of both the officially known Royal Guards and the Secret Cadre that included all of Genevieve's ladies-in-waiting and the handful of 'gentlemen-of-the-chamber' that had now been added to their ranks. If Marianna became one of Genevieve's ladies-in-waiting, Adam would likely see her every day and work with her directly to be sure her training in the arts of defense and protection were up to standard.

"I've been trying to figure out *how* to tell you," Jason told him.

"She can't possibly be old enough," Adam muttered distractedly, "She's just a little girl."

"She's eighteen, Adam," Jason said gently. His heart wrenched as Adam's face twisted in sorrow at all those missed years, and he stepped forwards to put an arm around his love. "Love..."

The Captain shook him off.

"You still have that prybar of yours out." He waved at Jason's massive broadsword. *"En garde."*

Practice had always been a way for Adam to avoid having to think about things, the focus on his sword leaving little room for abstract thought. But this time Jason didn't intend to let him do that; and he didn't mind losing to make his points.

The solarium began to ring with the sound of metal on metal again. Although he had the height and strength to handle a broadsword as long and heavy as Jason's, Adam's preferred style fit better with a lighter weapon. He began with his usual, relentlessly ferocious approach, and Jason let him wear himself out; an easier task since Adam had already been fencing Damien for some time, with Jason mostly serving to correct the King's form.

"Your mother sends us holiday greetings every year," Jason noted. "And your father signs the notes."

Adam missed his next stroke. He pulled back from his attack to look at Jason.

"If we're doing this, I think they'd like an invitation, Adam."

The Captain glowered at him. "*'If.'* What about *you*, Jason? *I* was willing to tell Damien 'yes' right then to adding our wedding to your coronation. *A thousand times 'yes.'* I would have, too, if you hadn't done that thing where your whole face shuts down." He eyed the Champion for a moment. "Like now. *Fight,* damn you." He launched another furious attack.

Wryly, Jason realized Adam was doing it to be helpful. They knew each other so well... Adam knew the Champion's head was always clearer when he was wielding his blade. "My family hasn't changed notably," he commented. "You had the joy of Mother pointedly ignoring you when she was here this Summer, you said."

Adam snorted. "I can live with Countess Alexa's disdain."

A couple of slices and a feint. Neither of them was actually letting the emotions affect their swordwork; a lesson they had learned long ago as squires, and which was why they trained their young King with edged weapons. Damien could be more frustrating than most of their other students, but he never lost his cool with the Monarch's Blade in his hand.

"How much gloating did she do about you receiving the Heir's Ring?"

"Not as much as you might have expected," Jason replied. "Though perhaps she's saving it until she can gloat in person. Or to other nobles."

Who would be a better audience for the tide of Jason's elevation raising her own boat. Though she'd said nothing to him about it actually, except acknowledging that she and the family would be arriving in time for 'the ceremony.' And that he should have the townhouse prepared.

"It's a good thing she's Bound through her land," Adam mused, fending off a handful of return blows. "I think she'd like being the mother of the king a bit too much. And Megan is going to importune you to name one of her children as *your* Heir immediately. *She'll* need watching."

Jason looked at him incredulously. His mother was ambitious for power, but surely Adam hadn't just implied that she would conspire to regicide... had he? Or that Jason's sister would? He almost missed parrying the riposte Adam tried to sneak under his guard after his first attack had been parried.

"What exactly *did* her letter say?" Adam pressed. "Did she actually say she was pleased that you've been named Heir?"

"Oh, you know Mother," Jason said vaguely. "She had more to say about how she wants the townhouse opened up. I'm sure she'll have much more to say in person." *That* was a guarantee.

Adam found himself abruptly on the defensive. With his *sword* anyways.

"Jason, your mother is never going to give you the appreciation you want from her. That you *deserve,* for all you've done and the man you've become. The appreciation the rest of us give you in *cartloads,"* he added, batting away a suddenly faltering blade.

He closed with Jason's blade, stepping in and binding it up with his own. It wasn't a maneuver he could usually pull against Jason's heavier sword, but the Champion was distracted and didn't make a serious attempt to resist.

With a sardonic smile, Adam reached around with his free hand, seized the back of Jason's neck and pulled him into a passionate kiss.

"And here I thought your concerns would have to do with circumventing our marriage vows to fulfill your promise to Genevieve," the Captain said when he ended the kiss, "but instead, it's your *mother* I have to worry about in our bed."

Now *that* was an horrific image.

Jason sighed and rested his forehead on Adam's shoulder. "Love..."

He didn't know what to say.

"She's still blaming you for what your father did to Megan. It's not fair and it's *not your fault* that you've grown up to look so much like him," Adam said softly. "How long are you going to let her steal you from me? Jason, we can be *married.* Just like Aryllis and Tim. Or Rosa and Zachary."

Jason tried to give him a smile. "Or Genny and Damien."

Though perhaps they... weren't the right model at the moment. All things considered.

Adam stepped out of his arms, sliding his sword back into its sheath with his usual smoothness. "Put up your sword, Jase." He was hunting for something in his belt-pouch.

Jason sheathed his own sword... the hand-and-a-half sword he had chosen as his primary weapon in part because he was one of the few who could wield it so effectively. And in part because of the other name for the style of blade: the 'bastard sword.' With his father's name stricken from the records – and never, ever mentioned in his presence – he was essentially fatherless. He didn't even have a memory of the man or know his name, nor did Jason particularly wish to, knowing why the records had been so altered. Megan had once thrown it in his face that he looked just like him. In Adam's presence, which was how *he* knew. And somehow implying, in her own inimitable fashion, that their choice of each other *proved* that he was just like his father.

It might not be his *fault,* but he couldn't really blame his mother and sister for not wanting him around as a reminder.

"Jase – Jason!" Adam called his attention back from the dark places it had been drifting. "I've been carrying this thing around for awhile. I... thought... hoped... that maybe even if it wasn't possible to get married in a temple, with a priestess and all... that we could have our own commitment ceremony in front of our friends. I just... was never sure how to bring it up."

In Adam's strong, capable, gentle fingers was... a ring. It was gold, a broad, flat band, with tiny diamonds embedded such that they didn't break the smoothness of the surface. A good ring for a swordsman to wear.

Jason took it with wondering fingers. Inside, it was inscribed: 'Yours till infinity... and beyond – Adam.' It must date from that period when Adam had been chasing their king down another set of intellectual rabbitholes – mathematical ones that time. Jason had come back from Minglemere with Genevieve to be subjected to explanations of 'different kinds of infinities' and other things that made as little sense after as before but that made his love... his *loves* happy to discuss in, hmmn, seemingly *infinite* detail.

He looked back at Adam. "How long have you... no. I don't want to know." Because then he would have to think about all the times and all the reasons Adam had found not to give it to him before. About all the reasons Jason had given him not to bring it out. About how *he* didn't have a ring to give *Adam.*

Jason turned the ring, looking at it, feeling somewhere between numb and too full of emotions to sort them out.

Adam cleared his throat, but he didn't press for an answer. Instead, he folded Jason's fingers around the ring. "Keep it. Think about it. We'll talk later. I... have Marcus waiting for me."

It was clearly an excuse to leave, but Jason didn't stop him.

He felt the shape of the ring in his palm, and tried to sort out what he was supposed to be thinking. What he was supposed to be *feeling*.

Chapter THIRTEEN

Dark Distractions

DAMIEN WAS TRYING NOT TO fume when there was a knock on his office door and Adam stuck his head in.

"May I have a word, my lord King?" he glanced around. "Where's Jason?"

"I don't know," the King bit out. "He never bothered to show up." He slumped back into his chair and finger-combed the hair out of his face. Trying to set aside irritation for concern. "Did I push him too hard, Adam? He *has* to stand up to Countess Alexa. I have to *know* he could stand up to her."

Adam came all the way in and shut the door, re-engaging the magickal wards. 'Typical Damien' the Captain had once called them, explaining that he meant 'understated, efficient, and usable by others' – they were simply short pieces of colored string that stretched from the door to a small hook set on the door-frame. One for sound, one for sight, one for magickal incursions. They were connected to a larger spell that the King had woven around the room, but it was set into action by looping the string over the hook – and disengaged simply by opening the door. Easy to tell at a glance if the wards were active.

He'd installed the same wards on Adam's office, and Aryllis,' and on their three apartments within the Castle as well. Ostensibly it was on the off-chance that someone spoke in their sleep, or so that Adam and Aryllis could safely conduct the Realm's business in their more private spaces as seemed appropriate, but in reality, it was as much a gift to his friends as for any other reason. He'd put the same wards on the solarium this morning.

Adam frowned. "I'm sure he wasn't looking forward to writing that letter, but it's not like Jason to put off unpleasant duties." He sighed and dropped himself into one of the extremely sturdy chairs that faced the desk.

Damien rolled his eyes. "I suppose everyone has his breaking point. I don't suppose you know where all these problems between Jason and his family come from? I'm tempted to blame it all on Countess Alexa, knowing her and Megan, and knowing *him*... It certainly can't be anything he did. *Ever.*" Jason was simply too *nice* of a person to imagine him doing anything that could have had such long-term repercussions.

Adam looked uncomfortable. "It's not my place to say."

Damien eyed him irritably. "If it weren't pushing the nobles just to accept a countess' younger son, I'd offer *you* the damned Heir's Ring. But a baronetta's son – even the oldest... It'd be a fight all the way. But *you* don't come with all these obnoxious relations."

"I do if we're married," Adam pointed out sardonically. Then he winced. "I'm the one that pushed him too hard, Damien. I... gave him the ring. *My* ring." He'd shown it to the King years ago. Not exactly intentionally, as Damien had simply come upon him contemplating it.

The King's grey eyes lit with joy. "That's – no, it's *not* wonderful," he caught himself. "Or you wouldn't look like that." He came around to the front of the desk, and perched on the edge. "What happened?"

Adam leaned forward, face in his hands. "Nothing. Nothing at all. He took it, but he didn't put it on. Didn't say 'yes.'"

"But he didn't say 'no'?"

"He didn't say *anything,* Damien." Adam sighed. "I told him to keep it. Think about it. That we'd talk about it later. Then I went to my office and..." He gulped a bit as if he needed more air. "I wrote to my parents. And invited them to come. And to bring the rest."

The King smiled. One good thing, at least, out of this unconscionably messy day. "They can stay in the Castle."

Adam gave him another sardonic look. "Where? We're going to be bursting the rafters as it is, Elista tells me. And there are... rather a lot of them."

"We'll find a place," Damien said serenely. "They took me under their roof when I needed a place to stay, Adam. I am hardly going to skip the opportunity to return the favor."

Adam snorted. "Speaking of which, have you invited *your* cousins on your mother's side?"

"Elderwyld received its invitation, yes."

The King had made his peace with his grandparents before they had passed on, and had no reason to believe his mother's siblings or their children had been part of the decision to deny him sanctuary as a young man. If he could forgive *Adam* and *Ciriis* for their part in that incident... he wondered idly if Jason had mentioned to his lover that he had admitted to Damien what they had done. Somehow, he doubted Adam would bring it up so casually if he had.

Open, honest Jason. Such a surprise to discover how many secrets he kept, both for himself and for others.

Now, *Adam*...

"So, you think Jason... just *forgot* he was to meet me here?" Damien asked.

Adam shrugged, his face a study of things he clearly didn't want to talk about. "He... usually wants time by himself when we disagree about something. Or at least, time away from *me*. I'd rather talk it out, but..." He shrugged again.

The King chuckled. "And here I've always thought that you and Genevieve were more alike than you and I. But she'd rather avoid a subject we disagree extremely on." He met Adam's eyes as the thought occurred to him. "Genevieve."

Adam looked tense. "It... would make sense, I suppose."

"I'll check."

The King blinked to shift his view to superimpose a see-through image of the Castle on his vision of the room. He turned towards the large table he'd recently had hauled in to spread papers and maps out on, because seeing Adam through the image was... distracting. Unexpectedly so. He concentrated on his *feel* of Jason, and quickly located him in the royal apartments.

"He's with Genevieve," he confirmed, and switched his awareness to the soul-bond. "She doesn't seem particularly disturbed."

The Captain relaxed. "Maybe... maybe she'll help him figure out what he wants."

Damien gave him a dry look. "I think that's obvious to everyone."

"Is it?" Adam asked softly. He looked as sad as he had while they had been traveling back to the city from his parents' home twelve years ago.

"It is to *me*," Damien said just as quietly. "And I've probably been watching you both longer than anyone other than Ciriis."

Adam's look turned sardonic. "Longer and more carefully, I hear."

The King blushed. "Um."

"I can't fault your taste, I suppose," Adam sighed, looking away.

"Adam..." Damien began apologetically, but he didn't know what else to say. Certainly not without giving anything else away. Adam likely hadn't even noticed his phrasing... but he would if Damien blurted anything *else* out without proper consideration. There were still some things that it would be better to leave buried, even still.

"*That's* not what the problem is, Damien." Adam looked at his hands. "I can... live with... the way things are. I'm not exactly *happy* about this, mind," he gave Damien a dark look, "but I can *live* with it. *This*... is temporary. The problem is that, after nearly twenty years, Jason still puts his mother's attitudes and nastiness ahead of *us*."

"If that were true, he'd have left you long ago."

Adam looked away again. "Maybe it was just easier not to. He could pretend that the problem with his mother – and Megan – was about our relationship, not about..." He gave the King a look. "About *other* things. I wasn't asking anything else of him than that he stay." He dropped his head. "Now I am."

For all that it hadn't been Adam's idea to push the option of marriage... Or at least not to do it right now, with all the other complications and changes and potential changes they were making Jason deal with. No... doing it *now* had been Damien's own brainchild – because Jason was absolutely right that he didn't have it in him to be king. At least not without Adam at his side... and it would be better for everyone if it was clear that Adam's position there was official and carried *weight*.

Well, done was done, even if – in retrospect – the timing was flawed.

Damien cocked his head to one side. "That doesn't sound like the Jason I know."

Adam's mouth twisted. "He's been... *different* these last few months."

"Um," Damien said again, because likely that had to do with *him* and his problems that he'd kept foisting off on his poor Champion.

"You have been, too," Adam added, but without particular bitterness or sarcasm. Though he now narrowed his eyes at his uncomfortable monarch. "You've been stirring up the entire castle. The entire *Realm* in some ways. You don't want me to double the Guard just to protect Jason, who's fully capable of protecting himself, when you didn't have me do any such thing for Genevieve. And it's not even for a baby Heir, who won't be moving around for the next couple years, and isn't even conceived yet. You've given still *more* power over to the Council, and moved up those blasted provincial elections, even as you bring Jason in and establish him as your proxy on the Council. And insist on an Heir's coronation in hardly any time. And now you want to add legalizing marriages between men.

"What's next, Damien? And *why?*"

The King looked away from his Captain's intense gaze. "Technically it's not about *legalizing*. It's just formally sanctioning the marriages. There's no law against it now."

"*Damien...*"

"You want to know what's *next,* Adam?" Damien looked back at Adam, eyes ablaze and tongue loosened as his unanswerable frustration and regret boiled up. "I *want* to clean out that rat's nest of crime down by the docks. *And* reunite us with the remaining Lost Provinces. *And* find a way to Bind the land through the *people* who live there, not just Bind the nobles who have been awarded those people as their charge not to harm them. *And...*" He bit off the rest of what was a much, *much* longer list. "It doesn't matter. I'm not going to have *time.*

"Who would be your choice as Captain of the Royal Guard right now, if you were no longer available?" He threw it out quickly, as a distraction and also so as to surprise Adam into giving him his gut-level answer.

"Tim Ancellius." Adam didn't look surprised at all, of course. "Marcus is coming along nicely, but there are still too many parts of the job he doesn't understand yet. He doesn't work with the Secret Cadre very much, and he doesn't realize how many administrative details there are, nor how much I have to interact with the nobles. He's certainly not ready to deal with *you.* Or Genevieve," Adam added more thoughtfully. "I'd've kept Tim on as my Second if he hadn't requested leave when their son was born."

"*That's* still an issue, though," Damien frowned.

"Less of one. The boy is old enough to tag along with either Tim or Aryllis most of the time. And he takes after his mother: he's a serious little lad. *My* duties," Adam said dryly, "rarely put me anywhere near danger. And Tim knows that."

"And if they have another?"

"I don't believe they intend to. Aryllis had enough trouble birthing Rico."

Damien wished he'd been able to spend time to get to know the little boy himself. As Adam clearly had. He folded his arms, pretending he wasn't doing it because he could practically feel what it would be like to hold a baby. His own child – the child of his heart, if not of his body. Adam's eyes echoed the feeling.

"How would you feel about taking the Champion's chain?"

Adam paled. "That's Jason's."

"He can't be both Heir and Champion," Damien replied reasonably. "By all rights you should have the place of the *Heir's* Champion... but someone has to be mine. You're the best qualified by your skills and... I think it will bother Jason less if it's you." He took a deep breath. "And I'll tell you the same thing I told him. It's not about skills, to me. You've been my Champion since you discovered me in the Library. You've pushed me to become better, stronger, kept me *alive* to get to the Throne... to get me to *this* point. And... I want you in a position more visible to everyone than Captain of the Royal Guard."

Adam frowned. "Damien, what's going on that you aren't telling us?"

The King stood up and paced over to the window, rested his hands on the sill. He stared out at the garden beyond, not seeing the Autumn-painted bushes and late-Fall flowers. "Women die in childbirth, Adam. It happens all the time. And Genevieve is old for a first child. And she's not going to be at her full strength and fitness. Even if she manages to carry Jason's child to full term... that's no guarantee that she – and I – will survive.

"And if this piece of Lord Prydeen's prophecy is true, there's reason to believe the rest of it. The Sword will never speak for this child. She'll never assume the throne. If she even survives. Babes whose mothers die in childbirth often don't.

"With the two of you married – with you gaining renown as King's Champion – you stand a chance of holding the Realm together. You'll be King-Consort, and Jason can name one of *your* nephews as Heir. He won't be limited to choosing from the Solway family... which I think we'll all agree is a good thing." Damien turned back, and his face was very fey; the face of a man anticipating his own death and the death of his beloved. "I remember Desirée. I think I can trust her to raise good people. I know I can trust you and Jason to raise a king. Again. This time you'll just have better starting material."

The smile he managed was watery rather than reassuring.

"You were *fine* as starting material," Adam said distractedly. "So, you want a contingent of Royal Guards sent to Lynncrag, to guard Desirée and the boys in my parents' home. *That's* why the increase in the size of the Guard."

"No one should have to grow up in this Castle," Damien said quietly. "I'd planned for my own children to spend as much time in Elaarwen as possible." He winced slightly. "It took several hours to convince Queen Marian of that, but my personal experience set against the unsuitability of her own offspring and grandchildren raised here... the fact that the Sword was willing to speak for both Genevieve and her father... and finally the fact that my father was the only royal child *not* raised here in the last century – and she has a sense that the Sword might have spoken for him if it'd had the chance... His mother took him back to Dawil for a few years, did you know?

"It wasn't just what King Reginald and Lord Prydeen were doing. I suspect the fact that this Castle is a concentrator for the Power of the Realm warps a developing mind."

Adam stared at him. "Your family lived in Elderwyld when *you* were born."

Damien inclined his head, wandering back to perch on the front edge of his desk again. "Until I was eight. And Kandy grew up there." He'd told Adam -and Genevieve – before that it should have been his older sister who ended up on the Throne. Kandy had surely been everything the Sword could have asked for. "A few of my aunts and uncles – and my father – spent enough time elsewhere to have had some redeeming characteristics. It's why I've encouraged Tim and Aryllis to take their child and go on long trips. Likewise with the others. Though it may only be children of the Alsterling line who are sensitive to the Power... I'd rather not take the chance."

The Captain rubbed his head as if it was hurting. "Damien... any chance you could get some food up here? This... is too much to absorb on an empty stomach, and I missed lunch."

Damien held his breath. "You mean... magickally?"

Adam waved a hand. "If you wouldn't mind. I didn't... I don't want to face anyone else right now."

The larger table was instantly covered with baskets of bread and cheese and cold cuts of meat. Damien hadn't forgotten condiments either.

"Thank you," Adam said gratefully, levering himself up out of the chair, and beginning to turn to the table full of food. He was entirely taken by surprise when Damien caught him in a hard hug, his face buried in the taller man's arm. It was only for an instant, but Adam's eyes softened.

"What was that all about?" he asked gently.

Damien looked embarrassed. "You're the only person who sees my abilities as something to be used, not hidden or feared or... somehow

inherently *wrong*. It's just... really nice. Not very kingly of me, I suppose..."
But he'd spent nearly as much time seeking Adam's approval as Jason's.
More in some ways. Their opinion mattered to him as much as Genevieve's,
and Adam's was the first *positive* reaction he'd had to his more casual uses
of magick.

He tried to shrug it off. "I guess we never completely outgrow some
things."

Adam's eyes said he understood entirely. He clapped Damien on the
shoulder, then turned to the serious business of assembling a sandwich.

"What else can you do?" the Captain asked over his shoulder. "You
never did tell me the other day. I suppose we had other things on our minds,
but..." He paused in the middle of drizzling mustard onto his bread and
meat. "Now that I think about it, Genevieve distracted me intentionally,
didn't she."

He turned back to see Damien looking frustrated. "She doesn't like it
when I do anything magickal – other than monitor the Realm. I suppose
that's partly because she can do that herself and has seen that it doesn't
imply any moral deficits." The King started putting a sandwich together for
himself as well, which gave him a good excuse to keep his eyes on his work.
"I'd been planning to send for food once Jason got here," he commented,
then added, "...*he* doesn't approve of magick either."

"Doing this sort of thing doesn't create the kind of problems you were
having before?" Adam asked.

Damien sat down on the couch that Adam had had brought in for him
to sleep on, and folded his legs up tailor-fashion while he ate. He typically
took his boots or shoes off when he was planning to spend any length of
time in his office. Adam had called it another relic of his time in the Royal
Library.

"No. I can't do this stuff when the Realm is feeding off my own Power,
but when the Realm isn't 'hungry,' the Power is just there." He took a bite
and chewed thoughtfully. "It's like a low drain, I suppose. When there's
flooding, there's nowhere for more water to go, but if it's raining, the water
will just keep building up. In a drought – the water drains away quickly and
the land is still parched."

"So... the Realm is *supposed* to be 'flooded' with magick?" Adam asked.

"I don't know about 'supposed to,'" Damien temporized. He actually
had very little idea what the Realm would look like if it were healthy. "But
it tries to drain *me* if it's not."

"What does your Queen Marian say about that?"

"She wasn't gifted with the ability to use magick herself. All she could do was sense where things were wrong in the Realm. Though she did have some ability to use the Sword," the King added in an effort to be fair.

Queen Marian had been quite as invaluable to him in learning to rule as Genevieve and her father – more in some ways, since neither of them had ever administered more than their rather economically impoverished duchy. On the other hand, his ghostly great-great-grandmother's failures as a queen and as a mother had led to this mess in the first place. So far as Damien had been able to determine, there had been no problems leading up to her reign.

The two men ate for a moment in companionable silence.

"Well," Adam said slowly, at last, "it seems to me that magick is just another tool. And there's no reason not to use a tool. Are there ethical limits?"

Damien sighed. Adam had read a great many of the same treatises on the subject that he had himself, so this felt less like the Captain was asking for more information and rather more like the way he had made the younger man think through moral and philosophical points during the years after they had lured him out of the Royal Library. Not that Damien had minded those long and convoluted and often frustrating conversations – he'd needed to explore the limits of what might eventually be his royal powers. He'd read through much of the philosophy section of the Library long before, of course, but hadn't had the context of imagining he might someday be king himself... and those elaborate arguments had come to life when it was Adam posing the questions rather than some long-dead author.

Jason and Ciriis had left them to those discussions, the King recalled. Ciriis had been more interested in the practical applications of royal powers – he'd likely learned whatever pragmatism and ruthlessness he possessed from her example... as well as Queen Marian and Duke Aldred.

And Jason had seemed uncomfortable with the deeper dives into matters of ethics and morality. After having heard what was apparently still just the edges of Jason's not-entirely-regretted time with Prince Oskar, Damien had a few guesses about why. He rather thought Adam would have understood enough to avoid making Damien debate those issues in Jason's presence... but a number of their conversations had happened over arms-practice...

"I think it was very wrong of Lord Prydeen to use the mice and birds to spy on people," the King replied. "We don't need that level of paranoia. I don't want to be *feared*. I wouldn't want to read someone's thoughts for the same reason, or use magick to kill someone. Or to torture them."

Adam's eyes had grown very startled, and Damien gave him a wry grin. Apparently, the tall knight hadn't thought about what those things they were reading about could be used for. Had Adam somehow managed to read all those things and yet think about it only in the abstract? Or was he startled because *Damien* had realized those things… despite all his efforts to get the younger man to always take the moral high ground?

"Yes, I *could* do all of those things. I can't *make* things, or alter them, unless I know how that would be done – it's not just wish fulfillment. For example, I know where the foods are stored in the kitchens – Elista and I have an agreement that certain things will be in certain places so that I can transport them. If it's more than this," he gestured at the bread and cold-cuts, "then I leave a note. Like with breakfast the other day. It prevents the servants for being blamed for items going missing."

"Thoughtful," Adam commented a little dryly.

Damien's expression grew even more wry. "I wish I'd thought of it myself."

He didn't elaborate on the commotion he'd caused and the maids who'd nearly been turned out over it. The whole thing had happened during one of the rare times that Adam and Jason had left the City for a private interlude. At the time, Damien had been relieved that he had managed to clean up the mess without word getting back to his erstwhile mentors.

"Now, I know better," he concluded, hoping there wouldn't be any further questions.

"What *can't* you do?" The Captain asked almost rhetorically, then smiled slowly. "Wait. You said you need to know how a thing is made. *This* is why we spend so much time wandering around in the crafters' district, isn't it?"

"I'd hardly call it *wandering*," the King objected. He'd heard plenty from any number of people about his explorations of the City. "I've always had specific destinations in mind. And we almost always have appointments."

"Not always," Adam muttered. "Remember the glassworks?"

The King rolled his eyes. "I thought they just hadn't had time to get back to me. I didn't know they were being intentionally secretive."

"You talked them into letting us in, though." Was that a note of pride? Or was the younger man still too sensitive to keeping watch for such things from his Captain.

Damien shrugged. "It's not like I was going to set myself up in competition with their Guild. All I had to do was make that clear. As you know."

Adam chuckled. "It helped when you explained that you wanted to see what they might need in order to be able to compete effectively with foreign glass." He narrowed his eyes at the King. "But you *could* set up as competition with them, couldn't you? Now that you've seen how glass is made?"

Damien shook his head. "It takes years and years to see everything in any craft, Adam. I have enough of an idea of how glass is made that I could create crude pieces if it became useful to protect the Realm. But I could never make quality window-glass, for example, or mirrors."

"'To protect the Realm...?" The Captain frowned. "Why would you ever need *glass* to protect the Realm?"

The King had spent a fair amount of time thinking about this before he'd come up with this idea. It wasn't to Adam's discredit that he didn't see this instantly, despite having read the same books. Most people didn't cross-correlate as well as Damien did. Rather, it was to the Captain's credit that he was putting the pieces together this quickly when presented with the entire jigsaw puzzle. Genevieve had had about the same reaction, and she was their unquestioned strategic genius.

"There are sorcerers out there who employ heat – or magnetism – spells to make weapons made of steel useless," Damien reminded his Captain. "Even fragments of glass can be very sharp. Or... I could throw the glass at the enemy and someone could shoot an arrow and make fragments rain down. My initial goal was to find out if I could mirror a *spell* back onto its caster – but I'm convinced that would take much more skill in glassmaking than I'm likely to put the time into developing."

He sighed. "Each of us who works magick seems to find a particular special set of skills to use – you've read the same books I have; you know that. I'm... still more of a generalist for now. And I can probably get away with it because I have the Power of the Realm backing me up. If it came to protecting the Realm, I could probably just overPower the attacker... though it might mean a few years of poor harvests thereafter."

Adam tilted his head curiously. "Are you really this concerned about us being attacked magickally?"

They hadn't discussed *why* Damien was so obsessively interested in reading about magick... what *else* had Adam thought his king was doing it for? A question for another day... because the younger man didn't really want to admit that he'd also been searching for how to ensure that no child of his would ever go bad, prophecy or no. Or how to suppress the soul-bond so Genevieve could recover.

Or how to Heal those malformed not-yet-babies they'd lost. He didn't think even his beautiful wife knew that he'd named each one in his heart... it had seemed cruel and blaming to tell her...

"By brute force attacks?" Damien shook his head. "Not terribly, not anymore. But I had to study the problem to come to that conclusion. By someone coming in pretending to be a friend, worming their way into our confidences, and then wreaking havoc through a more subtle play for power? Much more so."

"Like Lord Prydeen."

"Not... exactly." The King shook his head. "I've read as much as I can of the notes he and my grandfather both left behind. As far as I can tell, my grandfather had the gift of being able to use magick and was already abusing it – some – before he was even crowned. I've picked up some hints that *he* recruited 'Lord' Prydeen, though where from I've yet to determine. I'm... not clear on how much of an innocent Prydeen was when they began their... association."

Genevieve had looked determined, but extremely distressed, when he had tried to talk to her about this. Jason... had clearly wanted to know as little as possible and Damien hadn't even tried. Adam just looked thoughtful.

Time to prod a little more.

"Adam... I'm planning to make Jason Duke of Emeralsee."

The Captain's eyebrow lifted. "Good idea. He can use some real administrative practice. It took you awhile to sort all of that out as I recall. As Champion, Jason has always been a solo act." The last words looked like they were sour on his tongue. "It's traditionally held by the Heir to the Throne, isn't it? Who has the title now?"

Damien gave a sheepish grin. "I do. Genevieve already had Elaarwen, and Rosa had Dalzialest." He grew sober. "It will also let me Bind him to the land. Genevieve says she thinks it was easier to accept the whole Realm as Queen because she had already been Bound to Elaarwen and gotten used to that."

"So, you're preparing for your imminent demise again," Adam said sardonically. "I'm all for preparedness, Damien, but you're taking this down a very dark direction."

Damien shrugged apologetically. "I suspect Jason will find he has the ability to use magick once it's been... activated by the Binding."

Adam leaned back in his chair. "Well. That is... not something I was expecting to hear. Will he be able to do what you do?"

The King raised his hands. "I have no way of knowing. I could be entirely wrong about this. It's just a feeling I have right now."

"Hmmn." Adam stroked his chin. "Well, something to worry about if and when it happens."

There was a knock at the door, and Jason came in. He immediately knelt without looking around. "I apologize for my tardiness, my liege."

"So formal, Jason?" Damien said lightly. "You're late, not guilty of treason." He waved at the table. "Have you had lunch?"

Jason looked up, startled, and his eyes locked on Adam.

The Captain stood up too quickly, "I have work to get back to also. Thank you for lunch, Damien." He nodded at the kneeling Champion. "Jason."

"Adam..." Jason scrambled to his feet, but his lover brushed past him and out without another word. The Champion stared wordlessly at the closed door, his face gone blank and expressionless again with his inner turmoil.

Damien sighed. Clearly, he wasn't going to

Chapter FOURTEEN

Relations

WITH MERE DAYS LEFT BEFORE the Heir's coronation… *and* investiture as Duke… *and* wedding… the Castle had become a hive of frenetic activity. Most of the nobles who planned to attend had arrived – including, unfortunately, the Solway family.

Countess Alexa and Lady Megan had barely constrained themselves from seething directly at the King for his high-handedness – the mother, for the implication that she could not afford to pay for the enrollment of her youngest grandchildren as a page and squire, and the daughter for essentially forcing them to do so. While Damien hadn't made it a 'request and require,' it had been worded to make it next to impossible for the family to refuse without grave insult to the Crown. And then he had compounded their fury by keeping Jason too busy to dance attendance upon his mother's whims. The Countess had actually tried to corner *Adam,* when she couldn't pin down Jason.

That had gone about as well as anyone who knew the both of them could have predicted.

The Countess had accosted the Captain in the Great Hall, the huge main entrance hall where nobles of the Court often gathered to conduct business, to gossip, to spy on one another, or simply to keep tabs on the pulse of the Court. Several of the Secret Cadre were circulating through the hall at any time, and Adam made it a habit to check in with them several times a day; it gave them the opportunity to casually tell him things without anyone noticing, since he spoke to plenty of other nobles there as well. Adam was well known to have the ear of the King and Queen... and his new status as spouse-to-be of the new Crown Prince, as well as a member of the Royal Council, made him a target for those asking – or offering – favors all on his own.

Countess Alexa, however, began by trying to harangue Adam for Jason having passed off the task of opening up the townhouse to 'hired help.' Adam cut her off by saying it was by order of the King, and pointing out that the Royal Chatelaine and her staff hardly counted as 'hired help,' at least in the way Jason's mother meant it.

So, the Countess changed tactics and began insisting on special treatment for her grandchildren – the training of squires and pages falling nominally under the purview of Captain of the Guard; the aged knight who actually served as Master of the Knights-in-Training was Adam's subordinate. She also seemed upset that Elaina hadn't received an invitation to serve as a lady-in-waiting to the Queen, but clearly had not realized that Adam oversaw that program as well; instead, she attempted to enlist his help in 'dealing with' Lady Aryllis.

And – after years of ranging from completely ignoring his existence to being outright rude to him, Countess Alexa had the temerity to insist that Adam defer to her as 'his future mother-in-law.' Had she taken the time to know him at all, she would have realized he was already giving her – indeed had *always* given her – extra consideration for being Jason's mother. Anyone else with such outrageous requests would have been brushed off and thereafter ignored. In fact, the matter of how much time the busy Captain was giving her had already attracted attention.

Had she taken the *least* bit of time to know him, she would also have recognized the wicked gleam in his eyes that suggested he was going to rip her to shreds, verbally.

His Secret Royal Guards noticed, however, having seen that expression pointed in their direction all too often during training. A brief consultation resulted in a runner being sent for the King – as the only person capable of pulling rank on the Captain.

Damien didn't take the time to run; he simply transferred himself by magick from his office to a shadowed alcove along the side of the Great Hall and strode out from there. He arrived just in time to see Adam giving the Countess the cut direct and winced slightly inside. Though it surely took

Adam to be able to listen to a diatribe for ten minutes from the mother of the man he'd been paired with for fifteen years and then stare at her as if he'd never met her before... It was *probably* better than what he might have *said.*

"Ah, Captain," the King said in a nonchalant tone as he approached them and before the Countess could draw breath to begin anew. "There you are. Countess Alexa," Damien inclined his head to stately woman. It was meant as an acknowledgment and dismissal in one movement, but the steely-eyed Countess topped the King's height by several inches – it was obvious Jason's height didn't come entirely from his mysterious father – and she was able to pretend she didn't notice the dismissive part.

"Your Majesty," she sank into a deep curtsy... though Damien's trained eye noted ironically that it was only *precisely* as deep as it had to be for propriety's sake and not so much as a hair's-width deeper.

"My soon-to-be son-in-law here," she gave Adam a dark look as she rose – *without* awaiting the King's permission, "Does not seem inclined to find out for me why my granddaughter has not received an answer to her request to join Her Majesty's ladies-in-waiting. And my son claims – by *note* – that he has had no time to talk to me since I arrived. Perhaps Your Majesty can find some opportunity to assist a loyal vassal with these small concerns."

With both Duchess Rosa and Duke Tomas present and having edged closer to support their king, should he need it – which vaguely amused Damien – Countess Alexa's slight emphasis on the words 'loyal vassal' was surely no mistake. She still held herself above those who had rebelled against King Reginald, despite their social precedence.

Damien favored her with one of his vague smiles, quickly choosing between treating her with infuriating casualness and overformality. He'd spent most of his reign – most of his *life,* though the Countess had not deigned to notice him until he was Named Heir – in the former mode. She might not have yet realized that he had been in the latter mode since Lord Aldred's precipitous departure, though she was surely caught up on all the gossip.

"Applications to Her Majesty's personal service are made through the Mistress of Protocol, are they not, Captain?" He didn't wait for Adam's nod before continuing. "You would do best to apply there. And as for the Crown Prince's schedule... certainly you are aware that he has a wide-range of responsibilities that have fallen upon him rather suddenly. With the

Queen's illness, Prince Jason has been handling much of her work as well as his own."

"But surely he has time to greet his loving mother properly," the Countess persisted.

Damien let his look become reproving – and not the gentle, mildly reproving look he'd used in the past, but the hair-from-clap-her-in-irons look he'd been using for the last few weeks. He ached to ask who that person might be that Jason should greet thusly...

"I have the greatest faith in my Heir, Countess, and his ability to prioritize the needs of the Realm as well as the needs of propriety. Come along, Captain." Damien turned on his heel and strode out of the hall, not bothering to acknowledge the bows and curtsies as he left any more than he had the wave of them that had followed his entry. He knew Adam was a half-step behind him... and a half-step away from truly ripping into the Countess... and his goal was to get them into a more private space before his friend exploded.

The moment he knew they were out of sight, Damien transported them back to his office. Jason looked up in a sort of grim surprise, and the lady-in-waiting who had brought the earlier message looked absolutely frozen.

"Lady Lisa," Damien bowed over her hand as she dipped a belated curtsy. "Thank you for your service." He saw her out the door, shut it, and leaned back against it.

Jason strode up to engage the wards, glowering. "Your vanishing act is going to be known throughout the Guards by evening, Damien. Throughout the *Castle,* if they were the gossiping type."

"Which they aren't, because Adam and Aryllis would never let them join else," Damien said mildly.

"*Still–*"

"It might not be a bad thing," Adam said thoughtfully. "They all tend to underestimate him. That's not bad for enemies, but..."

"But it can be a problem with friends and subordinates who don't take me seriously." Damien gave his old friend a dry look. "I'm familiar with the problem."

He looked back at Jason as the Captain had the grace to give an embarrassed nod. "What would you have had me do, Jason? Leave Adam to your mother's tender mercies? Or the other way around? I wouldn't be surprised to hear that a betting pool had already been opened on how the confrontation would turn out."

Adam snorted. "I've wanted to say something cutting to that woman for fifteen years, Damien. I know how to restrain myself."

The King rolled his eyes. "Yes, and I'm sure that staring at her as if you didn't know her – after listening to her patiently for ten minutes – worked beautifully."

Jason groaned. *"Adam..."*

"What would you have had *me* do, Jase? Tell the old biddy hen that her precious Elaina has about as much chance of being accepted as a lady-in-waiting as of earning her shield? Or that if I have anything to say about it, the younger two will get a *harder* time, not the easier one she was after me to ensure? Or should I *really* tell her what I think of her for how she's treated you all these years?"

The Champion looked... frozen. Again.

Adam sighed, and went to put his arms around him.

"She *did* sort of point up a problem, though," Damien said thoughtfully, and they both looked at him curiously.

"I need a secretary," he explained. "And so do you, Jason. *And* Genevieve. We've been trying to handle this mountain of paperwork," he waved at his desk, "and schedule everything... my grandfather did it this way and I knew it didn't work. It's just that a secretary handles so much sensitive information and..." He stumbled to a halt.

"And you got burned when you appointed Lady Theresa," Adam finished for him.

Damien nodded, looking away. That betrayal still stung. Rather like a sword through the heart 'stung.' "It wasn't just that she was working with Lord Prydeen the whole time. It took months to sort out all the small things she'd done to undermine me."

"I remember," Adam said quietly. "But you're right. This," he looked at the piles of papers, "is even more out of hand since Jason started working in here."

Jason gave him a disconcerted and slightly offended look.

"Not your fault, Jase," Adam said absently. "You need *two* offices. Space for each of you to have meetings. And a secretary to serve as gatekeeper – someone should be handling routine messages, and my Guards can only do so much. And *scheduling.*" He gave the King an evil grin. "Maybe you can hire that man who did such a good job putting you off at the dockworker's union offices. If he can dare try to fuddle the Sorcerer-King, he should be up to handling Countess Alexa and her ilk."

Damien grinned. "Good idea. And it should be *three* offices. Genevieve will need one once she gets back to work."

Adam folded his arms. *"Not* until after the baby is born, Damien."

The King visibly deflated. "Agreed."

Jason gave him a wry look. "At least we shouldn't have any more trouble keeping her in her rooms with my mother and sister roaming the castle."

Damien gave him a small nod. "Hmmn." He looked at Adam. "Oh, some good news at least. Madame Elista has found rooms enough for *almost* all of your family. She wants to put your brothers in your sitting room. She has some plan that involves extra couches, though I'm not sure where she'll take them from."

Jason looked disconsolate. "Solway House could fit them all easily..."

Adam gave him a horrified look that melted to sympathy. As a son of the house, it should have been reasonable for Jason to ask his mother to house his in-laws.

"We can make this work, Jase." He looked at Damien. "And *after* we get a crown on Jason's head, I'll see about organizing office-space. And hiring a secretary. Or two."

Damien grinned. "Or three. Between the two of you, every future Champion of this Realm is going to find themselves with the unexpected duties of personnel management."

Jason looked ready to deny it, then hesitated, clearly remembering all the people he had vetted for Genevieve over the years.

"One other thing," Adam added thoughtfully. "You need a personal archivist to keep track of all *this–"* he waved a hand at the stacks of papers and reports that threatened to collapse off Damien's desk and overwhelm the room, "and all those references you keep shuttling back and forth to the Royal Library. I think Lena would be perfect for the job."

Jason nodded as Damien gave him a brilliant smile and added, "Tell Madame Elista that she can have any nonstructural walls removed to create the space we need... *after* the coronation."

Chapter FIFTEEN

Family...

ADAM'S FAMILY ARRIVED THAT EVENING, and had to be escorted up immediately to meet Genevieve – all eleven of them. Jason winced a little bit internally at how his mother and Megan would take that, but was generally so overjoyed to find that they really did accept him as family that he couldn't bring himself to worry.

'Immediately' was, of course, a matter of scale. First there was an incredibly teary reunion with Adam. In their private quarters, where Jason had needed to physically hold him to prevent Adam rushing down to meet them in the courtyard. Later on, he knew, his love would have regretted having let the whole Realm see him weeping...

There were apologies all around, until Desirée's little boys got everyone's attention by announcing that they were going to be pages starting *immediately*. Adam laughed, scooping both of them up in his arms – they were tall for their age like all of the family, but still just barely small enough for him to do it – and informing them that they had to wait a *wee* bit longer. Which brought a look of relief to their mother, if cries of disappointment from the boys.

The boys were also disappointed to find out that neither uncle had slain – or even fought – any dragons. They were *almost* mollified over the story of Damien's battle with Lord Prydeen – told when they reached the royal apartments so the King could fill in the story, since neither Jason nor Adam had actually been there. They swarmed over the delighted young King to get more details. When Aryllis and Tim arrived with little Rico, Jason noticed Damien and Adam exchanging a look of wistful hopefulness and caught Genny's eye himself. Not too much longer...

Marianna hit it off with Genny – and everyone else – instantly. Jason quietly informed Lady Alanna that Adam's sister was applying to join their special ranks, and the ladies-in-waiting nearly carried her off then and there to begin training.

At last, the Loveresses were bundled off to their own quarters to unpack, assisted by Guards both secret and official, including the Captain.

Damien held Jason back from the happy mob and watched with some concern as the tall knight collapsed into a chair after the door of the royal suite was closed behind the last of them.

"Jason?" the King asked tentatively.

"He'll be fine," Genny said, seating herself as well, but more decorously. She looked entirely healthy and normal, to the Champion's relief. "There's just rather a *lot* of them, aren't there, Jason?"

"Yes..." He was happy for Adam. *Really,* he *was.* And thrilled to be part of such a family. But they were... exhausting. It was like attending the three-ring circus that traveled from town to city across the Realm – too much going on and no idea how to keep track of it all. Genny and Damien understood, he knew.

"It's just for a couple of weeks, isn't it?" Damien asked. "The coronation is in eight days, and they're staying for four after that?"

Jason nodded heavily. "Most of them. Marianna is staying of course."

"I'm trying to talk Martin into staying here to learn from the Realm's best Healer," Genny smiled at her husband.

Damien raked the errant lock of hair out of his face. "I really don't have time to take on an apprentice, love. Even if his sort of Healing works anything like mine."

"Grandmother Marian told me we should try to talk him into it," the Queen said smugly. "She says it will be good for you to do something that isn't for the life and death of the Realm."

The young King rolled his eyes. "And I suppose she'll find me the *time* to do it, too?"

Genny gave him a sweetly menacing look. "I think you'll *find* the time if the alternative is listening to Queen Marian explaining to you why you should. You can only hide out in that office for so long, you know. She's still miffed that you warded it from magickal visits." She looked back at Jason. "You're worried about your mother. You have that look."

"She's going to go out of her way to be rude to the Baronetta, I know she will." Jason agreed heavily. "She's going to demand to know why the Loveresses were permitted up here and she has not been. She's–"

"Going to be her usual annoying self," Genny concluded. "I think Lady Loveress can take care of herself. Can *you?*" She gave him a serious look. "We talked about adopting you as an Alsterling, to break some of the hold Countess Alexa has over you, Jason. As Crown Prince – or as King – you can't be worrying about her reactions like this."

"*Adopt...*" Jason half-choked on the idea. He was a *Solway*. It was... who he was. He hadn't been home to Brindlewell in nearly ten years, but it was still *home...* wasn't it?

The Heir's Ring and coronation, marriage to Adam, losing the Champion's chain...

He felt adrift.

"We decided it probably created as many complications as it solved," Damien noted, sitting sideways along the back of the couch Genny was on, one knee propped up.

With his new hyperawareness of both of them, Jason noted that the King had kept a careful distance from his wife during the entire Loveress Family Visit. But they were drawn to each other – Jason couldn't count the number of abortive movements he had seen each make towards the other. The tension must be building again.

"I... can handle Mother," Jason said when it seemed clear that they expected some sort of comment.

Damien folded his arms, his expression skeptical. "Really? I won't crown an Heir who'll be a puppet of Alexa Solway if he takes the Throne."

Jason didn't want the throne. Or the Crown. Or any of it. But there was no one else...

"I *said* I can handle her, Damien."

Genny gave him a sympathetic look and stopped herself from reaching a soothing hand out to Damien. "It's just... we've never *seen* you stand up to her, Jason. Her *or* Megan."

It was true...

Damien came around the sofa and sat on the floor in front of his Champion, looking up at him earnestly. "Why does she ride you so? You're the best man – the best *person* that I know."

He flickered a glance of apology to Genny, who waved it off with a smile of agreement.

"There is *no way* you deserve how she treats you. How they *both* treat you. Even your nieces and nephew haven't shown you but the barest hint of respect." The King paused. "Does this have something to do with your father?"

Jason drew in a breath. "Is this my *king* asking? Or my *friend?*"

The dark-haired man seated on the floor gave him a long look. "I'm not sure the two can be entirely separate right now. If it's a danger to the Realm that your father's name has been stricken..."

"It's *not.*" Jason shrank into himself, hating the feeling of being small and vulnerable. "I've spent my entire life *proving* that it's not. That I'm not *him.*"

"Who was he?" Genny asked quietly.

Jason shrugged, feeling even smaller. "I don't have a name for him. Megan said once that I look just like him, but that's all I know." And she'd started crying hysterically after that, and her husband, David, had had to come take her to lie down, and he'd gotten another tongue-lashing from his mother for oversetting Megan so, even though he hadn't said a word... "Not even the servants in Brindlewell would tell me... and once I was old enough to understand what he *did*... I didn't *want* to know."

"What did he do, Jason?" Damien asked, looking up at him trustingly, so... trustingly with those lovely silver eyes that could see to the depths of one's soul it sometimes seemed.

Maybe they would see him as himself and not... not his *father.* Jason had helped Adam finish raising Damien and that had gone well... and he hadn't touched Genny that whole Summer they had played together, had ignored how much she had tried flirting with him and then pretending she'd done no such thing.

Or... maybe what he'd done so much more recently with Damien... what he was *planning* to do with Genny in... was it really only another week or so? Maybe that was evidence that he really *was* a monster just like...

"He..." The golden-haired knight took a deep breath. He had never told anyone but Adam. And really that had been his mother, not him, when Adam had demanded an explanation after Megan's collapse. Jason had never actually said the words aloud before. "He *raped Megan.* While our mother was pregnant with *me.*" Jason looked at Genny with tears in his eyes. "She was *thirteen years old.*"

Genny's eyes were shocked, but she shook her head. "That has nothing to do with you."

He wrapped his arms around himself, and stared down at his lap. "It wasn't just *once,* Genny. And... and he did what Oskar did to me. The first time."

He didn't elaborate, but he knew Damien would understand. Maybe Genevieve would, too. She'd lived through her own horror and it had wreaked havoc on her heart and soul. Damien had said she'd wept while Harald died a traitor's death. Making someone fall in love with you so that you could abuse them was clearly not his father's unique idea.

"Megan told me it took *years* before she forgave Mother for sending him away after she found out. That it took years for her to *understand* why Mother did it. She... Megan thought it was because *I* was born that he was sent away. So... I suppose she must have hated me from the beginning. Then she only had *more* reasons to hate me *later."*

Though it had been Megan he had run to when he was small... she had always seemed sad, but willing to give him the time and attention that their mother wouldn't... couldn't... hadn't. And... he had vague memories of Megan doing things with him... like reading to him... and smiling sadly as if the smile was for him, but it couldn't lift her sadness entirely. It hadn't been until David came into their lives that Megan had seemed to lose that sadness... Jason had always wondered if that was why his mother had approved her Heir's marriage to a mere merchant. Not that the Countess had seemed to have much more affection for her daughter than for her son.

"*Someone* must have loved and cared for you," Genny said with a frown. "Someone taught you how to love."

He didn't know what to say about Megan... not that either of them would be likely to believe those half-memories from his childhood. They'd *met* Megan after all. Though... they'd met her *after* she'd broken free of his father's 'spell.' When she was occupied with David and her children and Jason – and his monster of a father – were only bad memories that she was confronted with when the rest of the family came down from Brindlewell for the Summer social season at Court.

"My... my wet-nurse, I suppose... The other servants. They wouldn't break my mother's rule forbidding *his* name, but they said it wasn't my fault."

"It *wasn't.*" Genny told him firmly.

Jason shrugged again. Easy words.

She stood up and came closer to put her hands around his face, forcing him to look into her eyes. "It *wasn't* your fault, Jason. You weren't even born. It wasn't Megan's fault either. Some fault might lie with your mother for not seeing what kind of man her second husband was, but," she added pointedly, "I can give testimony to the fact that that is not as easy as it sounds."

"Genny..."

"Hush. Your mother has been punishing you to punish herself. It has to stop, but *she* probably can't. And if Megan grew up with this idea..." She paused. "Elaina and the other children know all about this, don't they?"

Jason nodded miserably.

"I'll send them home," Damien said instantly. "I thought perhaps we could do something with the younger two, but it won't be worth it to cause you more pain, Jason."

"No..." Jason shook his head. "Don't do that. They shouldn't have *their* lives ruined because of *me*. Like their mother."

Genny looked at him thoughtfully. "I agree. We should keep them here. But not because of that. *Megan's* life," she said dryly, "seems perfectly fine to me – unless you're going to claim that Rudolph decided to break that colt because of you."

"He *did,* though." Jason shook again – but this time it was all of him in a trembling that wouldn't stop.

He'd avoided thinking about this... His nephew that he'd wanted so badly to get to know... and love... and wouldn't have dared even if he'd been home to do it, even if his mother and Megan had allowed him... And then it was all too late to even *try*...

"Megan says he was always trying to prove he was as good as me at everything..." Jason managed to explain as Damien and Genny looked at him in confusion. "She and Mother wouldn't let him come here to train as a squire because *I* was here. So, he was always doing reckless things. Because... because of *me–*"

To his surprise, Genny interrupted him with a laugh as she sat back down. "I've seen – and trained – enough pubescent boys to know that recklessness is built into most of them. Girls, too," she reminded him with a grin that recalled the Summer they had spent together. "Oh, not *you*. Nor Damien." She smiled briefly at her husband. "*You* were too busy trying to be perfect enough to please your mother."

"And *I* was too busy trying not to be noticed by anyone," Damien added. His eyes gleamed a brighter silver, but he was turning to look over his shoulder at his wife. "But I've heard stories about a certain young lady who wanted to visit the docks at age twelve..."

"She wanted to live up to her great-grandmother's reputation," Jason said dourly. "Just like Rudolph wanted to live up to *mine.*" Though why Rudolph had ever wanted to be anything like him, Jason had never been able to fathom.

"I'll bet Megan wasn't easy on him," Genny mused. "Nor your mother either."

"They weren't."

It had driven Jason half-crazy that they hadn't let him start to teach the boy to hold a sword, or ride a pony, or... or *anything* on his brief trips home. Jason had taught Damien by then and knew how to teach all the manly arts and do it *well.* His brother-in-law, David, was barely able to do any of those things himself, as far as Jason knew, though Megan's husband *had* shown him how to hold a sword before Jason had been sent down to Emeralsee. David... and... but no, *that* 'memory' had to be *entirely* fabricated from wishful thinking and surely cast doubt on all the rest of what he *thought* he recalled. Megan was entirely too delicate and lady-like to have ever shown Jason...

Worse was that as the children grew older Countess Alexa's favoritism for Elaina became more and more obvious.

Jason had been so excited when Megan had Elaina and then Rudolph. He'd thought – *hoped* – that he finally had a chance to prove that he wasn't his father. And he'd always loved seeing the babies and small children in their village, though his mother had never allowed him to play with them out of some combination of snobbery and fear of his 'bad blood.'

But she and Megan hadn't so much as let him hold the babies or feed them or read them stories. David had let him hold Elaina as an infant – once – and had been reamed out for it by first wife and then mother-in-law far into the night, while the twelve-year-old Jason had hidden under a pillow and cried and tried not to listen. David's face had held a combination of mistrust, pity, and resignation the next morning when he saw Jason.

Jason had been sent to the castle as a page immediately after, and still had no idea why his mother had insisted he stay in Solway House when the rest of them came in to the city for the Summer social season, though it was probably about preserving the fiction of her perfect family.

Rudolph had been born a few years later; another hoped-for chance quickly proven otherwise.

And the stories Megan had told her children... by the time they were walking they shied away from Jason.

When Adam had brought him to Lynncrag, Martin had been seven and Marianna five... just a hair younger than Rudolph. They had claimed him as their 'other brother' and climbed all over him, demanding stories and attention. But by that time, at twenty-one years of age, and after Prince Oskar had built him up and broken him down and then rebuilt him to the Prince's own tastes and preferences... Jason was more than half-convinced his mother and sister were right about him.

He had treated Adam's littlest siblings like breakable glass, to the entire family's amusement.

After a few weeks, Jason had finally started to become more comfortable around the children... and then he and Adam had practically been thrown out of Lynncrag. And then Megan had the younger two children and it started all over again...

By the time Aryllis and Tim had Rico, Jason had not dared come close at all. And Adam's craving to be a parent scared him spitless.

Damien put his hands on Jason's knees. The tall knight had almost forgotten where he was and who else was there with him.

"You are in no wise to blame for *any* of it, Jason. I suppose I can understand Alexa and Megan's reactions," the King said reluctantly, "but they were still wrong to blame *you* and wrong to expect you to behave as your father did, especially when *they* had the raising of you. You, my friend, my *Champion* are a good person and worthy of every regard and honor we can heap upon you."

"And more than worthy to be the father of *our* child," Genny added. Damien nodded, and Jason – who had managed to persuade himself that he wouldn't be passing on his 'bad blood' to a prince or princess of the royal line – was brought up face to face with his own utter *un*worthiness for the role.

Not that they had anyone else they could ask.

Though... Damien *was* about to name Adam his Champion. Wouldn't that make the prophecy devolve onto *Adam?* To solve their 'Champion of a problem'?

Except... it wasn't Adam who was more than half in love – more than half *soul-bonded,* if Damien was right – to Genny. And Adam had even less interest in women than Jason did. Would he even be *able* to father a child with her? Even if it weren't rankest cowardice and unfair to heap his own troubles on poor Adam, who had put up with so much already...

And *that* wasn't even what Genny and Damien were worried about right now anyways...

Jason looked at them helplessly. "But you can see that I can't tell Mother or Megan 'no.'"

"I see no such thing," Damien retorted.

"*I* do..." Genevieve said softly, and the King turned to her in dismay. "Damien, love, Jason's been abused all his life by those women. And *he* still loves *them*. Maybe he shouldn't feel guilty – all right," she corrected herself at Damien's muffled protest, "he *definitely* shouldn't feel guilty. But they've trained him all his life to react like this. It took *me* years to shed what Harald did to me. This won't be a short path to tread... once he really *believes* he should be treading it at all." She gave Jason a very sympathetic look. "Adam's told you all these same things, hasn't he?"

Jason nodded, looking away to avoid Damien's compassionate silver gaze. "But what if they're right, and I *do* have 'bad blood'? What if I would... would *hurt* a child I had in my care?"

It was why he'd avoided training the pages and younger squires, making the excuse that until their skills were far enough along it was a waste of their time and his. He'd been able to make the argument stick due to his long absences with Genny; there really wasn't enough time during his short periods at home in Emeralsee to work with all the advanced squires and also train the Guards and help Damien, Genny, and Adam keep up their skills.

"Because you *haven't*," she told him bluntly. "You had *me* in your care that whole Summer and were never anything but a gentleman. And before you tell me that you were only a child as well, let me remind you that you were taller than some grown men at that point and you both outweighed me and outfought me. If you'd *wanted* anything else, you could have had it." She laughed. "And you don't know how many women have been shocked that all we did was swordplay."

"Well, not *all*." Jason felt himself blushing.

"Oh?" Damien's eyebrows had shot upwards.

Genny shrugged. "It was Summer, love. We climbed trees and swam in the beaver pond."

Jason coughed uncomfortably. "Naked. So we wouldn't get our clothes wet and torn. Her idea."

"I looked pretty much like a boy anyways at that age," she told Damien.

"Not... quite..." Jason muttered.

She grinned. "And here I thought you never noticed."

"You climbed trees naked?" Damien sounded fascinated, but Jason didn't dare look at him. "Didn't that hurt?"

"Not as much as the hiding I'd have gotten coming home with my fancy dresses all ripped to shreds," Genny said with a grin. "Not from Papa, but from my poor nurse who would have had to fix the things before he noticed... and would have had to explain how she hadn't known where I was, if Papa ever realized." Her grin grew broader as she added. "Papa never figured out why Storm was so well-behaved while we were in the City that Summer, either. He usually didn't take well to being kept up and Papa didn't have time to exercise him while we were here."

"Storm?" Damien asked.

"Duke Aldred's horse," Jason answered. "He was a fire-eater for anyone but Genny. She rode him out every day to the grotto. With me," he gave her a dry look, "on my little palfrey one step up from a pony."

Genny smirked and flung her braid back over her shoulder, as mischievous and irreverent and... *exquisite* as she'd been at twelve. "You couldn't ride Storm. You tried."

"Wait, a horse *Jason* couldn't ride?" Damien exclaimed, a look of mischief in *his* eye as well – and how, exactly, was a man to hold his own with these two ganging up on him, both of them as wonderful and kind and... *appealing* as...

Genny chuckled. "So, I guess there are *two* things he can't do wonderfully."

Damien blushed at that one, and Jason decided he didn't want to ask what that was about.

"Your Sunset is Storm's descendant, love," she commented and the young King looked enlightened.

Jason shuddered. "I knew there was something I didn't like about that horse."

Damien chuckled.

After a pause, the handsome young King asked tentatively, "Jason? Do you *want* to know who your father is? So you know the family and can see that there's no 'bad blood'? Just one... bad apple?"

Jason looked at his king. He'd put that idea aside so long ago. There had seemed no way to find out... "You... sound like you already know."

The younger man ducked his head in that *diffident* manner. "I had to find out what might come out of the woodwork to threaten the Realm, Jason. Just because your mother had the connection struck from the Solway family tree doesn't mean that you don't have aunts, uncles, cousins, grandparents and such who might suddenly come looking for favors once you're Heir. Or King. And it doesn't mean there aren't *clues* in the Archives. If you know how to look."

The blonde knight was all adrift again.

"I'd... understand if you didn't," Damien offered. "It wasn't until Genevieve made me that I visited my grandparents. They... I..." He stopped. But he'd told Jason about that before. Said he'd forgiven them. And maybe he had. But there was nothing left to build on.

Jason dropped his eyes again. Grandparents. Aunts, uncles, cousins. Who had never made any effort to contact him in thirty-four years. Perhaps *they* were ashamed of him as well. Even if his father was the only 'bad apple' in the family... Jason was still his father's son.

"They *tried* to contact you," Damien said, almost as if he was reading Jason's mind. Though he had promised once that he wouldn't. Or maybe that he couldn't. Probably this was merely the result of having his own estranged grandparents. He knew what Jason would want to know, because it was what *Damien* had hoped for.

"No, I haven't contacted them," the King went on. "I did some investigating. Letters were sent and returned unopened. There are records of such things, if one knows how to find them. And court proceedings – your uncle tried to get custody of you, or at least visitation rights."

Was there a slight, bitter emphasis on the word 'you'? But Damien was never bitter... even when he'd told Jason about how his own grandparents had repudiated him he'd been *sad,* not angry or bitter.

Jason felt even more lost. "So... *Aryllis* knows?"

Damien shook his head. "I have other ways to get information. No one you care about will know unless you want them to. Unless, of course, these other kin of yours try to claim you," he added dryly. "I have no way to control that *without* contacting them. Which I *won't* do without your permission."

Surely when most people received such potentially life-changing information they felt... something. Jason felt numb.

The King and Queen exchanged a glance.

"Take your time," Damien said quietly. "And do what you need to do to sort it out. I can manage without you until you're ready. Use my name if your mother or Megan – or Adam, for that matter – catches up with you before you're ready."

The King rolled to his feet, and left the suite, leaving Jason alone with Genny.

He... needed to spar. Jason's mind was always more clear when he had a swordblade in his hand. But the only people who could give him the sort of challenge that would occupy his mind sufficiently were Adam, Damien, and Genevieve. Adam was going to be engrossed with his family for the rest of the day. Damien had work to do. And Genevieve...

Jason looked at her and she gave him a steady look back.

"*I* think I'm ready to start rebuilding muscle tone," she said dryly. "But the three of *you* don't, and I certainly wouldn't be able to give you enough of a fight right now to free your mind." She knew him very well indeed. "You can stay and talk, or you can grab a few of the Guards and run them in circles."

The tall knight heaved a sigh. "Damien's not up to a real bout yet either. You both need to train with the Secret Cadre more than with me right now."

The Queen's eyes sparkled. "Is that a permission to do so?"

Jason just looked at her. "What do you think, Genny?"

She huffed, and pulled her legs up on the couch. "I'm not doing *anything* to delay this. *Or* to jeopardize the pregnancy once there is one. I want this done and over with as much as you do. More." Genny leaned her head back on the overstuffed arm of the leather couch. "Damien seems absolutely convinced I'm not going to survive. He's starting to make me think it might be true."

The knight frowned. "That's not a good way to start things."

She blew out a breath. "You're telling *me.*"

"He starts talking about these things more when the magickal tension starts getting to him, doesn't he?" Jason asked, distracted from his own conundrums by hers. "I noticed that you were being very careful not to touch each other."

Genny looked startled. "I... hadn't noticed that. But it might be true..." Her eyes darkened. "It hardly matters. We have eight days before the coronation. And then those three months are up. We can make it." Her mouth was firm with determination.

"Hmmn." He eyed her with what he hoped looked like skepticism and not an inordinate interest in the shape of her mouth. Because at the end of those three months...

She waved off his concern. "Bigger problems, Jason. Damien was absolutely serious about calling this whole thing off if he doesn't believe you can stand up to Countess Alexa."

The blonde knight gave her a wry look. So much for distractions. "I thought I was the candidate of last resort. He still needs an Heir. Who else can he pick?" And why hadn't he started with *them...?*

"Adam," was the Queen's prompt and startling reply. "Who wants this even less than you do."

"Oh." Yes, and it would be incredibly selfish to foist this off on his love, just as it would be to expect Adam to shoulder the weight of the prophecy when he took up the chain of the Champion. And it wouldn't get Jason out from under any of it, anyways. Prince-Consort to the Heir – or the King – would still put him in a position of power and influence that he most surely didn't want.

Genny nodded. "He'd still be stuck with your mother, but *he* has no problem saying 'no' to her." She chuckled. "Actually, I rather imagine he'll take an unholy glee in doing so. We were all rather lucky that he decided to take a different tactic yesterday, and that Damien got him out of there before he changed his mind."

Jason leaned forward and put his face in his hands. "I don't know what to do, Genny."

"I had eight years with Harald, Jason. You've had *thirty-four* with the Countess. Your relationship isn't going to change overnight." She snorted. "And *you* aren't going to find a catharsis by stringing her up on the Castle wall. At least, I hope not."

He shuddered. His mother was... impossible. But not a traitor.

"You have to be willing to try to believe this isn't about you, Jason," Genny said softly. "The rest of us can talk to you till we're blue in the face, but unless *you* are willing to try, it's not going to change anything." She paused. "It really isn't that hard to switch your part and Adam's in the coronation ceremony."

"I can't do that to him."

"Then you have to make peace with the idea that you're a good person who has been treated horribly by the people who should have taken best care of you." He looked up to see her blue-green eyes filled with sympathy. "I've been through it. Damien has. Even Adam has, though his story seems to be turning out better. Yours has gone for the longest and started the earliest. But think about the people who have helped you become the person you are *today* – the loving, thoughtful, intelligent person you are today. Think of your wet-nurse. Would *she* want you to think that you don't deserve to be loved?"

He looked back at the floor. He hadn't seen the woman since he was a very small boy, but...

"No," he admitted.

"And you've heard Damien's theory that it's pure chance that he and I are soul-bonded instead of you and I. I know, I know." She rolled her eyes. "It's probably one of the things that comes out as the *magickal* tension grows. Like thinking we're both about to die. But..."

She reached out across the short gap between sofa and chair and startled him as a trail of white sparks fizzed where her fingers touched his arm. Now Jason could see why it didn't bother her or Damien. The sparks felt... *good.* Better than *good.*

Genny withdrew her fingers and he felt a surge of disappointment.

"You said three months," she reminded him, but Jason could see her swallowing hard. "Damien... may not have been as wrong as I thought." She took a deep breath. "You know it was the soul-bond that helped convince the other leaders of the Rebellion that Damien was the king we hoped for... despite his *bad blood* as King Reginald's grandson."

Jason looked up sharply. "But Prince Eric–"

"Prince Eric was practically an unknown," she cut him off. "Princess Kandra was better known than her father, but even she had just begun to make her mark. When any of them – any of *us* – thought about Damien, the only hook we had to hang our thoughts on was his *grandfather.* And *we* weren't the only ones who felt that *any* option was better than a scion of King Reginald."

"I... hadn't realized it was that close," Jason admitted. Of course not. He'd concerned himself with Damien directly and left the scheming and politicking to Ciriis and Adam as much as possible.

Though surely it must have been, if Genny had felt it necessary to sneak off on her own to try to interview the new young King...

Genny – no, *Queen Genevieve* – nodded. "It was. But the soul-bond 'proved' Damien's good heart to those who needed proof." She tapped one finger on his arm again, eliciting another curl of white fire. "Can it do the same for you, dear Jason?"

Chapter SIXTEEN

Stresses

THE NEXT FEW DAYS WERE not any less frenzied, but Adam was happier than Damien could remember seeing him, and since the Royal Guards responded to their Captain's moods, the King found himself moving through an atmosphere of exuberance. It was a great spiritual lift, but even that could not alleviate the increasing stress he was under.

At least this time it was *only* the soul-bond. The Realm seemed satisfied for the moment, somnolent with early Winter and still surfeited with what he had been able to give it – with Jason's help – before.

And that left Damien the physical and magickal resources to deal with resisting the demands of the soul-bond. He'd taken to sleeping in the sitting room – discovering in the process that *both* of the leather sofas were really terrible for sleeping on. He couldn't have one replaced in the middle of everything else his poor chatelaine was dealing with for the coronation... or while Adam or Jason might notice.

He and Genevieve had never managed to abstain for so long. Part of Damien also couldn't help wondering if maybe, now that his beautiful wife's body had recuperated so much... maybe they *could* handle this without asking more of Jason and Adam...

When those thoughts started to seem more reasonable in the middle of the night, Damien made himself get up and go for a walk no matter how tired he was. Better than to blackout and wake in Genevieve's arms to discover the three months wait had all been for naught.

But he was counting down the days.

Occasionally the Guards on night duty were also on his training roster, though he'd never really trained with anyone other than Adam, Jason, and Genevieve before. It gave him something else to do in the middle of the night than wander – and it was giving his Guards a bit more respect for his own abilities. Damien was slowly but surely rebuilding strength and stamina, and he was all too aware of his vulnerability in case of an assassination attempt, notwithstanding Ciriis' accusations of his cavalier attitudes. There had actually been three such attempts since she left to 'take care of' his father-in-law – he had asked Aryllis not to tell Ciriis, knowing that she might feel obliged to return despite Aldred's need for her assistance.

Damien hadn't been sure if his request had been honored until Ciriis threw it in his face that there hadn't been any assassination attempts. It was nice to know where Aryllis' loyalties lay.

On the nights he could train, he returned to his chambers too tired to do more than close the door and collapse on the couch. Often without bothering about such niceties as removing his boots. On the other nights, he might wander the halls of the Castle for hours in order to reach the same state of exhaustion.

Ironically, as Damien wore himself out, Genevieve returned to the bloom of health. Or perhaps not so ironically, since her return to health was probably triggering the soul-bond's renewed demands.

The King was counting down the days, but it was a false count and he knew it. Once they had reached the day that... he didn't want to think about and couldn't help dwelling on... they would still have to wait to confirm that she was, indeed, pregnant. And every night until then, *Jason*...

Not to mention what a hypocrite he was to even be *thinking* like this...

It was enough to make him stare blindly into the darkness for *more* hours while his body was too worn to move. Rest for the body, but not the soul.

The result was that his focus was shot during the daytime as well. The thrice-weekly Royal Council meetings had been supplemented by *daily* Peer Council meetings – of the sworn and Bound nobles who were in attendance for the Heir's coronation – and side meetings with just about every other noble in the land. The friends he *actually* wanted to spend time with, such as Rosa and Zachary Miramar and even Tomas Elsevier and his lady, were looking at him with such concern that he felt he needed to avoid *them*, lest they ask questions which he could answer either honestly or accurately, but not both.

And to top it all off, Damien still had no real answer from Jason. Or rather *about* Jason. About whether he could stand up to Countess Solway such that the King felt safe placing the future of the Realm in Jason's hands. Not that even *he* knew for sure what would demonstrate Jason's independence sufficiently to reassure him.

Three days left before the *(probable? possible?)* coronation, and the only good thing Damien could find to consider was that he'd managed to avoid Countess Alexa Solway since her arrival except for the required greeting and that incident in the Great Hall with Adam.

He'd finally called a halt to the Council meetings until after the ceremony. The King simply couldn't focus on anything. He'd been called on a few times too often to weigh in on something consequential when he'd been daydreaming... *fantasizing*... about Genevieve and had no idea what had just been discussed. Damien knew that his friends among his noble peers were worried about him, but he had no answers to offer them just now; and there was no point in giving more ammunition to the ones that *weren't* his friends.

So, he was hiding out in his office – to which he had added a *new* ward.

Now, in addition to the ones preventing spying eyes and ears and magick, there was a longer strand that looped over matched pairs of hooks to actually *prevent* anyone else from entering. Three loops and it merely discouraged all but the most serious; five, and they would not be able to break down the door with a battering ram.

This last ward had become his favorite – despite Adam's contention about secretaries, he still didn't have one and with this office so much more accessible than his private one at the top of his tower, anyone and everyone tended to seek him out at any and all times. Which was what he wanted them to feel free to do... but maybe not just now when he already couldn't concentrate and there were triple the usual numbers of supplicants.

At least this new guarantee on his privacy was giving him a small respite. Even if Damien had felt too guilty to engage that higher level as of yet.

The piles of papers on his desk had grown significantly taller. His inability to focus and the greater social demands on his time – there were

Court banquets every night, for example – had left the reports to accumulate and him doing nothing about them.

Damien stared morosely at the slithery towers of papers just waiting to be knocked into complete chaos. It was going to take weeks to make up for this. *Weeks.* He put his head down on his arms in defeat. He was so *tired...* and it was taking all his effort simply not to fly up the stairs to Genevieve this very minute... or to 'vanish' himself there and not bother with the stairs at all...

Strong fingers began to massage the tension out of his shoulders, the knots so tight that even releasing them was painful. Painful, but so, so *good.*

Too good.

Damien came back to himself with a start.

"Jason. This isn't a good idea."

"You're as strung out as an addict missing their drug, Damien. This can't go on."

The King turned in his chair and looked up at the knight. "Yes. I am. And it won't. Just a few more days. I... only have so much willpower, Jason, and right now it's *all* going to prevent me from spoiling everything we've been waiting three months for."

The tall blonde man raised an eyebrow. "You're not the only one under stress here, you know. Has it occurred to you that *I* might need this?"

Damien choked on a laugh. *"You?* You have *Adam–"*

"Who hasn't touched me except passingly since his family arrived. It was supposed to be his three brothers sleeping in the outer room of our suite, but somehow Desirée's little boys have decided they belong there, too. The washroom is accessible only through our bedroom, and I understand it's much more convenient than the one down the hall, but it means that we leave the door unlocked, and they can wander in at all hours of day and night. And somehow our sitting room has *also* become the Loveress family breakfast room, and his parents are even earlier risers than *we* are..."

Jason looked nearly as harried as Damien felt. He'd grown up as the vastly younger of two children in a cold and strict household – the bustle and energy, and even the all-consuming *warmth* of the Loveress family was overwhelming to him, and the close quarters of the overstuffed Castle meant there was no place to get away.

Damien suddenly realized that he'd been finding Jason here in the office at all hours...

Jason, who *hated* reading reports.

216

"That doesn't sound at all romantic. Some guaranteed privacy is what *you* need!" Damien exclaimed. Perhaps there was a simple answer to at least this *one* thing.

Without bothering to wave or even blink, he transported both of them to Jason's bedroom. It was empty, luckily – he hadn't bothered to check ahead, his mind was so fuddled with exhaustion. The door was closed, of course, but the wards he'd given them so long ago were on the *outer* door of the suite and therefore not in the right position to protect this inner sanctum.

Damien fumbled in his pocket for a set of the hooks and threads he'd begun to carry everywhere, and began setting up a new set of wards that blocked only the bedroom and washroom. It was easy, even mindless, work for him now, and after just a moment he turned to his friend with a smile.

"They'll still need to use the washroom down the hall. I could try to create a second entrance for this one, but..."

Jason's eyes went wide and he quickly shook his head. Both of them – everyone in the Castle and half the City, actually, remembered what had happened the time Damien had tried some interior re-design by magick. Somehow his failures were always spectacular and public and his successes all too discreet; perhaps it was just lucky that the people weren't calling him the *Incompetent* Sorcerer-King.

Damien gave his Champion a lopsided grin. "I thought not. So, I gave you the same three wards as before, but I also added the new one I put on the office, so no one can barge in. And," Damien added shyly, "it's *longer.* Three loops to discourage, five to prevent entry entirely... and seven loops will even keep *me* from entering the way we did just now."

He'd added this extra as a matter of trust. Only Adam and Jason had a real idea that he could do this vanishing thing to get from place to place; he didn't want them to ever have to worry that he might interrupt their private time together.

And he was also hoping it would prevent Jason from expressing whatever disgust he might be feeling for having been subjected to the hateful magick again. Damien didn't think he had the energy to cope with that kind of rejection just now. He felt so tired and frazzled that he thought he might start crying – hardly the image of kingly dignity he should project, even with his closest friends.

It seemed to have worked. There was no distaste as Jason's eyes lit with interest and he came over to the door to examine the wards. Damien stepped back to allow the Champion to come closer to the objects of his observation.

"This may help," the knight admitted.

Damien sighed with tired relief. At least this *one* thing had gone all the way right, with no complications. "I'm sure Adam hasn't felt like being romantic with his mother right outside that door... Jason, *what are you doing?*"

The blonde knight was wrapping the long ward thread into place. Three loops. Five loops. Seven loops. Damien could feel each level of the new spells clicking into place.

"Testing something." Jason turned to face him. "That last level means you can't magick yourself in – or *out,* if I'm correct." He stepped towards the King with a certain look on his face.

"Jason..." Damien stepped back. No complications indeed. No such luck.

"I promised you a proper bed the next time, didn't I?" Jason's smile was... promising.

"Jason... that's *your* bed... and *Adam's...*" Damien took another step backwards, and another, and abruptly found himself *sitting* on the high edge of that very bed.

A spell. He needed a spell to get around Jason and then somehow figure out how to quickly unlatch the ward. That last one was tagged to require the person who set it to undo it... which had *seemed* a good idea at the time... maybe he shouldn't be inventing spells when he was this tired...

Damien cudgeled his tired brain for a way to get out of here without hurting his friend.

His Champion and Heir.

His sometime lover.

No.

Just a few more days...

"Damien, love," Jason said gently, patiently... just as he'd *always* been patient and gentle. Or, no, not *always,* but Damien hadn't at all minded the other night when gentleness had been superseded by something else. "*I* need this as much as you do. Wards or no wards, I don't think Adam is going to be comfortable with making love until his family is *gone.* And in the meantime, I'm dodging my *mother* and *Megan,* and now *Elaina* as well, *all* over the castle."

The tall knight's tone became a little less stressed-out and a little more... *wheedling?* "And then this damned *coronation...* I hadn't even realized you were handing over the duchy of Emeralsee to me as well, until I was looking over the details of the ceremony yesterday. The position of Heir is mostly ceremonial, but a duke-ship is an administrative position which I know nothing about."

That was guilt-inducing… Damien *had* more or less inveigled Jason into accepting the Heir's Ring and siring a child with Genevieve. This… *strong-arm* tactic to Crown him before the whole Realm and Bind him as Duke of Emeralsee had been both unfair and most likely unnecessary.

On the other hand, the King felt the trickling away of *time* all too keenly. If he'd taken the *time* to talk Jason around to this as well… there simply might not have been a *chance* for him to get everything straightened out. Jason would thank him posthumously, when his transition from duke to king was eased in the eyes of the Realm's fractious and untrusting noble class.

Not that that made it easier right *now.*

"It's traditionally part of being Heir to the Throne," he pointed out. "Besides, I thought you should be Bound to the land. Genevieve agreed that being Bound to Elaarwen made it easier for her to accept the rest of the Realm when she became Queen… And… Adam thought you could use the administrative experience."

Yes, put some of this on the other two. Maybe that would distract…

Oh. No, apparently not.

And apparently they really *should* have worked out something the other night to establish what sort of a 'no' really meant 'no.' Something simple, like a codeword, that Damien could manage before *exhaustion* and *tension*… and *desire* managed to overwhelm duty and *sense* and *responsibility.*

Damien swallowed hard as Jason stepped very close. Very, *very* close. Right up to the edge of the bed, in fact, and between Damien's knees.

The problem wasn't that he *didn't* want Jason to.

The problem was that he very much *did.*

"It might have been nice if you'd *asked* me." Jason might still be talking about the duchy of Emeralsee… but he was putting one hand on either side of the shorter man and leaning down…

Damien had to lean far back to dodge him. *Too* far back: the King found himself lying down on the mattress.

"Or if you'd at least *told* me what you were planning," Jason added.

He had Damien pinned now, their faces were only inches apart. The younger man cudgeled his tired brain to find some depths of willpower even as his breath became more rapid and shallow. Jason was still only leaning *over* him, the tall knight's weight was still mostly on his feet where he half-stood at the edge of the bed… but his hips were pressing against Damien's…

"I... was concerned you'd shut down again," the King said distractedly. "The way you've done about the coronation, getting married, finding out about your father's family..."

Yes, mention things that might distract *Jason* instead. *Upsetting* things, not *romantic* things...

Damien had sworn to himself not to take advantage of his friends any further than was necessary for the safety of the Realm. And Genevieve.

Although it wasn't really clear *who* was taking advantage of *whom* in this situation...

"Hmmn." Jason smiled, entirely *un*distracted, and leaned in that little bit more to give Damien a very enticing kiss. "It had nothing at *all* to do with being high-handed and manipulating all of us into doing your bidding all unknowing."

He punctuated each verb with another very... nice kiss.

Damien fought with himself over just giving in. "Jason..." The objection was largely meaningless when his arms had crept up around Jason's neck, a small part of him thought wryly. And when his legs had wrapped around Jason's.

"One last time, my Damien," Jason murmured. "And I show you how to do those things I did with you last time. You owe me that."

Well, he wasn't sure if *that* really made sense, but the word 'owe' reminded Damien that he *owed* Jason almost everything. In a weird complement to the way his Champion could not tell Countess Alexa 'no,' neither could Damien refuse Jason.

Not that he wanted to.

"One last time," he conceded.

In the washroom, Adam sat on the floor, covering his ears.

He'd heard them come in, with some consternation. Then been deeply touched by Damien's gift of another set of wards... although the reason for them was hard to hear. He hadn't realized Jason was feeling so neglected. And the last ward, the new one, had seemed rather dangerous. His strategist's mind had immediately seen the possibilities and the idea of his bedroom turned into the only prison cell that could hold his king was not appealing.

Adam had been drying his hands and about to step out into the larger chamber and point that out when it became clear that his lover – his *fiancé*, by all the Gods at once, and his *bridegroom* in just three more days – had come to the same conclusion, but had an entirely different idea about what that ward was good for. And then it had suddenly been *far* too late to come out where they could see him.

And so, he was stuck. Unable even to close the washroom door more securely – all the hinges of their doors creaked like mad, a security measure Adam had once thought useful and was now seriously re-thinking.

He'd known Damien was attracted to Jason. He'd observed the young prince's infatuation without concern from the earliest days, knowing from personal experience that Jason practically had to be hit over the head to notice such things and that the shy boy would never dare. It had even seemed *useful,* since Damien would fall all over himself to do things that *Jason* asked him to try, when he just sat in frozen terror at anyone else's request. It seemed to have faded away as such things usually did, but he hadn't been terribly surprised, when Genevieve had explained what the *next* part of the problem was, that Damien hadn't seemed particularly distressed. *Embarrassed,* yes; *upset,* no.

Adam hadn't been terribly *happy* when they disappeared to the grotto for a week, but figured it was better than ending up there himself, since that would leave Jason with Genevieve. The pair of *them* being alone together for several days seemed as likely to set back the Grand Plan as leaving Damien with her. And it was all too obvious that their margin for error in getting his dear friends through the next year *alive* was… razor-thin.

He knew Jason had enjoyed himself on the trip, but his love had been just as enthusiastic to come home, so he'd put it aside. With Oskar… Jason had had more than enough negative experiences. If this had to happen, he would just as soon his love had a good time.

The night Damien had lifted every piece of glassware in the Realm by three inches – several enterprising souls had actually had the presence of mind to measure – Adam had been as terrified as anyone else. More, possibly, since with all the reading about magick he'd done at Damien's side, he probably had a better idea than anyone else of what his younger friend's unintentional potential to wreak havoc might be.

Not that he'd dared show Damien anything but his own usual sarcastically serene exterior. The King needed – always – to have at least one person who took his magickal abilities in stride. Adam had picked up hints that that wasn't going to be Jason. It usually *was* Genevieve, but not *that* night… and perhaps not the rest of the time as much as Adam had thought, based on the almost pathetic look of gratitude the young King had given him when Adam had been so blasé about it all the next day.

That night, however, Adam had had his hands full, quite literally, with the overwrought Queen.

When Genevieve had flung herself *away* from Jason and *to* him, Adam had been baffled and frustrated. When he'd realized that it had been because she and Jason were both so attracted to each other that she didn't dare stay in Jason's arms... the Captain had eventually been hurt and angry. But he hadn't yet reached hurt and angry when he'd sent Jason to do 'whatever' he had to do to calm their king down. He'd sorted himself out after his desperate ploy had worked to shock Genevieve out of the hysterical sobs that were wracking her fragile body and his poor, sick friend had fallen asleep in his arms.

It wasn't Jason's fault that he had some sort of animal attraction to Genevieve, or even vice versa. It was a *good* thing – it meant that they would actually have a child of their *own*.

He'd fallen for *that* idea at the very beginning. After all, Adam had been trying to talk Jason into adopting a child for several years now. He knew exactly why Jason had been chary of the idea – damn those Solway women and Jason's mysterious father anyways – and he figured that the only way to get Jason over the fear would be to actually have a child of their own, impossible as that seemed. He knew that Jason loved children... but it was always easy to say 'later.'

What had kept Adam patient over the matter was the *Visions* that he'd had.

It was a gift in the Loveress line to *See* a little bit into the future. A help for parenting, his mother had called it, back when the worried and confused Adam had confided in her that he was having 'hallucinations' about Damien, back when they'd brought the prince to Lynncrag so long ago. Now that they were on speaking terms again, his little sister Desirée had confirmed that she had also *Seen* her boys well before they were born; even before she'd found her husband, actually. Mostly these consisted of things that had to do with preventing minor childhood disasters – his mother had told Adam of knowing when to send someone out to rescue him from a tree when he was five, for example, and Desirée had funny stories about keeping her boys from stealing the freshly churned butter.

Adam suspected that *Seeing* her children's true loves well in advance of meeting them was part of the gift... When the conversation had come up with Desirée, Mama had flickered a guilty look at Jason.

Well, guilty and *confused,* and Mama's reactions to Damien – and now to Genevieve – were making all too much sense. Adam hadn't dared confide any details of his own *Visions* once she'd reassured him that he wasn't losing his mind… not twelve years ago in Lynncrag and definitely not *now.*

Adam *knew* that the golden-haired little girl that Genevieve would bring to birth was his and Jason's daughter… he'd *Seen* her for years, though not her mother (possibly because he'd not wanted to *look).* And then there were the others he'd *Seen:* an energetic and anxious black-haired boy; an all-too-serious little girl with hair just as dark and eyes that same intense, almost magickal, silver as Damien's; …and a boy with light brown hair who seemed contented enough, but who always made Adam's heart contract with worry when he appeared in the *Visions.*

Damien and Genevieve's other children, presumably, who would surely be as dear to him as the first. Even if they would all grow up calling him only 'uncle'… they'd still be *his.*

He would know.

And then… there were the *visions* he'd had about Damien himself…

No, he'd been able to set aside his first, negative reaction about the King and Queen's problem… And then his reactions to the *other* problems that came from trying to solve *that* one… And Damien's attraction to Jason… And even Jason's attraction to Genevieve. He'd more or less *known* that these things were coming, after all (though somewhat less than more, since *Seeing* wasn't a terribly reliable guide until the context came clear, either in the *Vision* or in realtime).

Each piece had made sense at the time, but put altogether like that, it seemed far less reasonable to accept.

And now that he knew that *Jason* was also attracted to *Damien…*

The cynical, prickly Captain of the Royal Guard sat on the floor in his washroom, covering his ears – for all the good it did – and not even noticing the tears that rolled down his cheeks or that he rocked back and forth in misery.

They weren't trying to be quiet – why bother, with the wards up? And even with his ears covered, Adam could hear far too clearly what was going on. That Jason was… *teaching* Damien… *things.* Things that he could only have learned from *Prince Oskar.* Things he had never shared with *Adam.*

After too long – *far* too long – the noises from the bedchamber ceased. No, not ceased. Became quieter, deeper… lower. Pillow-talk. But at least it was an indecipherable murmur. Adam closed his eyes, resting his chin on his chest, and waited some more.

Giggles. *Giggles?*

"Jason, stop!" The King's voice was breathless with laughter, warm and relaxed in a way Adam had never heard it before. Full of... love. And Adam's heart constricted – again – in ways that he didn't want to think about.

"You can't fall asleep here, Damien. We have to get you back to your office. And you can't exactly walk out the door *here...*" Practical, practical Jason. Whose voice was *also* warm with love... a timbre to that voice that Adam had thought *he* was the only one to ever hear.

"I know, I know. Just let me put some water on my face so I'm not quite so sleepy. Then I can transport us both back. Once *you* undo the *ward,"* and the King's tone went very dry.

A deep chuckle. "You don't expect me to believe you actually minded."

"No-o-o..." The reluctant smile was almost audible. Or perhaps *not* so reluctant. "But that was a sneaky trick to play when I was trying to give you a gift. And you know I'm too tired to think straight."

"Oh, that was a *gift* all right..."

"Jason..."

"Just trying to keep the glassmaker's guild from profiting off the rest of us, Damien."

"Hunh."

There was nowhere to hide in the washroom. Adam didn't bother to get up.

Damien opened the door and stepped in... and saw him immediately. Exhausted or not – and, even in his own distress, Adam couldn't help noting the dark circles under his king's eyes, he'd been looking after the younger man for so long – Damien's quick mind instantly realized what had happened. His eyes went wide and apologetic...

...and then something changed, and a look of decisiveness came into his face as he pulled the door all the way shut behind him. That too-*focused* silvery gaze that so many found disconcerting...

The King knelt quickly down, cupped his hands around the Captain's tear-streaked face, and kissed him. With a passion Adam had never tasted from anyone but Jason.

"It was never just about Jason," Damien whispered, his eyes still shining.

Then he stood up, splashed some water on his face, dried his hands, and left the washroom, not looking back at his baffled Captain.

Baffled and... not. Damn those *Visions.*

"Ready, Jason?"

"Are you sure you aren't going to get us stuck in a wall somewhere or drop us in the Great Hall or something? You still look pretty out on your feet."

"Since I left the Monarch's Blade in the office, it's not like we have a lot of choices."

Silence.

Empty silence.

Adam stayed still for what seemed a long time.

For the first time, he understood how Jason could just... shut down. Too many different emotions at the same time was... numbing.

At last, Adam stood up, stretching carefully as he unfolded his long limbs. He had too many old injuries and scars from battles fought to ever not need to stretch after a period of stillness. A problem Jason was somehow still spared – but then Adam had actually seen more real warfare than his lover.

His fiancé.

Was he really?

Still?

Adam clung to the strange numbness. Once it dissolved, he didn't know whether he'd be raging or weeping... and neither emotion would get him through the rest of his duties for the day.

He'd only come back to the suite to get... oh, yes. Some papers he had brought back a few days ago that he needed to turn over to Tim. Who was supposed to meet him in his office to go over them. Since Tim would be taking over the role of Captain of the Guard *tomorrow*.

Adam washed his hands again by rote, then stepped into the bedchamber. It was exactly as he'd left it this morning – clearly Jason had made the bed while Damien... washed his face.

He found the papers and went to the door, lifted his hand to open it. And stopped.

The fourth ward hung long and loose.

A trap for his king. A trap for his heart.

Never again.

Adam pulled out his belt-knife and sawed off the end of the cord. Enough to prevent those last two loops from ever being used again. The remainder of the cord began to fray in his hand... then abruptly re-braided itself and developed a singed tip that bound the fibers from unraveling. *(In his office, just past the verge of falling asleep as he lay on the couch, Damien smiled.)*

The tall, blonde Captain grimly folded the few inches of cut cord into his fist and stalked out to meet with the man who was to take the position he had held for five years.

Chapter SEVENTEEN

Politics

Jason gazed with bemusement down at his sleeping king. He had already tucked a blanket around the slightly younger man. Something about watching Damien sleeping always drew him back to those first days, when he was still trying to tame the half-feral young prince. Perhaps he looked younger in his sleep; though that small, neat beard he'd grown recently should have aged him, somehow it did the opposite in Jason's opinion.

So *that* was the last time. He'd tried not to think about that while they made love. To pretend that they had all the time – all the *times* – in the world.

Some of it, he acknowledged, was fear – he spent more time with Damien than with anyone else these days and was all too aware that the younger man was convinced he wouldn't see the end of this sixth year of his reign. Jason feared he was right – either by poor luck or by believing it into happening. He also feared the thought of becoming king himself.

Or even 'just' Duke of Emeralsee.

That had been a shock, when he'd been reviewing the order of events with Aryllis in her role as Mistress of Protocol and seen his investiture as Duke listed. He thought – he *hoped* – that he'd covered his reaction. He should already have known about this.

Damien's – and apparently Genevieve's and Adam's.... why was he the last to know? – reasoning was sound, Jason had to admit. The King's ability to govern had been severely limited in the beginning because, although he'd held the title of Duke of Emeralsee, everyone knew that the old king had not allowed Damien to actually rule his own province. No more than King Reginald had given an ounce of real power to any of his previous Heirs.

Jason didn't try to pretend he had the combination of gifts and preparation that had worked for Damien in the end – the prodigious memory and the library he had read, the ability to see connections, the blazing compassion... the magick.

No, Jason would have to learn to rule the hard way, as he had done everything else. Practice, practice, practice, until there was no one better than him.

He eyed the piles of paper on Damien's desk with distaste. There *had* to be another way to do this. Damien's approach was to inhale every bit of information about everything, somehow match completely unrelated facts, and then explain the connections to everyone else. It was a feat Jason knew he could never replicate.

Perhaps he could talk to Tomas Elsevier. Or Rosa and Zachary Miramar. Learn how they managed their provinces.

A knock at the door surprised him. He'd disengaged the top level of what he'd privately nicknamed the 'thou shalt not enter' ward, but left it on the 'discourage' setting when Damien transported them back. 'Discourage' was a bit of a misnomer; would-be visitors whose needs were not urgent would simply remember somewhere else they had to be.

Adam stuck his head around the door and Jason felt his entire being light up at sight of his love. His soon-to-be-husband. Just three more days...

But Adam clearly had something else on his mind and barely glanced at him. "Where's Damien?"

"Asleep." Jason indicated the deeply sleeping King on the couch.

Adam walked all the way into the room and looked down at Damien sardonically, still not paying Jason any attention. He seemed to have something clenched in his hand that his fingers were fidgeting with. "For the first time in a while, to look at him. And to judge by the reports I've been getting from the Guards on night duty."

"Hmmmn. Speaking of which, weren't you meeting with Tim Ancellius this afternoon?" Jason asked. "The Changing of the Guard is tomorrow, isn't it?"

A spiral of disappointment wended its way down his spine as Adam seemed far too preoccupied for his hopes. With Damien so deeply asleep, they were effectively alone, as they hadn't really been since Adam's family arrived. Surely it was a moment to take advantage of for at least a *kiss*... but it was busy days for all of them. If Adam had too much else on his mind right now and needed to be all business, Jason could live with that. They had all the rest of their lives together, after all.

Though thank all the Gods for the little stress-relief session with Damien, or he'd be gritting his teeth to avoid tackling Adam right then and there.

Adam grunted. "Tim and Aryllis have things in hand. There's something to be said for having the direct commanders of both halves of the Guard literally in bed together. I've had a devil of a time getting Aryllis' attention for the past *month* to arrange for combined training sessions for the regular Royal Guards and the Secret Cadre, and for her people to train Damien and Genevieve. *Tim* has it set up already."

Jason chuckled. "So, what were you looking for Damien to deal with, then?"

The Captain shook his head. "Some nonsense with Count Emery and Duchess Laura. It can wait if he's finally getting some rest." It wasn't Jason's imagination; Adam's expression softened as he looked at their sleeping sovereign. Damien had been their first concern for fifteen years after all... it would have taken a harder man than his gentle love to not have a special place in his heart for the young King.

But Jason couldn't suppress a sigh as the reminder of politics caught up with him. As Heir, this was his mess to deal with, too... or so Damien was likely to point out once he woke up. "Alpinsward and Seasbourne don't even share a boundary and their economies are entirely unlinked. What can those two possibly have to bring to the King's attention?"

Adam gave him a sardonic look. "Well, well. And haven't *we* become the expert all of a sudden."

Jason gestured to the teetering piles of reports. "Read enough of those and you, too, will know every useless detail about the Realm."

"I've at least skimmed most of them," his love replied, to Jason's surprise. "It was *me* trapped in here with Damien for all that time you were hobnobbing about the countryside with Genevieve, if you recall. And *me* voting on the Royal Council. I get my own copies of most of these." He raised an eyebrow at the mess of towering piles of paper. "Though I haven't let *my* desk become completely swamped like this. And I've never seen his get *this* bad." He gave Jason a speculative look. "It's even worse than when I was in here a week ago."

The Champion-cum-Heir raised his hands in a gesture of surrender. "It's not my fault. He hasn't been able to focus on anything for days. He reads for a minute or two, then jumps up to do something else. You've seen him at Royal Council meetings. He was even worse in the Peer Council." Jason smiled ruefully. "I *think* I'm the only one who could see what he was doodling while everyone spoke. The decorated D's and G's linked together were rather sweet... but he's a better artist than I would have guessed and you know his memory. Every noble in the Realm doesn't need to see what Genevieve looks like undressed."

"Just y*ou?*" Adam suggested, his tone dripping sarcasm.

Jason flushed. "Not me either." No, him *seeing* her undressed wasn't what they were all waiting for. "So, what *is* the problem between Alpinsward and Seasbourne?"

The other knight gave him a look that said he wasn't fooled at all by the change of topic. "It's not between their *lands,* Jason. Count Emery claims he has a betrothal contract between the Duchess and his second son. Duchess Laura, of course, has long since married and has three children."

Jason tilted his head. "So, what does Count Emery want? The return of a dowry or something?"

Adam sighed. "If only. He wants the King to declare the Duchess' marriage invalid, and require her to marry his son. The son, by the way, looks less than enthusiastic about all of this, though he admits to a lasting fondness for Laura from when they were children. He spent several years living in Alpinsward as I understand it. Even before they rejoined Ilseador."

The Heir frowned. "The validity of Laura's marriage was one of the articles of the treaty."

His love nodded ironically. "However, marriages between two women – or two men – and the offspring thereof, have never otherwise been formally acknowledged in this Realm."

Jason felt the light dawning. "Until *we* get married in three days. Which is why the Count wants this settled now." He gave Adam a sideways glance. "And how *you* got involved, I assume. Duchess Laura came to you?"

Adam gave him a dry look. "Well, with you, Damien and Genevieve *all* so difficult to get a hold of... apparently *I'm* the next best option." He glanced out the window. "Speaking of which, it's getting late. If we're going to let His Majesty catch up on sleep, then *you* better go out and play host for this evening's banquet."

"I – *what?*" That took Jason unawares.

Adam gave him a deeply sardonic look. "Part of the duties of the Crown Prince, Jase. You probably have just enough time to get a wash and change into some of those fancy new clothes you've been acquiring."

Jason had just about wrapped his head around serving as proxy for Damien in Council. Filling in for his *social* duties... was something he hadn't yet thought about. At all.

Adam's look grew dryer still. "Surely you aren't going to object to taking Damien's place by *sitting* in his *chair,* Jason."

He seemed... irritated. And that surely wasn't meant to refer to the plan that Jason would take Damien's place with Genevieve to sire a child... was it? They'd talked about that, moved past it... hadn't they?

The Champion – for another few hours anyways – still hesitated. "One of us should make sure no one comes in and wakes him up."

Adam waved dismissively. "There's two Guards at the door. Granted Sir Drake isn't the brightest on the block, but even he will keep people out if I tell him the King is not to be disturbed."

"No... I mean one of us should be here if he wakes up." Jason looked at his love seriously. "They're sparking off each other again, Adam. That's why he hasn't been sleeping. He's been trying to wear himself out so he hasn't the energy to get to Genevieve. After a rest..."

Not to mention that while Jason doubted Damien's fears of abandonment would be triggered by waking up alone in his own office... it was still a cruel thing to do if it wasn't necessary. And being cruel to Damien was pretty far from his agenda – ever, but especially right now after...

The Captain's mouth twisted as if he was biting back something else he wanted to say. Instead, he waved again and thumped down into a chair. "Fine. *I'll* stay. Go on. That dinner won't wait for you. Except it has to." He looked without favor at the overpiled desk. "I'm sure there's *some* report here I haven't read yet... and should... if I can just figure out which *one...*" he muttered. He began to idly twiddle with whatever was still in his hand while glaring at the mounds of papers.

"The newest ones are on the pile to the far left," Jason told him and headed out.

Chapter EIGHTEEN

Motherly Love

JASON MADE IT INTO THE banquet hall – bathed and changed into one of what he privately thought of as his 'Crown Prince costumes' – just a little late. The company was assembled, but no one had begun to complain yet at the King's absence. Jason took a deep breath and strode to Damien's place at the high table.

"His Majesty begs your indulgence, but he is otherwise occupied tonight," Jason announced. "He has asked me to serve as your host in his absence." He sat down with no further ado, and nodded to Madame Elista to send in the servers.

"Is Damien all right?" Rosa asked quietly from his right. The Duchess of Dalzialest – and the last-before-Jason to wear the Heir's Ring – was a close friend as well, and had been spending most of her time with Genevieve. Her concern was genuine… and she would also be one of the people most likely to be able to guess about the Secret Plan to cope with Genny's miscarriages.

Jason nodded. "He's actually just napping. He hasn't been sleeping well lately and when he finally fell asleep, Adam and I decided to let him stay that way."

"Simply poor sleep?" Duke Tomas inquired. "That's a relief. He's been acting so fey lately… usually Damien has every last detail at his fingertips."

Jason gave the Duke a polite smile, but Rosa answered before he had to think up a reply. "I'm sure he's just been worried about Genevieve. Zachary didn't sleep much more than I did during my last trimester with Betha, and all I was dealing with was a very sour stomach." She smiled at her husband seated beside her.

Jason relaxed as the soup was served… but as soon as the server had stepped away, Rosa went on.

"When is Genevieve going to join us at table, Jason? I've been up to see her every day since we arrived, and she seems more restless than ill to me. But she said something dry about needing *your* permission. Not *Damien's,* which would have been odd enough…" The dark-haired Duchess raised a curious eyebrow.

"Damien deferred to my judgment on how healthy she really is," Jason heard himself saying glibly. "He feels he's too close to have an unbiased opinion. Though I'm not sure *I'm* unbiased, having had to carry her out of the negotiating tent after so many collapses," he admitted. "I'm erring on the side of caution. We'll bring her down for the various ceremonies, of course."

"Hmmn," Rosa did not look entirely convinced.

"Including for the Changing of the Guard tomorrow?" Tomas asked. "She's been close with both Sir Loveress and Sir Ancellius since the beginning of Damien's reign. Surely, she won't want to miss that."

Jason blinked. He hadn't thought of that.

He was saved from having to decide on the spot by a commotion at the end of the high table.

"You will make space for me," his mother was saying imperiously to a harried looking server. "I will have a seat beside my son, the Crown Prince." She brushed past the poor man, heading towards Jason at the center of the table.

He could feel the eyes of the entire room on him as Countess Alexa Solway strode past the dukes and duchesses of the Realm to demand that one of *them* be removed from the high table in order to seat *her.* Jason's stomach was full of butterflies.

"Don't rise." Tomas's fingers barely brushed his arm, and his words barely reached Jason's ear. "Don't turn until she asks for your attention. Polite but firm. Whatever you say, we'll all do without complaint."

Jason didn't dare so much as blink at the unexpected advice and support. His mother was at his chair.

"Jason."

He took a deep breath and started to turn.

Rosa beat him to it. Again.

"I believe you meant to say 'excuse me, Your Highness,'" she informed the steely-eyed Countess. On his other side, Tomas' fingers pressed down on Jason's arm.

"I was addressing *my son*, Your Grace," his mother bit out.

"Of course, Countess Solway. But in this time and this place you are also addressing the Heir to the Throne. You would not wish to reduce his prestige in any way, I am sure." Rosa sounded as serene as ever. She had hit upon it, however. Jason's mother was depending on his new position to elevate hers – something she had thusfar been stymied at since he had not been attending these dinners, nor been much in evidence about the castle at all.

There was a moment of grimly awkward silence.

"Your Highness, I request a moment of your time." Her tone denied the respect in her words, but it was a small victory. Pity that the victory wasn't his.

Jason turned in his seat and was startled to see one of the Royal Guards nervously barring her from approaching him too closely – with bared steel. They did that for Damien and Genevieve of course; a monarch was particularly vulnerable while eating in public, and even the high-backed, throne-like chair could only do so much to prevent assassination attempts without vigilant guards.

"Mother," Jason said politely. "Is there something you need?" He motioned to Sir Everett to lower his blade and allow his mother to come closer. Though for a brief instant he had felt a huge sense of reprieve at that sharp, shining barrier.

"It is not meet that the mother of the Crown Prince be seated so far from him. Kindly have the servants rearrange things." Hunh. He hadn't been aware that the word 'kindly' was in her vocabulary. Although she did seem to have a different definition of it than he did.

No more *sotto voce* advice from Tomas, but he could feel the Duke of Siovale's eyes... along with those of the entire hall. Rosa's face was serene, but Zachary beyond her showed a brief flash of concern.

The high table was filled with dukes and duchesses, ambassadors of foreign powers, and a small handful of Guildmasters and Master Merchants of undeniable wealth and economic power. Even the members of Damien's Royal Council had been demoted to lesser tables as the high Peers of the Realm had been gathered. If the Countess had made her not-*entirely*-unreasonable request prior to everyone being seated, instead of waiting halfway through the soup course, it might have been possible to accommodate her. Now, however...

"No, Mother."

Countess Alexa looked at him without comprehension for a moment. Apparently, *she* couldn't recall the last time he'd said 'no' to her either.

It gave him time to extend his answer. "You may apply to Lady Aryllis Ancellius to see if your request can be accommodated at a future meal."

"*Jason...*" There was a muffled noise from Rosa, and his mother glared at the younger woman. "Your *Highness*. Surely you want to reconsider."

Part of him most definitely did. Her tone promised nothing but suffering for him in the future. But he was not here as Jason Solway, the Countess' little-regarded son. He was here as Damien's Heir. And there was no one he could reasonably ask to leave the high table to make space for her.

"No, Mother." He turned back to his soup, feeling her anger radiating at him. Tomas' fingers tapped his arm once more and he flickered a glance at the Duke. Tomas made a small flicking motion with his fingers. It took Jason a second to realize that he had not dismissed his mother to return to her seat. Which she could not do without permission after addressing him in his official capacity.

There was no way to make this better. He turned his head back over his shoulder. "You should return to your seat, Mother. Your soup will be cold."

"*Jason Solway,*" she seethed, though too quietly for any but the very closest to hear. "*You would rather sit here between these traitors than beside the mother who sacrificed and stayed a loyal vassal that* **you** *might have no taint of treason upon* **your** *House and thereby earn* **your** *shield?*"

Jason decided that the best answer was none at all.

His mother stormed off the dais a long moment later. She did not return to her seat.

His sister looked daggers up at him while Megan's husband resolutely nibbled away at his soup. Megan, too, stormed away after a moment. David looked up at Jason in brief apology and returned his attention to his food. His oldest daughter, Elaina, looked torn, but stayed at her father's side, casting confused glances up at her uncle.

"Good lad," Tomas said quietly after the soup was cleared away and while they waited for the next course. "The family you're born to can make life... difficult."

Words of wisdom indeed from the man who had been magickally mind-controlled to support his cuckoo's chick half-brother in an all-too-successful, if brief, bid for the throne.

The Duke of Siovale took his lady's hand on his arm and smiled at her before looking back at Jason. "The family you *choose* should make your life easier."

"Thank you for your... help," Jason murmured.

Tomas shrugged. "Ah, mothers. Pray you that you need not deal with yours as I had to mine."

Rosa leaned forward to look at him. "I never did hear how that fell out, Tomas."

The glance she threw at Jason suggested that she was diverting the conversation to spare him. They'd all lived through the Usurpation five years ago, after all. Though there *had* been such a number of traitors to deal with that it was possible she'd missed this detail. Dowager Duchess Lydia Elsevier's disposition hadn't been of primary importance.

The Duke of Siovale sighed. "Had she been a hapless pawn of King Reginald and Lord Prydeen, I could have appealed to the King to give her an amnesty. As it was... she had made it clear since Harald was born that she expected something more of him than was due a second son. She was furious when our... *my* father would not send him to become a knight, and she spoiled him until he became that pleasant creature we all 'knew and loved.' She was pleased when I gave him in marriage to Elaarwen, referring to Genevieve as a 'princess' and therefore a fit bride for her son. When I made it clear that the marriage was to cement Siovale's entry into the Rebellion... she was *beyond* furious."

"So... what happened when you came home after..." Jason hesitated, not wanting to refer to the Duke's spellbound support of his half-brother's attempt on Damien's throne. "After you swore to Damien?" he finished.

Tomas gave him a sly look. "You have some potential beyond swordwork, lad. I'd not have expected such diplomacy from Evan Eldridge's son – nor Alexa Solway's, to be honest. But they do say such things can skip a generation. And you've been our fair Queen's right hand through all these long negotiations to restore the Lost Provinces. Seems you picked up a few things."

The sharp-eyed Duke somehow seemed to miss Jason's shock, as he heard his father's name for the first time in his life, and simply went on with his tale. "Mother... was preparing to join us in the capitol. To live the life of the Queen-Mother. If Sildra and the children hadn't pled for her life..." His eyes glinted, but he smiled again at his wife. "But they did. And the King granted it. We shut her up in a tower in Castle Elsevier. Anything she wanted, except her freedom. She died a few months ago."

"I'm... sorry." Jason felt that piece of information should have been in one of the many reports. Perhaps it was, just buried under the rest. He'd have to see if Adam had caught it.

"*I'm* not," Tomas said bluntly. "My father... we buried her without a fuss, but not in the plot he'd reserved for her. She got the unmarked grave she deserved, as a traitor to Siovale and to our true king."

"The whole concept of treason is... complicated for our generation," Rosa mused. "Was it treason to join the Rebellion or to support the tyrant destroying the Realm?"

Jason looked down uncomfortably at his food. His mother's staunch support of King Reginald – which had put her at such odds with her childhood friend, Duke Aldred – had given him the opportunity to become a knight, to find Damien, to help the prince grow into a man and a king. But her support had quite possibly extended his reign, hurting countless people. He had grown up a 'king's man' and would have fought in the Battle of Siovale *against* Tomas and Genevieve had Prince Oskar not prevented him. Adam *had* fought in that battle. And so had many others here tonight.

On one side or the other, anyways.

Jason didn't feel like that sort of discussion was fit for the table yet, but Rosa seemed to feel differently.

And perhaps Tomas didn't either.

The Duke of Siovale snorted with amusement. "Kind of you to put us into *your* generation, Rosa, when I've sons nearly your age – or at least His Majesty's."

His glance told Jason he'd thrown that out there to change the conversation and save the new Crown Prince from having to say anything on the issue of who counted as a traitor. The younger man was beginning to wonder how he would have survived this dinner without Tomas.

Duchess Sildra leaned forward to see Rosa. "Speaking of children, where are yours, Rosa?"

The younger woman's smile said that she knew she was being diverted, but for this topic was willing. "They're in our quarters. We have a wet-nurse for Betha – there are just too many times when I'm simply not available."

The older Duchess nodded. "I suppose it made some things easier, when the children were so small, that I was merely Tomas' consort, and not duchess in my own name. It's almost hard to remember now... though Gary is only seven, so I suppose it's not all *that* long ago." She smiled at her husband. "And a bit of an exaggeration to suggest that Mark is close in age to the king. He's twenty," she confided to the others at the table. "Closer in age to dear Duchess Laura and her sweet wife."

She dimpled at the pair of women farther down the table beyond Zachary Miramar, who had been chatting with the Head of the local Metreedi branch-House and the Pardasian ambassador.

Duchess Laura looked over quickly at the sound of her name.

"I had hoped to speak to His Majesty, Your Highness," she called down the length between them. "But *you* were there when the Queen negotiated the treaty with us. You might actually be more familiar with it than he. Has Captain Loveress had a chance to acquaint you with the situation?"

"Yes," Jason admitted. "And my... initial thoughts are in your favor. Their Majesties are unlikely to make any ruling which endangers the status of Alpinsward as a province of this Realm. But we'll have to look at the legal precedents and see what can be done to satisfy... um..." He wasn't sure what to call the other party in the matter and he didn't want to name Count Emery such that the man would take note and try to turn the banquet into the forum for hearing his complaint. Surely Jason's mother doing so was bad enough.

Duchess Laura and her wife both beamed at him.

Tomas chuckled. "When our young king wakes up, he's going to have some catching up to do."

Jason gave him a sideways glance. "Why?"

"You're making policy right and left, lad. *First,* you made it clear that Countess Solway may be your mother, but she's not going to displace any of the other Peers of the Realm. *Now,* you've basically stated that Damien will throw out a betrothal document – presumably a legal one – in favor of keeping one of the Lost Provinces." With that expression of worldly-wise amusement, Tomas looked every inch the grizzled warrior and senior politician that he was in this experience-denuded Realm, for all that he wasn't a full decade older than Jason.

Duchess Sildra reached across her husband and patted Jason's hand in her motherly way, and the tall knight was mortally certain that his panic was visible on his face. "There's not much else you could have done, dear. Don't worry about it. Damien would almost certainly have done the same."

Almost.

Jason had been at Damien and Genevieve's elbows while they ruled and negotiated... and no one had ever paid attention to him before. How had they ever managed to get through a meal without accidentally causing a war?

He wanted to put his head in his hands, but the next course was appearing. How much longer could this banquet last anyways?

Rosa and Zachary had been having a whispered conference. She turned back to Jason with a rueful look.

"Zachary tells me I was too hard on you," she informed him. "I was really thinking of your mother, and should have recalled that she is *your* mother." The Duchess of Dalzialest sighed. "There must be *something* worthwhile about that woman if she produced you."

Zachary heaved a dramatic sigh and shook his head, and Rosa looked at him and said "What?"

The Duke of Dalzialest leaned around his wife. "It's hard to believe that this woman was the chief negotiator for the Rebellion, isn't it, Jason? It's like all her diplomacy vanished when we had Talia. And then when Tally began to *talk...*" He rolled his eyes. "Let's discuss something more interesting. And less political. Sildra, how is it that you're letting Tomas talk to Jason as if he's the wise old man and Jason is a spring chick? By my count there's not a dozen full years between them... even if our Jason is a bit long in the tooth for a first marriage."

Less political. Dear Gods.

Jason found himself flushing as Duchess Sildra laughed. "Oh, Tomas will get into these moods. I'd say 'take advice from us old married people' and make no mind of it, Jason, but you and Sir Loveress have been a couple nearly as long as we have, I think. And certainly longer than Rosa and Zachary."

"How long *has* it been, Jason?" Rosa asked, curiously.

"Fifteen years, four months and five days," Jason mumbled, looking at his food. They'd agreed not to count the time he'd spent with Oskar in that second go-round... he was beginning to wonder uncomfortably if he should subtract the week he'd spent with Damien. The time out in the field with Genevieve didn't count against the tally, of course, that was just work.

He missed the amused silence for a moment.

When he looked up, Rosa's fingers were feathered across her lips to hide a smile. "I don't think I could answer that question so accurately... and instantly."

"I guess you pay attention when it's important," Zachary told his wife archly.

"And *you* could tell me how long?" she asked, plainly disbelieving. "That fast?"

"Well, we might have to argue about whether certain spans of time count or not," he said. "But I can give you an exact tally of something *else* right now if you want." He grinned as her cheeks matched her name, and looked at Jason. "I'll bet you have *that* tally down, too, eh, Jason?"

"Don't tease them so, Zachary," Duchess Sildra chided, as Jason's blush returned to match Rosa's.

"Yes, Auntie," the Duke of Dalzialest said with pretended meekness.

"Auntie?" Jason asked, sure that he was missing something. He wasn't Damien with the whole Realm's genealogical trees tucked away in his head.

Sildra wrinkled her nose at the Duke. "It's his idea of a joke. Zachary is my younger brother. My *much younger* brother. Mama and Papa had thought they were long done with having children. And Zachary was a roustabout as youngest children often are. We had an older sister who was the Heir, which is why I ended up married to Tomas." She paused to smile at her spouse. "And when poor Elsa died of a flux, since I was gone, Zachary ended up the Heir."

"Heir, nothing," Zachary was serious for a moment. "The flux took our parents also. I went from being the third-born 'roustabout' to ruling Dalziell in a handful of weeks. Sildra was pregnant with – was it Gemma or Denis?... so she sent what advice she could, but I was stuck figuring most of it out on my own. Luckily our near neighbors knew our plight. Gavin and I had been friends for years..."

"It was Gemma," Sildra cut in. "And Gavin Teraseel – now *there* was a roustabout. Begging your pardon, Rosa."

The younger woman's eyes glistened, but she smiled. "I knew my brother, Sildra. It's a fair description." It had been almost eight years since the massacre at Zialest...

Zachary put an arm around her. "Well, when Gavin's beautiful older-sister-the-Heir showed up to help me sort things out, I certainly wasn't going to tell her no. To tell the truth," he winked at Jason, "I'd spent all that time in Zialest with Gavin mostly to try to catch Rosa's attention. But she never noticed."

"Of course, I did. But how was I to know you were serious about *me* when neither you nor Gavin were ever serious about *anything* when you were together?"

"Wasn't it right after that when he got *very* serious?" Zachary asked. "About Ciriis?"

Jason was almost amused. He and Adam often used the same technique; playing off seemingly unrelated topics to bring the subject around to where they wanted it. Damien managed the same thing all on his own, though when he and Genevieve combined their efforts, the rest of the world had better watch out.

So, he was entirely unsurprised when Rosa's next question was about her sharp-tongued kinswoman. "What exactly happened with Ciriis, Jason? Gen won't talk about it at all. And I haven't been able to catch Aryllis. The castle gossips say Ciriis is pregnant – by Genevieve's *father*? And *he's* no longer to be called 'Duke'?"

Jason took a deep breath. At least he had his story straight for this one. "It's all true. They came back from Elaarwen to help us with Genny – she wouldn't stay in bed, no matter that she fainted if we let her up for more than a few minutes. After a week or so, they sprang the news of the pregnancy on Genevieve, and she collapsed again. Damien... well. That was the night all the glassware in the Realm went floating."

They all looked at the crystal stemware on the tables with misgivings.

"The Queen is on bed-rest to recover from all those miscarriages, isn't she?" Duchess Sildra asked thoughtfully.

Jason nodded. "We've been trying to keep her as quiet as possible. This... was a shock."

To his surprise, Rosa shook her head. "I'd've thought Ciriis would have better sense. Or Lord Aldred." She smiled sadly at Zachary over her shoulder, and placed a hand on the one he laid there. "She's barely looked at anyone since Gavin... and I know Lord Aldred hasn't been the same since Gen's mother died. They must be very much in love..."

"That still doesn't explain how they could be foolish enough to set themselves up in opposition to the King and Queen," Tomas noted disapprovingly. "I don't know the lady very well, but *Aldred* had better political sense when I knew him. It was the only reason I was willing to join his Rebellion. The risks to Siovale under Reginald were looking worse than with Aldred's motley crew."

Zachary sighed. "That's what Father was saying before he died... If Dalizell had abutted the Rebel front instead of being stretched so far away..."

"With Zialest in between, and Papa not at all convinced," Rosa added sadly.

"I always thought it was *Zialest* bringing *Dalizell* into the Rebellion," Jason commented.

"It would've looked like that," Rosa nodded. "So, Zachary had no choice but to wait."

"So why *did* you send Harald to marry Genevieve, if you were trying to make an alliance?" Jason asked Tomas. "You knew what kind of person he was, you said."

It was a question he'd always wanted answered. He knew that, despite everything, Genevieve had always liked and respected the Duke of Siovale.

And as long as they were going to throw every *other* uncomfortable and awkward topic out there on the table with the eel pie and the roast pheasant...

The Duke of Siovale gave him a long look, as the others grew quiet indeed. "I suspect, Your Highness, that you understand quite well about wanting to see the best in a relative. Despite all evidence to the contrary."

His mother... Jason looked down in embarrassed dismay, and Tomas sighed. "I hoped... I should have known better, since Harald was a man grown by then, but I *hoped* that Duke Aldred could do something with him. *If* he was out from under our mother's influence. Aldred agreed to try. And... I knew Genevieve. The love of a good woman can do tremendous things, and she is one of the best." He shook his head. "I should have summoned him home when Aldred told me things weren't working out. It might have already been too late – for all I know he'd been in contact with Prydeen from his boyhood. But... neither Aldred nor I wanted to do anything to disrupt our alliance."

His lady's face was sad, and faintly disapproving. And slightly relieved. Had she worried about Harald's influence on her own children?

Tomas looked at the younger three. "Before Aldred disappeared, we were discussing declaring our independence and crowning Aldred king. I don't know if Genevieve knew. We didn't want the word to leak to Harald – the stories of all his bastards had come to our ears by then, though it was nearly another year before Genevieve knew. His... 'discretion' was clearly not to be counted upon. And I knew Aldred was concerned that his only Heir might not be capable of producing an Heir herself..."

Jason... was stunned. And desperately glad that Damien wasn't here to hear this. More than the glassware would be floating... and for a moment he realized how much control the King must have had even in his fury, even without consciously being aware he was doing it, since not one piece of glass in the entire country was reported to have broken.

Glass. Notoriously fragile. And valuable. And sharp.

It could have been an unmitigated disaster.

Tomas had sent Harald to wed Genny *knowing* his younger brother's character... or lack thereof. Perhaps that could be forgiven. Jason knew how many times he'd hoped things would change with his mother, with Megan. But...

Aldred had accepted Harald as a husband for Genevieve *knowing* his history of violence. And perhaps he'd thought he could restrain the young man and teach him better behavior. After all, a treaty based around a marriage was a strong incentive.

But they had both *known* about Harald's infidelities. Even if they hadn't been aware of the abuses Genny was suffering – though how they couldn't have *known,* Jason couldn't fathom, as Damien had noted on the night of the floating glass – shouldn't that have been a sign that they needed to base their alliance on something else? Surely, a man who had so little self-control, a man who was so *indiscreet* – as Duke Tomas had put it – shouldn't have been in the position of consort to the likely next Heir to the Throne.

Aldred and Tomas had chosen to protect their ambitions for declaring Aldred king over Genevieve's well-being. Even after seeing the unmitigated disaster he was making of her life.

Aldred had been more concerned about who would inherit the throne he planned to seize than for the daughter and Heir who, Jason knew, still half worshiped him.

Tomas was frowning, as if putting something together. "Aldred was worried about Genevieve's ability to produce an Heir nine years ago. He told me he was looking into how to ensure the continuation of his line in case that was true."

"Gen and Harald *had* been married for eight years," Rosa said very quietly, as if she were seeing the same things. "Now it's been *another* eight and even a soul-bond hasn't brought children..." She looked up to meet Tomas' eyes with a worried expression. "You don't think...?"

"This pregnancy was *intentional,*" the Duke of Siovale said grimly. "Damn him. Haven't we been through enough war? Didn't he trust Damien to find a solution?"

Rosa looked stricken.

"How far along is Ciriis?" she asked Jason, who shrugged helplessly.

"It's *my* fault," the Duchess-and-former-Heir-to-the-Throne said. "I gave Gen – the Queen – back the Heir's Ring when you," she nodded at Jason, "came through Zialest on your way back from Elendria four months ago. With Tally and Betha – I didn't think I could keep that responsibility. I thought they'd name *you,* Tomas, honestly. And you've all those children of yours to secure a line of succession beyond you."

Tomas snorted. "Not likely. Not after Harald. But doubtless Aldred got word as well. And decided he'd solve the problem for them."

"Oh, that infuriating girl!" Rosa exclaimed. "Cirii, you always *were* too clever for your own good. Why couldn't you just have stopped with putting *one* king on the throne?"

"Instead of creating one from scratch, say?" Sildra sighed. "This *is* going to get messy, isn't it."

"They've already been exiled until Genevieve and Damien have a child," Jason said cautiously. He... shouldn't let them see his own reaction to all of this, probably. Speaking of getting through a meal without starting a war. "And Aldred has been sworn and Bound Lord of Cloudcroft."

"So, Damien finally Bound the old rascal?" Tomas' eyes were relieved. "I told him he should do it in the first place."

Jason looked at him sadly. This... was a step too far. "But you didn't tell him why, did you, Your Grace?"

The older man caught the sudden formality and looked at him warily.

"No," he admitted. "I didn't break my *oath,* Your Highness. I... couldn't. No more than Aldred can, now." The Duke of Siovale paused. "I *wouldn't.*"

"You walked perilous close, Your Grace," Jason said softly. "You suspected that Lord Aldred might pose a threat to Crown and Realm and you stayed silent."

The Duke of Siovale bent his head. "He's Genevieve's father, Your Highness. I'm just the brother of the husband who abused her and tried to usurp the throne. Whom would the King believe?"

It was Rosa who answered her brother-in-law. "*Damien* would have known the truth if you offered it to him, Tomas. He's never given you reason to doubt his trust from the moment you swore to him. I've heard the story from him, from Genevieve. From you. He placed his life – he placed *her* life in your hands from the moment you stepped into that sitting room to call on your men-at-arms to stand with you against Harald and that sorcerer's bullyboys."

Sildra placed a hand on her husband's back and looked up at them. "What are you going to tell the King?" she asked with fear in her voice. "My children..."

Jason winced internally. This... might have been how Lady Theresa Anvliyar began down her path. And that... had nearly destroyed Damien. They had waited for word from Baron Raphael, to know how he stood and to offer him the chance to take his mother home to Cedarwen and confine her, as Duke Tomas had done with his.

Raphael had come to the city and knelt before the castle gates, refusing to come in until Damien would come out and accept his oath. 'You look like your sister,' were the only words he had said before he took the Vassal's Oath. And then he had remounted his horse and turned to leave. Damien had called out to stop him, to ask if he had anything to say about his mother. Jason had known Damien was hoping the Baron would plead for clemency.

The Baron had looked back at the King with dead eyes and replied that he had no mother. And left.

And Lady Theresa had had to join the remains of Harald and Lord Prydeen and Prydeen's bullyboys on the castle wall. As with Harald, the King had not spared himself; if this was the fate of traitors, he would not set another to the task and pretend it was not as awful as it was. Jason and Genevieve and the entire Royal Guard had had to keep him off the wall and away. It had run nearly all of them ragged for two weeks and Jason was only glad Damien had not yet discovered his trick of vanishing from place to place or they would never have had a chance. He didn't think Damien had slept more than a few minutes at a time the entire two weeks, and he'd hardly been able to keep any food down.

It didn't matter that Lady Theresa had been hard and cold and hated him. It didn't matter that she had been acting on his grandfather's orders. It didn't even matter that it was really Elista – and not Lady Theresa as he had long thought – who had found him and begun leaving the food for him – though he was grateful to Elista and elevated her to Castle Chatelaine and befriended the capable, caring woman.

Lady Theresa had been almost his only human contact for four years. She had made sure he was fed and clean and clothed. She had talked to him. She had told him how to please his grandfather when he was summoned.

It was, Jason suddenly realized, a more extreme version of the way his own mother and sister had raised him. Though Damien had had a loving family for his first ten years, and Ciriis and Adam had rediscovered him when he was fourteen... but the damage had been done. He had made Lady Theresa into a mother-figure and wanted to please her... It had taken them *years* to wean him away from the library and the Dowager Baroness.

Her betrayal and execution as a traitor was almost a deeper wound, *still,* for Damien than his parents' murder before his very eyes. Because, Jason realized, the deaths of Damien's parents had been, in the end, both noble in character and entirely out of his control. But the young King still felt he should have been able to *win over* Lady Theresa, should have been able to *prevent* her treason. He had elevated her, honored her... and she had still sided with Lord Prydeen at the end. No wonder he could not stop wondering what else he could have done – not as a powerless ten-year-old, but as a grown man and a king. And he'd ripped his heart to shreds over wanting to, when setting it beside the knowledge that it was Lady Theresa who had betrayed his parents, his sister...

Jason looked out over the room filled with nobles of high and low estate... and his eyes met those of his niece. Elaina had stayed beside her father. Had David been able to provide some leavening against the 'brutal truths' that his mother and sister had felt it necessary to explain to Megan's children when they were far too young? Abruptly, Jason decided to make sure Elaina got her chance to try out for a position as a lady-in-waiting... no matter what Adam thought about it.

He looked back at the anxious Duchess of Siovale and gave her a reassuring smile. "I won't lie to my king, Your Grace. Not ever. Not even by omission. But I will find a way to tell him what I have heard that does not–" ...*throw him into a killing rage, make him break all the glass in the whole Realm...* "–give him cause to doubt Tomas' loyalty. He never has yet," Jason added, then gave the Duke of Siovale a wry smile. "If it makes you feel any better, Tomas, you *were* his first choice of an Heir after Rosa... and for a negotiator with Elendria after Genevieve. But he can't get the Royal Council to agree on the latter, so he didn't dare try for the former. *I'd rather you were to be crowned as Heir in three days, for that matter.*"

"*Damn* Harald," Duchess Sildra muttered, and Zachary gave her a shocked look. "Sildry!"

Tomas looked up, and pulled her close. "I think he is, dear. His soul certainly can't have ended up anywhere *good.*" He looked at Jason. "Thank you. And, Jason..." He hesitated as if unsure whether he should stay with the formal 'Highness.' "You'll do fine as Heir and as Duke of Emeralsee. As King, if it should come to that. You have the heart and the head. The hand – the doing – is something you can learn."

Jason inclined his head. "I certainly hope so."

Another course began to be served – the high table was last this time, as they had waved off hovering servants while in the middle of the discussion. Damien had long ago established that the other tables were to be served in such an instance.

Jason stared at the latest plates of food in dismay. "How long can one meal *last?*" he muttered.

Rosa laughed, breaking the tension somewhat. "You really don't attend these things very often, do you, Jason?"

Zachary rolled his eyes. "We should have brought all the children. Then you'd know just *how* long a meal can go on."

Sildra chuckled, though it still sounded slightly forced. "I wouldn't even subject Gary to this. Or us to Gary at one of these events. Mark and Arabella had no choice," she nodded to her oldest two, seated at farther tables, "but the younger four are all back in our townhouse." She gave Jason a speculative look. "Speaking of whom. 'Bella is a bit on the young side to serve as one of the Queen's ladies-in-waiting, but I hear that Adam Loveress' youngest sister is to join. 'Bella has several skills they may find... useful." She gave him a veiled look that suggested she did not mean embroidery and dancing. "And Denis and Gemma are of an age to join the ranks of the pages – as I hear your own niece and nephew are to do."

"Lady Aryllis is in charge of the ladies-in-waiting," Jason told her. "Arabella should speak to her. And of course, the younger two can enroll as pages. We'd be delighted to have them."

"Is it true that Roger and Esmerelda are here on *scholarship?*" Rosa asked, her eyes sparkling with mischief. "That must be driving your mother wild."

Jason gave her a wan smile. "Damien offered one. Mother turned it down. I'm not sure how word even got out..."

Zachary chuckled. "I'd say never underestimate the power of the rumor-mill, but it was Genevieve. Don't worry, we won't tell anyone."

"Hmmn." Jason noticed a calculating look on Duchess Sildra's face and wasn't sure if Duchess Laura had heard. Not to mention any servants who had happened to be near, or the Guards standing behind his chair. No wonder Damien warded any room he might have discussions in.

They survived the dessert course without any further terrible revelations, and Jason was able to make his escape. Thank all the Gods at once that there hadn't been a formal entertainment arranged for the evening.

He made it back to his rooms without incident or interruption, head still spinning. Though with a pair of Guards following him. Tim Ancellius had caught his eye and nodded – which Jason took to mean he had everything in hand.

And how did *Adam* feel about giving up the position he had worked so hard to attain and that he had held for five years – and two more before that as Captain of the Heir's Guard? Was he as torn as Jason was about giving up the Champion's chain?

By some miracle all the Loveress boys were elsewhere. The Guards – Sir Everett and Sir Angelos Eldridge – took their place at the door, and wasn't *that* something to get used to. Jason racked his sword and crossed the sitting room past all the cots and pallets, putting his hand on the doorknob before the name sank in.

Sir Angelos *Eldridge*. Damien was right. He needed to know. Tomorrow he would have to consult the genealogical record books – after the Changing of the Guard, perhaps.

How did Duke Tomas even know? Though on reflection, that probably wasn't so much of a surprise as all that. His mother's wedding would hardly have been a private affair. It was more of a surprise that it hadn't come up sooner in casual conversation. But Rosa was right – Tomas wasn't that much older than Jason himself. How was *he* familiar with... with Jason's father? Familiar enough to know the man 'wasn't a diplomat'?

It was too much to sort out. The tall knight shook his head, opened the door and stepped into his bedchamber.

Adam was already there, sitting on the bed, reading, his long legs stretched out in front of him. He was fully dressed, except for his boots. Clearly waiting for Jason.

Jason began to give him a smile, but Adam was giving him too serious a look, even for Adam.

"We need to talk, Jason. Close the door. And set the wards. *All* of them."

Well, he wasn't opposed to that.

Gamely, Jason turned and set the wards that Damien had installed that afternoon. Sharp eyes Adam had, to have noticed the change so quickly. He began winding the 'thou-shalt-not-enter' ward over its hooks and noticed... it was shorter than it had been. Too short to complete the sixth and seventh loops and the extra level of the spell. The end of the slender cord looked frayed and burnt.

"I cut it." He turned to see Adam pulling something out of his pocket. He threw a short piece of string across the bed. It fluttered and didn't go far. "I didn't want my bedchamber turned into a trap for my king. Again."

Jason looked at him in shock.

"I was here, Jason." Adam's face was stone. "I'd come in to grab some papers, went in to use the washroom. I was about to come out when... it became really obvious I shouldn't."

"Adam..."

"You called him 'love,' Jason."

No, Adam wasn't stone. Stone could not weep.

No wonder he'd said they had to talk.

Jason had to give him honesty... but gently. As he'd promised Duchess Sildra. Did his love deserve less than his king?

The tall Champion removed the silly, useless shoes that went with these new clothes, and climbed up on the high bed to face Adam. "I do love him, Adam. I always will. But it's not what I feel for you. *You're* the one I long for. The one I belong to."

Adam folded his arms, the book forgotten on his legs. "How can I ever be sure? By all the Gods at once, Jason, it's only three days till our *wedding*. How can I *trust* you now?"

He'd almost started wars over dinner. Words... were not Jason's best field, it was clear.

"The night... of the glass. You said to 'do whatever I had to do' to get Damien sorted out. This... was just more of the same." He hoped Adam could read his eyes.

"'Whatever you *had* to do.'" Adam said sardonically. "Seems like there's a lot of flexibility in that interpretation. I heard *everything,* Jason. I'm well aware that today was *your* idea, not *his.*"

Jason firmed his chin. "Then you're also aware that this was the last time."

Adam looked away with an angry shrug, arms still folded – no, *wrapped* around himself. "Damien this week, Genevieve next week."

"Adam, that's not fair." True, though.

He shrugged again, still not meeting Jason's eyes. "What about this whole mess *is* fair? If... if you were so, so... why didn't you just say something? To *me?*"

Jason began to unbutton his formal tunic. "And say what? That it was driving me crazy to lie next to you, touching, but nothing else? That with your brothers and nephews free to wander through our bedroom at all hours and your *mother* in the next room at an unGodly hour every morning, I wanted to make love to you?"

"We could have found somewhere else."

Jason laughed with real amusement. "In this castle? Right now? Stuffed to the rafters with nobles? Where? It's not like either of us have time to go find a room at an inn down in the city, even if *they* weren't all stuffed to the rafters with the nobility that doesn't fit in the castle or have their own townhouses."

Adam shot him a brief sideways glance. "There's my office."

"Where you've been working with Tim almost constantly to transition the Captaincy?" He was done with the buttons, and had the cuffs of the shirt loosened. Almost casually, Jason pulled off the upper garments and let them drop to the floor. On the other side of the bed. Where Adam's eyes were pointing.

Adam looked back at him sharply. Jason never, *never* just dropped clothes and let them lie. Except once. Or maybe twice... when there just hadn't... seemed... to be... *time...*

He drew in a ragged breath at the sight of Jason's naked upper body, and his fingers twitched as the taller man came up onto the bed on hands and knees.

Jason prowled a little closer. Within touching distance. *"You're* the one I love, Adam. You're the one I dream of. I was a hairsbreadth away from tackling you right there in the King's office today... it was as really *alone* as we've been in ages..." He began to undo Adam's buttons, hungry for the feel of Adam's strong shoulders under his fingers.

Adam had begun to reach out, attracted to the feel of Jason's heavily muscled chest as always, but he froze at those words. His face twisted. "You think you'd worn Damien out so much that he'd sleep through *that?"*

Jason didn't let that accusation slow him down. "Shall we see if I can wear *you* out so *you'd* sleep through anything?" he purred. Adam's breath caught. *"You're* the one I want to kiss goodnight," he breathed into Adam's ear.

The other man's arms slid around him, tracing every muscle as it flexed beneath Jason's skin. "Jase..."

"I know," Jason murmured. "I know, my love."

Chapter NINETEEN

Answers

"Jason?" Adam couldn't sleep.

A sleepy chuckle. "I guess I *can't* wear you out after all." Jason propped himself up on one elbow. "Nervous about tomorrow?"

"What? Oh." The Changing of the Guard. Giving up his Captaincy to Tim Ancellius. It had completely slipped his mind. "No. Not that."

"Then what's keeping you awake, lover?"

Adam shivered slightly. Jason didn't use that word often. "What you were doing with... with Damien, earlier..."

Jason groaned and buried his face in the pillow.

Adam forged on. "That... those were things you learned from Prince Oskar, weren't they."

In the low light of the lamps, Jason's eyes were almost violet as he looked up carefully. "Yes."

"You've never... shown... *me...*"

Jason regarded him calmly. "I didn't think you'd want to know. That there were good things."

"Hmmn." Adam was momentarily at a loss for words. "I guess... I didn't. Then. I was wild with jealousy when he took you from me. *Both* times." He startled as Jason reached out a caressing hand that *began* with his head...

"I know. *I* was more worried that you were going to challenge him than anything else. There was no way *that* could have ended well." Jason commented. "We both know you'd have mopped the floor with him if he actually agreed to fight you... and that King Reginald could never have let you live after that."

The obvious scenario – that Prince Oskar would have ordered *Jason*, as his Champion, to defend his honor and fight Adam... was one they had never discussed. And apparently wouldn't now. Perhaps it was one that Jason didn't want to think about himself. The late Prince had been cruel enough it was altogether imaginable that he would have insisted on a duel to the death.

"*Or* he might have appointed me Champion then and there," Adam objected, trying to stay focused despite the distractions. "He was often satisfied to control what he might want to use later, rather than destroy it."

"Mmmn. *Barely* possible," Jason traced Adam's lips with a finger. Adam kissed it, reflexively, and found that finger dipping into his mouth. Jason's ability to make commonplace things seem erotic was... possibly unparalleled. Not that Adam had had either desire or opportunity to look for 'parallels.'

"But you still wouldn't have had *me*. Winner's prize or not." The Champion's smile was dry, but... wistful? "Oskar was his only possible Heir by that point, besides Damien. He'd've given the Prince whatever he wanted... and you'd only have been making *sure* that was me." Jason shivered slightly. "Oskar was... possessive."

That hadn't entirely been a shiver of remembered *fear*, if Adam was any judge after all these years. He looked away. "I think... what drove me most wild... was that you seemed to be... happy with him. I *wanted* you to be happy, even if it wasn't with me... but I couldn't see how that was possible. Not with all I knew of Oskar's discarded lovers." He turned his eyes back to Jason's. "I don't understand. I saw what you were like when he was... done with you. Even the first time. How *could* you have been happy with him?"

Jason gave him a long look, and his hand stopped moving on Adam's body, staying quiet on his chest. "Are you sure you want to do this, love? It's been fifteen years."

Adam felt tears pricking his eyes. "Were you *in love* with Prince Oskar, Jason?"

The other man sighed. "Who was *your* first lover, Adam?"

It confused him. "What?"

Jason's eyes were... he didn't know what the word was. "You've never told me. Who was it?"

Adam lowered his gaze. It wasn't memories he'd wanted to keep to the fore. He'd known since he'd first seen Jason that they were meant to be together; Adam wasn't proud of himself for not having kept faith that it would all work out in the end.

"Sir Edmund Railston. Shortly after you were assigned to the Prince. And started to look so *happy*. It didn't last long. I think I was mostly hoping to make you jealous... and you never noticed, and after a while he sort of... gave up."

Though the man had done him a good turn thereafter, by somehow attracting Prince Oskar's attention such that the Prince had chosen Edmund his Champion and Jason had been freed. Likely it had been an inadvertent aid, as Edmund pursued the rise of his own ambitions... but Adam had to thank the man in his heart nonetheless, and nevermind that Edmund was a heartless son-of-a-bitch.

Jason winced, then gave him a lopsided smile. "Then... you never reacted like Damien with Ciriis?"

"You mean following him around like a puppydog and panting for his attention?" Adam snorted. "Certainly not."

Jason leaned forward and kissed him lightly. "Then you, my darling, are a most unusual man. For most of us, that first time is... magickal. And it sort of fogs up all the other senses."

"*Our* first time was magickal for *me*," Adam asserted a little anxiously.

"For me, too," Jason assured him. "But the *first* first time... Yes, Adam. I was in love with Prince Oskar. And I have some very wonderful memories of him. More of the other kind," he admitted candidly, "Especially of... when he took me back. But they can't entirely obliterate the other ones."

Adam struggled to wrap his head around that. His sweet, gentle Jason had been in love with that psychotic sadist?

"It was... just a physical reaction?" he said hopefully, but Jason was shaking his head.

"I don't know if there *is* such a thing, love. Our minds and our bodies are too closely linked. Oskar..."

His eyes grew far away as Adam had to think about that in the context of the current situation... and Jason's repeated protestations that his attraction to Genevieve was 'only physical.' Not that Adam hadn't *Seen* enough to guess...

"He could be absolutely charming when he wanted to be," Jason finished. "When it *suited* his purposes. The first time... it suited him to charm me very, very thoroughly."

"I suppose having the Realm's best swordsman at his beck and call made him feel important," Adam muttered bitterly. Though surely King Reginald's only remaining grandson – as far as most anyone had known – and only possible Heir shouldn't have *needed* anything *else* to make himself 'feel important.'

"Mmmn." Jason looked unimpressed with this assessment, but didn't argue. "Can we lay this to rest, love? The poor man has been dead for seven years."

'Poor man'? Surely Jason wasn't serious. But... Adam remembered how upset Jason had been after the massacre in Zialest that had allowed them to make sure Damien received the Heir's Ring. At the time, he'd thought it was out of sympathy for Ciriis, who had lost her fiancé, Gavin Teraseel, in the disaster... but with whom could Jason have shared his grief over Oskar when the rest of the Realm was quietly rejoicing over his death?

"No one was supposed to *die* in Zialest," he heard himself saying apologetically.

It was Jason's turn to look away. "Even the best-case scenario had Rosa sacrificing herself to Oskar's lust. On her wedding night. It's a miracle that she and Zachary could forgive the rest of us."

"It was her idea."

"It was a very bad one. As I told you at the time. You and Ciriis both." Jason's lips had become a thin line. "Can we *please* let this go, Adam? Those other memories... I'd like to leave them where they are."

But Adam couldn't... quite yet. It felt like a light was dawning. "That's why you wanted Damien. Here. In this – in *your* bed. Where *you* were in control."

It... sounded ugly to put it that way, for all that he'd heard enough to know it had been no such thing. And for all that Adam didn't doubt how deeply Jason cared for *'their* prince.' As deeply as he did himself.

But it was an inescapable parallel.

Jason looked at him with disfavor and pulled away slightly. "Damien is nothing at all like his uncle. The one has nothing to do with the other."

Adam wrapped an arm around to keep him from pulling farther away.

"That's the whole point, isn't it? You had no choice with Oskar. You do with Damien. *You* adored *Oskar.* Damien adores *you.*"

Never before had Adam used that name without 'prince' appended to it. His own small effort to set the man outside and beyond his relationship with Jason. They were both merely the sons of lesser nobility. Royalty had nothing to do with them. Not personally. Not *intimately*. Not... permanently.

Except Damien was all of those things and had been for as long as they had been a pair.

"I don't like where this is going, Adam. You... don't have any idea what you're talking about."

"So, tell me." Adam held his breath. *Years,* and Prince Oskar still came between them. Maybe this time they could change that.

"No." Jason took a deep breath and closed his eyes. Closed Adam away. Again. "I will not taint what we have. I will not have you *pity* me. *Again.*"

"Did you tell *Damien?*"

Jason's eyes flew open in surprise. "Some."

Adam tried not to feel hurt. Was it really what *they* had – or those *memories* – that Jason didn't want to 'taint.'

"Why?"

"I..." Jason closed his eyes again. "I wanted someone to understand. A little bit. And... he's carried around all this guilt all these years about... the second time. Apparently Ciriis told him some of what Oskar did to me the second time. She wasn't supposed to. The whole *point* was to preserve Damien's innocence."

"It worked, though," Adam couldn't help saying. "He was much more amenable to our training after that."

Jason gave him a disappointed look. "I should have known it wasn't just *her.* Thick as thieves the two of you were." He snorted. "He's well aware that Ciriis was trying to manipulate him using sex, you know."

"Oh?" Adam didn't like the sound of that.

Jason was absolutely right. He and Ciriis had hatched all their plans together – often leaving his more morally-minded lover out of the planning stages so that Jason would have no choice but to go along. More morally-minded... which had equated to *less driven.* Adam had no way, even now, to explain to Jason why he had sometimes needed to *push* things to happen faster than a *morally-minded* approach allowed for.

Why Ciriis had felt the same way, Adam had no idea.

Jason's expression was wry. "Yes. And he doesn't mind. He said it was better her than some of the less savory elements of his grandfather's Court. Though if you ask *me,* I think he turned the tables on both of you with that."

"What are you talking about?" Adam wriggled until he could sit up. This didn't seem like a conversation to have lying down. Jason looked up at him, head still propped on one hand, his long, lovely body stretched out and only lightly covered by the sheet. He'd recovered a sense of amusement.

"Just what I said. I suspect our prince was bursting at the seams with that magick he uses so profusely now, and that he used it – all unknowingly, mind you – to bind people to him. He's never Bound any of the three of us, or any of the Royal Guards – of either cadre – yet every single one of us willingly put our lives on the line for him."

Adam frowned. "That's just natural charisma. And the job." He hesitated, but in all honesty, he had to add, "And the fact that Damien will do the same for any of us."

"Ah," Jason waggled a finger at him. "But the ladies were willing to lay more than their *lives* down on his behalf. Zialest... would probably have gone very differently if Rosa and Gavin had ever met Damien in person." He sighed. "I strongly suspect that if Genny hadn't made herself so suddenly available, we would all have found ourselves in his bed sooner than later."

Adam guessed his face reflected some of his dismay, because Jason added, with a lopsided grin, "And been glad of it, one and all."

"Where are you getting this stuff, Jason?" Adam demanded before Jason could ask just why he was so disturbed by the idea. No, Jason wouldn't wonder that...

Jason frowned. "It's... cobwebs. It's like there are cobwebs on everyone Damien has ever Bound. I didn't notice it until tonight – I've been avoiding most of the nobles, as you know." He acknowledged Adam's snort with a flicker of his eye. "But looking down over the banquet hall... I didn't understand what I was seeing until just this moment, but it was pretty obvious. Megan and David and Elaina didn't have any cobwebs, for example, but Mother did. And Tomas, Rosa, Zachary, even Duchess Laura. But not Duchess Sildra or Duchess Laura's wife – I don't remember her name–"

"Carmencita," Adam muttered. "She's Mercasian." *Jason* might have been able to hide from the nobles on the pretext of doing work, but that had only left Adam to have to talk to more of them. Work or no work.

Jason nodded. "And there's only a few strands on the newer Guards, but Tim has more than anyone I'd seen other than Duke Tomas... and *you're* practically cocooned."

Adam frowned. All the things he'd read through these last five years, all the things Damien had begun talking about to him more recently... he had a notion.

"Take off the Ring for a moment, Jason."

"Our engagement ring? Why?"

"No, the Heir's Ring."

"Hmmn." Jason rolled onto his back to have access to both hands. He tilted his head to look at Adam once the Ring was off his finger.

"Well?" Adam demanded as his lover tilted his head back and forth and squinted at him.

"It's gone. Mostly. Here." He handed Adam the Ring. Then his eyebrows shot up in surprise. "On second thought, just set it down." When the baffled Adam did so, Jason nodded. "There's still the faintest haze around you, but the Ring definitely amplified the effect."

"What did you see when I was holding the Ring?" Adam wanted to know.

"I... think I should talk to Damien about this first," Jason tried to demure.

"Jase..." Adam made his tone promise nothing but pain in the practice-ring if his love didn't ante up now.

Jason shrugged. "You... glowed. And strands – not Damien's cobwebs, something else – strands of golden light seemed to be connecting you everywhere. I'm not sure what it means. I haven't had anyone else hold the thing since he gave it to me..."

"You have a suspicion, though...?" Adam pressed.

Jason put the Ring back on and made an exasperated sound. "*Now* it looks like our entire *room* is covered in cobwebs. The wards are nice, but I think I'm going to have nightmares of giant spiders..."

"I wonder what *you* look like if *I'm* practically cocooned..." Adam mused. "For all he's never Bound me magickally. To my knowledge." He frowned.

"To his either, is my suspicion," Jason reminded him. "We're talking about *Damien,* love. He's almost painfully honest."

"Not always open, though." Adam was still mulling over the idea that he was somehow more magickally Bound than Duke Tomas.

"No," Jason agreed. "He... keeps the secrets he needs to."

"Everything comes back to him, doesn't it?" Adam sighed at last.

Jason shrugged. "How would it not? We ensured he reached his throne – and that work started almost at the same time that you and I became a pair. We're his closest friends and deputies. Our relationship would be tangled up with Damien in one way or another."

Adam knew his smile was twisted. "This... is definitely another."

Jason put his arms about him. "Love, are you *still* worried? You are first in my heart, always and forever. And in three days... my *husband.*"

"More like two, now," Adam muttered, but he smiled.

Did Jason have any idea how his eyes lit up when he said that word? Whatever reservations had kept him from saying 'yes' immediately were clearly long gone.

Adam took a deep breath. "I want you to... show me. What you did with Damien. The... the *good* things you took away from your time with... Oskar."

Jason's breath caught. "Adam... You don't have to do that to make me happy. I'm deliriously, over-the-moon happy to be yours. To be with you."

Adam shrugged, a little uncomfortably. "If it's something you... *like,* Jase, I should be willing to try it. And..." His temper suddenly flared. "*Hellfires,* Jason. I'm not giving you any excuses to go hopping in Damien's bed again. *Ever.*"

Adam flipped them over so he was looking down at Jason, then kissed him as passionately – as *possessively* – as he knew how, and ignored away his own internal conflicts and feelings of hypocrisy. Let Jason's memories of Prince Oskar compare with *that.*

His love smiled. "That's the tiger I've wanted in my bed. I'm done with sweet surrender." Jason's smile became slightly predatory as his fingers began to explore in ways that were suddenly new after so many years. "I hope *that's* what you're wanting, too, Adam, beloved. Because *this* tiger *bites.*"

"We... should probably disengage the wards," Jason mumbled sleepily, happily.

Adam grunted. "I don't want to get up. Do *you* want to get up?"

"Noooo.... but your nephews... *our* nephews might need to use the washroom in the night. They're small boys."

"Not that small." Adam's voice was almost smug. "I told them all they'd need to use the facilities down the hall tonight. Besides. I might want to make love with you again in the morning. And my parents come into that room awfully early..."

Jason snuggled closer, feeling like his whole body was smiling. "Then let's leave the wards in place, by all means."

Chapter TWENTY

Change

THE CHANGING OF THE GUARD went smoothly the next day.

Queen Genevieve was seen outside of her tower for the first time in months, to the delight and relief of the entire Realm's nobility. She seemed hale and hearty, if rather pale and thin after her long convalescence. No one, except perhaps, the poor confused Guards on duty at the royal suite, wondered how she got down the tower stairs without being seen.

The formal Throneroom was the only site for an occasion of this formality. It had seen some renovations since Damien had re-taken the Castle: the old banners had been cleaned and repaired, the ancient torch-holders replaced with lamps, the heavy oaken doors that Lord Prydeen had blown to splinters had been replaced with new ones of a lighter shade of wood, though just as solid. The flagstones had been scrubbed and polished until a certain stain was no longer so obvious... though Damien still discreetly avoided it. Only a handful of people ever noticed, and Jason, Adam, and Genevieve were the only ones likely to make the connection to the assassination of Prince Eric and Lady Miria so many years earlier.

Little could be done to make the room more welcoming or less intimidating, however.

Damien, as had every monarch before him, refused to allow any major alterations of the room. No wooden flooring or wall-paneling, no opening up of the roof and ceiling to let in more light. And, also as with every monarch before him, he had refused to explain why he turned down every one of his people's well-intentioned suggestions... though he did, rather mildly, point out that there were times when any monarch needed to be able to overawe visitors and that the room served *that* purpose rather admirably just as it was.

As Queen Marian had advised him, the wise monarchs of the past had decided not to make it known beyond the Monarch and the Heir that the Castle, Hall, and Throne were concentrators of the Power of the Realm. If Damien chose to make that knowledge more widely known, it was up to him, of course, and she certainly could not *stop* him... but he should have a damn good reason before he did so.

For the Changing of the Guard, the King was seated upon the Throne, the Monarch's Blade unsheathed and shining across his thighs. The Queen stood at his side, fingers clasped with his, in what their subjects saw as a touching display of the love of the soul-bonded pair. None but the two of them were aware that it was that tight grasp that kept the King grounded to this reality and prevented the Throne from sucking his soul into the web that was the magickal underpinnings of the Realm. Damien had wanted Genevieve to sit, but she absolutely had to be touching his skin, and the dimensions of the Throne precluded any other positions than standing or seated at his feet. And the latter position robbed her of some dignity.

The Champion-and-Heir stood to the King's other side, one step down, his eyes shining.

The walls were lined with men- and women-at-arms in the Alsterling colors of dark blue and black. Her Majesty's ladies-in-waiting and gentlemen-of-the-chamber were much in evidence, mingling with the crowd of nobles. Lady Aryllis Ancellius stood to the Queen's side as Mistress of Protocol, her sharp eyes on everyone and everything.

The Royal Guard formed up and entered to a roll of drums; a brief flirtation with the idea of trumpets had been nixed by the horrified Adam. The Captain had perfect pitch, and most of their trumpteers... did *not*. Not to mention it would be in the enclosed space of the hall.

They marched in a double file of six behind their Knight-Commander, Captain Loveress, all of them in full plate armor, to the base of the royal dais. They all knelt, with a great crash of metal against stone in near perfect unison.

The half-dozen prospective members of the Guard watched enviously as the thirteen drew their swords in unison and laid them cross-wise in front of their bended knees, then bowed their heads respectfully. Only the Royal

Guard, the Champion, and the Queen were allowed to bear swords in the presence of the King. Even the men-at-arms in Alsterling colors stationed around the Hall were armed with halberds instead – not that the long-handled pike-axes were not just as effective weapons. This was supposed to indicate the trust the monarch had in his sworn people… though in Damien's case it was more for show. He had long since put in place magickal protections for himself and Genevieve as regarded edged weapons and had made Adam and Jason aware that he was going to do the same for them as part of the coronation ceremony.

"What haps, Knight-Commander?" Damien followed the script they had all agreed upon.

"I present to thee, Your Majesty, thy Royal Guards!" Adam exclaimed with a bit more enthusiasm than the King had expected. He faced Damien, as was proper, but his eyes sought Jason's, and his smile became more brilliant than those who knew him were familiar with.

"We are pleased, Knight-Commander," Damien recited. "And are inclined to offer thee a Boon. What would thee?"

Adam bent his head modestly. "I would lay down my office, Majesty. It is time for another to serve thee as Knight-Commander and Captain of thy Royal Guard."

"Canst not think of some other Boon, Sir Loveress?" Damien asked. "We are loath to see an end to thy most excellent service to the Crown in this capacity. Thou wert named Hero of the Realm for thy gallant defense of this Castle during the Pretendership."

The format they had decided on required Damien to ask him to change his mind three times to emphasize how much he valued Adam's service, and for Adam to insist each time that he was done. It gave a chance to air Adam's most significant public accomplishments… which made for some complications. Adam had been reluctant to include this first example, despite the medallion Damien had slung about his neck – and that he now wore – since he had, in fact, *lost* the Castle to Harald's forces.

Damien had been reluctant for a different reason. At least half the eyes in the room had slid over to see Tomas Elsevier, Duke of Siovale's, reaction and that of his wife and children ranged about him. Tomas had been named a Hero of the Realm and wore the same medallion – for his role in ending the Pretendership by restoring his forcibly turned coat when the sorcerer's power was broken over him. For some, however, the taint of his cuckoo's chick half-brother would never pall… or they refused to believe that he had been mind-controlled, despite the King's and Duke Aldred's word.

The Duke's expression was serene and interested, his gaze never wavering from the King's face, and his lady was just as calm. The younger children looked a bit overexcited, and the older ones somewhat strained, but they held up. Damien had to be careful not to look at them, letting his sense of the people in the room tell him what was going on. But he hadn't seen the entire Elsevier family together since their arrival... three sons and three daughters, an embarrassment of riches for which the King felt a deep envy.

Adam's second challenge named him Mentor to the King for his role in having helped Damien reach the throne in the first place. They had argued about *that* one as well, Adam thinking it wasn't a good idea to remind people that their king had lived in the Royal Library for nearly ten years.

He had shut up about including that one when they decided that the last one would honor his role in the Battle of Siovale. For which Adam had *definitely* been decorated, but which was a potential political tangle... given that he had actually faced the Queen herself in battle.

The problem, of course, was that the things Adam did were usually either kept quiet because they were sensitive or were vital but not impressive. Such as training Damien and Genevieve, or serving as administrator of the Guard. Adam had suggested that they only do one refusal, or simply skip that part altogether. Aryllis had responded by pointing out that the format was traditional, and that there had been far less accomplished Knight-Commanders in the past and *they* had gotten full honors. That she hoped her husband's upcoming tenure in the position would be one of the quiet ones, but still wanted to see *him* get full honors when he retired went unspoken. As all of them had remarked at one time or another, they had all seen enough excitement to last several lifetimes.

The argument had finally been resolved by Damien simply deciding.

After the refusals, Damien bowed his head in acquiescence, feeling an odd reluctance for this change despite having instigated it himself. Adam had had the care of his honor and safety since he and Jason and Ciriis had managed to lure the young prince out of the Royal Library... and before that, since the Captain had first discovered him there when he was himself merely a senior squire. Some fifteen years of trust – vindicated and validated by the fact that Damien was sitting here right *now...*

He'd known Tim Ancellius nearly as long, of course, and had trusted to the effervescent knight and to his more sober-miened lady, Aryllis, as well. Nothing was *really* changing except who wore which choke-chain...

"We cannot justify refusing thee the Boon which thou hast requested. However, We find Ourselves in need of a Champion for the Crown. Sir Adam Loveress of Lynncrag, in merit of thy place as the foremost swordsman of the Realm – not also of royal blood – and thy longstanding place as Our Good Righthand, wilt thou accept this office?"

They had also argued long about whether to include this part here or in the coronation, In the end, it had been Jason who didn't want Adam's shining moment in front of his family to be eclipsed.

"Your Majesty, I would be honored to offer my sword and my service to thee as thy Champion." Only the handful on the dais could see the ironic twinkle in Adam's eye at being called the 'foremost swordsman of the Realm.' Only Adam probably noticed that Jason's jaw was a bit tight over that description... although it was traditional to say, regardless of the truth of the statement. Indeed, the office of Champion had become entirely ceremonial during King Reginald's reign, awarded as often as a political plum as for any real prowess.

Damien had inserted the words 'not of royal blood' – though he hadn't explained why, and it had not mollified Jason. It was traditional that the Champion could not be a member of the royal house... but although Jason was about to be crowned Prince and Heir, he wasn't of royal blood.

The King rose from his seat on the Throne, balancing the Monarch's Blade on his palms and releasing the Queen's hand. Genevieve turned towards Jason, who knelt down before her and bent his head.

"Sir Jason Solway of Brindlewell shas served as Our Champion with distinction and honor," Damien stated. "He has served Us as Mentor to the King, Hero of the Realm, Bodyguard to Her Majesty, and Advisor to the King. We ask that he yield up the chain of office of the Royal Champion only that We may bestow an higher honor upon him. Let it be known to all and sundry that We lay claim upon Sir Jason, Our claim having seniority and supersedence over any other." Damien's intent gaze focused on Countess Alexa Solway. This... had not been in the script but the glimmer in her eye suggested to him that he had better say *something*.

Just over one full day left till the coronation...

One *single* day wherein Jason was neither Champion nor crowned as Heir... though he still wore the Ring of the Heir.

The King had no idea what the Countess might do with that slender margin of time, and simply hoped he had spiked whatever plan she had.

Jason lifted the chain over his head and handed it to Genevieve, then rose and stepped back. His heart might be conflicted over the loss of this office – the highest *he* had ever aspired to – but his eyes shone with love and pride as Adam stepped forward to receive the chain from Genevieve's hands. It was yet another piece of tradition.

Adam bent his knee again to the King.

Damien rapped him sharply on each shoulder with the Monarch's Blade, just enough to make the steel of his pauldrons sing. "We name thee our Champion, Sir Adam Loveress of Lynncrag. Rise and assume thy position."

One step below and behind the Named Heir. At Jason's side, just as he was always wont to be.

"We now stand in dire need of a Knight-Commander," Damien announced. "Stand forth Sir Timothy Ancellius of Elmirscroft." He heard Aryllis suck in her breath. Timothy was the third son of an unlanded knight-turned-man-at-arms in the service of the Duke of Reyensweir. Elmirscroft was on Crown lands – little more than a house and a few farms to support it – but it would be *theirs*. Damien and Genevieve had made the decision last night.

Tim came forward as called upon. He was dressed in the Alsterling colors – as a sworn king's knight, not a man-at-arms, he had the right to turquoise-and-gold. No sword, since he was not currently serving in the Guard. He knelt before Damien.

His little son tagged after him, and Damien smiled. There had been a discussion of what to do with Rico, and Damien had stated that his Court should be a place welcome to all. It simply wasn't fair to exclude the boy from a ceremony involving both his parents.

Four-year-old Rico knelt on one knee beside his father, looking very serious, and a ripple of amusement washed over the crowd, with only a few eddies of disapproval. One from Countess Solway, of course.

"Wilt thou, Sir Timothy Ancellius, accept from Our hand the office of Knight-Commander and Captain of Our Royal Guard?" Damien spoke clearly.

"Your Majesty, it is my honor to serve thee in this, or any other capacity, as thou dost see me fit."

Damien veered off-script again. That serious little boy deserved to be taken seriously. And Aryllis and Tim deserved to know that the gift of Elmirscroft was not one to be revoked casually... to feel more secure than Damien's own grandparents had felt when faced with an impossible request from their royal grandson. Not that any amount of entitlement could have – or, really *should* have – lightened their fear with regards to his other grandfather, the king.

"And wilt thou, Enrico Ancellius, accept Elmirscroft from my hands unto thine, to be a good lord for its people, and to listen to thy parents in the ruling of it until thou art old enough to take oath for thine ownself?" Damien could *feel* Aryllis trembling behind Genevieve... *felt* Genevieve reach a hand out to the other woman.

Tim looked startled, and the boy, confused. Tim smiled and put his arm around his son and stage-whispered "Say 'yes, Your Majesty, Uncle Damien,'" as he sneaked a wicked grin at his king.

The little boy gamely repeated what he was told.

Damien sheathed the Sword and came down the remaining stairs to take Tim's hands in his. Tim kept his son in the circle of his arm, moving the boy in front of him so he could offer Damien both his hands.

"Timothy Ancellius, wilt thou guide and guard my fair property of Elmirscroft as its Lord-Regent, placing the needs of thy people before thy own and caring always for their prosperity and well-being?"

"I so swear." Tim said, and Rico whispered the same words.

"And wilt thou take me as thy liege-lord, accepting the rule of my fair property of Elmirscroft in my name? Wilt thou further swear to be a loyal and faithful subject of this Realm and to raise arms only in the defense of thy people of Elmirscroft or of this Realm?"

"I so swear."

"Then accept my fair property from my hands unto thine and rise. From the Power granted me by the Gods as King of this fair Realm, I create thee Timothy Ancellius, Lord-Regent of Elmirscroft."

He felt the magick settling from his hands into Tim... and a thread to little Rico. Tim gave him another startled look, and Damien smiled gently. He'd seen that same look of shock on every noble he had Bound as they connected with their land for the first time. On the few faces where there had been shock and dismay – like Aldred's – it was clear that there had been an intent to do something with which the Realm disagreed.

Little Rico's eyes widened and then he grew very thoughtful.

Damien had a sudden horrible thought that he might have damaged the child... but no. The Realm sought to Heal all of its beings, from grass to oak trees, from water-striding insects to humans. It wouldn't harm a child. He hoped. In five years, Rico was the first child-lord who had been Bound when Damien gave the oath to a regent; was it because his father's arm had been around him? No way to tell right now, though the matter surely bore looking into...

Tim rose, and Rico stayed stuck to his leg.

Damien turned to the Royal Guards, still kneeling in their neat rows. "What say you, my loyal Guards? Will you accept Sir Timothy Ancellius, Lord-Regent of Elmirscroft, as your Knight-Commander?"

As one, the kneeling knights crashed their fisted metal gauntlets into their chests in acclamation.

Damien slowly re-mounted the stairs, his royal cloak of scarlet and miniver brushing two steps below where his feet trod. He took his time as he turned about to face the crowd again, trying to meet the eyes of each member of the Secret Cadre, scattered throughout the room, before he finished his pronouncement. Each one lifted his or her chin a little to approve the choice as well, and gave him a small smile.

Last of all he met Lady Aryllis' eyes, which were full of tears, but she was smiling.

Damien looked out over the room. "I name thee Knight-Commander and Captain of the Royal Guards from this day forth, Sir Timothy Ancellius, Lord-Regent of Elmirscroft. Let the word be given."

He reclaimed Genevieve's fingers before unsheathing the Sword oncemore to lay across his lap as he settled back on the Throne.

"Be this Audience ended. Let the celebrations begin."

The Royal Guards stood with another massive clang, saluted their new Captain with their swords and crossed the swords for him to walk under. Tim hoisted Rico in one arm, then held the other out to Aryllis – she was the commander of the Secret Cadre and therefore his partner in this, as in all other things. She joined him gracefully, giving her husband a kiss on the cheek, and they went out arm-in-arm, each pair of Guards sheathing and following them as they went under.

Beautiful, dignified, dramatic... and somehow little Rico's clear voice saying, "Papa, why is Mama crying? I thought we were happy today?" seemed to add to the moment in Damien's opinion.

The entire Loveress clan mobbed Adam as Damien levered himself back up. He released Genevieve and sheathed the Sword only after he was safely free of the Throne, and by that time Adam had been carried off by his family, laughing. And clanging. His sister Marianna seemed to take particular delight in making his plate armor ring by knocking it with her bangles.

"Why aren't you with them?" Damien asked Jason, who had hung back. "They're *your* family, too." For once they were nearly the same height, with Jason standing a step below he was only barely taller than the King.

Jason tilted his head, looking at Damien a little... quizzically? "I was looking in the genealogical records this morning. Tomas... mentioned my father's name at dinner last night."

Damien froze. "Oh?"

Jason nodded. "It's probably more of a surprise that I hadn't heard it before. It's not like my mother would have kept her wedding secret. More like the social event of the season, if anything."

"And... what did you learn?" Damien asked softly.

"That your mother and my father were cousins. And that my father was... inexplicable to everyone at Elderwyld. In his looks as well as his behavior." He took a deep breath. "They said... They said that he looked like an Alsterling."

Damien winced, though not in surprise. "This... just doesn't get any easier, does it, my friend?"

Jason sighed. "Yes and no. I'm... becoming very sympathetic to Tomas."

"Did I hear my name?" The Duke of Siovale had come to stand beside the dais. He couldn't come up the steps without invitation, but he was as close as he could get.

Damien smiled at him and came down to greet his friend. "I hadn't seen your whole herd together in a long time, Tomas. They're... beautiful. You are an incredibly lucky man."

The Duke's eyes went soft. "Yes. I am." He looked up at Jason. "As I was telling the Prince yesterday, the family you *choose*..."

"Should make your life easier." Jason finished. He was looking over Tomas' head. "The family you're born with however..."

Damien followed his gaze. Countess Solway. Of course. And she looked far too pleased for the King's peace of mind. Or Jason's, clearly.

He needed to send Jason on an urgent errand, but he was drawing a blank.

Just one full day...

"I *know* the coronation is tomorrow, Jason," he said, putting as much exasperation into his voice as possible, "but we need to make a decision *tonight*. I can't *believe* you didn't finish reading that report." Jason's eyes flickered with hurt confusion, then relieved understanding.

Duke Tomas merely looked amused.

Damien turned to his wife as Countess Solway came within reasonable speaking distance. She had surely heard at least *part* of what he had just said... and *heard* through the soul-bond enough more to know what he was trying to do. "I'm sorry, sweetheart. Can your ladies escort you back upstairs to lie down? Jason and I have some last things to get done today."

Genevieve raised an eyebrow until she noticed Countess Solway, and nodded almost absently to her husband.

"Oh, Alexa," she said casually. "*There* you are. We haven't had a chance to talk. Perhaps you could come upstairs to catch up with me since Damien is apparently co-opting Jason for the moment. *Again.*"

Genevieve rolled her eyes as if she was rather done with having to put up with such things.

Damien turned about quickly, as if surprised to see the Countess. "Lady Solway. My apologies. I thought we had this matter squared away, and it simply will not wait. Tomas, I'll talk to you tomorrow. Jason, come along." Damien began walking away, listening as he went.

"Jason, we have to talk."

"Mother, it will have to wait. The King needs me."

"You're not his sworn Champion now, Jason. Your duty to Brindlewell and House Solway takes precedence. If only for this little while."

Jason must have held up the Heir's Ring. "I'm still the Heir, as long as I wear this, Mother. And I've been a sworn king's knight since I was eighteen. When my king summons me, that *always* takes precedence."

Damien turned slightly and inserting a note of impatient exasperation into his voice. "*Jason.*" He raised an eyebrow. "You can have him when I'm *done* with him, Countess Solway."

He began walking again, and felt deeply relieved when Jason's long stride caught up with him and left the Countess fuming behind them.

"'When you're *done* with me'?" Jason asked, his tone mixed amusement and relief.

"Which will be *never,*" Damien replied, as they strode quickly through the crowd of nobles, nodding acknowledgments but not stopping to chat.

Jason snorted as they reached more empty corridors. "That might distress Adam."

Damien fought down a blush as he looked up at his tall friend – his *cousin* at a few removes, as Jason had just discovered – and forced himself to remember that they had both agreed yesterday was the *last* time. Again. There was nothing more to blush *about.* "Not like *that.*"

He looked around and, on seeing that they were alone, he transported them to his office by magick. Damien had defeated that incipient flush, but it was just as well he didn't need to touch a person in order to take them along with him.

"I feel like that was a close call, but I'm not sure why," the King said, taking off his royal cloak and carefully hanging it up before engaging the wards and collapsing into a chair. Hopefully there would be no larger problems to deal with today than keeping Jason out of the Countess' reach and feeling a little awkward about it.

"Hmmn." Jason had stayed standing, his arms folded. His expression was very... closed. And never mind the joke he'd made a moment ago... Gods, it *had* been a joke, hadn't it? "Mother *did* have that *look* she gets when she's planning trouble for someone."

Damien sighed. "Jason, are you alright?"

The tall knight shook his head, and now he looked more *bemused* than anything else. He sat down on his usual, firmly upholstered chair. "I... was very proud to see Adam named Champion. It just... still feels wrong that the chain isn't on *me.*"

"And *that's* why you didn't go with the Loveresses." Damien nodded in understanding.

Jason heaved a sigh. "Perhaps it was all for the best. Mother wouldn't have hesitated to wade in among *them* and drag me off."

Damien snorted. "Somehow, I think the Baronetta might make a better defender than *I* do. Besides, Jason, you rank her. I heard about last night's dinner. You did a fine job of standing up to her."

The knight shrugged. "I didn't have much choice *then.* Turning anyone off the high table to make space for her halfway through the soup... I've heard of wars started for less."

"Well, feuds anyways," Damien half-agreed. He regarded his friend thoughtfully. "So. You'll stand up to her for the good of the *Realm.* For the good of *others.* But not for *yourself.*" Jason started to reply, but Damien waved him to silence. "The problem then becomes re-defining what is good for *you* in terms of what is good for the *Realm.*"

Jason eyed him warily. "That way lies tyranny, Damien."

Damien boosted himself out of his chair and began to pace. He was tired still, but the stresses of the situation made him restless. "You have a point. So... not to that extent."

"You look much more energetic," Jason remarked dryly. "And focused."

The King grinned at him. "I slept in a *bed* for the first time in two weeks last night instead of on that lumpy couch. It helped." He fought down another flush. Nothing more to blush about, remember? "No sparks. You were right. Thank you."

"Mmmn." Jason gave him an odd look. "You know... Adam was there in our washroom the whole time."

Damien looked down. "So... he told you. That's... good. Better than secrets. I *didn't* know until *after.*"

"I thought you said you know where *everyone* is in the castle all the time."

"Jason, I was so tired I barely knew where *I* was." Damien hesitated. "Are the two of you... okay?"

Jason nodded. Then he smiled and leaned back in a languid stretch that popped and crackled enough to make Damien wince just listening. "We... talked. A lot. About Oskar. About *you.*"

"Wonderful company to be in," Damien muttered, remembering that Jason had made the comparison before.

"Damien. You, of all people, know that I have some very positive memories of your uncle. No person is all bad. Or all good." Jason smiled. "Though *you* come pretty close to the latter. So does Genny. And Adam, of course." As usual, his eyes glowed a bit just saying Adam's name. It always made Damien smile to see it. "We talked about *us,* also. And... we did a lot of *not* talking, too." His smile became a smug grin. "A *lot* of not talking."

"Um." The younger man fought down another blush that seemed even more determined to escape. "Good for you. Did... you tell him about Evan Eldridge?"

Jason deflated a bit. "No. It... there were other things that were more important. And... I wanted to look things up before I told him. Know for sure. I'd recognized the family name, of course, but I didn't know how... *he* fit into... that clan. And now... I still don't know what to say."

He being Evan Eldridge. Jason's father.

Damien looked down. "I... looked into where the Baroness – Mother's aunt, *your* grandmother – might have come into contact with... an Alsterling. She... wasn't married at the time, if that helps any. Her first husband had passed some years earlier and her older children were half grown. He... wasn't a cuckoo's chick."

Not like Harald Elsevier.

"No father given. I saw." Jason sighed. "Same problem, just moving back a generation."

"Do... you *want* to know?" Damien asked hesitantly.

"You already know this, too, don't you?" the knight asked wryly. "I should have just let you tell me the other day, instead of letting myself feel like I was blindsided by Duke Tomas. Not that he *meant* to do that to me. Or even really *noticed.* I think." He gave Damien another odd look. "Speaking of whom, I have something else to tell you."

The King rolled his eyes. "You all get on *my* case when *I* go off on a related tangent."

Jason half-smiled. "I thought we were just killing time until it's safe for me to come out. Or figuring out how to spike whatever plan Mother has hatched that we haven't the faintest idea of. How much farther off can we get?"

"Hmmn. Good point." Damien perched on the back of the sofa. "So. What do I need to know about dear Tomas?"

Jason shook his head. "Sit down properly, Damien."

"Oh, come now. It can't be all *that* bad. The man is loyal, honest, a good duke, and a good friend."

But Damien obligingly threw a leg over the back of the sofa and plopped down on the cushions, stretching himself almost full-length and crossing his arms behind his head. Surely this would be easier than facing more uncomfortable truths about Jason's parentage.

Then he looked at Jason's face and sobered. "It *is* that bad?"

"You'll have to decide. Just... please leave the magick out of it this time. And leave the glass on the tables." Damien's eyebrows flew up and Jason actually cringed.

"Jason. I'm as calm and relaxed as I can be. And in control of myself. But this lead up of yours is creating more anxiety. Is this something current?"

Jason shook his head. "Tomas... says Aldred knew how volatile Harald was. Before Genny married him. That they both knew things were... bad... all those bastard children of Harald's, for instance... *before* she did, but they didn't *act,* either of them. They chose to preserve the Rebel alliance. Instead of... to protect *her.*"

Damien nodded. He did have to swallow down – anger maybe? It was disappointment at least. If he'd grown to think of Aldred as a father, helping him learn to rule, Tomas had been perhaps an older brother, advising on any number of small things without seeming to condescend over all that the sheltered young King hadn't known. "That's really no more than I expected."

"There's more," Jason sighed. "They were close to declaring that part of the Realm independent when Harald abducted Aldred. They apparently had some suspicions of Harald already, so they didn't tell Genny to make sure it wouldn't get back to him."

Damien nodded again. It was a logical direction for the Rebellion.

"One of the things holding them back was Aldred's concern that Genny hadn't conceived in eight years with Harald," Jason took a deep breath. "Apparently... he was already considering *'other solutions'* for an Heir of his own. Tomas and Rosa are both convinced that there's nothing coincidental about Ciriis' pregnancy. I wasn't sure about the timing, but Rosa thinks it might be that they heard she had given the Ring back and that *that* is what precipitated their... action."

Damien sighed and closed his eyes. "It's nothing that I hadn't already figured out, Jason. Though I suppose there's some satisfaction in hearing that someone else came to the same conclusion independently and I'm not just weaving paranoid fantasies all on my own. It broke my heart to have to tell Genevieve that her father has always put his ambitions above her well-being... and thereby failed as a ruler as well as a father, since ensuring the mental and physical health of his Heir is one of a ruler's prime responsibilities. Although, I suppose that, arguably, he was doing that when he was duke by considering seeking a new Heir. It's only doing it *now* that creates a problem, since it's not *his* problem to solve anymore."

Jason still looked trepiditious. "Tomas says he told you that you should Bind Aldred... but not his suspicions as to *why.*"

"He did tell me. I'm not sure how likely I would have been to follow his suggestion if he *had* told me these things, though." Damien admitted.

Five years ago... he hadn't wanted to believe anything less than perfection of the old man who had become a surrogate father. Five years ago, Damien was still starry-eyed with his Binding to the Land and his new soul-bond; while he was savvy – or at least well-read – enough to have seen the truth if Tomas had told him of Aldred's ambitions, he'd believed that *love* could solve any such problems.

Even now, Damien didn't question that his father-in-law *loved* Genevieve... *or* himself. But now he was a bit older and wiser – and there had been time to grow accustomed to the Land and soul-bond both. Time for rationality and skepticism – or perhaps that was *cynicism* – to corrupt some of his idealistic views.

Love could lose out to ambition, the King had learned.

"He said that's why he didn't tell you. He thinks you wouldn't have believed him because... because he's Harald's brother." Jason felt he had to add, "Duchess Sildra is very worried that you'll declare the whole family traitors by omission."

The King rolled his eyes. "I hope you put paid to *that* notion, Jason. And I'd have *believed* whatever Tomas told me. It's just that five years ago I was still pretty unsure of myself and I needed Aldred's advice to learn how to rule." That was a good enough explanation. Jason *knew* him, after all, if anyone did. "I was also pretty starry-eyed," he smiled, "with actually being with Genevieve. And you know how *she* sees – she saw... she *sees* – her father. If she had asked me to bring the moon down for Duke Aldred's enjoyment, I'd probably have tried."

And *he* still loved the old man as well, despite how very flawed Damien now knew him to be. It wasn't just Genevieve who was conflicted. And it wasn't like there wasn't anything he wouldn't do for her *now*.

"Could... could you *do* that?" Jason asked, in what was obviously an intentional, if morbidly fascinated, distraction from the topic.

"No!" Damien replied, then paused. "I don't think so... Gods, I hope not." He shook his head. "Nevermind. We need some food. These late afternoon events always mess up my sense of when to eat.

"My point was that I don't blame Tomas for not alerting me to the problem. I knew there was a potential for trouble. Not *this* trouble precisely, but something. Capable, clever people without enough to do and problems that need solving... I should have found them something to apply their talents to." He smiled wryly. "And possibly not put two of the sneakiest people in the Realm together on their own for so long."

Jason looked nervously at the door. "Do you want to bring some food in here?"

"You mean by magick?" Damien raised a surprised eyebrow when Jason nodded. "I can. I suppose we should all be grateful that there wasn't a banquet planned for tonight."

"Why wasn't there – oh, right. Aryllis."

The King nodded. "We didn't feel it was right to take Aryllis away from her family's celebration."

"You did a very good thing there, giving them the croft," Jason told him seriously. "I know you didn't do it for this reason, but you've given every landless knight a hope, and every younger son a reason to try for their shield."

"And *daughters*, I hope," Damien added. "Though there are plenty of other worthy ambitions, as Adam's brothers have found. No, that's not why... I'd've given you and Adam a place, too, by the way, except..."

"Except you're making me Heir to the Realm and Duke of Emeralsee." A wry look. "It's not like I've *forgotten*."

The King shook his head. "Not what I was going to say. We all hope those are temporary."

He stopped before repeating just why both appointments should be temporary. They were so close to making everything turn out that he was afraid of jinxing it, even though he knew, knew that wasn't the way magick, or even luck, worked.

"No, it's that Adam is still officially his mother's Heir. I could still grant you – either of you, both of you, your own private estate, of course, but if he's going to be Baronet of Lynncrag at some point... I wasn't sure if it should be *close* to there so that you can get away regularly, or *far* so that when you go it would be a real retreat. And then... if she was going to choose *another* Heir... whether it should be close enough to visit or far enough away to be left in peace." He turned a hand open upwards. "As long as he wasn't on speaking terms with them, I didn't want to ask... but now..."

Jason blinked. "I... hadn't thought about any of that."

Damien gave him a bemused look. "For someone as intelligent as you, Jason, you're strangely good at not thinking about certain things."

The tall man gave him a reproving look back. "You've had different challenges is all, Damien. And there's other things *you* haven't been willing to think about."

The King shook his head with a mild smile. "Sure, Jason. Though in your place *I'd* have spent half my time daydreaming about marrying Adam and when Lynncrag would be yours and his." He waved a hand at the table that had become covered in sandwich supplies while they were talking. "As you know, that *is* pretty much what I did. Daydreaming about marrying Genevieve. And having a home with her – though I didn't really dare imagine it being *this* heap of stone. I imagined it would be Elaarwen, and I'd never seen what her castle looked like at that point. And our chil–"

He cut himself off and sprang to his feet to begin filling a plate, hoping Jason hadn't seen the sudden sparkle of tears in his eyes. Damn, but he was jealous of Tomas' large family. And Adam's. Even the obnoxious Megan Solway had managed to have four children, though he wouldn't have wished the pain of losing one even on her.

"You and Adam," Jason sighed as he put together his own meal. "You're both utterly obsessed with children. Him, I understand. Growing up in that madhouse it probably feels unnatural to have just the two of us. You..."

"I was born in Ravenscroft and grew up in *that* 'madhouse' for the first eight years of my life, I'll remind you," Damien said archly, nibbling on a tiny, crisp, sweet pickle. "Mother was the oldest of seven... and with Kandy being twelve years older than *me,* there was plenty of time for my aunts and uncles to begin having babies. The older ones anyways. Place was overrun with children and pets."

"Moving here must have been a terrible shock." Jason gave him a wry look. "It was pretty different for me. And I'd been coming to Court every Summer since Mother could have me stuffed in a suit and expect I would mind my manners."

Damien raised an eyebrow. "Meaning you were what? Two? Sorry about the food, by the way. Elista will probably roll her eyes at me, but we have an agreement that I can magick away whatever I like from one particular cold cabinet. She keeps it stocked with this stuff and I don't need to leave a note. I know she has fancier stuff ready for today, but I don't know what's where and I'm not messing any of it up by 'stealing' part of what they have set up."

"Very... organized of the two of you," Jason commented, eyes on his sandwich.

"Oh, I made her give me a tour of the Castle closets when you and I came back from the grotto," Damien told him blithely. "There were any number of little things would have made the trip more comfortable, but I didn't know where any of them were before. I'm probably the only king in history to know where all the mops and buckets are stored here." He laughed. "Which would sound like bragging if it weren't so odd that no one – *utterly no one* – but me cares."

Jason tilted his head. "Is that where you got that mattress from, on the tower top?"

Damien flushed. "Um. Yes."

The golden-haired knight chuckled. "It's still up there, isn't it. Soaked by rain, covered in fallen leaves... snow soon..."

"It's still in a protected bubble of warm, dry air, thank you very much," Damien was almost offended, then realized what he'd said and blushed harder. "Mostly I just forgot about it," he muttered, focusing carefully on his food. "I haven't had a reason to go up there since."

"Damien, you're a gem," Jason chuckled again and took another bite of his sandwich.

"Hmmn. So, *do* you want my guesses on who your Alsterling grandfather – assuming you have one – could have been? Or..." the dark-haired man hesitated and carefully kept his eyes on his food. "Nevermind. Probably wouldn't work anyways."

Jason gave him a look. "You know that I'm aware you do that intentionally to make me curious, don't you? You've been doing it since you were fifteen."

"It works so well, why would I stop? And sixteen. At fifteen I'd just stopped hiding when you came looking for me."

"Fair enough. All right, I'll bite. *What* probably won't work?"

Damien knew his smile was stretched between smug and delighted. He loved creating a clever new spell and only wished he had time to do more of that sort of work. Though, admittedly, it was the rest of what he had to do that inspired his creativity. Necessity being the mother of invention and all.

"I *think* I've perfected a spell that will let me trace your ancestry through your blood."

"'You *think*'? And how does it work? Do you... need a sample or something?"

"Nothing so crude. 'Blood' is what we call our lineages, but really the information is in every bit of our bodies." He had been so excited to discover this. It wasn't mentioned in any of his books, and Damien wondered if he was the first to notice. It felt like the sort of thing other wizards would find useful, but he had no idea how to share the knowledge. Wizards were not exactly thick on the ground after King Reginald's tenure.

"Damien. Stop." Jason held up a hand. "You have that look where you're about to launch into a lecture on all sorts of details that make no sense to me. Just tell me *what* it does. Skip the *how*."

The King gave his friend a disappointed look. "After you're Bound as Duke, you're going to discover a talent for magick, Jason, I just know it. And then you're going to wish you'd listened."

The golden-haired knight rolled his eyes. "I'll deal with that if and when."

"Fine. I tried this out on Genevieve, and I got the results I expected, but I haven't had a chance to try it when I don't know for sure what I'm going to find out. I should be able to just hold your hand and tell how we're related."

Jason frowned. "But will it work since we already *know* I'm your cousin through the Eldridge family? Won't that confuse things?"

Damien shrugged. "Maybe. Maybe not. Like I said, I only tried this with Genevieve, and we know precisely how *we're* related. I *think* I have the spell tuned for the Alsterling bloodline." He hesitated. "And... there's only so many options, Jason. At the time of your father's birth there were only so many men of the Alsterling line in existence."

"Hmmn. And not that many particularly *great* options." The other man sighed. "I know you've had to come to terms with your family tree, Damien, but this is all new to me. Just... I really don't want to find out that my father was Harald of Siovale's half-brother." He shuddered.

The King gave him a wry grin. "That one I think I can rule out based on a couple of things. First, proximity. I couldn't find any records that my grandfather was anywhere near your grandmother at the appropriate time. *My* father was in Dawil with *his* mother, Queen Rena, at the time and my grandfather seems to have spent much of that period sending threatening letters to King Eldrig of Dawil about having her sent back. Baroness Eldridge seems to have been in Elderwyld the whole year before she became pregnant... though of course records aren't always what they should be. For another..."

Damien hesitated.

Jason sighed. "I'll bite," he said again. "'For another'?"

"Grandfather was pretty snobby. Planting a cuckoo's chick in the Elsevier family to tweak the Duke of Siovale is one thing. But an insignificant widowed baroness... wouldn't have been worth his time." Damien tried to look apologetic and relieved at the same time. Most of his bastard cousins had been born of commoner mothers. No real threat to the line of succession unless the Sword should unexpectedly develop a fondness for one of them... and as far as King Reginald had known, the Sword had completely disappeared.

"Also, his own notes don't make any mention... and I've found some gloating references to the Siovale situation. I... don't think he was fond of Duke Hector."

"Was he fond of *anyone?*" The knight was mildly curious.

"Nooo. But he seemed to dislike Duke Hector *almost* as much as he did Duke Siegfrid of Elaarwen... who was married to his cousin, the Grand Duchess Alicia and was therefore a direct threat to his throne. It just seems... excessive." Damien frowned. "He gloated about having brought Duchess Lydia on board with his scheme and misleading her to think Harald would ever have a chance at the Throne, but his *actual* plan seems to have been to make her dissatisfied to be a 'mere' duchess and to reveal Harald's birth at the most potentially embarrassing moment. The whole thing is scratched off with the comment 'Hector dead, no point.'"

"So... who is left on your list of possibilities?" Jason asked. "And would it even necessarily be a *legitimate* Alsterling scion? There's plenty of King Reginald's bastards scattered across the countryside... and they've had children and even grandchildren by now."

"Yes and no," Damien answered. "We're talking over fifty years ago, mind. Of my twenty-nine legitimate aunts and uncles, only about ten of them were old enough to be possibilities, and only three of them were male. My research suggests that it was only some ten years before that – so about sixty years ago – that King Reginald became more... hmmn... *undiscriminating* in producing offspring. However, he hadn't completed his purge of all the Alsterling cousins by then – Princess Alexandria was hiding out in the mountains of Elaarwen, and while he didn't even know that Alicia had been born yet, he was more focused on eliminating the Princess than on lesser threats."

Damien sighed. "He'd had his own brother and sisters and their families executed for treason earlier on, of course. And 'accidents' had begun to befall Queen Marian's other children and their families even before he had her assassinated. He was still fairly young when the first ones happened... I'm not sure if they can be traced to Reginald himself, or if his father, Prince Anthony, had anything to do with it. I haven't come across anything that suggests Anthony was anything but sickly and even weak-minded."

Jason looked faintly ill. "I'm... not so sure I *want* to find out I have a connection with that side of your family tree, Damien."

The King shrugged. He'd more or less come to terms with all of this even before they'd gotten him out of the Royal Library. All that time with the Archives and Chronicles and the piles of reports that looked far too pristine to have had much use before being rather haphazardly shelved there... Damien had had a very thorough *academic* education in the dark side of his lineage. And his tenure in the Library had begun with the only *practical* lesson he'd ever really needed in order to believe the rest.

"It's your choice, Jason. The possibilities, however, narrow down to Princess Lindrea's three sons. None of whom were known to have produced any legitimate offspring before their father – or Prydeen – had them killed." He gave his oldest friend a very dry look. "You *could* be the only child of the eldest son of King Reginald. Who was himself the eldest son of Prince Anthony. Who was the eldest son of Queen Marian."

He let Jason take a moment to swallow that. Except for Evan Eldridge's illegitimacy, and his being struck from the Solway family tree... Jason would have been more closely in line for the throne than Damien in that case.

"Now, that's just a guess at this point," the King warned. "And since the Sword hasn't spoken for you, and Queen Marian has barely acknowledged your existence – though she's more of a snob than a ghost really has a right to be, in my opinion – I could be entirely off-base." He smiled. "If I was right, I can't imagine why the Sword wouldn't have at least *glimmered* when you held it."

"I... need to think about this," Jason mumbled. "I'd... been thinking about all of this more in terms of finding out *who* my father was... and *how* he became the awful person that he did. And... what happened to him after my mother threw him out."

"Oh." Damien pursed his lips and looked up at the ceiling. "Well, you know the first part now. The Baroness apparently adored him as a small child, but she died when he was still quite young. He wasn't much regarded by his much older siblings and began to rely on his stunning good looks to get him whatever he wanted. Naturally he had to be charming to make that work... which is how I assume how he won your mother. After... well, his own family was just as shocked and wouldn't take him back. I believe he put to sea to seek his fortune somewhere else."

Jason stared at him. "How do you find all of these things out, Damien? This seems... much more involved than you could pick up from old records."

"Oh, you can read a lot between the lines," Damien said slightly evasively.

He hadn't even told Genevieve yet that he'd started to be able to get a sense of the emotions of the people who had touched an object in the past. If they had been focusing on something of interest – say, writing a record entry or a letter about someone, he could pick up the things they *hadn't* written. Of course, that left him prey to the biases of whomever wrote the documents... or whatever they felt at that time anyways.

"I don't think Evan Eldridge was born bad... like Harald and, um, Oskar, circumstances created him." Referring to his late uncle without the title made him seem rather too much like family for Damien's taste, but he was trying to be thoughtful of what Jason had told him before.

The knight raised an eyebrow. "You almost sound sympathetic."

Damien shrugged. "Who knows what path *I* might have trod if I'd been left to Lady Theresa's tender mercies until my grandfather decided to train me himself? Or if Lord Prydeen had noticed my magickal potential? Whatever I did would be as little forgivable as what they accomplished, but... there but for the grace of you, Adam, and Ciriis... Especially you."

Jason looked uncomfortable. "You give us too much credit sometimes, Damien."

The King smiled diffidently. "It's hard to see how."

"Without the foundation your parents laid..."

"Of course," Damien agreed easily. "But a solid foundation is just a hole in the ground without walls and floors and a roof." He glanced at the darkening garden behind the window. "Adam will be worrying about you.

And I really should make sure my sweet lo – I mean, *Genevieve,* made it back up to our rooms safely."

He flushed at his slip of tongue, but Jason just smiled.

"She's probably worrying about you, too," he suggested.

Damien winced. "No, she's probably waiting to give me a tongue-lashing for setting her up to have to invite your mother up to our rooms." He stood up and offered Jason a hand to stand up out of the slightly-too-comfortable chair.

Jason accepted it with an amused look. "Am I looking so old these days, my king?"

Damien gave him an abashed look. "Not *looking,* it's the sound from your joints. I was hoping to sneak some Healing in when you weren't paying attention." And something else, but if Jason didn't want to know yet, he'd leave it be.

"I'd be more than happy to accept a gift of Healing," Jason admitted. "Though Adam could probably use it more than I can."

His offer hadn't entirely been a bluff. Damien gave him a relieved smile and sent a tendril of magick to soothe some aches and pains Jason probably hadn't consciously noticed for years. They'd have to plan time for a more extended session to make more significant and long-lasting changes. Time for *both* his friends. He already did for Genevieve what he could, every night they were together; it had taken *years* for him to replace the scar tissue of that sword-wound in her thigh with healthy muscle and ligament. Worth every moment of effort if it made her agile enough to dodge another such injury.

"Good. It helps to be able to do what I *can.*" As close as he would come to referring to all his Healing *hadn't* been able to do for Genevieve and their unborn children. As close as he *could* come without his frustration and despair surfacing again. *Not today.* "Give Adam a clap on the back for me, would you? And Tim, if you see him. I don't know when I'll have an informal moment with either of them in the foreseeable future."

Jason nodded. "It... seems strange after all the moments that the four of us have celebrated together – and with Ciriis and the Miramars."

Damien shrugged. "I think the rest of us can all be envious that Adam has a family like that to co-opt him from us." He smiled. "And so do you, especially after the wedding."

"Yes..." Jason's eyes glowed happily again. "Say, if anyone asks, what was it that was supposed to be so urgent for us to decide on tonight?"

"Oh!" Damien went over to the desk and flipped through the most recent stack of reports – the ones he hadn't so much as glanced at, to Jason's best knowledge, but he didn't really need to pore over them anymore. Most of the current batch were updates, and once he saw the titles, he knew most of the contents. There were advantages to having a finger on the pulse of the Realm through its magickal web.

"Here it is. The sewers on the west side of the city need to be repaired before the expected annual flooding in the Spring. It's been on my to-do list for the last several years, but I've been fighting the Council for the funds. I wanted to make it a gift from the Crown to you as the new Duke – bypassing the Council – and needed you to approve the amount I'm gifting you. It had to be done tonight in order to get the monies transferred before the coronation... and the work needs to start now or it won't be completed before the Spring floods." The King paused thoughtfully. "We're cutting it close as it is."

Jason blinked at him. "You just came up with all that right now?"

Damien grinned. "I'd love to say 'yes,' but you already have an exaggerated idea of my intelligence. No, I've been playing with this idea for a week or so. I don't really need your approval for the amount, of course. But we're going to say that you thought the amount I proposed was too small and I said that unless you'd read the report, and proved it to me, that I wasn't going to give you more."

"Oh."

"You won the argument, by the way," Damien informed him. "You pointed out that with the typical cost overruns to be expected in a project like this it would just barely work, and that I hadn't paid attention to the fact that we are going to have to pay to put up a number of families while workmen dig around or under their homes."

Jason shook his head. "Damien... I'd never think of all that."

"Maybe not the cost overruns, but you'd definitely have noticed how many families are going to be temporarily displaced. *If* you'd read the report." The King cocked his head. "It's the kind of thing you usually *do* notice, Jason. The human cost to decisions of the King and Council."

"You overestimate me..."

"I don't. But you'll have to see that for yourself, eventually." Damien smiled wryly. "*I* didn't believe Genevieve when she told me I was good at this either. It took, oh, six or seven years to believe her."

Jason frowned. "You've only been crowned – and *married* – for five."

Damien raised his eyebrows. "So what does that tell you? Go on. Your mother is at the other end of the Castle from the path you need to take back to your rooms. Where Adam is surrounded by his family. He feels a bit anxious, and I assume that's because you haven't turned up yet." He looked over at the ravaged buffet and it disappeared without a trace, even to the dirtied plates and crumbs.

"Handy, that," Jason nodded. "Thank you for bringing it in."

Damien's smile had more relief in it than anything. Perhaps Adam was right and he simply needed to use his skills more frequently to wear off the novelty for other people. Like Jason. And Genevieve.

Jason stepped to the door and opened it, then looked askance at the unguarded threshold. "I shouldn't leave you to make your way back to your rooms unguarded, Damien."

The King waved him on. "I'll go the other way. Magick," he reminded as Jason gave him a questioning look.

"All right," Jason nodded. "Good night then. Tomorrow is supposed to be a day of rest before the coronation, so I don't suppose I'll see you."

"Rest is what *I* plan to do. Go on, Jason."

The door shut behind the tall knight.

Damien reset the three simpler wards – and the almost invisible thread that not even Jason knew about that would warn him that someone had invaded this space. There were too many sensitive documents in here not to take what precautions he could. The regular latch that he also set could too easily be picked, and he had yet to figure out a way to magickally secure the room from the outside without causing other complications.

Cleaning the room presented other problems. It annoyed the staff that he did it himself, magickally, but he had established a détente with Madame Elista over the matter. Damien had promised not to extend his magickal housewifery to the rest of the Castle and obviate her people's jobs, and she didn't fuss at him over the mice that might be attracted by crumbs he didn't notice.

Humming softly to himself, Damien gave everything one last check before vanishing himself back to his own quarters. He and Genevieve should have at least a few more days without sparks and he intended to enjoy every last minute of them.

Chapter TWENTY-ONE

Revelations

THE KING AND QUEEN WERE intent on a game of chess following a late lunch when there was an urgent rapping on their door the next day. It was their *fifth* game of the day, actually. They rarely had the opportunity to devote to such pastimes, and the brief respite was providing a chance to test their improved skills. Genevieve had had the opportunity to play a number of games against Countess Miraly of Elendria and the Deltheran Ambassador – both of whom had attended an event in neighboring Perdi a few years back and had played renowned Grandmaster, Premala Kalingana. Damien had spent some of his more lonely evenings reading books on chess – new ones that he had sent for from Mercasia.

They gave each other a rueful look, and Damien climbed up off the floor to answer the door. He was expecting any of a dozen minor calamities, most likely regarding minor adjustments to the schedule of events planned for the coronation tomorrow, but he'd pulled in his senses of the Castle to be able to concentrate on his time with his wife. Aryllis and Elista were two of the people *not* taking the day off... he suspected his new Knight-Commander was not either, though surely all the plans for the security of the occasion had already been laid. Perhaps Tim was entertaining their small son while Aryllis was busy; Adam was nothing if not thorough.

Adam was nothing if not standing wild-eyed on the landing at the top of the stairs. Sir Drake and Sir Everett were eyeing him nervously, having never seen their former Captain in such straits before.

"Where's Jason, Dam– Your Majesty?" Adam demanded. It wasn't like him to slip in public like that and call the King by his given name as he did in private.

Damien glanced at the two Royal Guards, who both snapped to attention, eyes forwards but ears still all too obviously alert. He towed Adam inside and shut the door firmly.

"What are you talking about?" the King asked. "He hasn't been by today."

"I was hoping he was here with you. *Either* of you. *Both* of you. He didn't come home last night," Adam said, his eyes anguished, his body tight with tension. His very admission suggested how worried he was. "I – is it this chain? I know how important it is to him. But I... I thought he was happy for me..."

Genevieve uncurled herself from her favorite spot on the couch. "Of course, he was. Even if he was disappointed that he had to give it up, anyone could see how pleased he was for you." She put an arm around Adam and drew him over to a chair. "Damien and I ran some interference for him after yesterday's investitures. Countess Solway was trying to get him to come with her. I had her come up here for awhile, and Damien took Jason to his office on some fabricated pretext. Damien came up here an hour or so later, shortly after Alexa left."

"I made sure she was on the opposite side of the Castle from Jason's path home before he left the office," Damien said. "He should have been back in your rooms before she had a chance to catch up to him."

"You should have just taken him there in the first place," Genevieve told her husband. "And be-damned with this subterfuge. It's not like the Countess bought your excuse anyways."

He waved her to silence. "Just a moment."

It wasn't so long ago that assassinations were *de rigeur* in this Realm. And plenty of the targets – like his sister, Kandra – had been fine warriors. He should have insisted that the Royal Guards be doubled *years* ago – or at least assigned Castle Guards to Jason as soon as he named him Heir. Or *Adam* should have. They'd all just trusted Jason's own skills to protect him...

Damien hunted for his sense of his oldest friend among all the other people in the Castle. He wasn't there. But there was still a sense of him... he wasn't dead. Desperately unhappy, but not dead.

Grimly, the Sorcerer-King extended his search. It had been on instinct, and with some sense of guilt, that he had used that brief handclasp when he'd pulled Jason out of his chair to try out his spell to find Jason's Alsterling connection. But any vestiges of guilt now evaporated because he had a much stronger connection to the tall knight than he would otherwise after that – blood, it turned out, was stronger than mere love and friendship. Only if you knew about it, though... magick apparently depended on perception as much as any objective reality.

"He's in Solway House," Damien knew his tone was grim. "But not for long."

He stepped to the door and jerked it open to order *both* Sir Drake and Sir Everett on errands.

"At your very top speed!" he shouted after them, as they scrambled down the stairs.

Even in his distress, Adam frowned. "They shouldn't be leaving you unguarded no matter what orders you give them."

Damien favored him with a glower. "They aren't. My Champion is right here."

He strode into the bedchamber, trying not to dash. It would take time for Drake and Everett to fulfill the instructions he had given them. More time than it would take for Damien to make his own preparations.

Genevieve stepped into the room and closed the door behind her.

"Care to enlighten *me?*" she asked with a lifted eyebrow.

He eyed the comfortable old gown she'd worn while they luxuriated in a quiet day. He could do this without her... but she looked healthy enough to manage, and it would *better* if he could do this from the Throne...

"You need to wear something more formal. I can do your laces. Can you do your own hair? I don't think we have time to wait for Lady Alanna to get here."

She frowned, but went to her wardrobe and began to change. Ladies' styles were still rather confining, but Genevieve used the same tailors and seamstresses as their ladies-in-waiting. Not only could she fight or ride in any but her most fragile outfits, she could put them all on and off with only minimal assistance at need.

"I didn't want to explain in front of Adam," Damien told her as he changed into his own more formal garments. "I only hope that Drake gets to Solway House in time, or I'm going to be doing more than merely throwing out Count Emery's betrothal document for Duchess Laura today."

Genevieve gave him a horrified look, but didn't slow her movements as she pulled on layers of petticoats and an elegant gown. Bless her for not being the type to demand explanations faster than he could give them.

Damien moved close to do up her laces, for once completely oblivious to the lure of the creamy skin of her back as she held her hair out of the way. Almost completely oblivious. "She's found a girl who's willing to marry Jason, and doubtless a priestess who's offended by the fact that Mother Alayana is willing to wed Jason and Adam. It seems like the latter would be easier than the former..."

"Oh, please," Genevieve scoffed. "Have you *seen* Jason? There's hardly a maiden in the Realm who wouldn't be willing to try to 'save' him with the blessing of a priestess. Especially if it turns out that she has a chance to be Queen. Too tight, love." She gasped slightly, and he quickly gave her some more give.

"Sorry," he said as Genevieve went over to sit before her mirror to dress her hair.

"You can't just have them all show up in the Throne-room – that *is* where we're meeting them, I assume? – without giving Adam a heads-up," Genevieve pointed out as she brushed out her hair. "He's frantic already and you haven't done anything to relieve his worry. I'm surprised he hasn't burst in here already."

"I warded him into the sitting room," Damien admitted.

"*Love...*"

"I know, I know." He opened the door to meet Adam's glower as the man stood bare inches from the threshold. Not for the first time, Damien wished he were taller and more imposing. He looked up into Adam's eyes... then on impulse stepped forward and gave the man a hug. "It will be all right, Adam. I will *make* it turn out all right."

"Damien...?" Adam's voice was wavery. "Is he... is he alright?"

Damien looked up at the man who had found a terrified boy in the Royal Library and turned him into a king. "He's as unhappy as you might guess with Countess Solway forcing him into a marriage he doesn't want." He had made sure he was braced, so that when Adam staggered, he didn't let his friend fall.

"H – how?" Adam stuttered.

Damien guided him over to sit on the bed. He needed to finish dressing to play the part of the frosty-tempered king who would brook no argument and whom no one dared cross. Like... his grandfather. Dammit. But Countess Alexa would never have dared put a *toe* wrong in King Reginald's day. "She thinks that as his liege-lady – for less than two whole days – she has the right. I would have thought her Bond to the land would prevent this. The Realm made its wishes known to Lord Aldred–"

"I *told* you that you put too much trust in that Bond," Genevieve commented, as she stared fixedly into her mirror, her arms doing... something... over her head. "The Realm didn't appreciate Father setting up a potential conflict for the throne, but you've already Named Jason as Heir."

Damien was grateful that she forbore to mention that the Realm might actually be *pleased* that the Heir might be able to produce his own Heir. A tendril of thought across their soul-bond told him that it had occurred to her, however.

"Damien," she added, "I need a hand here."

The King gave his wife a look of trepidation. "You're not going to ask me to do something more complex than a simple braid, are you?"

To his surprise, Adam stood up and came over behind his queen. "What do you need, Genevieve?" She described something using terms with which Damien was only vaguely familiar, and he grunted and began to do... something. "I had to take care of Desirée for a few years when Mother was pregnant with Fontaine and then she was such a difficult baby. And the boys were... wild and it was all our poor nurse could do to keep track of them. Siri was four years old and wanted nothing more than to be a 'fairytale princess.' It was more interesting to create exotic hairstyles for her than have endless tea-parties with her dolls."

Genevieve laughed. "You are a man of many talents, Adam Loveress."

A few minutes later, Genevieve's hair was put up, her crown somehow solidly embedded in it, and Damien had his own crown on – the Crown of the Realm, this time, that he'd worn yesterday for the Changing of the Guard, and not the coronet he'd used to send off Aldred and Ciriis – and his sumptuous royal cloak. Genevieve looked critically at Adam, and adjusted his collar and chain slightly.

"Time to go?" Damien indicated the door.

Genevieve reached up and pulled Adam's head down for a kiss on the cheek. "We'll fix this, Adam."

He tried for a smile. "I know you'll try..."

Damien turned to face him. "Not *try,* Adam. I can and I will."

The King strode out of the room, leaving his Queen and his Champion to follow the swirl of scarlet and miniver.

Chapter TWENTY-TWO

<u>More</u> Revelations

I SHOULD HAVE AGREED WHEN *Damien offered to adopt me into the Alsterling family,* Jason thought miserably as he walked into the Throne-room behind his mother and Megan... and beside his *wife.*

The escort of Royal Guards were doing their best not to look at her. Or him. Or the smug-faced priestess and the portly legal scholar who trailed them. His brother-in-law and oldest niece completed the party.

David had actually tried to object to Mother's plan, and had looked like a thundercloud when hushed – but then he'd looked at his own children and contained himself. Countess Alexa, and not their father, was their guardian by law as liege-lady of Brindlewell and Head of House Solway both. David had no real say in what happened to his own children any more than he did for his young brother-in-law. David's younger two – Roger and Esmerelda – had been brought along as well, but Sir Tim – Captain Ancellius, now – had left them in an antechamber with stern orders to obey Lady Alanna.

Jason didn't plan to look up at the dais once they were in the room. He knew what he would see. Damien, Genevieve... Adam. All their faces limned with disappointment.

How many times had each of them told him that his status as Heir to the Throne out-ranked that of his mother as Countess? It sounded like sense when *they* said it, but the legal scholar she had unearthed from who-knows-where claimed it wasn't true. That in this limbo period between being Champion and being crowned Duke and Prince he was no more than Sir Jason Solway, younger son of the Countess.

He wasn't Damien, to know the law well enough to quote it back and defend himself.

Or Adam or Genevieve, who could simply *argue* anyone into throwing their hands up.

And then the priestess had stood there, claiming he was an abomination before the Gods, and that she was there to 'save' him by binding him in marriage to this girl... Jason didn't even remember her name. The girl looked at him like he was a prize she had won – or a meal to be devoured – not a person. Knowing her name hardly seemed worthwhile. Even after the priestess said the words of the marriage binding over them – his mother affirming his acceptance as his liege-lady when he couldn't make himself speak the words at her behest– the girl's name had seemed inconsequential.

Tim and the Royal Guards had arrived minutes too late.

His sister – who had been the one to accost him on his way back to his own quarters last night – had looked vindictively satisfied. David, her husband, had settled on cautiously sympathetic and pitying. His nieces and nephew, even Elaina, seemed more fearful and confused than anything else.

His *mother* had looked *triumphant*.

A pair of women in elaborately flounced dresses made in a style that was more Mercasian than Ilseadoran, brushed past the Solway party and their escorts on the right. Jason was startled enough to look up and identify Duchess Laura Marseill of Alpinsward and her wife, the Lady Carmencita. He saw his mother twitch her skirts away although she was nowhere near them, heard the disdainful sniff of the priestess behind him.

Lady Carmencita gave him a look of deepest empathy and determination as she ruffled past.

The two women curtsied to the dais...

Jason had not meant to look, but his eyes were drawn all unwilling...

He hadn't realized Damien could look so severe. Nor Genevieve. Adam wore that stern look often enough as he'd trained his Guards, but as his eyes met Jason's, they shone with so much love that Jason nearly stumbled.

No censure.

No disappointment.

Not from *any* of them.

"Your Majesty," Tim – no, Jason should think of him as Captain Ancellius now – bowed. "I have brought the... parties you requested and required."

"We are pleased, Captain Ancellius," Damien said evenly. "Countess Solway. You will explain why you abducted Our Heir."

Jason's mother curtsied not a hair's-width deeper than she had to by protocol. "I did no such thing, Your Majesty. I merely invited Jason to come home and spend some time with his family."

"Invited? An invitation is an offer that can be refused. Countess, shall We inquire of Our Heir as to whether he felt he had a choice?" Jason had never been so aware of the Monarch's Blade naked on Damien's lap. He didn't really understand why the King always had it there when he sat upon the throne... any more than he really understood why the King and Queen's fingers were always clasped at the same time.

Or so he'd always told himself.

Suddenly Jason realized he could see those cobwebby threads everywhere throughout this room. There were actually two different sets – different 'colors' he would have called them, except color wasn't a part of the way he could describe them. One set extended from Damien to Adam, to Tim Ancellius, to Genevieve... to all the members of the Royal Guard. To himself.

The other extended from the throne – and Jason abruptly understood why Damien always said it as if it had a capitol letter. This set extended to Genevieve, to Duchess Laura, even to Jason's mother. But it most tightly bound Damien himself, in fact seemed to be tightening upon him as he spoke as if seeking to pull the King down into the source of those threads. The Throne.

It didn't do that to **me,** a grumpy lady's voice said in Jason's head. *It wouldn't have* **dared.** *The boy just needs to take a stronger hand with it.*

Jason shook his head. Something was wrong with him if he was hearing voices.

Nonsense. I've just decided to acknowledge you, Grandson. Not your fault that your grandparents couldn't formalize things properly.

"I gave my son over to the king's service when he was twelve, Your Majesty," his mother was saying. "During that time, he has served to the honor of our House. And as king – first your grandfather, and now you – you have kept him sworn to your personal service, making you his liege-lord above and beyond what most knights give up to serve their king. For this brief span of time my son is free of royal servitude. Free to do what most any *other* knighted son of a noble house might do." She lifted her chin. "It is my prerogative to see my son wed as befits his station and to the benefit of my House."

"Your Majesty!" Duchess Laura burst out.

Damien quelled her with a glance.

"Do go on, Countess," the King invited. "Explain to Us how thy reasoning supersedes those plans which We have approved and would implement upon the morrow."

Never a good sign when the boy starts using his thees and thous, the nonexistent grumpy old lady chortled in Jason's ear. *I'm not sure Alexa will notice, though. The Solways never were that sharp. I can't imagine what her father was thinking to name her after my daughter while Reggie was trying to hunt Alexandria down –* **and** *my little girl was running circles around the fool.*

Jason twitched.

Oh, not **you,** *boy. Clearly you inherited your brains from the other side of the family. Mine, to be precise.*

"A man or woman should never marry below their station," the Countess repeated. "There's no benefit for the higher ranked person to such a match unless the dowry is consequential. The son of a Countess should marry no lower than the daughter of a Count. Hence, Isabelle Laidly, Heir to Seasbourne. An excellent match."

Oh. So that was the girl's name.

Genevieve raised her eyebrows. "And tomorrow, when Sir Jason is elevated to Duke of Emeralsee and Crown Prince of the Realm? Shall it not be clear that he wedded *far* below his station then? Should he not then wed a *princess* by your reasoning?"

Jason's mother snorted. "As if *that* was likely to happen. We all know this appointment of his is temporary, Genevieve. If you're ever able to carry a child to term, Jason will lose his fine titles. But he'll still be *my son,* and *Isabelle Laidly's husband.* We've arranged some excellent trade deals between our Houses as his dowry."

Jason felt both Damien and Adam bristling at the insult to the Queen that his mother would refer to her miscarriages or dare address her in such an informal manner in this venue. Or ever, really. But they stayed silent, letting Genny handle it herself; she'd long ago proven that she could defend herself quite well.

"You speak out of turn, Countess. The affairs of House *Alsterling* are none of your concern." Genevieve said coldly.

"I'm not speaking of House Alsterling," his mother said smugly. "I'm speaking of House Solway and House Laidly."

And she just lost, right there! The old lady crowed triumphantly in Jason's ear.

"Hmmmn," Genevieve glanced at her husband. "Do you say so, Countess?"

"It's all done anyways," Alexa Solway added. "The priestess has spoken the marriage vows over them. You can't do a thing about it... any more than you would Duchess Marseill's." She looked at the pair of young women to her right with an expression better suited to an alley-cat.

Duchess Laura looked like she wanted to dive in scratching – at least verbally, but her wife seized her arm and began whispering rapidly in her ear – in Mercasian, if Jason caught the intonation. The Duchess subsided, but gave Jason an apologetic look.

They were trapped as neatly as were he and Adam. If Damien declared this marriage-bond between Jason and Isabelle Laidly null and void, especially on the grounds that Jason was already betrothed to Adam, then Laura and Carmencita's marriage was also at risk on the same grounds. And then they would lose Alpinsward back to Mercasia... and now that Jason could *See* what hold the Realm had upon Damien *that* clearly wasn't an option for the King...

He rubbed his fingers over the betrothal band – Adam's love-gift, carried in secret until *Jason* was ready to accept it – that he had discreetly shifted to his other hand before Isabelle or his mother... or Megan... could notice and demand he remove it. The frilly, delicate wedding band Isabelle had shoved onto his finger – barking his knuckles as she did – was a sharp contrast in more ways than one.

"And did my dearest friend accept the vows of his own free will?" Genevieve asked.

"*I* accepted on his behalf. As his liege-lady and mother," the Countess stated triumphantly.

"That seems... of some legal concern." The Queen raised an eyebrow, turning slightly to regard her husband.

"It's perfectly acceptable, Your Majesty," Countess Alexa's lawyer huffed, though she had clearly been addressing Damien.

"And you are?" Genevieve inquired with an almost excessive politeness.

"Rupert Dolschael, Attorney and Legal Scholar," the portly man said self-importantly. "My credentials are on record with Judge Emberdeen."

Genevieve nodded. "Ah, yes. His Majesty's Judge of Docks and Locks. I fail to see how that commends you to Our notice as an expert in this matter, barrister."

The priestess surged forward as Dolschael looked offended. "There is also the matter of saving this poor soul, Your Highness. I pronounced them man and wife that you might not allow this heresy to take further root in our fair Realm."

She glowered at the Alpinsward noblewomen.

Genevieve gave her a look of deep disfavor.

"The Realm does not agree with your assessment, priestess," Damien's voice seemed to come from a deep well, and even Genevieve looked startled. The King shook his head slightly, blinking, and continued on in a more normal tone. "Nor does the discourtesy you show to the Queen stand you in good stead in this hall. You are dismissed from Our Presence."

The priestess stared at him, mouth agape and unmoving, until Sir Drake took her arm and began to escort her out. She came awake at that point and began to scream nasty things about how Damien would damn the souls of every person in the Realm. Even Countess Solway didn't seem to mind when the door shut off the priestess' string of curses.

Jason's eyes sought Adam's again. It still didn't look good to him, but Adam didn't look discouraged. An amused light came into the newly-named Champion's eyes as the girl – Isabelle – threaded her arm through Jason's elbow possessively. Adam regarded Isabelle momentarily, then met Jason's gaze. Something – Jason couldn't have said what it was – about the look in his love's eyes made him flush slightly and smile back almost shyly. And if there had ever been *shyness* in their relationship these many years it had never been on *his* part before. A frisson of relaxation took some of the painfully correct starch out of his spine at the confidence in Adam's expression.

Isabelle frowned and tightened her grip on Jason's arm, but the tall knight barely noticed. He still didn't know how, but he was beginning to believe this *might* actually work out after all.

"As for you, Lord Barrister," Damien looked at the lawyer. "While your claim is not entirely without merit, the precedents you cite apply better in other contexts. Forced marriage has not been permitted in this Realm since long before Queen Marian's time."

"Your Majesty does not have a legal credential," the man huffed. "You are most certainly mistaken."

Genevieve laughed disbelievingly. "Where *did* you find these treasures, Alexa? Master Dolschael–" The Queen denied the lawyer the coveted title that Damien had overgraced him with. "You are perhaps unaware that the *King* does not *require* a legal credential. The King *makes* the law. The King *sets* precedent. Doubtless these five years of Our more genteel reign have caused you to forget such trivialities... though you might be grateful it is not King *Reginald* whom you face with such impertinences on your tongue."

"My Queen..." Damien began reprovingly.

"Nevertheless," Genevieve went on, ignoring her husband's attempt to interrupt, "since it *is* King Damien you stand before and challenge, you might do well to remember that he does not need to file a *legal credential* with one of his own lower courts. He has the finest legal mind in the Realm."

Pffmph, muttered the grumpy old lady's voice. *And this is why she was the Sword's second choice. Too hotheaded. Just like my daughter. And granddaughter. She's letting them take this in the wrong direction.*

Damien broke from his severe expression to give her a bemused look. "While We thank Our Queen for her gallant defense of Our capacities," he said mildly, "the matter at hand is not whether Countess Solway had the right to speak for her son as his liege-lady, but whether she is rightly his liege-lady at all."

"What are you talking about?" Jason's mother cried.

Damien eyed her, waiting patiently until she wilted under that intense silver gaze.

"What are you talking about, Your Majesty?" she said more quietly, if not more humbly.

Damien acknowledged her submission only by answering.

"It has long been understood that a legitimate child will inherit their name and rank from the parent of higher status. And it has become well-established that the Monarch's Blade will speak for only those descended of House Alsterling." He looked directly at Jason. "Come forwards, Sir Jason."

Jason frowned, but wrestled his arm free of his would-be wife and did as his king commanded, stepping past his furious mother and sister to do so. He knelt, without being told, at the foot of the dais, though his relief at being separated from his family made him want to run up the broad stairs to claim his place beside Damien. And throw himself into Adam's arms. Or at Adam's feet in apology for this entire fiasco.

The King rose from the Throne, and Jason could see now how he gently disengaged the tight grasp of the Realm – loosening the threads without denying them their hold on him until, like persistent children, they gave him space to move. Damien took the Sword by its blade and offered the hilt to Jason.

Automatically he reached for it, knowing that nothing would happen. He'd done this before, after all.

*Ah, but **then** I hadn't acknowledged you as my own, Grandson. Took the boy awhile to convince me I should, I can tell you. Not that I don't wish you and your young man all the best – and would be pleased to put paid to another presumptuous Solway – but the Alsterling name isn't something to be casually offered.*

The Blade glowed instantly to life, casting bright, rainbow corruscations off from it. And it seemed to be... *purring?*

Jason looked up at Damien in surprise.

"My oldest uncle, Crown Prince Robert," the King explained, and his voice mesmerized not merely Jason, but the entire hall. "Eldest son of King Reginald by his first wife, Princess Lindrea, himself the eldest son of Prince Anthony, himself the eldest son of Queen Marian Alsterling. My uncle Robert – as so many of my aunts and uncles and cousins – sought some other life beyond what his father, King Reginald, permitted. And they one and all were executed for such temerity, including my own father, Crown Prince Eric.

"Prince Robert, as did so many of his younger siblings, fell in love with a woman of more modest means and of whom his father would never approve – in his case a recently widowed baroness. They wed in secret and produced one child before Prince Robert was 'killed by bandits' after leading that famously successful treaty negotiation with Mercasia."

He nodded at Duchess Laura and Lady Carmencita, who nodded soberly back. It was Prince Robert's death that had put paid to that treaty... leading eventually to Alpinsward's eventual defection to Mercasia.

"The Baroness died soon after, and *supposedly* no one remembered who the child's father had been, though he had been recorded as legitimate. A protection for mother and child both, no doubt, in that perilous time. Some fifteen years later, my father came hunting the missing child, having inherited his brother Robert's effects in addition to the Ring of the Heir. He found the young man... and the young man's beautiful cousin. My father married the cousin – my mother, Lady Miria – and sponsored the youth to come here, to Our Fair City of Emeralsee. His own father could, after all, hardly claim that the Eldridge family of Elderwyld was unworthy to provide a bride to the Crown Prince... when they had clearly already done so."

Damien took a deep breath. "But there the tale takes its dark turn. My father's goal was to raise his eldest brother's child up out of obscurity and set him in his proper place as a Prince of the Realm. But the youth was a country boy, unused to the bright lights of the city... and the shadows that lurked beneath. He ended up on what seemed to be his own father's path. Barely of age to wed, but blessed with the height of a man and the looks of one, he too wooed – or *was wooed by* – and won a recently widowed noblewoman. And fathered one son."

He looked directly at Countess Alexa Solway, who looked like she dearly wanted to speak up but didn't dare interrupt the King. "But in *his* case, the noblewoman had been tasked with this marriage and the bearing of a child by the word of King Reginald. And once the child was born neither she nor the King had any use for the country boy – his grandson – who had fathered it. So, they cast the young man out and sent him to sea, where pirates might steal him away and thereby end their problem for them.

"And the child that the noblewoman had borne at her king's demand... The *son* who was to mend her growing rift with the Duke of Elaarwen by offering him for the hand of the Duke's only daughter, and give the noblewoman her fondest wish... That child was forgotten by the King, his grand destiny but one more of a dozen such schemes King Reginald had planted about the Realm to sow dissension and havoc when and where he might."

Damien held out his hands and Jason laid the Blade across his palms – carefully, most carefully. He'd always known the thing was precious, but now it was the means of feeing him from that farce of a marriage...

The King gave him an ironic look and wrapped his own hands around the sharp, shining metal, then handed the hilt to Genevieve. The Sword blazed up brighter still in her hands than it had in Jason's.

"The man you know as Sir Jason Solway should more properly be named Jason Alsterling. Eldest and only son of the eldest and only son of Prince Robert Alsterling." Damien looked at Countess Alexa Solway. "And thereby his only liege-lord or -lady would be myself and the Queen. And thereby, Countess Solway, inasmuch as thou didst know this and yet seek to subvert Our will, and inasmuch as thou hast no standing to make vows upon Sir Jason's behalf, I declare this marriage null and void."

He looked back at Jason. "Rise, Cousin. And take thy rightful place by Our side as Heir. By Our Choice and by the Choice of Our Blade... and by thine own birthright."

And there we go! The old woman chortled.

Jason looked up into Damien's clear, grey eyes. The fey silver had faded back to the King's normal, if oddly intense, gaze. He looked to the right and met Adam's stunned, but pleased eyes. So, *he* hadn't known where Damien was taking this either...

Then Jason stood, turning to look at the crowd gathered there in the Throneroom.

Duchess Laura smiled at him, her expression filled with relief.

His niece, Elaina, was clearly stunned. Her father, Jason's brother-in-law, looked thoughtful more than shocked.

Megan... her gaze traded back and forth between her mother and Jason, a sense of betrayal evident in her mien and posture, no matter which way she looked.

His mother... regardless what other history there was, she was still the woman who bore him. He looked – for a last time? – for some maternal feeling in her gaze. Some hint that she had his best interests at heart. Some clue that she cared for him.

And saw nothing.

Nothing more than the ashes of ambition and a vicious lack of concern for any consequence to him. To *anyone* besides herself?

"Evan *Eldridge*," declared the Countess in ringing tones, "*raped* my thirteen-year-old daughter while I was pregnant with his *son*. And was struck from our family tree for the horror of it. Tell me again, Your Most Gracious Majesty, how you dare claim the scion of such a man as your Heir!"

Isabelle Laidly gasped with shock, and Megan went absolutely white. Her husband moved carefully forwards and put an arm around her, looking with disgust at his mother-in-law... and sworn liege-lady. Her eyes still confused, Elaina stepped up to her mother's other side.

Damien held out his hand without looking, and Genevieve reversed the Sword and laid the hilt into his grasp. The light from the Sword burst forth until the hall was nearly as bright as day. It was entirely clear that the *King* was the first choice of the Monarch's Blade.

"Did he *really*, Countess? I left a part of the tale aside – out of respect for Lady Megan." The King nodded to the white-faced woman, who stood trembling in the circle of her husband's arm.

Megan shuddered away from the King's gaze, her eyes meeting Jason's as she did so. And he had no words for what was in her expression – surely nothing he had ever seen before on her face...

Abruptly Jason was thrown back to the memory that had surfaced recently: of looking up adoringly at Megan while she patiently showed his chubby little fingers how to hold a very tiny sword. If the end of the memory weren't of his mother coming upon the two of them and berating Megan, he would have guessed it was his own wishful fabrication. His child's ears hadn't understood anything but that his mother was angry – as she was *always* angry – but Megan had gone as white-faced as she was now. And thrust him away from her, telling him harshly to go back to his nurse and stay away from her. Was that the last time his sister had shown him a kindness? He'd all but forgotten that she'd ever viewed him with anything other than disgust and hatred... and something else that was deeper and somehow even harder to look at.

But in that odd, orphan memory from – surely Jason couldn't have been a great deal older than Tim and Aryllis' little Rico – Megan's expression had been tender as she spoke to him. And he'd trusted her implicitly... hidden behind her when their mother had come bursting in upon the lesson.

It had to be wishful thinking. *Megan* couldn't use a sword. And he'd never in all these years seen her wear anything other than elegant ladies' gowns and show disdain for women who were more practical. She managed Brindlewell as their mother's assistant, but she didn't ride out to check on things herself.

Still... that fragment of wishful thinking had seemed so *real*...

But why would he invent such a fantasy around *Megan*? Wasn't it always his *mother* from whom Jason had hoped to win approval?

"You don't know *anything* about that time! You were not even born!"

Did his mother have a desperate look to her eye as she railed rudely at the King? Jason had no idea what that should look like. She had always been so in control – of herself, of him, of everyone and everything around her.

Until she arrived two weeks before to find that Jason had disobeyed her directions about the townhouse and that the King was offering a scholarship to Roger and Esmerelda...

Damien raised an eyebrow at the irate woman. "Do We not? Do you suppose, Countess, that one can know only what one's own eyes have seen, what one's own ears have heard? What one's own heart has pulsed through?" He shook his head. "A paltry way to live. Even had We not discovered the truth through other means, surely it would be obvious that a boy of fifteen and a girl of nearly the same age might begin to fall in love.

That a sophisticated and graceful girl, educated in the ways of the Court might find a newfound countrybred Prince charming."

"Nooo..." Megan put her face in her hands, shaking.

"And surely it would not be surprising that when the countrybred boy – with his countrybred values – woke to find his sweetheart in his bed, that he would pledge to marry her on the instant. Realizing only later that it was her *mother* he had pledged himself to." Damien looked like he was trying not to be judgmental. "As to why you were there – I suppose we have my grandfather to thank for that. Though it seems an unnecessarily convoluted scheme when he could have let nature take its course between the younger people." The King shrugged. "Not that leaving things alone was King Reginald's forte."

"You *lie.*" But Countess Solway was nearly as pale as her daughter.

Damien inclined his head. "The legend goes that lies cannot be spoken by one who holds the Monarch's Blade. But if it pleases you to believe it, Countess, there is proof. Lord David of Solway." Jason saw his brother-in-law's head jerk up in startled – though not exactly *surprised* – acknowledgment of perhaps the first time the King had ever bespoken him. "Did Lady Megan come a virgin to your marriage-bed?"

David flushed, glancing at his wife and daughter, then pulled Megan into his chest to shield her from the avid eyes of the Court. "She did, Your Majesty."

Jason stared at the man. Twenty-four years he had been married to Megan... allowing her and the Countess to perpetuate this lie to their children, divide him from his nieces and nephews. And all the while he had known the *truth?* That Jason *wasn't* the bad seed offspring of a rapist?

David met his eyes as if seeking forgiveness... and dropped them.

Jason struggled to make sense of it. The man had always been weak, he knew. But could he not have done *something?*

A small part of the tall knight tried to remind him that David had always been kind. And that he'd had few options to help Jason unless he was willing to risk losing his own children.

But it was a fairly small part, and Jason's entire world had been turned upside-down and inside-out. He might muster up forgiveness for David – or even Megan – eventually.

But... not today.

Damien nodded. "Prince Eric's personal papers... and Lady Miria's... record the progress of your romance, Lady Megan. My lady mother wrote often to her cousins of Elderwyld to update them on Evan's progress. The

Eldridges were preparing to make an offer to betroth the two of you, contingent upon you both coming to marriageable age, and there was much back-and-forth regarding what dowry would be suitable. A dowry for a countess' Heir to wed a royal prince... or a dowry for the youngest brother of a country baron to wed a countess' Heir."

Megan was weeping quietly.

"Your Majesty," David spoke up, for once not sounding timid, his faint, foreign accent more distinct than Jason usually recalled it. "Give over. Please."

Damien gave him a long look. "And what dowry did Countess Solway demand from your family, Lord David? And how much has she held it over your head that, despite your family's ships and trade enriching her House's coffers, you are no more than a 'jumped-up merchant's son'? No matter," the King added pointedly, "that your family is merchant-*princes* in the land of your birth and you served as captain of your own ship?"

David looked up with clear eyes at the King... and then at *Genevieve* with what could only be a... *warning glance?*

"Megan is worth it, Your Majesty. My *children* are worth whatever *she* heaps upon me." His eyes flickered to Jason. "Though I cannot say it has been the same for others."

He *had* been the only source of kindness in that House for twenty-four years. And... despite his own lack of skill, it had been David who first put a sword in Jason's hands and showed him the basics of what to do with it when he was still courting Megan and Jason had been only nine years old.

"Mother, you *lied* to me," Megan burst out, twisting in David's arms to look at the angry older woman. "You told me Evan crept into *your* bed. You said... you said..." Her eyes turned to her brother, unreadable – almost un*see*able behind the sheen of tears. "Oh, Jason, what have I *done...?*"

Her husband of nearly a quarter century turned her again to weep into his chest over the first-love she had lost so long before he ever met her. Jason saw the same patience and compassion with which David had cared for his children... and that he had extended to Jason himself whenever he could do so out of sight of the Countess... or of Megan.

David's eyes asked the King to end this... but did not beg. Perhaps David was not so weak as Jason had thought. Perhaps he was a different kind of strong.

"Countess Solway," Damien said. "Thou hast broken no law of this land, save those natural laws that speak to moral character. Keep thou, therefore, thy title. Howe'er, thou shalt absent thyself from Our Court from this day forth, and from Our Duchy of Emeralsee. We expect that thou shalt confine thyself to thy lands at Brindlewell, there to stay for the remainder of thy days. Be aware," he added, "that thy Vassal's Oath still doth Bind thee and take care in thy choices of guests and correspondence."

While she spluttered in fury, the King turned to Megan and David. "Lady Megan, We do seek thy forgiveness for the harsh nature of this inquiry. Do thou take up the reins of thy House and prosper it, but lay the underpinnings with kindness above all else."

It was David who nodded on behalf of his still-overcome wife, accepting for both of them though he officially held no Ilseadoran title beyond mere courtesy and had no legal binding upon Brindlewell beyond his marriage and children.

And now Damien looked at Duchess Laura and Lady Carmencita. "We trust that you are satisfied with these outcomes as well, Your Grace. My Lady."

They both curtsied in acquiescence.

Damien turned to mount the dais once again, pausing as he saw that Jason still stood with but one foot on the first step.

The King frowned. "Jason?"

Jason wrenched the frilly, sharp ring from his hand, not caring that it scraped his barked knuckles still more raw.

He tossed it at Isabelle Laidly's feet, the tiny ornament making a tinny sound as it struck the ancient, flagstoned floor... precisely where there was no longer quite a stain.

"You might want that back," the Heir to the Throne said, stepping smartly over to his true love, and kissed Adam fiercely, passionately... and for the very first time in *public.* Ten years of hiding their relationship from King Reginald and Lord Prydeen – or trying to – and Jason's own natural modesty and private nature had made his mother think... had made *Adam* sometimes think... that he was ashamed. That he shared his mother's biases and only loved Adam reluctantly.

Not true.

Never true.

Jason laced his fingers tightly with Adam's – as tightly as Damien had held onto Genevieve – as he stepped away, and kept the grip tight as he took one step higher on the dais to claim his place as Heir. As an *Alsterling,* for all that the thought of being *adopted* into the royal family had horrified him not so very long ago.

The look Jason gave his mother was defiant in a way he had never dared look at her – never dared to look at *anyone* – before.

Adam's face was... smug. The sardonic look with which he favored his soon-to-be mother-in-law clearly declared that he had won.

"Oh, Isabelle, what have you *done?*"

Count Emery bustled into the room, summoned by rumor, not royal decree. Jason noted that the room had filled up – he could not say at what point Damien had had the doors flung open. Lady Alanna had finally allowed Roger and Esmerelda to enter; they clung to their parents, looking far younger than thirteen and eleven, and casting fearful glances at both their grandmother and the King.

"I made a play to be Queen, Father," the young woman admitted candidly, in a high, thin voice that made Adam, with his perfect pitch, wince. "Or at least Princess-Consort and Duchess." She shrugged. "I failed. But the King broke *my* marriage, so now you have what you need to see Raymond properly wed to Laura."

"You foolish child," the Count raged at his Heir, while his son – the estimable Raymond – stood behind him shaking his head. "Have you no political savvy at all? I was looking for *bargaining* strength, and now you've *squandered* it! Your Majesty," he addressed Damien, who had paused on the second-highest step of his Throne dais to observe the new drama curiously. "I petition to set aside Isabelle as my Heir in favor of Raymond."

Damien glanced at Genevieve, who shrugged, before answering. "That choice does not require Crown approval, my lord. Nor my approval as Duke of Emeralsee." County Seasbourne resided within the duchy.

"I don't *want* Seasbourne, Father. I want to go *home*." Raymond was striding across the room to Laura and Carmencita. "To raise my *children*. I'm so sorry for getting us all caught up in this, my dear ladies. Father wanted to be able to acknowledge the babies as his grandchildren."

"I *want* to be able to adopt one of them as Raymond's *Heir*," Count Emery blustered. "Damnfool girl." He glowered at his daughter... who didn't look in the least bit cowed.

Damien did raise his eyebrows at that one. "That would seem to be a matter for Lord Raymond to choose, not yourself, my lord Count. Though there are *precedents*," Damien cast a wicked glance at the lawyer who was now trying to make himself scarce against a wall, but not daring to leave without a royal dismissal. "For adopting an Heir from another House."

The young man had his hands out to the Duchess and her wife. "I thought I was visiting my parents for a few weeks once the border was open and we were part of Ilseador again," he was saying. "You *know* I meant to come back home to all of you. I didn't think it would take nearly three *years*. But then Father had this mad idea of using the betrothal document and the treaty to leverage the King into making the children legally mine as well. And then he wouldn't let me come home to Alpinsward so he would have more leverage. Do they even remember me?" he asked wistfully.

Jason tried to extract his thoughts from the excess of relief fogging his mind after the messy swirl of his own close-call and all of the stunning revelations in order to focus on this.

He was *Damien's* Heir, dammit, and this was important. He could focus. Was Raymond Laidly really saying he was the sire of Duchess Laura and Lady Carmencita's children?

"Should make a legal threesome of it. They do it in *Dawil*," Count Emery grumped. "Don't make a man choose between his son and his grandchildren."

"They are *considering* such marriages in Dawil," Damien corrected punctiliously. "And only in the port-city of Wave. And even there, it's only because of the tradition that the Lord – or Lady – of that province is ceremonially wed to the Sea-Queen and therefore any regular alliance already involves three people. We have no such traditions here," though he glanced ironically at the hungry Throne, "and simply getting marriages between *two* men or women worked out is turning out to be a bit of a challenge."

Isabelle Laidly didn't seem clever enough to realize he was talking about her until her father cuffed her ear lightly. Presumably her erstwhile marriage to Jason had been his mother's seed, though planted in fertile ground.

Countess Solway simply seethed... though she did it silently. Jason couldn't quite believe that Damien could possibly have put paid to all his mother's devious and multifaceted plans by simply exiling her to Brindlewell... though what else she could possibly do, he had no idea. At least her reasons for not joining the Rebellion were now clear – as the mother of a potential Royal Heir, surely she hadn't dared, lest King Reginald discover her faithlessness before Duke Aldred could extend his protection. And that explained at least some portion of her bitterness towards Jason himself.

Damien's voice had faltered as he looked at the young Duchess, her lady-wife, and the young lord, still talking about their children. The women had each given Raymond a hand and a kiss on the cheek, though their arms were around each other. The young man seemed to expect nothing more.

All three of them were barely in their early twenties – Alpinsward had declared its allegiance to Mercasia not long after Prince Eric and Lady Miria had been murdered, so Laura had grown up a Mercasian. The duchy had returned to the Realm but three years earlier – Genevieve's first successful negotiation for one of the Lost Provinces. The Duchess had been pregnant at the time, Jason recalled, and her lady-wife had had the care of two other toddlers, one from each mother. It had made him wonder who the father was, and Adam had later expressed envy that it seemed to be easier for a pair of women to have children than it was for the two of *them*. Laura could not have been above eighteen when the oldest was born.

Jason could see the hunger in his King's eyes that *he* should suffer such problems. Genevieve's eyes were shuttered as if she dared not even *think* too hard about this.

It wasn't Jason's place to speak.

Or was it?

As Heir, did he have the right? King Reginald had permitted no one else to have so much as a smidgeon of power. Damien... was all about giving his power away.

"I'm sure there is some way we can accommodate the needs of all the parties involved," Jason heard his own voice saying before he had consciously decided to speak. "The wellbeing of the children is surely the paramount concern." Adam squeezed his hand approvingly.

Even if it worked out for Laura and Carmencita Marseill and Raymond Laidly, Jason realized, it wouldn't for himself. The accepted standard would not bend so far for the child of the King. Not within his lifetime anyways, though perhaps in some distant future... A *king-less* future if Damien had his way, thereby negating the problem before it began.

"Well said!" Duke Zachary Miramar had appeared in the Throne-room as well, and *his* baby daughter was snug in his arms. "And with that as a goal, can we not let the lawyers and the Council meet to determine the details, Your Majesty?"

Damien started. "Yes, of course..." His child-hungry eyes were now fixed on Betha Miramar in her father's arms.

Jason sighed internally, wondering if he was going to have to step in still further.

Genevieve seemed to come out of herself just before Jason couldn't deny any longer his duty as Heir to keep things moving. "Captain Ancellius, do assist the Countess in carrying out His Majesty's commands. This is a day of rest, dear people. Let us return to our private pursuits in contemplation of the demands of the morrow. The day beyond that is surely soon enough to sort out any *other* complications."

Oh, she was good at moving people along when she wanted to be.

Practice makes for better, as you know. You didn't do so badly yourself, Grandson.

Jason shook his head. Hearing voices was a sign of madness, he'd been told.

Well, I never! A brief pause, then, *You know exactly who I am, don't you, you naughty boy. The feeling of someone chuckling inside your head was... distinctly odd. There may be hope for you yet, Jason* **Alsterling**.

His mother gave him a blazing look as poor Tim escorted her from the room, and Jason shuddered. Old as she was – and his mother approached seventy years, slightly older than Lord Aldred – he couldn't doubt there was more trouble she *could* cause. And *would*.

Adam pulled him down a step to slide his arm around Jason's waist.

"And here I was wondering if I'd get so much as a polite little kiss at our *wedding* – out in front of everyone," his love said teasingly. "I certainly didn't expect you to practically *make love* to me in the Throne-room in front of all and sundry." His tone held as much relief as humor, and a faint tremble in his ever-steady arm told Jason of just how fearful Adam had been.

David caught Jason's eye again, and he saw a certain wistfulness in his brother-in-law's gaze. David might love Megan with all his heart, but twenty-four years under the Countess' close supervision and with Megan believing a lie had surely done some damage.

Nothing but pride shone from three other sets of eyes – and more – and Jason suddenly realized he had *other* brothers-in-law. Nascent ones, anyways.

"You... missed our celebration last night," Adam was saying shyly – *Adam? shy? outside* of bed? – as the Loveresses converged about them both. "It... wasn't right without you."

"Then we'll have to have a re-do," Jason told him firmly, and to the delight of the younger Loveresses.

He and Adam both glanced over to the King and Queen, who were not-quite-drooling over baby Betha. Sir Angelos nodded at his former Captain from nearby, and Lady Alanna smiled at the baby as well, but her eyes were alert and moving. They were guarded.

Sir Angelos *Eldridge,* Jason suddenly realized in shock. This must have been nearly as uncomfortable for the young Royal Guardsman as for the rest of them. The man was his own cousin… Jason glanced in his direction, and Sir Angelos gave the Cham– the *Heir* a wry nod and a slight smile. The younger knight had been one of the more promising members of the Guard; Jason remembered Adam commenting that, if Marcus didn't start to show a bit better, Angelos might make Second… for the sense of humor that Marcus notably lacked, if nothing else.

Marianna dove between him and Adam, unlacing their arms from about each other's waists and shoving them apart with a laugh. "Don't you two know you're supposed to give each other a little space on the day before your wedding?" she teased.

"Are we supposed to be pretending to something we're not?" Adam asked his youngest sister with a raised eyebrow.

She considered. "Well, I've seen your wedding outfits, and since neither of you are being so bold as to wear *white* as if you were virgins… I suppose not." Her forthright evaluation made Jason blush, but apparently Adam was even less prepared to hear such words from his baby sister, because he began to choke.

Choke with *laughter,* Jason finally realized, as everyone tried to pat Adam on the back at once. And Marianna sent him into a fresh paroxysm when she inquired where they were both going to sleep tonight – because it was bad luck to sleep together the night before your wedding – and Desirée commented dryly that she doubted *sleep* would be much on the agenda for either of them. Charley then punched Lorry in the arm and suggested that that explained his two divorces.

Somehow Jason realized they were being swept out the door with fair efficiency despite all the horseplay – and that at least one of them had a hand on him at all times. "We're not letting *anyone* steal you away this time, big brother-to-be," Marianna whispered in his ear when it was apparently her turn, and Jason felt warmed inside and out.

Chapter TWENTY-THREE

Ceremony

JASON'S INVESTITURE AS DUKE OF Emeralsee the next day went smoothly, except for the usual part where the Realm reached out and Bound the new Duke.

They were all used to the newly sworn Vassal being somewhat boggled after and had planned time to allow him to recuperate. Those very few nobles with a more-than-marginal talent for magick – like Lord Aldred – took a little longer, since their vision was distracted by newly seeing the sparkles of magick as well. Damien anticipated that Jason had a talent, and had advised Aryllis to give him some extra time.

What he hadn't anticipated was Jason being near-*blinded*.

Damien himself had been Bound when he accepted the Sword from Queen Marian's statue. It had been broad daylight, and he had still been quite dazed by the magick imbued in the citizens, the buildings, and most especially the City gates as they had escaped Emeralsee, even though the brighter light of the sun had washed out much of the sparkle. The flows of magick out in the countryside were easier to take – perhaps because they weren't unnaturally Bound in place – and it had still been broad daylight. He had gradually recovered himself once in the protected space of the grotto.

Genevieve, he had sworn and Bound as his First Vassal in the grotto. At night and outside of the city where the flows of magick were more naturally distributed... more... *peaceful.*

Because Jason's investiture was of interest to the entire City, they had decided to hold the ceremony at dawn in the City's central market square. The place where Damien and Genevieve had formed a soul-bond in full view of the citizenry on the last day of his own coronation festival – it was the obvious place to hold major public events because of its size. And dawn because... they had two more ceremonies to conduct that day and because the City workers preferred it, as it meant there would be an entire day for the festival that would follow and therefore a longer opportunity to sell food and memorable fripperies to the revelers.

Dawn was never Damien's favorite time of day. Perhaps he would have thought harder about the location if he hadn't been grumpily focused on being overruled about the time.

Or perhaps he and Genevieve were simply so used to the magick they saw everywhere that they had forgotten how overwhelming it could be at first.

In any case, the pale light of dawn did nothing to dim the coruscating sparkles, and as Jason rose from his Vassal's Oath – still also dazed that Damien had named him 'Sir Jason *Alsterling,* Duke of Emeralsee' – he literally could see nothing *but* magick.

"Damien, I can't see," he said, trying not to move his mouth very much and betray his state to the watching crowds. "I can't see *anything.* It's all colored light."

The King managed the rest of the ceremony – minimal as it was – by guiding him by hand and with *sotto voce* instructions. It would have been hard to tell which of them was more relieved when it was over and they could turn away from the crowds and sit down at the top of the reviewing stand.

"Close your eyes," Damien instructed, and placed his warm hands on either side of the new Duke's face.

"What's wrong?" It was Adam's voice, harsh with anxiety.

"He'll be fine," Damien said calmly. "I've been warning Jason for a while that I suspected he has a strong talent for magick. He just confirmed that rather dramatically."

"Oh, no." Now Genevieve's voice, caught between amusement and concern. "I forgot how much more there is to see here in the City."

"And at dawn, with nothing to wash some of it out..." Damien's voice was also amused, if slightly grimly so.

"What are you two talking about?" Adam demanded.

Genevieve explained. "The Binding wakes any latent talent for magick, Adam. The first thing that happens is the sense of one's own lands and people sinking into you... and then you can see the magick. It's generated by ever–"

"Yes, yes, I know where magick comes from," Adam said impatiently. And then, patently responding to some expression on her face. "It was – and *is* – my job to protect you both, Genevieve. I had to learn what I could about magick to that end."

Jason could imagine the speculative look on her face and realized he hadn't spoken to her or Damien yet about the way Adam had seemed to *glow* when he held the Heir's Ring...or the cobwebs of Binding that he'd been seeing everywhere.

"All right then. The way we see magick, it looks like colored sparkles," she went on. "In the countryside at night, it's like... fireflies. Everywhere, but ebbing, flowing, concentrating briefly here and there... After a while you get used to it and it's only faintly distracting from whatever else you're doing. In Emeralsee City, though, every person has their spark and there is magick Bound into nearly every wall and cobblestone. We'd never realized how *much* magick was used to build this city until Damien and I began to look around..."

"So, the problem is that he can see it all at once, all of a sudden?"

Damien snorted. Whatever Healing he was doing was... not making that much difference. Jason's eyes still felt slightly... burnt. "Genevieve calls it fireflies. I think of it more like fireworks. Jason just stared right into a firework as it exploded. Close up." He stepped back. "I've done what I can for now. He needs a blindfold and rest." Jason imagined the King raking that eternally errant lock out of his face. "It'll be a miracle if he can see well enough to make it through the coronation at noon. I *told* you crazy morning larks that a dawn ceremony was a terrible idea."

"Yes, love," Genevieve's voice was close enough that it must be her winding his head with something soft – one of the scarves that had been in her hair based on the sweet fragrance. Adam would doubtless be dismayed that he could identify the smell of the Queen's hair. Though for all the times he'd had to carry her... Her voice was amused as she rebuked her husband. "If you'd given us a *reason* instead of just sounding like you were grumpy at having to get out of bed..."

"I always have a *reason,*" Damien retorted. "I just can't always *explain* it."

"That's called a *'hunch'* or an *'instinct,'* Damien. Not a *reason.*"

"Call it what you like, but the sudden shock of that much light – it's not even *actually* light or I could Heal his eyes. We just perceive it as light because our minds know how to interpret light." He paused. "It could have been *worse,* I suppose. We could have done this in the Throne-room."

"Jase? Are you ready to go lie down?" Adam's voice was in his ear. What was doubtless meant to be a quiet, private query while King and Queen argued amicably had... quite a different effect as Adam's warm breath proved a delightful contrast to the more-than-brisk air of late Autumn.

"Only if it's with you." Jason replied. The blindfold was helping.

Adam chuckled. "Insatiable, you are today."

Jason's lips curved in a smile. Desirée had been more correct than she might have guessed. They hadn't gotten nearly as much sleep as they should have to cope with a long and harrowing day. But the fear of losing each other that they had both faced so directly the previous day... and the relief of knowing that there could be no further hindrances... had combined into a deep and desperate need for each other. Some things were more important than sleep.

Though the need for sleep usually caught up with you quickly enough, in Jason's experience.

"Actually, love, I just want a nap," the newly-made Duke admitted. "But... I'm not sure I can fall asleep without you..."

He heard Genevieve chuckle. "Damien, I'll go talk to Aryllis about adjusting the coronation. You take these two directly to their rooms so we don't have to explain about the blindfold to every noble, servant and citizen in the capitol."

"Very well. Don't forget to tell the Baronetta what we've done with them. I'm going to take my *own* nap after I see them settled."

"Of course, my handsome night owl. I wouldn't *dream* you would do otherwise."

"Join me?" Was the lack of his eyes making his hearing more keen? Surely Damien had pitched that for Genevieve's ears alone, that hopeful, breathy tone one Jason knew well...

"Not... a good idea, love. Not today." The disappointment in her soft voice was just as hard to miss. "There's likely to be a number of things we women will need to take care of, with all you big, strong men fast asleep through the mid-morning," she added in a more spritely, teasing tone...

though to Jason's suddenly acute hearing it was all too clear that she was making excuses. Surely, they couldn't be reacting to each other again *already?*

"Of course," Damien copied her bright tone as best he could. "Whatever could we do without you? Come... send someone to wake me in time to prepare for round two of this crazy day, if you please. Adam, Jason?"

The air stopped being cold and fresh and filled with the smell of the sea and damp leaves and the morning's baking. Instead, it was warm and smelling of fresh linens and Adam's favorite scent.

"Do you need anything else?" The King asked.

Adam barked a laugh as he eased Jason onto the mattress of their bed. "Fewer years so I didn't have to rest my poor body like an old man after such an easy morning?"

He began to pull off Jason's soft, ornamental-looking boots and the fancy overtunic in turquoise and gold. There was a different one for the coronation, but he'd wear both again in the course of his upcoming duties and there was no need to make the maids' work harder by creasing it as he slept. He'd felt guilty about the tunic he'd tossed on the floor so blithely two nights before until Adam had shown him that he'd placed it in the clothespress and it seemed fine. Clothing was expensive – a fact his mother had impressed upon him despite the wealth she spent on her own wardrobe.

How could he *hear* the King hesitating?

"I resemble that remark," Damien said lightly at last. "But... perhaps we can do something to make you feel those years a little less. Later." There was no sound or even a whoosh of air, but there was a sense that the King was no longer in the room.

"Did... he just make a pass at me?" Adam asked uncertainly.

Jason loosened his belt once Adam had removed his overtunic. It had seemed very strange indeed not to have his sword at his side today. He laughed as he lay down carefully, feeling his way to make sure he didn't try to lie down half off the bed. "Believe me, love, if Damien had made a pass at you, you wouldn't need to *ask* that question. I think he was offering to Heal some of your old injuries. He made me the same offer a couple of days ago."

"Hmmn." Adam made his own preparations – which included removing *his* sword, which as Champion *he* wore all the time. Though, to be fair, as Crown Prince Jason would as well. It had merely been decided – by Aryllis and Genevieve, he thought – that his sword would be an unwelcome distraction from his investiture as duke. Dukes, after all, did not usually wear swords in the presence of their king.

Adam snuggled in around him. Jason felt much of the tension flow out of him, and even his eyes felt a little better.

"Besides," he added sleepily. "Damien didn't even want *me*, really. Just an old... fancy... of his..."

He drifted off, his magick-stunned mind craving rest and almost missed Adam's soft, cynical snort.

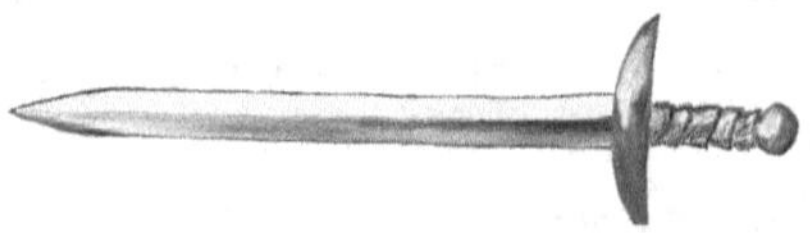

The coronation ceremony went off smoothly. Aryllis and the Queen had cobbled together ways to give Jason staging directions without anyone noticing. The basics of the ceremony were quite simple, after all; simply the placing of the Heir's Coronet on Jason's head. The rest was window-dressing and theatrics, but that was what the crowds gathered for.

By now everyone had heard that the Sword had spoken for Jason, so they had to repeat that display, of course. And the story of how the son of Countess Solway could actually be an Alsterling was making the rounds as well. Martin and Marianna had gleefully reported that there were at least three different songs about it already. Apparently none of them very *good* songs yet; all the Loveress siblings were sensitive to the quality of music.

Jason had winced at that. For all that Megan had made his life a misery growing up, she didn't deserve to have her private business spread all over the Realm like this. Nor did his nieces and nephew deserve to be the targets of mockery.

Tim had stopped by and promised to give the squires and pages a talking to before Roger and Esmerelda joined their ranks. But Jason knew what it was like in those training halls and Tim just wasn't fearsome enough to enforce decent behavior. In point of fact, the new Captain had laughed at his dubious look and promised to put the fear of *Adam* into the boisterous children. And Adam had offered to stroll around at unexpected intervals in the squires and pages halls. It wasn't as if he wasn't going to have the time, he noted cynically.

Jason had tried to give him an offended look at that, but his vision was too blurry to accurately glower in Adam's direction... and Adam wasn't far wrong. Compared to his duties as Captain of the Royal Guards, Jason's as Champion had been light: training the more advanced swordsmen and serving as Genny's bodyguard. He hadn't had a problem fitting in the time to sit in that stuffy office reading reports with Damien.

The light curling and sparking off the Sword was, apparently, *real* light, not just magick made visible – or so Damien surmised when it didn't set back Jason's slowly recovering vision. More rest, the King prescribed, and he *might* even be able to see Adam's face enough to kiss him in the right spot after the wedding. Adam snorted at that and said he'd take care of it... regardless of how much Jason could see.

So, it was another blindfold and another nap in the afternoon. Jason would have been shocked that he could sleep so much... if he weren't too tired to be shocked.

This time, however, Adam didn't bother trying to pretend to sleep and simply got up after the other man was clearly out. He put on his tunic – dear Gods, his *third* for the day, but at least this one was just an old, comfortable thing, and belted his sword back on before sneaking out of the room carrying his boots. Jason didn't even stir as the door hinges made their usual squeal, and Adam frowned with concern.

To his not-complete-surprise, Damien was in his sitting room, playing a card game with Desirée's little boys. The King acknowledged him with a glance, but finished the hand with all due care before telling the boys he had to talk to their uncle for a bit.

"He's fine," Damien said as soon as the door had shut behind them and Adam had reset the wards. "And, no, I can't speed the process along. He's not sick or injured. His brain is just dealing with the sudden shock of having an entirely new set of faculties available."

Adam looked at the King dubiously. "I don't remember *you* being this tired."

Damien shrugged. "I had several years to get used to the Heir's Ring before the Sword found me. And the soul-bond. And... I didn't exactly have an opportunity to *be* tired, if you'll recall. They had me carrying a carpet all the way to the grotto."

Adam relented slightly with a reluctant chuckle. "Because you couldn't let go of that damned Sword."

"Now, now, be nice." Damien touched the hilt of his Blade lightly. "It's saving you from that dreaded curse of a mother-in-law."

Adam abruptly racked his own sword in the wall clasps where it was meant to go and threw himself into a chair. "And *that's* a bloody mess." He glowered at his king. "Did you have to air their dirty laundry in front of half the Realm? Asking David if Megan was a virgin, by the Gods!"

"Jason needed to know," Damien said simply. "And so did Megan. She's lived a lie most of her life."

"David gave up a great deal to marry her. His dignity, among other things. You did him no favors there."

The King cocked his head. "Didn't I? I suspect he and Megan will make their home here in Emeralsee at Solway House and leave Brindlewell to Alexa until she eventually suffocates in her own venom and dies like the snake she is."

Adam's eyebrows flew up. "That's... the most vindictive thing I think I've ever heard you say."

Damien looked down. "She hurt Jason. And she hurt *you*. And for no good reason. I mean, she had her *reasons,* but I don't think they were very good. I put her in the same category as Harald."

"And Lord Prydeen?" Adam asked sardonically. "And Prince Oskar? And your *grandfather?*"

"Hmmmn." Damien stood up to pace. "Those are... more complicated."

"Really?" Sarcasm dripped off of Adam's words.

"Really." Damien sighed. "Adam, hasn't it occurred to you yet that Grandfather shielded the two of you from Lord Prydeen? He knew exactly who Jason was. He knew what you were to each other." He snorted. "He knew what you were doing with teaching and training *me*. He made all that very, very clear when we came back from Lynncrag. Not about who Jason was, I only just figured *that* out this week. Yesterday, mostly, after I was able to confirm that Prince Robert was his grandfather. And I only sorted that out after the Changing of the Guard."

Adam frowned. Well, at least that answered the question of why Damien had sat on the information. He hadn't. "When did you have time? I thought you spent the evening and morning with Genevieve."

"Oh, you know how I don't sleep well at night." The King would not meet his new Champion's eyes. "I had all the pieces. I had to re-check my father's and mother's correspondence to be sure. They both knew Jason's father rather well."

"Twice your cousin..." Adam shook his head. "And King Reginald *knew.*"

"As long as no one but Alexa – and Megan – Solway did, Jason posed no threat. And Jason has never shown the slightest bit of political ambition. I... almost think King Reginald took some pleasure in watching us each grow up." Damien sighed. "He was very lonely in his own way."

Adam stared at him. "Damien, you're talking about the man who had your parents murdered in front of you."

The King looked down. "I know. And it's not like I forgive him for that. Or for leaving me to Lady Theresa. Or for giving Jason into Prince Oskar's hands." Adam had noticed that while Damien referred to the other children of King Reginald occasionally as his aunts and uncles, Oskar was always 'Prince Oskar.' He did more or less the same thing himself, after all. "Or for half-killing the Realm. But... he let me *live*. And he let Jason. And he could have separated the two of you, just on a whim..."

Adam remembered Damien's shamefaced admission of having sent knights on far assignments simply for having looked too interested in Genevieve. He hadn't yet been able to determine just which knights those were, or how fresh they had dared get before the King responded.

"And he let you both – all three – raise me." Damien added, then hesitated. "I assume you've realized that – *someone* – is going to eventually decide that Jason's claim to the Throne is better than mine. Eldest son of an eldest son, and all that."

Adam shrugged. "That's why you made sure to hold the Sword after he did, I assume. And had Genevieve do it. It burns brighter for her than for him, but brightest of all for you. And you're already crowned. And Jason doesn't want it. Nor do I."

The King nodded. "But sooner or later one or the other of you will be approached by... dissidents. I don't pretend they don't exist, and you've read all the same reports that I have."

The new Champion shrugged. "They won't make any headway with us."

"I didn't think so. Still, it might be an opportunity."

"You want him to play along and spy on the dissidents?" Adam shook his head. "Jason's almost painfully open. No one would believe him. And I am *not* going to let him go into some dark part of the city just to try it out. He thinks he knows how bad things are, down in the Docks District, but he has no real clue."

Adam knew that *Damien* knew, exactly. If the reports they both read hadn't made it clear, his sense of the Realm would have done it.

"Adam," the King's expression was almost pitying. "Jason is Bound to Emeralsee. He's going to *know*."

The knight frowned down at his hands in his lap. Yes, he'd realized that. He didn't want to think what it was going to do to his love's bright, fragile, hopeful heart.

"He'll be a light in that darkness, Adam. The way I can't be. Emeralsee needs more than I can give it, with the rest of the Realm also needing my attention." Damien sighed and perched on the back of the couch. "It's not easy to pace in here with all these cots, is it?" He eyed Adam. "Nevermind. Neither of you are pacers, I know that. I wasn't imagining that *Jason* could be an ear with the dissidents."

Adam looked up. "Me?"

Damien gave him a half-shrug. "You're widely considered to be the mastermind who placed me on the throne. Well, you and Ciriis," he amended, "but she's not here. And there are places where a man will find out more than a woman. Aryllis has ears in most of them," he admitted, "but anyone who thinks they're savvy enough to try to suborn the husband of the Crown Prince... the man who put me on the throne... you'll be hearing from a different quality of dissident."

Adam regarded him for a long moment. "And knowing you, you won't want to know *who,* you'll want to know *why* they don't agree with your rule."

Damien smiled. "Got it in one, Adam. If it's something I can address, it gives me the chance to do that before it gets out of hand. If not..." he turned a hand palm upwards, "it's an early warning." He gave his new Champion a wry look. "You *were* saying you'd have too much time on your hands as Champion."

"Nothing may happen – ever," Adam warned him.

"I know."

"And I'm giving Aryllis the names."

"I imagined you would."

"And Genevieve."

"No." Damien shook his head. "She'll feel she needs to do something about what I won't. No. You clear it with me before you share what you learn with Genevieve."

Adam looked at him. "And if I don't agree, will I even be able to?"

The King frowned. "What are you talking about, Adam?"

"Jason has started *seeing* your Bindings – he told me a few days ago. Apparently, they look like cobwebs to him. He says that I have so many on me that I'm almost cocooned." The knight glowered. "When and how, and bloody *why* did you Bind me, Damien?"

"I don't know what you're talking about..." The King squinted as if he was trying to see what Adam was describing. He shook his head, rubbed his eyes and tried again.

"I'm sorry, Adam," he said at last, "I can't *see* Bindings like that. It must be Jason's own gift, activated by the Ring. You... *sparkle* more than other people," he offered a little *diffidently*. "With magick. But I don't believe that's due to anything *I've* done."

"Jason thought it might be unintentional." Adam suggested.

Adam found himself laughing.

The King gave his friend an irritated look. "This isn't funny, Adam. And I'd think *you'd* be more upset than I would." His expression grew even odder. "Are you actually laughing so hard you're *crying?*"

Adam shook his head, wiping tears away. "It's just... your face..."

Jason stepped out of the bedroom with an expression of good-humored concern. "It's good to hear you laugh. But this seems a little extreme for you."

Adam was up in an instant, and at Jason's side. "Are you alright? Can you see?"

"I'm fine... and I wouldn't want to try to read anything yet, but I can see well enough to get around without bumping into furniture and walls." He looked quizzically at Adam. "Care to tell me what was so funny?"

Adam snickered again. "Damien's face when I told him about the cobwebs you see – or saw–" he added judiciously. "And your idea that he might have been placing Bindings without knowing it."

The King was pale. "I don't see how I could have. It takes energy and intention. I... This would be such an incredibly big problem."

Jason frowned at him. "Why?"

"Bindings need to be warded," Damien explained. "Otherwise, there can be... I don't know what to call them. Secret doors maybe? That a clever and determined wizard can find and use to turn the Binding to their own uses."

"Hmmn." Adam tried to stop laughing as Jason looked at him... but it felt good to laugh. It released stress in a completely different way than sex.

"I can't *see* what Adam says you did, Jason," Damien said earnestly. "I can't tell if there's something there I need to fix... or something there at all. The Bindings I placed intentionally – or set intentionally, like the Vassal's Oath – those I can sense. But not this other... this whatever it is. Who all is affected – other than Adam?"

The newly-crowned Heir to the Throne took the time to think about it. "Your Guards, including the Secret ones. Madame Elista. Tim, even before you made him Lord-Regent of Elmirscroft. The retired Guards I've seen around. I only started noticing this a few days ago. The night I hosted the banquet for you, actually."

Jason lowered his eyes as if not really wanting to remind the others of the other things that had happened that day.

"Your vassals are, but there's some sort of difference in the webs. And Genny, of course. She has both kinds. So does Tim, last I looked." He hesitated. "And I figured out why you hold onto Genny when you sit on the Throne. There were a huge number of threads that seemed to be almost trying to pull you *into* the Throne. I... saw that yesterday."

Damien blinked. "That's... a lot of people. And all people I care about."

He seemed neither surprised nor disturbed by Jason's description of webby things trying to pull him into the Throne. Though the idea made *Adam* cringe.

Jason was still thinking. "Tomas Elsevier, Rosa and Zachary. But Duchess Laura only has the other kind. And... Aryllis and Lena had more than anyone but Adam or Genevieve."

Something clicked in Adam's mind. "It *is* all people you care about, Damien."

The King looked guiltily at him. "Yes..."

"Could it be that it isn't magickal Bindings – at least not these other ones? Could it just be a... visual manifestation of... love?" Adam asked.

Jason's eyes softened, as Adam had expected, but Damien's, surprisingly didn't. If anything, he looked more upset.

"So, I've inadvertently *labeled* everyone I care about. In a way *I* can't detect or affect, but others potentially can. Wonderful." Damien's eyes widened further. "What if someone already *has?* What if that's why our, our *soul-bond* doesn't seem to be working?"

Jason folded his arms and put on his 'imperturbable swordmaster face,' as Damien had nicknamed it one particularly frustrating day when he was nineteen. "What have we taught you about 'what if'?"

The King sagged. "Don't think about 'what if' unless you have some solid reason behind it," he mumbled.

Adam suspected that while the younger man might be able – no, was *definitely able* – to quote anything and everything they had ever said to him, their words had made more of a difference mostly by kicking that overactive imagination underground. He hoped that the repetition had worn some grooves in Damien's thought patterns, but the suppressed panic at the back of the King's eyes made him wonder. Damien's entire governing style seemed to be to collect so much information that he could outflank the 'what ifs' before anyone else even noticed they existed. It seemed... exhausting.

On impulse, he threw an arm around Damien's shoulders. "It's not a bad thing to love someone, little brother," he said, and as Damien looked up at him in surprise and delighted shock, Adam realized that he had once given the younger man a fair amount of physical affection before... before he was married. Somehow, after Genevieve came into the picture, he'd stopped casually touching Damien.

"You haven't called me that in years," Damien confirmed his memory, as he leaned into the comfort of Adam's arm. He didn't say anything about the embrace, but it clearly made him feel better. It made Adam feel better, too, the new Champion noticed for himself. After the break with his family in particular, but even just with the distance between Lynncrag and the castle, Damien had somehow come to substitute for the younger siblings he had missed so fiercely.

And if the phrasing kept Damien clearly in the category of 'younger sibling' and let them all forget about the events – and exchanges – of a few days ago... Well, so much the better.

"Well," he said sardonically – because they would expect that of him, "You're younger than Charley and Lorry, and even Martin is taller than you. So, you'd be the only 'little' brother I have left."

Jason chuckled. "I don't think we fed you enough when you were younger."

Damien gave him a tolerant look. "If I was underfed and missed some growth it was definitely *before* I met you." He grinned suddenly. "Or we could just admit I take after the Eldridge side of the family. They're all short and dark and delicate."

Adam barked a laugh – a more normal laugh than his outburst earlier – and ruffled the King's hair. "Delicate you better *not* be, after all the work we've put into you."

Damien snorted, then ducked out from under Adam's arm. "Delicate we'll *all* find out we are, if we don't stick to Aryllis' plan after all the work she's put in. Time to get dressed for your wedding, my dearest friends." He grinned. "At last, a ceremony where *I'm* not involved at *all*."

He stepped to the door, then suddenly whirled back and caught the startled Adam in a fierce hug. A moment later, he was gone, the door closed firmly behind him.

"Should we have made sure he had a Guard with him?" Adam asked, somewhat bemused.

Jason gave him a stunningly relaxed smile, as if the weight of the world had been taken off his shoulders. "That, my love," he said, turning back towards their bedchamber and the waiting suits of wedding clothes, "Is now your problem and Tim's. And *not* mine!"

Adam shook his head as he followed Jason. "Like you'll ever stop worrying over that one."

Nor would he himself, of course.

But for now, worries could take second-place to dreams about to be fulfilled.

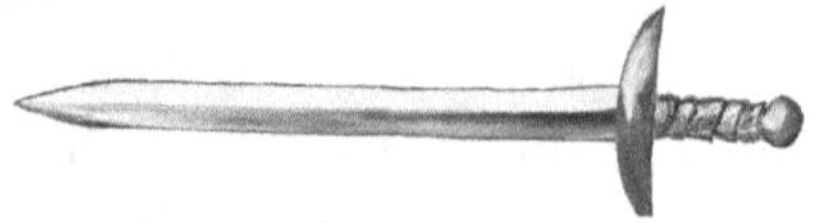

Investiture at dawn. Coronation at high noon.

The wedding, of course, was timed for sunset.

Aryllis had spent out Damien's private purse to acquire every hothouse flower in the city, not to mention having the King himself turn one of the more obscure castle gardens into a nursery with the exact temperature and humidity and light the gardeners claimed were necessary for the flowers she wanted.

And – for just the couple hours of the ceremony – the air around the capitol city was still and almost summery warm. Damien had first winced at the idea, and then just warned everyone that weather-wizardry had to be paid for, and he couldn't predict what kind of howlingly insane storm they would see after this. The city and countryside had been warned, but almost everyone was intrigued enough by the idea of a truly warm evening less than five weeks before the Winter Equinox to not complain. The ships in the harbor were braced, and storm shutters had been put up all over the duchy.

A few small changes had been made by Aryllis and Genevieve during the afternoon break.

Damien and Genevieve were already part of the wedding party as Jason's closest friends, as well as his liege-lord and -lady. Now, given that Jason was using the name Alsterling instead of Solway – whether or not he wanted to – Damien was given a place of precedence as the Head of his family. The King ruefully recalled his blasé comment about not being involved in the ceremony.

Truth be told, Megan didn't seem to mind having a less prominent position in the public ceremony. She'd even offered, Genevieve later informed her husband, to stay out of it entirely. The Queen and Lady Aryllis had had to talk her out of that; Genevieve could only imagine how hurt

Jason would have been, not to mention that Lord David and their children had shown no inclination to be excluded.

Adam, of course, had the entire Loveress clan on his side, not to mention Sir Tim and Aryllis and the current Royal Guards. The knights who had retired from the Guards over the last five years – and their ladies, who had similarly been founding members of the Secret Cadre – stood with Jason. The remaining members of the Secret Cadre had been split. Those ladies who were married to current Royal Guardsmen could reasonably stand with their spouses, but the younger men and women had to be content with watching from the sidelines, there being no reasonable explanation why they should know the former and current Champions well enough to join either family. There would be a private celebration for current and former members of both Secret and Official Royal Guards and they would have to be content with that.

The new positioning placed Damien across from Baronetta Linda Loveress, and she looked pleased about it. She had all but mother-henned the King when she saw him, until her own children had pulled her off to remind her that Damien was no longer the scraggly seventeen-year-old who had sought refuge in her home. Of course, her energetic smile might also have been simple relief at not having to face Alexa Solway's sour face during the whole ceremony. Or that she – and Lord George – seemed to be trying to make up for all the years when they hadn't been on speaking terms with their son... and to reassure both Adam and Jason that they adored Jason *now*.

The marriage rituals were rather more involved than the coronation. Mother Alayana invoked the Gods by various names, and had altered some of the wording – the numerous references to fertility and fruitfulness of the couple seeming both egregious and potentially embarrassing.

None of it could possibly have mattered to Jason and Adam, who knelt on the cushions provided, smiling into each other's eyes.

Damien and the Baronetta were handed garlands of flowers by Mother Alayana's junior priestesses; Damien handed his to Jason, and Baronetta Linda handed the other to Adam... apparently murmuring something into his ear that made her oldest son flush and shift slightly. She winked at Damien as she straightened up, and – surely the motherly woman couldn't be giving Jason such a *wicked* smile. At Mother Alayana's instruction, they put the garlands around each other's necks.

Next, Marianna and Elaina each came forwards with their wedding rings. Damien and Genevieve had set a new fashion, wearing rings instead of the more traditional wedding necklaces. But for someone who had reason to fear assassins, a necklace was a garrote just waiting to happen. It had been Adam's idea... or more like his order. He had basically told them that he would resign as Captain of the Guards if they were such idiots as to put their own necks in a noose. In so many words.

Genevieve had spent the next couple of years touching her collarbone as if expecting to feel a necklace... for all the King knew she still did, just not when he could see her anymore. He'd had to harden his heart against her wistful comments that at least the ring didn't tangle in her hair... and teasingly point out that it didn't bop him in the nose when they were in bed. Damien suspected she had wanted it in part to replace her memories of the wedding necklace that really had been more of a choke-chain. How much more, he didn't want to know; there had been a certain look in her eyes and she had acquiesced with much less fuss than Adam had apparently expected. Damien spent as much time as he could kissing that long, lovely neck so that it wouldn't feel neglected by the lack.

Marianna gave Adam his ring for Jason with a kiss for his cheek.

Elaina was more circumspect in handing Jason the ring he would give to Adam, but Jason caught her hand and smiled at her for an instant and she smiled hesitantly back. Her inclusion had been a matter of some debate. Genevieve and Aryllis had considered having Megan and Charley, as the oldest siblings, or Megan and Desirée as the oldest sisters. Megan, however, had declined the honor. Marianna as Adam's youngest sister could have been paired with Esmerelda as Jason's youngest niece, but Jason had suggested Elaina, ostensibly on grounds of symmetry, since both young women were close in age and of similar height and coloring. Elaina had been... surprised. Since the evening of the banquet, she had looked somewhat confused, and since the denouement of the day before she'd hardly spoken. It was very different from the Elaina Solway the rest of them had learned to know and not exactly love.

When the two young women had withdrawn, Mother Alayana blessed the rings. Then Adam and Jason placed them on each other's fingers, ending by holding each other's hands.

The priestess moved the fire-bowl under their out-stretched hands, then called forth Genevieve and Adam's father to slowly pour the libation of melted butter and sacred brandy over their joined hands and into the licking flames of the fire-bowl. The spirits caught fire and the flames shot up, enveloping Jason and Adam's hands briefly before the liquid smothered the flame.

Damien tensed as he watched – this part of the ritual never failed to make him nervous. If something went wrong, if the Blessing of the rings didn't go right... Only couples that were marrying out of love underwent this part, and supposedly the flames would not burn their hands if their love was true; couples who were wed by arrangement merely held hands over the flame momentarily. It seemed a rather... drastic... way to find out that your new spouse didn't reciprocate your feelings, and of course there were always stories floating around of people who had found out just that way. It was always a second cousin's friend's uncle – someone too far away to trace. After his own wedding, Damien had spent some time trying to determine if any of the stories were real. He hadn't yet found any he could verify.

Ironically, at his own wedding, the young King had had no doubt in his mind that the flames would leave him and Genevieve unharmed. Though *he'd* had a soul-bond to lend assurance. He'd never asked if his wife had undergone this part of the ritual with Harald of Siovale.

During the brief conflagration, Mother Alayana spoke the words that bound them as a married couple. Adam and Jason only needed to murmur assent at the proper places, much as when Damien Bound his nobles with the Vassal's Oath. Again, she had altered some of the wording to make it less *specific* regarding the expected outcome of children... though, interestingly, she did not preclude it. She had spoken briefly in the past few weeks with Adam and Jason each, separately, to make sure they both really wanted this; she must have seen how much Adam hungered to have a child.

She finished with the traditional words: "–and just as Fire is never the same twice, an Oath taken in the presence of the Holy Flame can never be taken back. You are now bound as spouses so long as your souls inhabit these bodies. May joy find you in all the shared days that are to come."

She pulled the fire-bowl away, using tongs, and gestured to them to rise.

The proper way to do this was without relinquishing the grip of their hands... or breaking their gaze. Not all couples could manage that, and their attempts often broke the tension of the wedding ceremony. Damien recalled that it had been harder than he had anticipated, despite the fact that he and Genevieve were both naturally graceful and their bodies were well-trained... and comfortable with each other. While he could easily stand up without using his hands, doing so while looking into her eyes and holding her hands while she was also rising... had been a different challenge.

Adam and Jason made it look as if they did it every day.

The junior priestesses snatched the cushions out from between them, and Damien and the Baronetta stepped forwards again. This time their job was to first try to pull the pair apart – and then give them a sharp shove together when that failed. All the symbolism of how one had to cleave to one's spouse despite the difficulties one's birth-family might cause in one grand gesture.

And another poignant moment for the King – Jason had done this office for *him* at his own wedding… He and Genevieve had fallen into each other's arms…

Of course, the little play was far less effective when the marrying couple severely outmassed the representative family members. Adam and Jason simply stayed steady, and then stepped together for the kiss that signaled the end of the ceremony.

Damien reached out without looking as Genevieve came near, and she snuggled into his arm to regard their dearest friends enjoying their moment. For just an instant the King thought perhaps it could work… but the sudden crackle and spit of white sparks where their bodies touched gave the lie to his hopes. He stepped apart from his wife, feeling intensely bereft despite her nearness. He didn't dare look at her, and simply prayed that no one else had noticed. The story of his early attempt to deny the soul-bond had become local legend, and he'd had to endure more than one lecture from the priestesses about it. The King didn't care to share the ultimate irony of that effort.

The entire city seemed to rouse up with a cheer that startled the two men out of their kiss. For once not flustered by being the center of attention for something other than swordskill, Jason slid an arm around Adam and turned them both to face the crowd and wave. Somewhat startled – or so Damien guessed from his body language – Adam waved as well and inspired a renewed round of cheering.

There was a coronet that would normally be worn by the spouse – the *wife* – of the Crown Prince. And another for the spouse of the Duke of Emeralsee. After some debate, it had been agreed that they would skip crowning Adam with either of the delicate, feminine pieces of jewelry which had last been worn by Damien's mother. A more appropriate piece had been commissioned for those occasions when Adam would need a crown to support the title of Prince-Consort – or Lord-Consort when Jason played the part of Duke. Even Queen Marian could not guess what had happened to the pieces her first husband had worn when she held the titles.

The next part of the tradition for a reigning Duke's marriage had made Tim and Adam have conniptions. The couple was to walk – *walk* – throughout the City to greet the people.

330

Genevieve had felt it was important to stick to the tradition, especially given that Jason was so little known and would so newly be crowned Duke. She had waxed almost lyrical about having done so after the repeated wedding ceremony she and Damien had done in Elaarwen.

Adam had responded by pointing out that they had *not* taken such a walk in Emeralsee, despite Damien's title as Duke. His role as King and the recent coup had made the whole prospect seem rather too dicey.

Damien in his turn had noted that he went all over the City *now*, usually with just a handful of Guards, which had only brought out Adam's growl. And a load of sarcastic comments and half-serious threats about ending that bit of folly.

They had compromised on a stroll around the market square... with the Royal Guard and Secret Cadre spread well out around them. Damien had been required to swear upon Genevieve's wedding ring that he would not leave the top of the reviewing stand where the Castle Guard could protect him... and upon the Sword not to let Genevieve leave either. Adam had a fair sense of what oaths would bind Damien most thoroughly, and had laughed sardonically at the Queen's offended complaint that he wasn't asking for *her* oath.

"I know you too well, 'Erawan,'" he'd told her, and she had flushed.

On their way down to the crowds of well-wishers, however, the newly married couple had to pass by the members of their wedding parties. The various Guards would be following – or leading – them, but the Loveresses and Solways were to wait with the King and Queen.

Damien and Genevieve stepped forward together and gave Jason simultaneous kisses on his cheeks. They nodded congratulations at the Baronetta and her husband as they stepped past to do the same to Adam.

A surprised, feminine yelp caught their attention and made everyone turn.

Jason had *picked up* his sister and spun her around, much to the amusement of her husband. He ended with a hug that clearly stunned her. Damien couldn't quite hear what he was saying, and Genevieve bopped him on the shoulder before he could use magick to sharpen his senses and sate his curiosity. But he did hear Jason call his sister 'Meggie' and wondered how long it had been since he'd done that. Since he was a toddler, perhaps? Lady Megan burst into tears, and hugged him back, then spun away into David's arms.

"Good," Baronetta Linda said firmly in Damien's ear, her voice that of sad experience overcome. "There might be some hope for that one yet."

Chapter TWENTY-FOUR

Resolution

"Ready for bed, Jase?" Adam murmured as they took a break from dancing at the ball thrown in their honor. The event was being held in the Grand Hall and was attended by all the glittering nobility of the Realm, most of whom had taken the opportunity to take one man or the other for a spin around the room.

More dancing was going on in the streets outside, but Adam had drawn the line at carousing by torchlight with the populace. The City Guard Captain had reluctantly agreed. There were enough conservatives who were unhappy with their marriage that it would be a stretch to say they could guarantee the Crown Prince's safety.

"Mmmn." Jason slid his arms around Adam from behind, resting his chin on Adam's shoulder. "I didn't want to tear you away from your family... but I've been hoping... We should take our leave of Damien and Genevieve before we go."

Adam leaned his head against Jason's. "You *are* my family. But thank you. I'm glad Martin and Marianna are staying on. They were so small when..."

"Yes."

"It's been nice getting to know them as adults."

Jason chuckled and straightened up. Adam was hyperaware of every square inch where their bodies no longer touched as he did so. "'Nice' might not be quite the right term. Your baby sister has the wickedest sense of humor I've ever heard. Except maybe for your not-quite-so-much baby sister – Desirée might be even worse. Marianna's going to quite corrupt the other ladies-in-waiting. Come on, we know where our fair sovereigns will be."

He offered his hand, and Adam clasped it tightly.

"Where *do* they get that sense of humor anyways?" Jason asked.

Adam was spared having to answer because they had come upon Damien and Genevieve.

Normally, the King and Queen would be dancing until the musicians retired, lost in each other's eyes. The handful of Royal Guards protecting the section of corridor where they stayed out of everyone else's eyes would rotate throughout the evening.

Now they caught Tim's concerned gaze as the pair leaned on opposite walls, looking at each other and talking quietly. Jason shrugged and Adam put on his most sardonic expression. They couldn't explain to the new Captain why there was no real cause to worry about his friends and sovereigns but perhaps their nonchalance would serve to reassure him some. For the first time, Adam wondered if putting sharp-eyed Aryllis' easygoing husband in place to so closely observe the King and Queen had been a good idea. Tim's relaxed manner made it easy to forget how clever he was... and how he might see things that they didn't want him to.

Though there was no one better to keep the pair of them – and Jason, and eventually their daughter – safe. At least if Adam couldn't do it himself.

Damien noticed them first. "Done for the evening?"

Adam sketched a bow. "His Highness and I beg your permission to retire, Your Majesty."

Genevieve snorted. "As if either of you would ever *beg* for anything."

Damien's eyes flickered, and Adam was thrown back to remembering how he had pleaded – though only with his eyes – for the King not to let Jason sacrifice himself in some bold gesture the night of Harald's coup.

Damien said nothing of it, however. "Walk us back to the tower."

Adam glanced at his love – his *husband* – and Jason shrugged. What was a few more minutes? "As Your Majesty commands."

Damien smiled slightly and led off. Genevieve took Adam's elbow and his manners made him automatically bend his arm... though bedamned if he was going to let go of Jason's hand. There was a slight tremble in her hand, which made him look more sharply at his beautiful, red-headed Queen. She seemed warmer than normal, though they had patently *not* been dancing, and her eyes were slightly glazed. She had better not have a fever, Adam mused, not so close to their deadline... His fingers tightened on Jason's.

They chatted lightly as old friends will, but didn't talk of anything of consequence. They most particularly did not mention absent friends – but Ciriis' absence tonight was keenly felt by all of them.

The entire party stopped when they came to the foot of the stairs that led up to the royal suite – and were in front of the door to the windowless rooms that had once been Genevieve's... and had once been used to imprison Duke Tomas Elsevier.

"We part ways here," Damien commented, then nodded at the doors. "I promised Madame Elista–"

"*We* promised," Genevieve corrected and the King rolled his eyes.

"*We* promised," he gamely re-stated, "to get you here. This is the Castle staff's wedding gift to you. They've been decorating for days, as I understand it."

Adam looked at the door with mixed emotions. This was definitely more private... but after the long day, he'd kind of been looking forward to his own familiar bed...

"I added wards," Damien went on. "And... here. It's my personal wedding gift to you, Adam." He slid a bracelet made of a single red thread off his wrist and handed it to his Champion. "To you both, but I want *you* to keep it. If you pinch the knot, it will come open. You can pinch it onto another thread and it will join with it until you pinch the knot again." He didn't say just *which* threads it might be used to lengthen... or why he was handing it to *Adam*... but he didn't have to. And in company with Guards and Genevieve... probably shouldn't.

Adam took it as the trust it was, and slid it onto his own wrist.

"Congratulations again," the King said, then held out his hand to his wife. "Sweetheart?"

Genevieve let go of Adam's arm and reached up to ruffle his hair. "Congratulations, my friends." It was heartfelt, but her focus was on Damien, as it had been while they walked. She put the barest tips of her fingers in his grasp and used her other hand to lift her skirts to mount the tower stairs.

Adam wondered if they would make it through the night. It hadn't passed his attention that she hadn't touched Jason any more than she had her husband. Or that there had been an almost unnoticeable fizz of white sparks between the royal pair's fingers where they touched. If he hadn't been looking for it...

He was startled out of his thoughts by a clap on the shoulder from Tim. "Go on in, you, two. These miscreants," he waved at Sir Drake and Sir Everett, "will be on duty out here if you need anything." He stepped back with a bow. "Your Highness. Prince-Consort." The easygoing knight grinned at them. "Gods but that sounds strange to say. I still look around for you, Adam, when someone calls out 'Captain!'" He gave them a second, slighter bow and strode off, whistling, the remaining two Royal Guards following in his wake.

Sir Drake grinned at his former Captain and opened the door for them...

Adam didn't try to look around at first, being more interested in making sure the door was properly closed and setting the wards. He paused for several long seconds, contemplating the final ward, and the bracelet. At last, he shrugged and attached the cord as instructed, looping it the last two loops to keep even Damien out. While the King could technically walk through *any* of the castle walls with the help of the Sword, it had not surpassed Adam's attention that the magickal escape route from the King's bedchamber led straight down through this suite.

When he turned around at last, he took a few steps forward almost without noticing.

It was *beautiful*. Every surface that could hold a candle did, and most of them had small mirrors tucked beside them to double the number of lights. It was still more dim than he had seen this place when the lamps were turned up – he could see that the lamps were lit, but their steady glow was turned down to allow the gently flickering candles to dominate the lightscape. A banked fire in the hearth added a deeper red tone and the slight sizzle of smouldering wood added to the ambiance.

Someone had even placed a few twigs of sandalwood in the hearth, and he was touched by the fact that the maids who cleaned their quarters had even noticed that he always added a bit of sandalwood to his clothes drawers.

It was... utterly cozy and romantic.

He turned to Jason with a soft smile on his face, only to find his love – his *husband* – backed up against the wall beside the door. Jason's eyes were wide, and he was trembling with the look of someone experiencing a flashback of the worst kind. Adam only wished that he didn't have so much experience in recognizing that look – on Jason's face, as well as on others'. Damn King Reginald and his eighty-three-year reign of terror.

"Jase," he said gently, moving slowly and deliberately so as to not startle the other man. "Jason. Talk to me. Tell me what's wrong."

Jason took a long, shuddering breath, but he still seemed not to be able to focus on Adam. His eyes were on the multitude of candles. "It's... the room. Oskar..."

Adam frowned. Prince Oskar's rooms had been in a far wing of the Castle – which had been a consideration when they had chosen the upper part of this tower for Damien. At that point in time, they had not known that King Reginald's youngest son would never return from Zialest... and what should have been Rosa and Zachary's wedding. They had wanted to keep the former Heir as far from their protegé as possible... and Ciriis and Adam had silently agreed to also keep him as far from *Jason* as possible.

"These aren't his rooms, Jase," Adam said carefully. "We're nowhere near his old rooms. And... Prince Oskar has been dead for seven years."

"He *had* a room like this, though," Jason explained, his eyes still fixed on the candles. "No windows. Only the one door. Soundproof. And... he would bring me in and have it all lit like this..."

Oskar had ruined *romance*? Would the specter of the vile prince never quit haunting them?

Adam stifled a sigh. It was what it was. "Tell me."

He'd long ago learned that speaking fears aloud sometimes – *sometimes* – made them less powerful. He hoped this would be one of those times.

"He... would bring me in and say it was time to take our relationship to the 'next level.' The first time... the first *few* times... it was romantic. Exciting. Then... then it began to be something else." Jason seemed to come back to himself, almost focused on Adam, though his gaze kept going back to the flickering candles. "I shouldn't tell you this."

Adam stepped close and put his arms around his love. "What you need to say, I can bear to hear. If there's any chance it will release his power over you... But if you want, we can go back to our usual rooms..."

Jason shook his head. "We can't. After all the effort they went to preparing this for us? That Elista even kept these rooms aside, with how tightly packed the Castle is... We *can't.*"

Adam kept his tone even. "If you can't bear to be in here, we *can.* Elista will understand. You're not the only one with... memories."

Jason dropped his head, at last breaking the mesmerizing power of the candles. "I can't show that kind of weakness, Adam. I couldn't as *Champion.* I can't as... as *Prince* and *Duke* and *Heir.*"

A fair admission of how delicate Jason's position was, even after all this fanfare and festivities. And Jason's position was now one of the most critical supports of Damien's... Any number of those glittering nobles they had left behind in that decorated and well-lit hall would happily turn on them if there were some way to do it without breaking their Oaths and Bindings. Damien was assured the support of the duchy of Emeralsee through Jason, Elaarwen through Genevieve, Dalzialest through Rosa and Zachary, Alpinsward through Laura, and Siovale through Tomas... But their minor nobles – like Jason's mother – had their own opinions and the duchies of Reyensweir and Embervest were nowhere near so close to the throne. Duke Quillian of Reyensweir seemed to harbor a dislike of the King even leaving politics aside, and while the Duchess of Embervest should be pleased that Minglemere had been returned to her, Damien had as yet done nothing about Everfields.

Or perhaps that was an admission of Jason's own insecurities about holding these titles.

Either way...

"Then tell me. Tell me what you need to in order to be able to cope." Adam started to turn away. "I'll blow out the candles..."

"No!" Jason's voice was spiked with an old fear that was no less powerful for its age, and his fingers pinched Adam's shoulder as he gripped tightly. "No! That's when the... the *bad things* would start."

Adam closed his eyes and counted to ten backwards, fighting with his famous temper. He'd spent all his life containing that temper, fighting it and winning. For his brothers and sisters, his shield, his young king, the men under his command. Jason had been the only person who had weathered his highs and lows without judgment or complaint. Prince Oskar was too long dead to take the brunt of Adam's anger, and Jason certainly didn't deserve to. He could master himself now and be the gentle breeze beside the peaceful lake that Jason needed.

"Let's sit down, Jason."

He removed both of their swords and stood them in a corner before he towed the other man to the overstuffed, brocaded sofa – a relic from when they had decorated for Genevieve's presumed tastes. Who had done the presuming about the Rebel Duchess who had arrived in hunting leathers as a spy that ended her up with this excessively feminine lounge, Adam could not guess.

Jason sat down, but wedged himself deep into the corner. Adam sat down in the middle, one foot tucked up so that he could face Jason. "So. Tell me."

"He would have me sit down on the leather couch. It was always hard leather couches with a smooth finish... Easier to... to clean." Jason swallowed, the pause giving Adam too much time to think about that. "Then... he'd bring me to a fever-pitch of desire. And then. Stop. And ask if I was ready to... to go on." The candles had mesmerized Jason again. "I'd say 'yes,' and he'd laugh... this soft, seductive laugh... and say 'let's just see, shall we?'

"And then he'd take one of the candles... and... put it out." Jason had wrapped his arms around himself, and now he rubbed at his upper arms, not even seeming to realize what he was doing. Adam wondered if he looked as greenish as he felt; this... seemed to explain a number of scars he had discovered on Jason...

"If I jerked back... or seemed upset at all, he'd say I wasn't ready and that we had to... to start over. And he would. Until I was so... so... out of my head with wanting him that I didn't even notice. And then he'd have me beg." Jason almost-focused on Adam again. "I'm sickening you. That I should have submitted to this... that I should have *wanted* this enough to *beg*..."

"Not you," Adam said forcefully. "It angers me to hear this. Yes. But *you* don't sicken me. And I'm not angry at *you*. Never at you, Jase."

Jason's eyes flickered away. "I... I won't tell you what came after that. It was... different every time anyways."

There was a long moment of silence.

"Well..." Adam said at last, "It's not a leather couch."

It was a stupid statement. Nearly completely irrelevant. But what do you say when nothing will help?

It confused Jason long enough that his eyes actually *focused* on Adam. "What?"

Adam wondered if he looked as foolish as he surely sounded. He tapped the overstuffed brocade of the sofa. "It's not leather." He gave Jason an embarrassed smile. "Do you want to leave, Jason? This is no way to spend our wedding night..."

Jason gave him a stricken look. "Oh, love, I'm ruining everything."

Stricken, but *present*. He wasn't off in that neverworld of the past with Prince Oskar anymore. He was *here* and *now*.

Adam shook his head and stretched out to place his fingers on Jason's lips. "No. You're not. First, it's not your fault. And second..." He hoped this would work the way he wanted, not make everything worse... "Nothing has been ruined that we can't fix." He hoisted himself until he was sitting astraddle Jason's lap. He put his arms around his husband's neck and kissed him lightly. "Can you be in the here and now? With *me?*"

Jason closed his eyes for a second kiss, but he didn't respond with the enthusiasm he had earlier. At least he didn't seem to have to fight himself not to pull away.

"I'm sorry, love," Jason said, his head sagging into Adam's chest. "I want to... it's just been such a long day..." It *was* that. But it was more than that, too.

Adam suppressed another sigh. He wasn't quite giving up yet on pulling Jason out of this. This funk, this... this *flashback.*

"That it has been," he said, making it sound like he was conceding.

He pulled himself off of Jason, and laid down with his head in Jason's lap. The sofa had never anticipated accommodating two such large men – Adam propped his calves on the far arm and crossed his ankles casually, toeing off the silly little grey half-boots that completed his wedding outfit.

He felt Jason's breath hitch slightly and hid a smile, but wriggled a bit as if trying to find a more comfortable position. Which indeed, he *was...* but it also gave him the opportunity to rub his head against Jason's groin. His love would have to be made of iron not to react to that... and indeed, he wasn't.

"So, what did you say to Megan?" Adam asked conversationally.

Jason's fingers began to twine through his hair. He'd keep it shorter than Damien's if not for these moments. He loved to feel Jason's fingers in his hair.

"I told her that I hoped we could find a new way to be siblings."

"Hmmn. You called her 'Meggie.'" Adam tilted his chin upwards to see Jason's face, and got the satisfying little whimper he'd been aiming for in response. "When was the last time you called her that?"

Jason was clearly struggling for nonchalance on more than one count. Adam hadn't watched him skitter away from criticisms of Megan even more than of his mother for all these years without seeing that deep and baffled attachment his love had to the impossible woman... Nor without unwillingly having kept a close enough watch on Megan to realize that the woman was desperately, deeply unhappy, and had been even before her son had gotten himself killed. And that, somehow, that unhappiness seemed sharpened and pointed and painful around his Jason.

Adam would lay odds that Megan's husband knew the whys and wherefores... but the man was as closemouthed as any Metreedi Adam had ever met, for all that he'd lived nearly half his life as a Solway. Not that *they* were usually chatterboxes either.

"Oh, I don't know. When I was five or six. I was still trying to follow her around at that point. I'd given up on Mother long before then, I think." Jason paused. "And... I told Elaina this evening that I'd see what I could do about helping her become one of Genny's ladies-in-waiting. If she still wanted to." He was clearly waiting for Adam's reaction.

The new Champion shrugged, his head... rubbing... again. "It's Tim's problem now, not mine."

"I begin to think," Jason breathed, "that your sense of humor is just as wicked as your sisters.'" His fingers were exploring the inside edges of Adam's shirt collar. Unfortunately, there wasn't very far he could go with this, given the overly formal and fitted state of their wedding outfits. Though at least he was now interested in *trying*.

"Why leave my brothers out of it?" Adam asked. "Or have you not *heard* them?"

That... might be a good thing, all things considered.

"Hmmn." Jason was experimenting with undoing the too-numerous buttons on Adam's formal jacket with just one hand. "I'm fairly sure you all didn't pick this up from your father... Lord George is practically prim. No, it couldn't be your sweet lady *mother?*" His tone had grown warm and teasing.

"My very *earthy* lady mother you mean? The woman *did* have seven children, after all," Adam did not really want to talk about his *mother* just now... and guessed that Jason knew exactly that and was paying him back.

Jason's fingers trailed through the beard-stubble on his chin, pressing the hairs the wrong way. It was a move he knew well never failed to make Adam very amorous. "Just what did the Baronetta tell *you* when she handed you my wedding garland, love?"

Adam sat straight up, narrowly missing Jason's nose and chin – which would definitely have ended any more interesting plans for the evening. "Nevermind."

He was facing away, and the light was almost certainly too low and too ruddy to tell that he was blushing. Furiously.

Jason seemed fully recovered at least. He scooted forwards until he was close behind Adam, and slid his long arms up under Adam's... to start working on those buttons again, while his mouth nibbled at the strong stem of Adam's neck. "You're not going to start keeping secrets from me, now that we're married, are you?"

Adam snorted, but there wasn't much force behind it. It was hard to concentrate with Jason's lips... "There's always been secrets I've had to keep, Jase." His voice went unexpectedly up an octave as Jason's hands left off the recalcitrant buttons and went somewhere else entirely.

"State secrets don't count, lover." Was he, oh, dear Gods, yes, he was *biting* delicately... Adam shivered convulsively and Jason's soft laugh teased his skin almost as much. "Tell me what she said and I'll do that again."

"She said 'This may not net me any more grandchildren, but don't let that slow you two down tonight,'" Adam said, blushing furiously.

Jason's hands withdrew, and Adam couldn't interpret the small choking noises behind him. He turned around to check, and realized that Jason was holding his stomach as he convulsed in nearly silent laughter.

"Oh, you all *definitely* get it from her," he wheezed as he saw Adam looking at him. "Oh, you are a *beautiful* shade of red, love."

Well... this *was* better than Jason being terrified and stuck in the past.

"Shall we see if you're still as ticklish now that you're a married man, Jason?" Adam half-threatened to cover his embarrassment.

"Promises, promises..." Jason purred, and his strong hands slid around Adam again. "I believe I have a promise to fulfill first, though..."

EPILOGUE

DAMIEN MAGICKED HIMSELF INTO HIS office, and collapsed onto his couch. He did not *want* to be here. He *wanted* to be in his bedroom. In his bed. With his wife. Who was probably cursing his name for abandoning her.

No. She wasn't. Of course not. He could feel her through the bond.

Calling to him.

A siren's song, and no matter what he stuffed his ears with, he would hear her because she was singing to his heart and soul.

They could *not* go on much longer like this.

Genevieve was healthy again.

Damien rejoiced over it, but it meant the soul-bond was reactivating with its mindless demand for reproduction. He'd been able to fool it so far – with Jason's help... but the sneaky thing was now acting on Genevieve directly. If she wasn't a woman of iron self-control... they would never have made it all the way up the stairs tonight, let alone would he have been able to escape when her self-control eroded so suddenly and...

...deliciously...

The King tried to make himself smile at the thought of how much they would have startled and embarrassed their poor Guards... it didn't help, of course, since then he was put to imagining *that* scenario...

Soberly, Damien withdrew another bracelet of red thread from his sleeve and regarded it. He'd sensed Adam's destruction of his first sleepy-headed creation and been grateful. He'd made these... extension cords... out of a sense that they would come in handy.

If he sealed himself into his office... Would he remember how to undo the spell when the soul-bond – and Genevieve's loneliness and desire – tried to draw him back to her? He wasn't sure he wanted to find out what it felt like to try and fail to vanish himself through the ward...

...but what other choice was there?

Grimly, the King went to the door and set all the wards. Then he added the red cord and magickally sealed himself into his office.

Genevieve was healthy. Once Adam and Jason were done with their honeymoon they could all do what needed to be done to end this insanity.

Did you miss the FIRST BOOK in this series?
Turn to page 361
(just past the MAPS)
to check out an exerpt from
The Rebel Duchess
Book One of the Chronicles of Ilseador!

Alsterling Family Tree

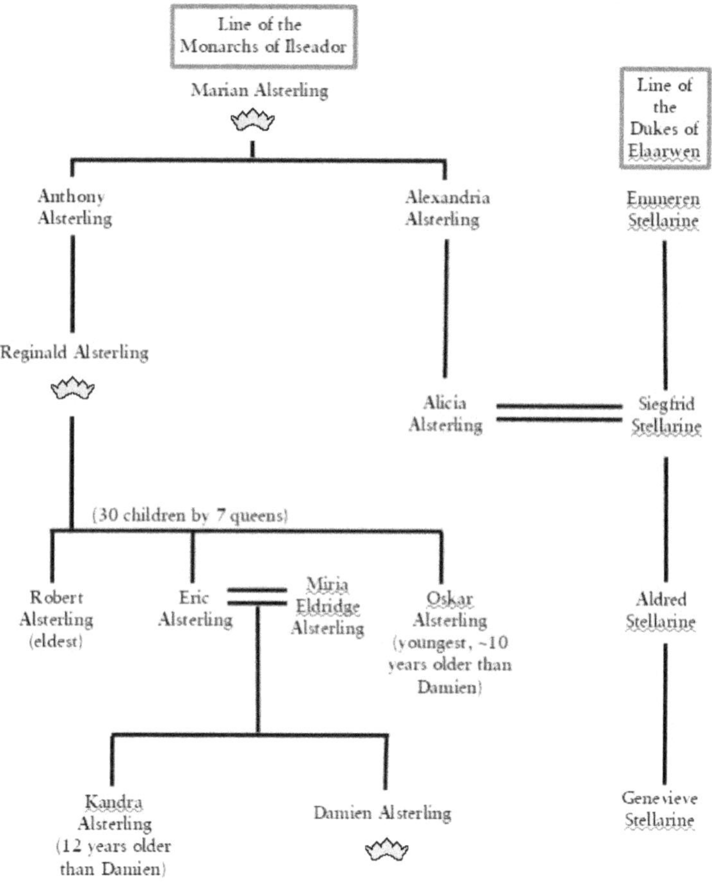

Index of Characters
(for an Index by alphabetical order, go to
https://www.RisingDragonBooks.com and click on the link for this book)

Characters that appear in this book are <u>underlined.</u>
(Characters that are referenced, but do not actually appear are in plain type.)
Deceased characters are in *italics*.

The grandchildren of a reigning king or queen are officially grand dukes and grand duchesses in Ilseador, but are also referred to as princes and princesses when the question of their position in the line of succession is not in question.
Damien was Crown Prince after Oskar died.

Contents of the Index:
- Royal Family of Ilseador
- Provinces of Ilseador in order of precedence and relevant ruling family members
- Emeralsee contains the following fiefs named in the story: Seasbourne, Cedarwen, Eldyrwyld, Lynncrag, Elmirscroft, Ravenscroft
- Elaarwen contains the following fiefs named in the story: Brindlewell, Cloudcroft
- Siovale
- Reyensweir contains the following fiefs named in the story: Zialest
- Embervest contains the following fiefs named in the story: Minglemere, Everfields
- Alpinsward contains the following fiefs named in the story: Dalizell
- Dalzialest, duchy
- The Lost Provinces: Alpinsward, Minglemere, Elendria, Farivera, Everfields

Royal Family of Ilseador
(and noted individuals in the Royal City and Province)

- **<u>Damien Alsterling</u>,** King of Ilseador
    - **<u>Queen Genevieve (Stellarine) Alsterling</u>**, Duchess of Elaarwen (a.k.a. 'the Rebel Duchess'), King Damien's wife
    - ***<u>Queen Marian Alsterling</u>*** (a.k.a. 'Marian the merciful'), King Damien and Queen Genevieve's great-great-grandmother (common ancestress)
        - *Eric Alsterling,* son of old king Reginald Alsterling, former Crown Prince, King Damien's father
            - » *Queen Rena (Tindilaar) Alsterling,* a princess from Dawil; mother of Prince Eric Alsterling; grandmother of King Damien; sister to King Eldrig Tindilaar; her parents were Queen Marlerite and King Ezerial of Dawil
        - *Miria (Eldridge) Alsterling,* King Damien's and Princess Kandra's mother; wife of Prince Eric; daughter of a minor noble family in the countryside of Emeralsee Province; oldest of seven children
            - * *Miria's father, David Eldridge,* was a failed squire, son of the Baron of Elderwyld
            - * *Miria's mother, Alexa,* was a blacksmith's daughter
            - » *Grand Duchess (or Princess) Kandra 'Kandy' Alsterling,* King Damien's sister; Prince Eric and Lady Miria's daughter joined the army as a common foot- soldier at 18, worked her way up. Was to have married Lord Raphael Anvliyar of Cedarwen (love-match) and helped her parents and brother escape to the Rebellion in Elaarwen

        - *King Reginald Alsterling* (aka 'the old king' or 'Reginald the Ruthless'); King Damien's grandfather
            - » *'Lord' Prydeen,* his Apprentice Evil Wizard
            - » *7 wives*
            - » *1st Princess Lindrea Alsterling (died before he was crowned)*
            - » *2nd*
            - » *3rd*
            - » *4th*
            - » *5th*

- » *6th Queen Rena (Tindilaar) Alsterling* of Dawil, Prince Eric's mother, King Damien's grandmother
- » *7th Eliza Alsterling* (Oskar's mother, married to King Reginald simultaneously with Queen Rena)
- » *Oskar Alsterling,* the youngest son of Reginald.
    - * <u>Sir Jason Solway</u>,   Prince Oskar's bodyguard before he was Heir, his Champion while he was Heir
    - * <u>Sir Edmund Railston</u>, Prince Oskar's Champion and bodyguard at the time Ring was taken from Prince Oskar (also Adam Loveress' first lover)
- » 30 legitimate children (all dead), including the following:
- » *Crown Prince Robert Alsterling*
- » *Princess Selda Alsterling*
- » *Crown Prince Eric Alsterling*
- » *Crown Prince Oskar Alsterling*
- » Some 100 grandchildren (all dead besides Damien) including the following:
    - * *Alric Alsterling*
    - * *Grand Duke Salleen Alsterling*
    - * *Grand Duchess Kandra Alsterling*
    - * Crown Prince Damien Alsterling

- **King Damien's Royal Guards**
    - » **Champion: <u>Sir Jason Solway</u>** (mother is Countess Alexa Solway), a close advisor of King Damien's.
    - » **Captain and Knight Commander of the Royal Guard: <u>Sir Adam Loveress</u>** (shield is puce with a rose, argent, crossed by a black sword), a close advisor of King Damien
    - » **Original Guards**
        - * <u>Sir Timothy Ancellius</u> (a.k.a. 'Tim'), Second-in-Command of the Royal Guard when Damien is crowned, marries Secret Cadre member Aryllis after Damien is crowned, has son Enrico (a.k.a. Rico)
        - * Sir Leverett Childress (a.k.a. 'Lev'), marries Secret Cadre member Terellie
        - * Sir Otto
        - * Sir Randolph

- **Newer Guards members** (five years into Damien's reign)
  - » Sir Marcus (Second-in-Command)
  - » Sir Mikal 'Mik'
  - » Sir Rodney
  - » <u>Sir Everett Ladler</u>
  - » **<u>Sir Drake Milbourne</u>**
  - » <u>Sir Angelos Eldridge</u>
- **The Secret Cadre of Royal Guards**
  - » **Original twelve King's Ladies:** the Secret Cadre of Royal Guards (all but Lena and Ciriis marry one of Damien's original Royal Guards following his coronation)
    - * **<u>Ciriis Celavell</u>**: Mistress of Protocol and Spymistress, Commander of the Secret Cadre under Adam Loveress, later King's Advisor and then Assistant to Duke Aldred
    - * **<u>Lena Devergnon:</u>** Poisoner/anti-poisoner, later Assistant Royal Librarian
    - * **<u>Aryllis Ieldore</u>**: marries Royal Guardsman Tim Ancellius; mother of Enrico Ancellius (a.k.a. Rico); becomes Mistress of Protocol and Spymistress and commander of the Secret Cadre under Adam Loveress
    - * Felena
    - * Terellie: marries Royal Guardsman Leverett Childress
    - * Sasha
    - * Elsa
    - * Emerie
    - * Thielda
    - * Nalda
    - * Kamauri
    - * Licia
    - * Mirabelle
  - » **Newer Secret Cadre** (five years into Damien's reign)
    - * **<u>Lady Alanna</u>**
    - * **<u>Lady Lisa</u>**

- Castle Personnel
  » Elista, senior maid, later Chatelaine. Began work the day
    Prince Eric and Lady Miria were killed, fed Damien
    until Lady Theresa discovered her. Married to Robert,
    Captain of the Castle Guard during the Usurpation
  » Captain Robert of the Castle Guard, married
    to Elista, died during the Usurpation
  » Maree, knife sharpener for the kitchen, had
    a huge infatuation with Damien
- Others
  » Master Fenric, lawyer, specialist on treaties
  » <u>Mother Alayana</u>, priestess willing to marry same-sex couples
  » <u>Rupert Dolschael</u>, Attorney and Legal Scholar
    with the Royal Court of Docks and Locks
  » Judge Emberdeen, presides over the Royal
    Court of Docks and Locks
  » Old farmer with a haywagon who helped
    Genevieve during the Usurpation
  » Hay farmer's wife: Marabell

Provinces of Ilseador

in order of precedence and relevant ruling family members

- *Emeralsee,* duchy – Alsterling family, gold and turquoise
  (guards wear dark blue and black)
  - <u>Duke Damien Alsterling</u> as Heir and then continuing as King-and-Duke
  - <u>**Duchess-Consort Genevieve (Stellarine) Alsterling**</u>
  - <u>***Ghost of Queen Marian Alsterling***</u>, great-grandmother of both
    Damien and Genevieve
  - *Dead-and-gone:*
    - *Prince Anthony Alsterling,* eldest child of Queen Marian
    - *King Reginald Alsterling,* eldest child of Prince
      Anthony (see 'King Damien Alsterling' at top
      for details of King Reginald's offspring)

- *Other siblings of King Reginald* (and their families and Alsterling cousins)
- *Other siblings and half-siblings of Prince Anthony*
- *Princess Alexandria Alsterling,* youngest child of Queen Marian (fled Emeralsee with the Monarch's Blade shortly before Queen Marian was assassinated by Prince Reginald; played the role of 'Erawan the Kind Robber' while hiding out in the mountains of Elaarwen)
- *Grand Duchess Alicia Alsterling,* only child of Princess Alexandria; married Siegfrid Stellarine, Heir to the Province of Elaarwen, had one child, Aldred Stellarine

- **Others of note within Emeralsee** (see under 'King Damien Alsterling' at top)

- *Fiefs within Emeralsee*
  - *Seasbourne,* county – family Laidly
    - » <u>Count Emery Laidly</u>
      - * <u>Isabelle Laidly</u>, eldest child of Count Emery and Heir to Seasbourne
      - * <u>Raymond Laidly,</u> second child of Count Emery; was betrothed to Lady Laura Marseill of Alpinsward as a child, prior to Alpinsward's defection to Mercasia and Laura's investiture as Duchess of Alpinsward
  - *Cedarwen, barony* – Anvliyar family
    - » Baron Raphael Anvliyar (intended husband of King Damien's sister, Princess Kandra)
      - * Dowager Baroness Theresa Anvliyar, mother of Baron Raphael, former Royal Librarian and guardian of King Damien as a child after his parents were slain; died a traitor's death for having conspired to betray Crown Prince Eric, Lady Miria, and Princess Kandra, as well as for Conspiracy Against the Crown due to her role during the Usurpation of Harald Elsevier

- *Elderwyld,* barony – Eldridge family
(Note: names in the Eldridge family aside from Miria, Alexa, Angelos and Evan have not been given in the story yet; they are included here to make the family connections clear)
» Baron Eugenio Eldridge
    * <u>Sir Angelos Eldridge,</u> one of Baron Eugenio's sons
    * Previous Baron Eldridge, grandfather of the current Baron, father of Dara and David
    * *Baroness Dara Eldridge,* mother of the current Baron
    * *David Eldridge,* Lord of Ravenscroft (gifted to Prince Eric and Lady Miria and deeded to her parents), younger son of the former Baron, a failed squire, husband of Alexa, father of seven (Lady Miria was his eldest)
    * *Alexa Eldridge,* David's wife;a blacksmith's daughter, mother of seven
    * *Lady Miria (Eldridge) Alsterling,* Damien's mother, eldest child of David and Alexa Eldridge
» Unknown fate
    * Evan Eldridge, a cousin of Lady Miria's, son of Baroness Dara Eldridge, half-brother of Baron Eugenio
- **Lynncrag,** baronetcy – Loveress family
» <u>**Baronetta Linda Loveress**</u>
    * <u>Lord George Loveress,</u> husband of Baronetta Linda
    * Their children (ages given for the 5th year of King Damien's reign)
    * <u>**Sir Adam Loveress**</u> – 34yo, Captain of the Royal Guard
    * <u>Charles (a.k.a. 'Charley') Loveress</u> – 32yo – a forest ranger
    * <u>Lorenzo (a.k.a. 'Lorry') Loveress</u> – 30yo – married and divorced twice
    * <u>**Desirée Loveress**</u> – 28yo
        * <u>**Desirée's 2 little boys (8yo and 10yo)**</u>
    * <u>Fontaine Loveress</u> – 24yo – priestess novitiate (but left before final vows)
    * <u>**Martin Loveress**</u> – 20yo - healer
    * <u>**Marianna Loveress**</u> – 18yo – lady-in-waiting applicant (Secret Cadre)

- *Elmirscroft*, property
- *Ravenscroft*, property
  - » David Eldridge, grandfather of King Damien
    - * Alexa Eldridge, grandmother of King Damien

- *Elaarwen*, duchy – Stellarine family, violet and silver
  - Duchess Genevieve (Stellarine) Alsterling
    - Duke-Consort Damien Alsterling
    - Duke Aldred Stellarine, widowed husband of Duchess-Consort Giendra (Topasirre) Stellarine, father of Duchess Genevieve, only child of Duke Siegfrid Stellarine and Grand Duchess Alicia Alsterling
    - *Duke Siegfrid Stellarine,* father of Duke Aldred, husband of Grand Duchess Alicia Alsterling, son of Duke Emmeren
      - » *Grand Duchess Alicia Alsterling,* wife of Duke Siegfrid Stellarine, mother of Duke Aldred
    - *Duke Emmeren Stellarine*
    - Others in the duchy:
      - » Lord Adsel Topasirre, Chatelaine and Regent of Elaarwen, from Genevieve's mother's family
      - » Istvan, man-at-arms, childhood friend of Genevieve's, wife had miscarriages, so they adopted
      - » Raymond, man-at-arms

  - *Fiefs within Elaarwen*
    - *Brindlewell*, county – Solway family
      - » Countess Alexa Solway, mother of Megan and Jason
        - * Lady Megan Solway, Heir to Brindlewell, oldest child of Countess Alexa, wife of David
        - * Lord David Solway (a.k.a. Captain Daffyd Metreedi), husband of Lady Megan
        - * their children (ages given for the 5th year of King Damien's reign)
          - * Elaina Solway – 22yo
          - * Rudolph Solway (deceased) (would have been 19yo)
          - * Roger Solway – 13yo
          - * Esmerelda Solway – 11yo
        - * Sir Jason Solway, younger child of Countess Alexa
    - *Cloudcroft*, property – Stellarine family
      - » Lord Aldred Stellarine

- *Siovale,* duchy – Elsevier family, forest green and silver (guards wear dark green and black)
  - <u>Duke Tomas Elsevier</u>
    - » <u>Duchess-Consort Sildra (Miramar) Elsevier</u>
    - » Their six children (ages given for the 5th year of Damien's reign, not all of their names have been given in the story as of yet)
      - * Mark Elsevier - 20yo
      - * Arabella Elsevier – 17yo
      - * Lorinda – 14yo
      - * Denis Elsevier – 12yo
      - * Gemma Elsevier – 10yo
      - * Gary Elsevier – 7yo
    - » *Duke Hector Elsevier,* father of Tomas, husband of Lydia
    - » *Dowager Duchess-Consort Lydia Elsevier,* mother of Harald and Tomas, died a traitor's death for Conspiracy Against the Crown for her role in the Usurpation by her son Harald
    - » *Harald Elsevier,* cuckoo's child of Duchess Lydia by King Reginald, died a traitor's death for Usurping the Throne after Damien was crowned
  - **Others in the duchy of Siovale**
    - » man-at-arms Douglas

- *Reyensweir,* duchy – family Mirion
  - Duke Quillian Mirion
    - **Others within Reyensweir**
      - » Sir Ancellius, father of Sir Timothy Ancellius, is a man-at-arms for the Duke

  - *Fiefs within Reyensweir*
    - *Zialest,* county – Teraseel family (adjacent to Dalizell, across some challenging mountain passes from Elaarwen; HOWEVER see also DALZIALEST below)
      - » <u>Countess Rosa Teraseel</u>
        - * *Gavin Teraseel,* Rosa's brother; he was to marry Ciriis Celavell

- *Embervest* duchy – family Eledor
  - Duchess Tariana Eledor
    - Duke Istvan Eledor, father of Tariana

  - *Fiefs within Embervest* The Lost Provinces of Minglemere (returned) and Everfields (still Lost to Vindalia) are part of Embervest
    - *Minglemere,* barony – family Krakenroost
      - » Baron Densal Krakenroost
      - » Lost to Vindalia some seventeen years before King Damien was Crowned
      - » Regained in the 4th year of King Damien's reign
    - *Everfields*
      - » Lost to Vindalia some fifty years before King Damien was crowned

- *Alpinsward,* duchy – family Marseill
  - The last of the Lost Provinces to defect (in their case to Mercasia after Crown Prince Robert Alsterling's negotiations failed following his murder by 'bandits')
  - The first of the Lost Provinces to return, following King Damien's coronation and negotiations with Queen Genevieve
  - <u>Duchess Laura Marseill</u>
    - » Duchess-Consort Lady Carmencita Marseill (a noblewoman of Mercasia)
  - Their three small children

  - *Fiefs within Alpinsward*
    - *Dalizell,* county – Miramar family; HOWEVER see also DALZIALEST below
      - » <u>Count Zachary Miramar</u>
        - * <u>Sildra (Miramar) Elsevier,</u> Zachary's next elder sister, was already married to Tomas Elsevier when parents and Elsa died
        - * *Zachary's parents* (died of flux)
        - * Elsa, eldest child and Heir to Dallizell; Zachary and Sildra's older sister; died of the same flux as their parents

- ***DALZIALEST**, duchy,*
  combined of Dalizell and Zialest when Rosa Teraseel and Zachary Miramar married just after King Damien's coronation – the Miramar family was granted the promotion to a Duchy in recognition of their loyalty to the new king (the counties had been asking for royal permission to merge for several generations)
  - <u>**Duchess Rosa (Teraseel) Miramar**</u>
  - <u>**Duke Zachary Miramar**</u>
    - 2 children in the 5th year of King Damien's reign
      - * Talia Miramar (a.k.a Tally), 3yo
      - * Betha, newborn

- The Lost Provinces
  1. Alpinsward, duchy – family Marseill
  Duchess Laura Marseill
  Lost to Mercasia some five years before King Damien was crowned
  Regained in the 3rd year of King Damien's reign
  2. Minglemere, barony – family Krakenroost
  Baron Densal
  Returned to Duchy Embervest
  Lost to Vindalia some seventeen years before King Damien was Crowned
  Regained in the 4th year of King Damien's reign
  3. Elendria, county
  formerly part of Duchy Alpinsward
  Countess Miraly
  Lost to Deltheran some twenty-five years before King Damien was crowned
  negotiations begun to Restore Elendria to Ilseador in the 5th year of King Damien's reign
  4. Farivera – formerly part of Duchy Siovale
  Lost to... Sindalla? Some forty years before King Damien was crowned
  5. Everfields – formerly part of Duchy Embervest
  Lost to Vindalia some fifty years before King Damien was crowned
  (return to top)

MAPS

Ilseador

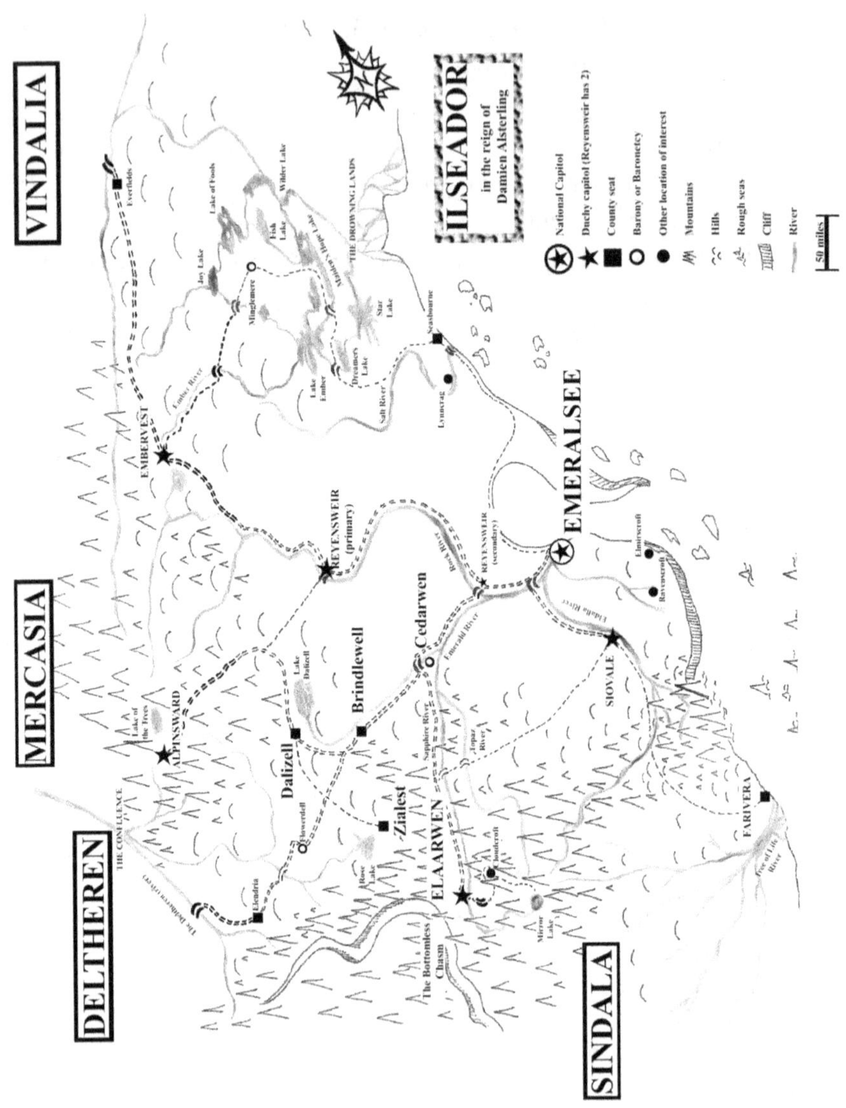

LANDS Around the MERUTIAN SEA

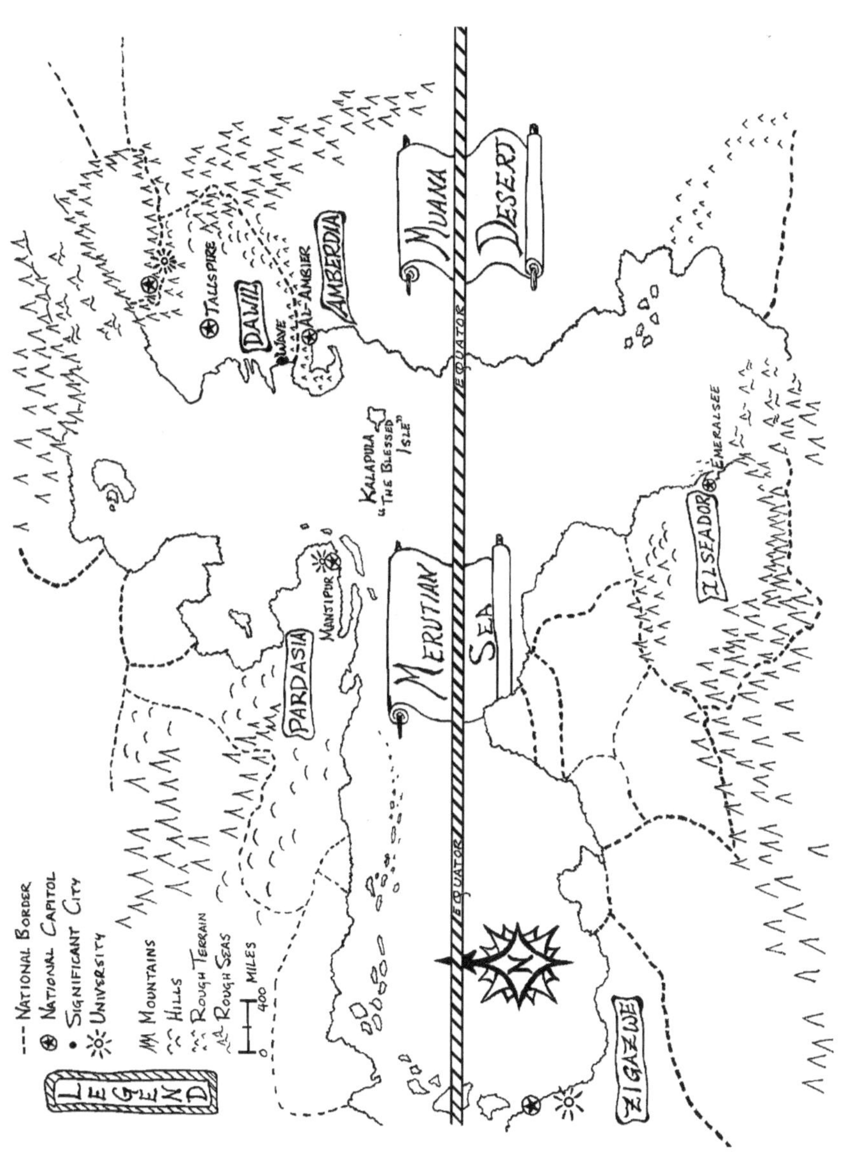

The REBEL
DUCHESS
Book One of the
Chronicles of Ilseador
KERRIDWEN MANGALA McNAMARA

Chapter ONE

Caught!

GENEVIEVE HAD NOT FORGOTTEN THE old king's pet sorcerer. She *had*, however, assumed he would not be a problem. This was clearly not the case.

She ducked into a rubbish-strewn alley and prayed that one of the doors leading off of it would open to somewhere that was not a dead-end. Unlike the alleyway itself. Genevieve really wasn't familiar enough with the layout of the capitol to be doing this sort of thing. As her advisors had repeatedly told her. Her chagrined memory replayed the scene of her tossing her head as she assured them that "the Rebel Duchess" could handle anything.

Not that she had *planned* to have to handle anything at all. She was just going to come in as part of the crowds hoping to get a glimpse of the new young king, on this last day of the coronation festivities. Just another gawker from the countryside. She still had no idea how Lord Prydeen had identified her.

The second door on the right opened at her frantic tug, and Genevieve hurried into darkness, pulling the door tightly shut behind her. She could hear people talking somewhere off to her right and the darkness seemed a little less dark in that direction. Perhaps there was a way through the building and back to the main street she had veered off of so abruptly. She needed to get back to the streets to complete her mission. The inhabitants of

the room ahead would be startled, but if she could get past them quickly –
before they decided to hold her for a thief – she might make it.

Just as the young woman started towards the sounds, the door behind
her crashed open and the sorcerer stepped through.

Lord Prydeen was a master of dramatic effect, some odd corner of her
mind noted absently. He stood framed in the doorway, too deeply cowled to
see his face, his ankle-length black cloak flapping and curling about him in
the sudden cross-currents of air between building and outside. The alley was
brighter than the room – so perhaps he merely paused to let his eyes adjust
– but in that moment he was more silhouette than shape, more demon than
man.

Genevieve could not – *could not* – lead him towards those unsuspecting
innocents in the room beyond. Perhaps the completely unexpected would
gain her – well, *something*.

She took a deep breath, but carefully did not think too hard about what
she was doing – though whether it was because Lord Prydeen was rumored
to be able to pull one's thoughts from the air itself or because she wouldn't
have the nerve if she did–

She spun on her heel and charged directly at the sorcerer, startling him
sufficiently that she shoved past him and back out into the dead-end alley.
Then to her left and back out to the main street – perhaps she could lose him
in the crowd. She had to try.

In her haste, however, Genevieve's own hood was pushed back, exposing
her signature red-gold hair – and confirming what had surely only been
Lord Prydeen's guess about the identity of his quarry.

Fool that she was for not having dyed it.

Thrice a fool for deciding to skulk about the coronation festivities – like
any small child playing "Erawan the Kind Robber" – instead of listening
to the reports of her spies as the mature, careful, strategic leader of the
rebellion should do. That stupid, romantic title – "Rebel Duchess" – really
had gone to her head, as Rosa had accused her. She would do the Cause
no good by being taken by the king's sorcerer. Even if the new young King
Damien lived up to his month-old reputation for fairness, Lord Prydeen
would never give her a chance to find out.

No time for this.

Genevieve jerked her hood back up and tried to blend into the crowded
market square, trying to outguess Lord Prydeen. Which direction would
the sorcerer be unlikely to go? – or which way would he be unlikely to
follow? Surely the feared and hated Royal Sorcerer could not make his way

through the crowd without causing an uproar that would let her dodge away... though he had before, when she first caught him following her. Could there be *any* safety for her here in the capitol, just six days after Damien's crowning? Surely the old guard was still in place and *no one* (not even the young king?) would dare to gainsay Lord Prydeen.

Abruptly, and entirely on instinct, not daring to look back to measure her pursuit, Genevieve swerved and tore for the royal viewing stand. Damien, if the stories were right – the stories that she had not believed and had come in person to verify – would merely have her executed for a traitor. Lord Prydeen – as she had reason to know – would sell her soul to demons and wring every last memory and secret from her shrieking heart.

The fine bright day taunted her travails, small poofy clouds ambling across a sky as blue as her own eyes. The market square – packed with a crowd of pleasantly frolicking merchants and peasants – impeded her swift progress. The swarms of children playing games of tag nearly tripped her up. The very *joy* of it all nearly derailed her thoughts, for such gaiety could never have been shown in the old king's rule, and part of her could not leave off trying to determine if there was still the undercurrent of desperation that she expected from her previous, and more successfully clandestine, visits to the capitol city.

But the Rebel Duchess knew exactly where the royal platform stood, both due to having marked it well when first she arrived and for the fact that it stood as tall any of the half-timbered two-story buildings surrounding the square. She had hoped to catch a glimpse of the young king from afar when first she arrived, and the royal platform had seemed like the right place to start. She had perhaps stayed still too long, staring too intently at the brilliantly bunting- and flower-clad structure, trying to discern which, if any, of the milling nobles on its three ornately decorated levels was the young king. Then, as now, the top level was empty, save for a matched pair of guards.

Part of her – the part that had insisted on this mad mission against all rational thought and advice – was certain that, if she could but look into his eyes, she would know if Damien was all that the reports claimed... or if he had been corrupted by his grandfather and Lord Prydeen.

Part of her – if she dared admit it – wanted to believe, even if it seemed beyond belief, that he could have been untouched. That the Cause was won, the need for a Rebel Duchess was done. That the Rebellion could quietly fold itself up and her folk could slip back to their homes, to their lives...

though perhaps not the Rebel Duchess herself, recognizable as she was as a symbol...

Yet – how could those two old, evil men *not* have insured that the crown prince was a "fit successor" to the king who had controlled a creature such as Lord Prydeen?

Genevieve had met the prince once, when they were both children. He had barely been of an age for his first pony, and she – a few years older – had just graduated to a mild-mannered horse... and her father's half-tamed, firebreathing mare that Duke Aldred had no idea she would even attempt to ride. Her father had brought her to Court to make her curtsy to the old king and see her named his Heir. Damien had been but one of a pack of the old king's grandchildren – a nondescript royal child, good-looking as they all had been, but special in no particular way. They had spent perhaps minutes in each other's presence, on separate ends of the audience hall that had seemed miles-long to her then.

Now those other siblings and cousins, aunts and uncles, were all gone and Damien – unremarked offspring of an unremarkable parent – had been named Crown Prince, and now King. For him to have inherited would seem to signal that he had done something to earn the old king's approval – perhaps by being ruthless enough to have ensured no other contenders were available. Certainly, he had made no mark by protesting his grandfather's policies while the old king lived, no mark of any kind, in fact. Despite all the time Genevieve had spent at Court, she did not recall ever noticing him again.

Yet she could still remember a certain clear-eyed gaze from that long-ago child. A gaze that seemed to recognize and promise to right all the wrongs that existed in the world. A gaze that had haunted her dreams since she had heard he had been crowned, and had kept her skepticism from becoming outright denial when rumors of the new king's beneficence came to her. And so, she had come to see for herself...

She had reached the royal platform at last, and hunted for a spot to clamber up. Not an easy endeavor, as it was so heavily be-ribboned – in every color, not merely royal gold and turquoise – with bright buntings stretched between triple rosettes made of actual rose petals. An elegantly illuminated sign noted that these were the coronation gifts of the Weavers' and Florists' Guilds – but the small barrel that the sign rested upon was of more interest to her, as it gave her a leg up to the first level, which was filled with younger noblemen. These young men were here to satisfy fathers and mothers who wanted them close to the source of power. They eyed her with interest – her cloak had of necessity been pushed aside to climb and she was dressed in hunting leathers fit tight to her athletic frame – and she in turn ignored them, using the spigoted ale kegs at which they were amusing themselves to give her a step up to the recessed second level.

The older noblemen and -women – and their maiden daughters – on this level looked at her quite askance. Genevieve hoped her hood shadowed her face enough to keep any of them from recognizing her, for she knew no few of them, though she did not recognize the barely-grown girls, nor more than a handful of the hardly-older lads below. These nobles had toadied up to the old king while Genevieve – and her father before her – had sought to protect their people. She knew all too well that they would as soon sell her out to Lord Prydeen as look at her. Even now they were trying to toady up to King Damien, bringing their marriageable daughters to parade before him – an array of maidens scarcely past puberty, for their elder ones had been taken to serve the old king and Lord Prydeen in years gone by, many never to be seen again. They, too, must surely be hoping for better from Damien, yet she saw nothing but avarice in the faces of even the children.

A good-looking young man – unusual only for being the only *young* man on this level of the platform, did someone think the new king's taste ran to boys? – with very dark hair and clear grey eyes offered her a hand onto the level. Genevieve was not too proud to accept help, even from a scion of one of *these* families. They exchanged a startled look and nearly let go of each other as an electric spark seemed to jump between their hands. Surely it wasn't dry enough today for such things, and so close to the harbor besides.

Putting such irrelevant details aside, Genevieve brushed off her hands on her breeches as she looked up towards the highest level of the reviewing stand, but saw only the pair of Royal Guards – two blondely handsome men so perfectly matched as almost to be twins – decorating that august space. Knights chosen for their beauty, just as were the horses that pulled the royal carriage. She wondered who they were – might they have enough real skill at arms to have faced her in the Battle of Siovale seven years earlier? She'd caught no more than a glimpse of either of them so far, as they turned, watchfully, eyes raking the crowds. Perhaps they were more than merely decorative.

Hopefully the king himself was sitting down and merely out of view. Genevieve needed for him to be there, before Lord Prydeen caught up with her. It was a wild gambit – praise all the Gods at once that Rosa really could handle the Rebellion, since it looked like she was going to have to. Rosa – would never forgive her for getting herself captured and killed. The

Rebel Countess – surely that sounded just as impressive. They had known it couldn't last – this would free Rosa to wed and produce the Heir that she needed. Genevieve's own proper title – Lady Stellarine, Duchess of Elaarwen (she dared not think "Princess of the Realm", though her bloodlines were as good as the king's) – would pass to a collateral line...

No matter. The issue at hand was to get up there to the top level and there was no obvious stair or ladder.

Genevieve dropped her useless disguise of a cloak before it could hinder her further in climbing higher, ignoring the massed gasp from the gathered nobles, and looked for a convenient way to boost herself to the king's level. The balustrade of the king's level – still festooned with those slippery buntings and banners – was more than head-high to her. It was higher than she could hoist herself on arm-strength alone.

That young man was still watching her – looking slightly amused, damn him. Or maybe that was *bemused*. Surely, he had little idea what to make of her and her sudden arrival. But he seemed to come to a decision and wrenched a ring with a large grey pearl on it off his finger, thrusting it towards her. It was the sort of thing a nobleman might offer a noblewoman to indicate interest – a sort of "let's get to know each other" offer, not quite a tryst, but more than an offer of acquaintance. The ring would have a house sigil on it, perhaps even a personal seal – enough information for her to find him again later on. A crazy thing to hand to the highly recognizable Rebel Duchess as she attempted to single-handedly besiege the new king's festival viewing platform. The young man must be completely daft.

And then he bent and cupped his hands as a stablehand might do to help someone into the saddle. The sparkle in his eyes suggested he was prepared to toss her high enough to pull herself up over that balustrade.

Again, the gathered nobles gasped, but this time there were also mutters and a fearful eagerness... and she guessed someone had spotted Lord Prydeen approaching.

There was no time for this. Genevieve stuffed the ring onto her finger – her beltpouch would take too long to open – put her foot in his hands and leapt up in concert with his toss.

And got the – third? fourth? – shock of the day as her reaching hands were grasped from above and an all too familiar voice gruffly said "Young miss, this is the king's place, you can't be climbing... up... her–" The voice cut off as and the hands fumbled and nearly dropped her back down, as their owner peered over the edge and then grabbed her more securely and helped her over the balustrade.

The Royal Guard was looking at her in exasperation and some of the same confusion Genevieve was feeling. It was the strangest and least appropriate timing on anything ever – but the touch of his hands had inflamed her with desire. *Not now, not now!* The Rebel Duchess thought frantically. She'd heard of this, but thought it a fairytale... Rosa, *Rosa* was her love...

"Jason Solway?" she managed to gasp out.

"Genny?" He was as flabbergasted as he was, and if the blush rising in those perfect cheeks was anything to judge, he was suffering from the same reaction. Suffering...

"Here now," said the other Royal Guard, coming forward from his ceremonial position. "Jase, what's this all about?"

She looked almost gratefully at the other man, just as gratefully *not* recognizing him as yet another childhood friend. But his familiar behavior towards Jason – were they lovers? Why did that thought make her heart – or something lower than her heart – do flips? And why, oh, why, *was this all happening at once?*

"Stand back, gentlemen," growled a low, cultured voice.

Lord Prydeen.

Apparently, she wouldn't have to sort any of this out after all.

The two Guards obediently stepped aside, though she rather thought that Jason only reluctantly let go of her hands, and she could see that the sorcerer had come up a set of stairs at the back of the reviewing stand. A brief surge of wind whipped the cowled hood from off Lord Prydeen's spotty, balding head, and tossed his long, drooping mustaches. He had not aged well since the old king's death; his hair had been thinning, but was still full when last she had gotten a good look at him, some months earlier, and the lines around his mouth were graven deeply, where once they had been entirely masked by his whiskers. Genevieve had heard tell that evil sorcerers cast vile spells to keep themselves young – by sacrificing true youths and maidens to demons, some said. She had scoffed, even as she wondered. The old king had lived long past his age, and Lord Prydeen, some said, had not aged at all, even as those noble daughters came to serve them both and were rarely seen again.

"Lady Genevieve." Lord Prydeen greeted her, coldly, but not correctly. He needed nothing besides himself to emphasize his authority, but he had brought a squad of his personal guards up with him. They fanned out behind him, blocking the path, even to headstrong young women who might push past a sorcerer.

She tilted her chin up – her nose was too snub to properly glare down it, but she was tall enough to try... and the arrogance might mask the tremble that the tumult in her stomach had settled into. "The proper title is '*Your Grace*', messir." She was actually in line for the throne herself, with all of Damien's family gone, and 'Lord' Prydeen was, after all, a sorcerer of no particular breeding.

And if she told herself that a few more times, perhaps she could dare to face him.

A wintry smile passed over Lord Prydeen's lips – gone as quickly as snow in the Summer. "No longer, I fear. My former master stripped you of your titles for your treasonous activities."

Genevieve inclined her head. "So, I have heard. But even a Royal Decree does not make a thing reality. Even His – belated – Majesty never put it to the test in *Elaarwen*."

Something sparked in the sorcerer's eyes. Anger, perhaps? Could such a one as he even feel something as tender as grief? He gestured to his men. "Bind her and bring her."

Jason bestirred himself to protest, "My lord–!" but the other Guard pulled him back and Genevieve found herself being roughly seized and turned around by hands that made no pretense of not enjoying their task. Even the king's own Royal Guards, it seemed, dared not speak against the sorcerer. Not yet anyways. If only she had waited to see if the young king could consolidate his power; if, indeed, he would continue in the way he had begun!

"My Lord Prydeen! What passes here?" The mild voice interrupted from the direction of the stairs, but was no one Genevieve recognized. She had been turned to face outwards towards the square whilst they bound her, and could not see the speaker.

Lord Prydeen's voice was a curious mix of ingratiating and dismissive. "Nothing you need trouble yourself over, my lord. Some rabble found her way up here, clearly to cause some trouble to you. It is my task and my privilege to safeguard Your Highness. We'll be away momentarily."

Gentle hands cleared away the thongs that had begun to lash her wrists. "Surely you are mistaken, my Lord Prydeen. This is no rabble, but Her Grace, the Duchess Genevieve Stellarine of Elaarwen."

"Yes, my Lord, the so-called 'Rebel Duchess'," Lord Prydeen's voice was growing impatient. "I am taking her to the castle dungeons to have out of her what she knows. You can make an example of her later on – you must not detract from your coronation festivities."

"Nonsense, Lord Prydeen," the mild voice replied. "That isn't how we treat visiting royalty... not to mention that the people would rise in protest and not even you could put them *all* down at once."

He came around to Genevieve's right side, and before she could register that this was the same young man who had cupped his hands for her boot like any stableboy, he gave her that same enigmatic smile, and faced the crowd – who had begun to turn as they saw their king. Damien lifted Genevieve's right hand in his left, holding them high above their heads and called out, "I give you Genevieve Stellarine, the Rebel Duchess!"

It was the sort of moment a Duke's Heir is trained for and – bemused as she was at the turn of events – Genevieve flattened her palm against the king's and stood tall before the crowds, the errant breeze tossing her red-gold curls like a mane. She smiled fiercely, trying to think if this would be taken as some sort of inadvertent admission of surrender.

Even as the people roared their approval – and Lord Prydeen fumed behind them – a sudden, strange crackling noise erupted and ribbons of white fire fountained up between their pressed fingers. It wreathed down to wrap their hands and curl around their arms.

For all that she was the reigning duchess of a province, the leader of a rebellion against an unjust king and an evil sorcerer, and had spent most of her life in that struggle... Genevieve was tempted to faint right then and there. This was absolutely the *last* thing she had expected. If she hadn't seen this happen before, she would have thought it was some new and clever attack by Lord Prydeen.

But she *had* seen this before. And, likely, so had every member of the crowd below.

At least young King Damien looked nearly as befuddled as she felt.

He, however, recovered more quickly than she.

"And your future Queen!" he announced in what sounded like a calm voice.

He pulled her in and kissed her.

And the crowds went absolutely wild.

**Read the rest of this exciting story of rebellion and romance!
The Rebel Duchess
now at your favorite online ebookseller in print or ebook!**

Also by Kerridwen Mangala McNamara

ADULT Fiction:
- The Chronicles of Ilseador
  - Book One: *The Rebel Duchess*
  - Book Two: *The King's Champion*
- Knightess of the Realm series (Book One is YA)
  - Book Two: *A Not-So-Simple Mission*

More Adult coming soon...
- *The Pirate-King:* Book Three of the Chronicles of Ilseador
- *A Not-So-Unexpected Problem:* Book Three of the Knightess of the Realm

---

YOUNG ADULT Fiction:
- The Knightess of the Realm series (not-YA with Book 2 and on)
  - Book One: *A Not-So-Sacrificial Maiden*
  - *Out of the Woods... Hopefully* (K.of the R. Prequel Novella)
- The Prankster Prince series
  - Book One: *Thony and the Much-Anticipated Adventure*
  - Book Two: *Thony Goes Astray! (in the deep, dark, and dangerous Fairy Wood)*

More YA coming soon...
- *So You Want to Be a Hero:* Book Three of the Prankster Prince
- *Scaredy Cat:* A Knightess of the Realm Prequel Novella

Non-fiction:
- *The Homeschooling Parent: Self-care and Feeding of the Person Who Makes It All Happen*
- *The Homeschooling Parent Teaches MATH! Bringing Math to the Math-Averse (Parents and Kids Both!)*

More homeschooling books coming soon...
- *The Homeschooling Parent Handles High School: Raising Capable Adults and Seeing Them on to the Next Stage*

Author's Note

(I'm keeping this Note short – I still have Book Three of the Knightess of the Realm to get out to catch up with where I thought I would be by the end of 2023, so I need to get back to work.)

Boy, was this book a challenge to get out the door!

When I set my initial publication date (back in July 2023?) getting it out before Thanksgiving seemed entirely do-able. And now it's the New Year... Eeep!

What I wasn't counting on was: ill-health (mine) that took me out most of the Summer; traveling up to the NorthEast to visit my family – our first trip there since the pandemic; the amount of time it would take to do Counselor Statements and fill out the other paperwork for my next-out-the-door college student; a three-day model government conference that knocked me flat for at least three days after that; an early Christmas so we could celebrate with Young Adult #1 before she headed North to spend the rest of Winter Break with her boyfriend'd family; and another trip all over the SouthWest to see my husband's family. Not to mention how much Time and Emotional Energy it takes to try to sell books in person!

It was great getting to meet so many readers (and potential readers). I hope some of you reading this book are folks I met at the Louisville Book Festival, LouisvilleCon, or the Georgetown Farmers' Market.

Great but... it took time away from writing, book formatting, and cover preparation. When you are a one-woman publishing operation and also a full-time homeschooling mom... things have a way of getting out from under you!

The book itself also bucked and reared a bit. I dithered and argued with myself about putting out an incredibly long book – or splitting it into something easier to hold in the hand. In the end, the Glossary and an alphabetical version of the Index of Characters is moving to the website (https://www.RisingDragonBooks.com) and click on the button for Maps or Maps & Lore. I'll be adding periodically to that page, so keep checking it.

Eventually there will be a timeline connecting all the different series as well as more family trees.

And because I was seeing the whole thing as a cohesive piece, it took awhile to see that Jason and Adam's wedding made a natural break-point.

It makes a good break-point also in terms of the flow. Book Three (The Pirate-King) is much more action-oriented, as – literally – all Hell starts to break loose!

I'm shooting for getting that one out by Summer 2024…

Contact me at RisingDragonBooks@gmail.com for updates on that publication schedule… as well as exclusive Sneak Peeks of book covers and the initial chapters before they are published for everyone… and the occasional extra treat, such as a novella or short story that will only be available for a limited time and then disappear until I get around to getting it published broadly.

And, of course, please, please, please leave a review for The King's Champion – or any of my other books – on whatever site you like to look at books. I'm new at this, and getting the word out there that my books exist is big!

Other AWESOME options if you want to help me out (because maybe reviews aren't your style): request one of my books from your local LIBRARY… tell a friend about them… or even give a copy to a friend!

And do email me and let me know if you did any of that! I will THANK YOU BY NAME (first, last, or both) in my newsletter!

Because READERS are why WRITERS can do all this fun stuff – thank you for being a great reader and helping me find more wonderful folks like you!

About the Author

KERRIDWEN MANGALA MCNAMARA IS AN Indian-American with a Master's degree in Bacterial Genetics who lives in Flyover Country (the far northern end of the US South) with her husband, The Professor, and four of her six children. Professor plays chess, and the children largely unschool while Mangala writes. (The remaining children are in college – you can blame the oldest for the excessive amounts of math showing up in Mangala's fantasy novels, the second one for better attention to staging of scenes, the third for all the economics, and the fourth for great attention to history – and all of them for a focus on political science!) Mangala is a former professional bellydance instructor, currently coaches a model government team, runs homeschool parent support groups, and used to enjoy knitting, crotchet, and embroidering Temari balls but now is much more boring as she rarely does anything but write, argue economic theory with her 18 and 15 year olds, and wonder loudly if her 12 and 10 year olds do anything other than watch Minecraft videos. She owes her love of books and reading to her mother, who was a professional folklorist and could recite – from memory – stories from every nation in the United Nations.

(The picture was taken at one of her favorite local bookstores: The Rosewater in Louisville, KY.)

Learn about Mangala's upcoming projects (fiction and nonfiction both) and sign up for email updates at
https://www.RisingDragonBooks.com

www.ingramcontent.com/pod-product-compliance
Lightning Source LLC
Chambersburg PA
CBHW070206310726
48976CB00001B/227